Playing The Field

GRAYSON LONG

Contents

Copyrights	1
Dedication	VIII
Malcolm	3
Five Years Earlier	
1. Kate	17
2. Kate	25
3. Kate	38
4. Kate	43
5. Malcolm	51
6. Kate	64
7. Malcolm	75
8. Malcolm	87
9. Kate	93
10. Malcolm	107
11. Kate	112
12. Kate	119
13. Malcolm	131
14. Kate	139

15.	Malcolm	148
16.	Kate	154
17.	Malcolm	166
18.	Kate	180
19.	Malcolm	191
20.	Kate	201
21.	Kate	214
22.	Malcolm	221
23.	Kate	233
24.	Kate	245
25.	Malcolm	257
26.	Kate	264
27.	Malcolm	274
28.	Kate	288
29.	Malcolm	297
30.	Kate	314
31.	Malcolm	327
32.	Kate	333
33.	Kate	343
34.	Malcolmm	352
35.	Kate	359

Malcolm	372
Eight Months Later	
Acknowledgements	380

About The Author 382

Copyright © 2024 by Grayson Long

All rights reserved.

No part of this publication may be reproduced, distributed, or transmitted in any form or by any means, including photocopying, recording, or other electronic or mechanical methods, without the prior written permission of the publisher, except as permitted by U.S. copyright law. For permission requests, contact the author.

Playing The Field is a work of fiction.

The story, all names, characters, and incidents portrayed in this production are fictitious. No identification with actual persons (living or deceased), places, buildings, and products is intended or should be inferred.

Book Cover by Cindy Ras.

To my friends,
For being a form of love I didn't realize I needed,
and for putting up with me for longer than I deserve.

Malcolm

Five Years Earlier

"Oh my gosh, ew."

The young woman grimaces at the bag of mealworms the customer ahead of me places on the checkout counter. Irritation swells inside of me as she uses a ruler to scoot the bag across the scanner and rings him up.

"Excuse me, ma'am," I grumble when it's my turn in line. She barely acknowledges me, turning her eyes to the giant cell phone in her hands. "Where can I return this?" I ask, shaking the large roll of fencing slung over my shoulder.

The look she gives me is filled with disdain as she smacks her gum. "Returns are in the back." She *shoos* me away before focusing back on the screen in her hand.

This interaction annoys me, but I press on. I turn around, readjusting the cumbersome roll on my shoulder. As I navigate through the aisles of the hardware store, a chick runs across my path.

Not the human type of chick. An actual baby chicken.

A tiny, feathery escape artist, plush and yellow.

"I don't have time for this," I mutter under my breath, feeling even more annoyed that this place can't contain their livestock. I scoop up the chick with my free hand, almost losing the wire off my shoulder in the process. Tucking the fluffy nuisance in my jacket pocket, I readjust the wire and continue toward the back.

"Hey! Hey!" a high-pitched voice shrieks behind me.

"Geez, what is with this place?" I try to ignore the voice. But it's my lucky day, and the shrill voice persists, following me like a shadow.

"Hey, bozo, that's my chick you're stealing!" The voice increases an octave, nails-on-a-chalkboard level. The accusation cuts through the air like a knife. It's also accompanied by a few disapproving glances by other customers.

"Keep it contained next time," I retort, setting the chicken back on the ground. I have to remind myself I'm a Southern gentleman and resist the urge to snap at the lady bickering at me as I walk away.

The chicken follows me. I can hear the pitter patter of its small talons against the tile.

"Lady, get your chicken before I take it home for a meal."

A gasp of horror follows me. "You wouldn't dare!" I'd bet she's clutching the poultry to her chest, *protecting* it, all while the bird just wants to be let free. Poor, pitiful thing.

Finally reaching the back of the store, I see an older gentleman sitting behind a large wooden counter. Heaving the wire on the counter, I glance at the floor to ensure there aren't any other tiny creatures near my boots as I step them together and pull out my wallet.

"What can I help you with today, sir?" the older gentleman asks as he looks the wire over.

I hand him my receipt. "I need to re—"

"Don't help him, Gary!" *Lord, help me.* The shrill woman is back. No longer five feet behind me either. No, now she's standing right next to me. I refuse to look in her direction and keep my eyes fixed on Gary. She huffs at me, as if I'm the one with the rude behavior in this situation, and begins tapping her foot at me. This is my hell.

"Miss," I sigh, scratching my chin, "can you please take your poultry and get out of my hair?"

Lucky for me, Gary can tell I'm in a hurry. Or maybe he just has sympathy for the man getting harassed by a psycho chicken lady, because he spares me from the assumed customer service banter.

"Gary, this man eats chicken!" Her shriek grates my nerves even more—didn't think that was possible at this point.

I pinch my eyes shut, feeling the pressure build between them, when I hear Gary say, "It's either him or me, girl." He chuckles under his breath. Chicken Lady gasps in disgust, and I have to bite the inside of my cheek to keep from laughing at Gary's and my solidarity.

"Ya want store credit or a refund?" Gary asks me.

I keep my head down and give him a subtle thumbs-up. I can't resist glancing to my left toward where the woman is standing. A pair of bright-pink high-top tennis shoes are pointed at my muddied work boots.

She clears her throat at me. Who does this broad think she is? I refuse to respond to anything that isn't actual words, so I continue to wait in silence.

Throat cleared *again*, she says, "So you like to kill animals, then?"

Gary whispers, "Here we go," at the jab as he hands me the handwritten gift card with my store credit on it. I take it, continuing to ignore the gal to my left, and turn right, keeping my head as low as humanly possible as I head for the door. No reason to entertain this crazy animal rights advocate any more than I already have.

"Hey, old man!" she calls out.

I can't help the harsh laugh that leaves my mouth. *Old man.* Who would've known thirty-two is considered old these days? I let the laughter overtake me as I give her a dismissive wave, leaving the store and not looking back.

My orange truck is at the end of the parking lot, and to my dismay, Animal Rights is hightailing it behind me. I hear the stomp of her feet against the gravel driveway and the chirp of chickens—not just the one, but an entire flock.

"Hey! I'm talking to you!" she yells, closing the distance as I make it to my truck.

"Sorry, lady. I ain't got time for your nonsense." I wave over my shoulder then open my driver door. Before I can escape, a small hand with multi-colored fingernails shoves the door shut. I let out a sigh as she keeps it planted against my window. And then, she has the audacity to start tapping her finger at me. Pink, yellow, and blue drum against the glass impatiently. The nerve of this woman.

I follow the line of her arm, noting smooth, dark-olive skin. Like those arms you see in commercials, convincing you to buy some weird lotion. There's a slender definition in her bicep and shoulder, making it the most distracting arm I've ever laid my eyes on. My gaze travels up the smoothness of her arm, finally meeting her face, and I'm greeted by a set of brown eyes.

And they're *pissed*.

"Ma'am, could you please remove your hand from my vehicle?" I ask as frustration pulses down my temples. Her hand flexes as she pushes harder onto my window. As I tower over her small frame, I have no doubt I could throw her over my shoulder in one swift motion, so removing her tiny hand shouldn't be a problem.

"Not until you apologize."

"Apologize for what?" I snap my head back at her. "For rescuing your chicken from my boot?" At her feet is a large wire crate with at least ten baby chicks in it, all chirping up at me.

"No." She removes her hand and crosses her arms. "For eating animals."

I cock my head back and bark out a laugh. The afternoon sun pierces my vision for a moment before creating a glowing halo around this woman, illuminating her flawless skin like it thrives in sunlight—again, distracting.

"I'm not going to apologize for the naturally created food chain. You gotta take that up with God." She gapes at my words, probably offended, but I don't care. I open my door again and try to climb in. "Have a nice day."

The lady grips my door, *again,* drawing a low growl out of my throat. This woman is maddening.

"Fine." She huffs. "You could at least apologize for trying to kidnap Nugget."

"Nugget?"

She nods, pride pinking her cheeks as she smiles down at the crate. "Cute, isn't it?"

The chicks chirp as if they are agreeing with this woman. Nugget sits front and center, eyeing me with her permanent scowl and brown mohawk. Hard to miss, and yes, kind of cute. The corner of my mouth twitches up as they all chirp up at me.

"Sure, whatever. Take care now." I attempt to close my door.

"Could you at least give a stranded woman and her animals a ride?" She leans her arm on the inside of my door, staring at me expectantly. Does this woman not have any sense? What if I'm a serial killer? "It's the least you could do since you were trying to steal my chicken." The balls on this woman. Crossing her arms again, she waits.

Now I'm gaping at her. No, gawking, as I take her in.

Dark-brown hair, wild and curly, is tied on top of her head with a bright-yellow scarf. Strawberry-pink cheeks with plump lips to match sit beneath dark, doe-like eyes. It's like they're filled with raspberry chocolate, a swirl of browns and reds looking back at you. Someone might even think there's a sweet, intense passion about them, but based on the last few minutes of dealing with her, that passion is almost loony. Her small frame is swallowed by ratty blue coveralls, the top half unbuttoned and tied around her waist. A white tank top covered in dirt—and who knows what else—hugs her slim torso.

"I won't bite," she jokes, hoisting the crate of chickens into the bed of my truck. I haven't even said yes yet.

I watch as she whispers something to the chickens then skips to the passenger side of my truck and climbs in. Again, please let the record show, I have *not* told this mystery woman I will give her a ride. *What if she's a serial killer?*

"We're losing daylight, Grandpa." Patting a hand on the dash then adjusting the back of the seat, she makes herself comfortable, as if riding in a truck with a complete stranger is nothing to her. She even goes as far as plopping her feet on my dashboard.

My neck and jaw tighten watching her. It could be my imagination, but I swear I hear her force a sigh, *rushing* me. I drop my head and rub the back of my neck before accepting that I have no control over this situation, and I climb into my commandeered vehicle.

"Are you going to murder me?" I hesitate to start the truck and watch her carefully.

"Are you going to murder *me*?" She raises an eyebrow at me. Something about that look makes my stomach dip. *Weird.*

"Alright," I huff, "where to, ma'am?" I shove the lump of anxiety forming in the back of my throat deep down and try to ignore the fact that I am at the mercy of a fearless woman with a very specific agenda. Having a plan is the only thing I need to function these days. Knowing the basic details of where I'm going and what I'm doing is a necessity. Yet, somehow, I have succumbed to the requests of my polar opposite. In what world have I ever let this happen?

"First of all, do I really look like a ma'am to you? Second, 71st and Hilltop, please," she says without looking at me, cranking the window down. Now I have to turn the air conditioner off. Summer heat is thick and oppressive outside, and this strange woman is just wasting my cold air.

"First, ma'am has nothing to do with age and everything to do with respect. Secondly, that's, like, an hour away." I'm forced to crank my window down now so I don't suffocate.

"It's, like, twenty minutes. You'll be fine." She gestures toward the road. "Don't worry, you'll be back for the early bird special." Her giggle fills the cab of the truck like a symphony.

I relent and head in the direction she instructs. We drive in silence for a bit, and everything about the situation sirens in my head to drop the crazy broad off on the side of the road. But something else in my chest is telling me to enjoy the ride with the pretty girl in coveralls.

It has been a long time since I have had this much one-on-one interaction with another person. The last few months have been nothing but packing up, moving, and settling into my new life, alone. Peaceful and miserable all at the same time.

I scratch the top of my head and flatten my hair as I switch lanes on the highway. What could this lady be doing on the outskirts of the city? To any onlooker, she may give off the independent, country-girl vibe with her coveralls and livestock, but as a true farm boy, I can tell she's anything but. The way she was carrying those chickens, like she's never touched an animal in her life, was a clear indication.

"Where are we going?" My words come out harsh, and her eyes grow in size at the tone. "Sorry... This grandpa just likes to know where he's headed." I smile faintly, and I see the corner of her mouth twitch up in response.

"I have a friend there, and I'm hoping she'll take these chickens for me."

"The chickens aren't for you?" My eye roll is involuntary at her side smirk, answering my question with an obvious *no*.

I have to force myself to keep my eyes on the road, not on the hands that fidget with the knobs, the air vents, her pants, anything she can reach. She messes with her nails then with the dial of the radio, turning it to a station I've never heard of. A guy with obvious mother issues starts rhyming to some repetitive beat. She taps the windowsill a few times before pulling out her phone and typing frantically. I see her glance this way a few times then bite her lip. That's distracting too.

I clear my throat. "You good over there?"

"Just a little antsy." She cracks her neck. "It's not every day I get in a stranger's truck and travel an hour with him."

"I can say the same." I turn on my blinker to switch lanes, checking over my shoulder and noting the chicken crate is still in the bed as I do.

Mystery Woman turns in her seat to face me. "So what's your deal?"

What a loaded question.

"Well, I woke up this morning, planning to have a nice quiet day running errands. Then I was accosted by a strange woman and her chickens."

She lets out a soft kind of chortle, and it does something to my stomach I'm not familiar with. I glance at her and then back at the road. The wind whips tendrils of her hair around her face as she stares at me. It's something you'd see in slow motion in a film: pretty girl in your passenger seat with the sun setting behind her and nothing but the whistle of the wind passing between the two of you. I could watch it on repeat.

I shove the thought away and remind myself that she is a stranger.

"What?" I squint at the road, resisting the urge to stare back at her and wrecking this truck.

"Is that all you're going to say, Mystery Man?" She taps her colorful nails against the back of her cell phone. Distracting again. Everything about her is distracting.

"Yes." What else is there to say? I'm a simple man. And I don't usually tell my entire life story to anyone—and definitely not to this woman who's hijacking my afternoon.

Pulling the visor down, she messes with her hair and picks at her teeth. Pretty comfortable up here, aren't we, lady?

"I don't even know your name, so that's all you get."

"I'll give you three guesses." She pops the visor closed. "And you'll turn at the next marker." She points ahead at a marker indicating a turn off the stretch of concrete onto a red dirt road. Something about it warms my chest. Up until now, I hadn't realized how much I missed the Oklahoma roads since I'd been gone. It feels good to be home—most days. Other days, it feels just as lonely as the desert.

"You're running out of time, Gramps."

"Grace?" The first name I could think of would, of course, be my mother's name.

"Close!" Her eyes widen in excitement, and that also does something to my insides. "Two more guesses."

"Glenda?" I wince, making the turn down the dirt road. Crackling and popping happens below the tires, and a red cloud of dirt swallows us as my tires turn up the ground. I lean closer to the windshield for a better view.

She giggles at me. "Bad eyesight there, Pops?"

"No, *Gloria*. Just trying to figure out where I'm going." I turn the windshield wipers on, worsening the view. I growl and pull over.

"Three guesses, but no luck." She's laughing as I put the truck in park. She hops out and walks toward the bed of the truck, the cloud of dirt still blocking our view.

I climb out of the cab and walk to the front, escaping the cloud of dirt and checking my surroundings. A small farmhouse sits at the top of a hill straight ahead, about fifty feet from us. The lady clanks the chicken crate out of the bed, almost turning it over and killing the chicks in the process.

"Do you need—"

"Nope. Thank you." She heaves the box onto her hip, with struggle all over her face as she does. I have to rub my jaw to prevent laughing at her. She wobbles toward the house, and chickens roll all over each other with each step. Little chirp screeches beckon to be rescued. "Lola! Lola! I'm here!" she yells toward the house.

The flimsy screen door swings open and slams against the side of the house. An older woman in rubber boots and a straw hat walks out, her demeanor changing when she sees the girl walking up to her porch. "Kate Stanley! What are you doing?"

"Lola, shut up," she tries to shush her, looking over her shoulder at me.

I mouth, *"Kate,"* to her, and she groans in defeat as she heads to the steps of the house.

Kate Stanley. Mystery gone. The other woman comes down the steps and meets us in the driveway. Kate grapples with the crate she's losing grip of and sets it down as gently as she can before wiping her hands on her thighs and tapping the toes of her shoes on the ground, ridding them of any red dirt remnants that collected by the truck.

"Katherine Joy, I can't keep these." The woman points at the flock of chickens in the cage. I could be hallucinating, but I feel their little chicklet eyes on me as the ladies bicker back and forth.

"They're going to get eaten," Kate argues.

"That's what they're bred for, sweetheart." The woman puts her hands on her hips, looking very much like Kate at the moment.

"Lola, you have to." Kate's voice sounds fragile as she tries to coax this elderly woman into accepting responsibility for the animals. She clasps her hands together under her chin and pouts at her.

For a grown woman, Kate seems to have no shame in pulling out all the stops.

"I said no." Lola's face has a look. I've seen that look from my own mother. Disappointment. Never goes away, even as an adult. She eyes me, clearly suspicious as to why I'm here. "Did you encourage this?" She waves to the birds.

Her tone sends a chill down my spine. "No, ma'am." She looks satisfied with my response and looks back at Kate. A breath of relief leaves me. I can tell I don't want to end up on her bad side.

I'm not sure what it is, but there's something about this farm woman that terrifies me. Fifteen years as a naval nuclear engineer, three deployments, and dozens of short tours, but this woman in her flowery boots and t-shirt covered with kittens is one of the most intimidating things I've encountered.

"What am I supposed to do, then?" Kate groans, and the chicks chirp, like they also want to know what will happen to them.

"Take them back," Lola says, unfazed.

"They'll die!" Kate practically whines out, and Lola just shrugs. *Pretty savage, lady.*

She rubs Kate's arm. "I'm sorry, honey. I just can't," she says, turning to head back into the house.

"What am I going to do? Gary's gonna fry them the first chance he gets!" Kate calls after her.

"I'll take them." The words come out quicker than my brain computes them. Taking home a crate of chickens was not on the agenda for my Saturday, but seeing the defeat all over Kate's face is enough to gut me—that and the crate of innocent eyes staring up at me like I'm their mother bird.

Kate whips her entire body toward me. "What?" Her voice is faint. "Are you serious?"

Am I serious? "Sure." I shrug. *What's the worst that could happen?*

"Are you going to eat them?" She eyes me suspiciously.

I can tell that eating any of these yappy birds will hurt Kate. And for some unknown reason, that is the last thing I want to do. I hold up a hand and say, "I will keep them safe, ma'am."

"Oh my gosh, thank you!" Within seconds, her arms are around my shoulders, pulling me flush against her for a hug. Her head nuzzles perfectly in the center of my chest. It would be nice…if the force of the hug didn't knock the wind out of me. I give her a pat on the back in reciprocation. "Thank you! Thank you!" she squeals.

"You're welcome." My words are muffled by her curly bun pressing against my mouth and nose. The smell of lavender swirls around me. She steps back and beams at me, bouncing on the balls of her feet. Kate's glee is palpable, and I feel lighter just looking at her.

"Malcolm Geer, you are a saint."

"It's not a big—wait…" The bemusement I feel is clearly on my face as she bites her lip. *Distracting.* "How do you know my name?"

"Google." She shrugs. "Duh, Gramps." She turns on her heels and reaches for the crate, the chickens chirping in protest. I instinctively grab the crate and hoist it onto my shoulder. The chicks go quiet. *I got you, buddies.*

As we head back to the truck, I ask, "So how do you know my name?"

"I know people." She shoves her hands in her coverall pockets. "And Google. I saw your ID when you gave it to Gary."

"Clever." I smile. "Nothing incriminating on there?"

"Not that I've found yet." She winks at me, and I almost trip over my foot at the sight. *Pull yourself together, Geer.* "But I'll find something. We all have issues." She jokes, but it feels forced. There's something about her tone that weighs on me. "Anyhoo"—she pats me on the shoulder—"thanks again!"

I set the chickens in the bed of the truck and cover them with a blanket from the backseat. Her clear concern for the safety of these birds is somewhat amusing but also confusing.

"Not a problem. I promise I won't—"

"I know. You have a very trusting face." Her cheeks go pink with her words.

I nod and shove my hands in my pockets as awkward silence fills the air. The next thing for me to do would be to leave. But I have this weird desire to stay and keep talking to the pretty chicken lady. "Well...I guess I should go." Probably for the best anyway. Since history tends to repeat itself, the only thing I would probably get from this girl is heartbreak.

"You're our new math teacher, right?"

"Umm, yes. How did you—"

"I work at Glendale. Got an email about you yesterday. I teach science and coach volleyball." She lifts her chin up proudly and reaches out to shake my hand.

"So you didn't actually Google me?" I shake her hand.

"Oh, I 100% did. It was just a wonderful coincidence that you were at the store today." She chuckles at herself. "A little hazing opportunity just presented itself. Couldn't pass it up." She gives me a wink, her thick lashes fluttering with the movement.

"So this entire—"

"Yep, I knew who you were the moment you scooped up my chicken." She smirks.

"My chicken, you mean." I smirk back, and her head falls back as another laugh bubbles out of her. It's an entrancing noise, and I can't help but laugh with her. I'm enjoying talking to this girl a little too much. Her laughing slows, and her smile widens as she looks me up and down. What could possibly be going on in that head of hers? And why do I have this desperate need to know?

"I think we're going to be good friends, Malcolm Geer."

Chapter One

Kate

Sweet mother of pearl.

What have I gotten myself into? Three years. I gave up three whole years of nightly sweatpants and ice cream for *this?* As I shift uncomfortably in the heels I borrowed from Ellie, I can't help but question every little decision I've ever made in my life. The unnatural angle of my feet is so painful I'm even starting to question my sanity.

A little too New York for my taste, Ellie.

"I guess I shouldn't have assumed that the first time I got back out there I would be swept off my feet, right?" I muster a laugh and take a sip of the complimentary Mai Tai. "But doing it this way is fun too! Like pulling off a Band-Aid, don't you think?"

The gentleman across from me—*Larry,* per his blue name tag—does not respond.

"Maybe not a Band-Aid," I backtrack. "More like chopping off—"

A buzzer blares, cutting me off and rescuing Larry, based on the exaggerated sigh of relief he gives before power-walking to the next table. "It was nice meeting..." I trail off when I see him eagerly approach the pretty blonde's table ten feet away. She's wearing a bright-red, low-cut dress with a slit up to her hip bone, unaware of my existence as she laughs and swoons over the very perky Larry.

Where was that perkiness two minutes ago, Larry?

Glancing at the clock, I realize I only have to endure this night for thirty more minutes. I've been here for almost two hours, and what do I have to show for it? A half off coupon to the Hot Dog Hut down the street and a phone number written on the back of a parking ticket.

"Hello there." A bald man wearing a white turtleneck approaches my table. "How you doin'?" Using a *Friends* pick up line? Do better, my man.

Summoning all the energy I left behind in my early twenties, I inhale, slow and deep, focusing my attention on the potentially harmless man with a shiny head in front of me.

What if he's the one, Kate?

He picks his teeth with his pinky finger, retrieving a rather large piece of...spinach? Broccoli? Something green and rotten. Then, he proceeds to wipe it off on the white satin tablecloth between us.

Nope, not the one.

"You know what..."—I eye his name tag—"*Tom*, I'm not doin'." I feel like air-quoting the word is essential for added effect in this moment. "I'm at a singles mixer on a school night. I haven't dated anyone in three years, and after months of loneliness and self-reflection—I even took up knitting and made a sweater—I figured it was time to get back out there, find myself a man." My tone deepens on the word *man* involuntarily. I tend to ramble, and when I do, my voice gets gritty and, according to my cousin, Benny, can be a tad macho.

"A man, huh?" Tom gives me a slow wink, adding another level of cringe to this interaction. I check the clock—thirty more seconds with this one.

"Yes, Tom. A man. Someone to share a life with. Not even a crazy, extravagant, world-traveling life. Just someone who sees me for me, someone who fixes the sink when there's a leak, someone who gives me the comics while they read sports. I've been burned. I gave love a chance before, and it led me down a long road of unhealthy carbs and binging *Sweet Home Alabama* before I finally realized that most men suck."

"So why do you want a man now, then?" Tom's eyes don't communicate sincere curiosity. No. His wiggling eyebrows and heavy stare at my chest communicate creepy. That and the trailing hand sliding toward me across the tiny bar table that separates us.

I clear my throat. Just a few more seconds of this guy. "Because my best friend just got engaged to my cousin, and I realized how lonely I am. I realized how much I want what they have. Someone to laugh with and share those lingering touches in the hallway. I'm a teacher, by the way," I say defensively, feeling the need to clarify to Tom here. "I don't just loiter in random hallways. But anyway, I just want what they have. I don't want to inhale a pint of Phish Food every night by myself. I want to share that with someone." My words come out fast and whiny, collecting glances from fellow speed-daters. The music crackles out of the duct-taped speaker at the front of the room, and the singular disco ball light flickers like it's running out of juice.

A perfect picture of how this night is going. I am the disco ball.

The buzzer sounds. Thank the heavens.

"Well, maybe we can circle back to this," Tom writes his number on my call log, shooting me another slow wink and a small pucker of his lips. Disgust shivers its way up my spine as he backs away slowly, eyes still pinned on me. You aren't winning any points here, Tommy.

My next visitor, *Julian*, joins me, sporting a blue button-up and board shorts with birds on them. He sways on his feet for a moment then regains his balance. Oh boy. "Hey there, good lookin'!" His slurred words blare at me from all cylinders. Wincing, I plaster on a smile and attempt to respond.

Before I can, Julian loses his balance again, tumbling forward into the table and flinging his drink all over me. Streaks of pink and orange splash my chest and arms, staining my brand-new shirt. It's a white shirt with cute puffy sleeves that is both flattering and feminine.

Wearing white...ugh, rookie mistake.

Okay, Kate, just stay calm. Maybe he's just nervous. Julian, the thirty-nine-year-old dog groomer—because yes, he wrote his age and job title on his name tag as well—was so nervous to put himself out there that he got blitzed drunk. Just your old, run-of-the-mill, singles mixer shenanigans, right?

"You were supposed to catch me!" Julian yells at me as he climbs to his feet from the floor. It's more of a stumble to his feet with his eyes glossy and chest heaving rapidly, like he just ran a race. I can't help but gape at him as the remnants of his drink drip off my cheeks, and goosebumps travel up my arms from the icy cold of the liquid. Julian storms off, heading straight to the bar, leaving me to clean up his mess.

Surely this is all part of a poorly thought out prank. I'm sure, any second now, a man in a bunny suit is going to jump out at us and yell, '*GOTCHA!*' Then, this painfully awkward moment will turn into a hilarious one, followed by a knight-in-shining-armor entrance of a tall man with a deep voice, who sweeps me off my feet and says, "Let's get you cleaned up," filling my stomach with giddy butterflies and my head with a happily-ever-after soundtrack.

It's a silly thing to think—being swept off my feet. Yet, here I am, suffering through this night with that small flicker of hope that this could have been the night everything changed. But based on the last few options and the poorly curated line of subjects awaiting their turn to join my table, I'd say this is definitely not the night everything will change.

A young waitress, shaking like a Chihuahua, rushes to my side with a towel in hand. She's more chivalrous than Julian. "That was..."—she bites her lip—"painful to witness."

"Had to make the night memorable." The liquor smell soaking into my hair will probably speak for itself the next few days. A constant reminder of this night. I chuckle at the ridiculousness of it all, wiping pink sludge out of my hair as I do. The waitress eyes me warily, unsure at first if she can laugh with me, until we're both in a fit of giggles as she helps me wipe up the table. "Thank you."

"Can I get you anything?" she whispers, looking at the bar then back to me. "Dessert?" The offer is served with a recoiling smile.

Kindly refusing the offer, I take a seat at my table and wait for the buzzer to signal my next assailant. My phone dings in my pocket as I wait. Checking my phone is off limits. That's rule number one of date etiquette—per my lola's instructions, anyway. "You young people and your phones. Put it away, and focus on the man in front of you."

Another ding sounds, drawing my attention even more. *What if it's an emergency?* This isn't a real date anyway. I watch the clock at the front of the room count down ten seconds, an absurd internal battle of phone checking waging a war in my head, before finally checking.

Panic, or embarrassment, or just sheer terror courses through me when I read the text that pops up on my screen.

> **Malcolm:** I've never seen someone so bored.

I'm an hour away from home. How does he know what I look like right now? How does he know I'm bored? My heart pounds in my chest as I scan the room. In the sea of singles, no one resembles my grumpy friend. A crowd of people isn't necessarily his ideal hangout spot anyway. But that doesn't stop me from looking.

"I have to take a phone call," I lie to the new gentleman trying to join my table, then I weave my way through the bodies lingering too closely to each other. I keep scanning the room. Still no sign of him. Even standing on my tiptoes, I don't see a big, brooding man in a fishing shirt, mentally growling at everyone behind a glass of brandy. Dodging the handsy man from earlier, I make it to the front door without being intercepted by Malcolm.

Did I want him to intercept me? Maybe. It might have been enough to save this painful night.

I wave bye to the hostess and rush out of the bar. The cool air is harsh against the sweat on the back of my neck, a combination of fear and embarrassment of being seen here sizzling through my veins. It's like I just ran a marathon.

Wobbling in the heels, I scope the sidewalk and across the street—still no Malcolm. Assessing my shirt, that is now sticky, I accept that tonight was a complete dud and head back to my car. I continue my search for Malcolm as I climb in. I wouldn't put it past him to jump out and scare me once I try to pull out of the parking lot.

My fingers get tangled in my hair as I try to smooth it out. I have to yank to separate some of the sticky strands that are now knotted and plastered to my cheek—another very literal representation of my current situation. Dating is sticky and messy and can ruin your favorite clothes if you aren't careful. Why I thought going to a speed-dating mixer was the best way to get back out there is beyond me. Maybe I'm not mentally sane, and I need to see a therapist. Maybe I should talk to Ellie.

Unlocking my car, I realize Malcolm isn't anywhere around me. Did he stay inside? Of all the people I would want to see me enduring a night like this, he is the last. There's just something about telling my very surly, dating-the-traditional-way friend that I'm getting back out there that terrifies me. His opinion is annoyingly the most important to me. Don't ask me why. I haven't figured it out yet. It just is, and I have no doubt he is in stitches over seeing me tonight.

Wait. *Why is he here tonight?*

Is Malcolm speed-dating right now? My best friend getting back out there, too, is something I should want. The man deserves his happy ending, just like me. A pit forms in my stomach at the idea of him chatting it up with the pretty blonde from inside. They'd probably have cute blonde babies within a year, and I'll still be alone.

My car engine rumbles as I let the heater warm my skin and throw my head back against the seat. I guess if any part of my getting-back-out-there plan was going to be a train wreck, I'm glad it was tonight. Ripped off the Band-Aid.

Another text dings on my phone—a photo of Frankie, my cousin's cat, perched on top of Malcolm's chicken coop, staring blankly into the camera. It's followed up with another text.

> **Malcolm:** Isn't she supposed to try and eat them?

Uncontrollable laughter bubbles out of me, leaving me borderline teary. I remember now that he is babysitting Frankie for the night. She must be the one who is bored, not me. Malcolm isn't actually here, an hour from home, also at a singles mixer. I panicked for nothing. Relief feels like a balloon deflating in my throat.

The relief fades quickly as I drive home, reminding myself to stick to the plan. *You're dating again, Katherine. It's time.* Once I'm home, I do the thing I swore I would never do. I sign up for a dating app: Playing the Field.

Chapter Two

Kate

"You are immersed into a gallery of different species, with a variety of shapes and sizes, all ranging from whales to *Homo sapien* genitalia."

Horror. Sheer horror.

A creepy sensation moves up my spine, and my stomach retches from dread as I stare at the poster board hung on my chalkboard that is covered in graphic images and stickers. Charlie Henders, the senior class clown, continues his presentation on the Icelandic Phallological Museum. An actual museum he visited with his family over winter break. Pictures of animal and human phallic shapes are scattered across my whiteboard along with a picture of Charlie, himself, grinning from ear to ear as he stands next to a whale replica.

I shove my reading glasses onto the top of my head and rub my temples, praying the pressure erases the images. He continues discussing the details of each sculpture, the size comparisons, and the history of the museum. That's right, the *history* of a penis museum. To my dismay, the class is completely engrossed in this presentation, giggling and whispering as Charlie continues. I should probably stop this...but the kid is so focused on his work and getting the extra credit—he hasn't been this motivated to participate all year. Maybe the tornado alarm will go off so we can end this before someone walks by.

"They even had a cafe and bistro!" Charlie holds up a restaurant menu. "If any of you are looking for a cultural experience ..."

26 GRAYSON LONG

A cultural experience? What is happening? I sneak my phone out of my desk drawer, desperately needing to share this horror with someone.

> Henders presented his senior project today.

> I'll give you three guesses on what it was…

Malcolm: Hmm…

> You'll never get it

Malcolm: Do I get any hints?

> Of course not!

Malcolm: Is it over a place?

> ….yes

Malcolm: A museum perhaps?

> yes….

Malcolm: Does this museum showcase art of the penis kind?

> **HOW DID YOU KNOW?!**
>
> **Malcolm:** I know everything.
>
> **I hate you.**
>
> **Malcolm:** Don't lie to yourself.
>
> **Fine. I don't. But you took away my fun**
>
> **Malcolm:** Just doing my duty.

I roll my eyes at my know-it-all best friend, sliding the phone back in the drawer. Refocusing my attention on Charlie's presentation, I see he has now started a slideshow with more images, and the rest of the class is taking pictures of the ginormous phalluses.

"Alright, then." I stand, slapping my desk to interrupt Charlie mid-sentence. "Let's not get me fired today." I gesture for Charlie to take a seat and hide all evidence of his presentation. "Thank you, Mr. Henders, for that in-depth presentation."

"Yeah, Charlie, real *deep* presentation, bro," Travis Van says from the back of the class. The students cackle and cheer at his innuendo. Charlie bows. *God, help me.*

I drag a hand down my face and groan. "Moving on." I eye Charlie as he high-fives his friends on the way back to his seat. I fold up his posterboard, quickly hiding it from the world underneath my desk. "Who else would like to present?"

A few hands shoot up at the same time the class bell rings. Time flew by, and I feel flustered for not monitoring the time more efficiently.

"Alright, then, we'll get through the rest of the presentations tomorrow," I say to the rest of the students as they rush out of my classroom. "Don't forget the exam on Friday!" No one acknowledges my reminder.

I fold up Charlie's board and shove it under my arm before he can snag it back. This one will not be on display. I feel the thick foam give way to the bend and crack a tiny bit. I ignore it, grabbing my phone out of the desk and heading out into the busy hallway. The minutes in between classes are always a blur—students racing to their next period or, the complete opposite, blocking the hall with their group chit-chat.

My phone buzzes in my hand.

> **Malcolm:** Iceland is calling.

Hilarious. I weave around the kids and make my way to the teachers' break room, penis poster in hand. The death grip I have on this thing makes it difficult to text and walk, but I *cannot* let its contents be seen. I reach the door to the teachers' lounge and stare at my phone screen, desperate for a funny comeback.

> Your mom is calling.

> **Malcolm:** Kate Stanley, you can do better than that.

> I stand by my comeback!!

> **Malcolm:** You sure about that?

> Ugh! YOU DIDN'T GIVE ME TIME TO BE WITTY.

> **Malcolm:** The definition of witty is quick humor, dollface.

> Hush, you bearded dragon.

I stare at the screen, awaiting Malcolm's response. Text bubbles pop up and disappear for what seems like an eternity. Then, a picture of his face, squished cheek to cheek with mine, pops up on my screen as his call comes through.

"Do we need anything else for tonight?" His voice is breathy on the other end.

"What are you doing?" I lean against the lockers in front of the lounge and clutch the poster to my chest.

"Working out." Another heavy breath pulses through my phone speaker. "Why?"

"You sound like a dying old man." I laugh as his erratic breathing slows down. He's clearly trying to hold it in for my sake.

"I am a dying old man." Malcolm clears his throat. I hear movement on the other end of the line—a slam of a locker door, a thud, a zip.

"Answer the question, Kit Kat." A quiet, breathy chuckle moves over my speaker.

The nickname Malcolm gave me five years ago hits me in the chest. It wasn't the first time someone tried calling me that, and I always hated it—loathed it actually, with a deep passion, my entire life. But for some reason, I don't hate it coming from Malcolm, and I definitely couldn't tell him I hated the nickname, especially not when it took him six months to warm up to being my friend.

Malcolm was like a baby deer the first year he was at Glendale. Any sudden movements or unplanned conversations were avoided by him at all costs. And I sure as heck wasn't going to be the one to scare him off, especially after giving him such a hard time with the chickens. So when he called me Kit Kat, I let it happen. Then it just stuck.

"I think we're all set! Be there by eight."

"Yes, ma'am. I'll see you later."

"Wait!" I click over to a video call, and he answers immediately, his bright-blue eyes peering at me through the screen. "Did you get a question today?"

His chin dips with a silent laugh, pulling the phone closer to his face. Every inch of my screen is covered by Malcolm—piercing blue eyes, smile lines, and his perfectly trimmed, light-brown beard on full display. "Oh, I got one," he whispers, eyes darting around, checking if the coast is clear. "Did you?"

I pout. One of the highlights of my day is sharing the ridiculous questions and anecdotes I endure as a high school teacher. It's rather startling how *out there* some teenagers can be in their thought process. Even if the majority of my classes are filled with seniors who are children approaching adulthood in a matter of months, I am constantly shocked at the things said in my classroom. Today, though, I came up short. No revelatory remarks or bizarre inquiries to share. "Aside from the penis museum, I got nothing. Now you go!"

"Well, to maintain the student's dignity, I will keep their name off record." He waves a tsking finger at me when I try to retort. Clearing his throat and raking his fingers through his damp hair, he says, "I was asked if you can get cancer from smoked ham."

"What?" We stare at each other through the phone, both rolling our lips and cheeks splotching red as we fight the inevitable. I break first, a wave of cackling laughter bellowing out of me. Laughter overtakes us, and I have to hang up without speaking.

"What are you bringing tonight?" Benny's voice startles me as he approaches.

"Cheese and rice, you scared me!" I jump, somehow hitting the back of my head against the locker then dropping the poster and my phone onto the grimy hallway tile.

"Maybe you should check your surroundings, then." He chuckles as he picks up the poster board. "Oh, is this the infamous penis poster?" His eyes are full of mischief and delight as he attempts to unfold it.

"Did you know about this too?!" I snatch it from his greedy paws and hit him in the arm with it.

In one swift motion, my annoyingly athletic cousin jukes to my left then to the right, grabbing the poster board so fast I don't even have time to respond. He walks into the teacher's lounge, opening the poster and reveling in all its glory. A cackle leaves his mouth as I follow him.

"Whoa," Ellie giggles over our shoulders. She must've snuck in behind us. "What a detailed presentation." She points at different pictures on the board, belting out a trill of laughs. Benny joins her. Their synchronized pre-marital chuckling is so adorable I almost forget what they are laughing at.

Almost.

Unfortunately, the images are burned into my brain, so I'll probably never forget.

"Anyway," I say through gritted teeth, "are you guys coming tonight?"

"Of course," Benny says, still heavily focused on the poster. "You think this could be used for actual scientific research?" He bites his fist to stifle his laughter. It's unsuccessful.

"Alright, that's enough out of you!" I snatch the poster board and wave my finger at him. "I would think our vice principal wouldn't be favorable of this kind of presentation."

Benny shrugs nonchalantly. "Charlie put in a lot of effort. I couldn't tell him no. Plus, I figured it would end your week on a high note."

"A hard note," Ellie corrects with a laugh. "No, a limp note!"

They both burst out into hysterics, and all I can do is groan as I storm out of the break room. What's the point of enduring their jokes if Malcolm isn't here to enjoy it too? He is the first person I want making fun of my classroom torture, and he's missing out on it.

"Kate, wait!" Ellie calls after me as I head into the hallway.

The crowd of bodies has slimmed to a few wanderers as we mosey back down to my classroom.

"We're sorry. It's just so funny. You know it is." She hooks her arm around mine.

"It is."

"Then what's wrong?" She follows me into my classroom as I shove the poster board into the supply closet. I'll just give Charlie a *B* and call it a day. No need to endure actually evaluating this thing any more than I already have. I definitely won't be checking his sources of information either.

"I'm just distracted." I sit at my desk and pull out my phone.

"Do you want to talk about it?" Ellie sits at the student desk directly opposite me.

"Will this be a friend talk or a therapist talk?" I roll my eyes.

"Ouch." She crosses her arms, leaning back in the chair. She's not offended by my words in the slightest, I'm sure. My attitude doesn't hold a candle to the people she's had to deal with as a therapist. But maybe receiving a reaction like that from a friend isn't ideal either.

"I'm sorry." I blow a curl off my face. They're crazy and untamed today, my hair clip hanging on for dear life. "I just had a long night. Then a long morning."

Ellie stifles a laugh. "Long, huh?"

"I hate you." I throw a pen at her but can't help giggling with her.

"What's going on, Kate?" She leans over the desk, resting her chin in her hands.

She's so effortless when she talks to people. I mean, yes, it's kind of a requirement for her job, but she's so freaking good at it. I bite at my thumbnail as she watches me. I can't hide anything from her. Not that I want to. She's my best friend. But it doesn't bode well that, on top of her seeing right through me, keeping secrets from a therapist in general is downright impossible for me. Those two things together make Ellie my secrets' kryptonite. When Benny told me he was going to propose, I had to fake sick with contagious diarrhea for a week just to avoid ruining the surprise.

"I don't know. I just don't feel like myself." I grab a rubber band from my desk and twirl it between my fingers. "I'm stressed about the party. My students already have a case of senioritis. And I haven't told Malcolm..."—I pause, pulling the band back farther—"my plans...yet." The rubber band snaps against my finger, and I wince in pain, shoving it in the trash can in protest.

"I see." She pauses, doing that therapist thing where she chooses her words carefully. "One, of course the kids have senioritis. They graduate in three months. Two, don't stress about the party. It happens every year. And lastly, why haven't you told Malcolm?"

"I don't know." I chew on my nail again. But I do know. I'm afraid of what he'll think of my random decision to start dating again. He's so protective and opinionated, like a German Shepherd sniffing out the drugs. I'm already anxious enough about getting back out there, but I know as soon as he finds out, he'll be watching like a hawk. Some might find it annoying, but I'd do the same for him if he were to get out there. But he's never liked dating—or so I think, since I've never seen him with anyone. And I haven't dated since—

"Are you afraid he'll be mad?" Ellie asks, cutting off my thought.

"Kind of."

"Why?" Her green eyes flicker at me as she leans forward.

I shrug as she stands and walks down an aisle of desks, her black high heels clicking against the floor. The fluorescent lights and baby-blue sweater she's sporting today are harsh against her pale skin, yet she still glows like an angel. She's really come out of her shell, going from all black or neutrals to an array of colors in her wardrobe, since she's been with Benny. I guess that's what happens when you find love...the color comes back into your life.

"Malcolm is a grown man. The guy is almost forty—"

"Thirty-seven," I correct her.

"Years old," she continues. "He's been single a long time. I doubt he'll be upset that *you*, a grown woman of child-bearing age, is ready to find a mate."

"First of all, ew. Do not use those weird fairy book terms with me again. Second, children? Also, ew. Calm down."

"You don't want kids?"

"That's not—no, I don't—I'm not sure. Maybe. Can we focus please?" Leaning my head back against my chair, I spin around in circles, noting pieces of Scotch tape left from my Christmas decorations last term.

"All I'm saying," Ellie says, refocusing as she keeps walking around my classroom, "is that Malcolm is an adult. You both are. Just tell him you're ready to date, and he'll support you. He wants you to be happy, and if getting back out there makes you happy, then so be it." She makes her way across the back of the room, noting the science presentations on display, before pivoting on her heel toward me.

"I know he just wants me to be happy. He's the best. We've just been single pals for so long I don't want him to feel abandoned or something."

I've been single for the last three years. After Eric left Glendale, our relationship didn't last longer than a month. Long distance just never works—not for me anyway. And Malcolm was there for me when it happened. He ate ice cream with me. Watched sad movies with me. He even went to a *Mamma Mia* production with me. The poor guy was so out of place, but it made the night a million times better. So, of course, when I was tipsy off two glasses of wine one night, I told him we should make a pact. Stay single until we're old then live off our retirement together.

"I just can't help but feel like he's been holding out on dating because of me. Because I wasn't ready. Being a good friend and all." I do one final spin around in my chair, bringing my knees to my chest for momentum. "Now I'm just jumping back in the sea and leaving him on land."

"Malcolm won't have any issues finding someone. Just tell him you're thinking of dating again." Ellie sits on the edge of my desk, straightening my stapler and clicking my pens so they *don't dry out*. She does this every day. Sometimes I leave my pens unclicked or uncapped just to drive her a little crazy.

"Well, here's the thing..." I hesitate. "I already am...dating...again." My voice cracks at my words, and Ellie gives me an incredulous look.

"What?" She grits out, pressing her lips into a tight line, nostrils flaring. I half expect to see smoke come out of her ears at this information.

"You're mad," I whisper, looking down at the discolored tile under my feet.

"Am not."

"See, if *you're* mad, then can you imagine how Malcolm will feel? What will he think when he realizes his best friend has been lying to him for weeks about her extracurricular activities?" I groan, throwing my head into my hands.

"Weeks?" she exclaims, jumping off my desk, her heels screeching against the floor. Such a horrible noise. I wince as she towers over me, tapping her foot. "Why didn't you tell us? Why didn't you tell *me*?"

"I don't know." *I really don't.* Maybe I'm embarrassed. Embarrassed that it's taken me this long to get back out there. Embarrassed I let the Eric situation knock me down so hard. Embarrassed that every time I see my family, they hound me about getting married and giving them grandbabies. The embarrassing truth stings my eyes.

I look up at Ellie, her eyes softening at the sight of my pitiful self. The pain I feel about this conversation is probably all over my face, because she doesn't press me any more.

"And I thought Benny was Malcolm's best friend?" She smirks, changing the subject for me. I hate conflict. Avoid it at all costs. Ellie figured that out early on when she found me pacing in the girls' bathroom, a cupcake squashed in my fist. Patsy, our old school counselor, was mad at me for bringing vegan cupcakes to her fundraiser bake sale. I was too chicken to defend myself and my efforts, which is not out of character for me. But Ellie saved the day and bought every last cupcake, taking them to her office. She is a friend above the rest—well...behind Malcolm. But no one compares to him.

"We can let them believe that. Benny is his favorite *guy* friend," I answer her question. "But we both know I'm Malcolm's *all-time* favorite." She nods in agreement at this fact, both of us refusing to acknowledge the elephant in the room.

I'm dating again.

Chapter Three

Kate

"It's not high enough." My grandma—my *lola*, as she's referred to in our Filipino culture—is graciously bossing me around as we decorate her house for her party tonight.

"What, do you want it hanging from the ceiling?" I wince and groan, reaching as high as possible, attempting to pin the garland to the wall. My five-foot-two stature is less than ideal for this task, but it still beats her five-foot-nothing with a recent hip replacement. I know if I wasn't here, she'd be climbing this stepladder, unsupervised.

"I don't know why Malcolm isn't here doing this." Her voice sounds like a pouty teenager as she sits in her rocking chair behind me.

"Because that man has a life outside of putting up with my family." I push the final pin in the garland and assess my progress. It looks *presentable*. "Plus, I think I'm doing a fine job." My unstable knees pop as I hop off the ladder.

"Oh please, he lives for this stuff."

"I don't think Malcolm's ideal Friday afternoon is decorating for a party for his friend's grandma." I roll my eyes and sit on the squeaky porch swing perpendicular to the house. Tracing the lopsided K carved into the armrest with my finger, nostalgia warms my chest as I swing back and forth, the rusty chains squeaking loudly as I do.

Lola scoffs. "Aye, is that all I am to the boy?" A scowl pinches her eyebrows as she lets out a huff and crosses her arms. Pouty teenager, indeed.

"You know you're more than that." The number of times I need to reassure this woman that Malcolm does love her like his own is ridiculous. It's borderline unhealthy, the obsession she has for the guy. "But he has a life away from here, and I don't want him to feel obligated to you."

"Afraid your internet boyfriends won't like it?" She snuggles deep into her chair, a cocky smirk shining at me as I gape. How dare she.

"First of all, I don't have internet *boyfriends*. I'm internet dating—two different things. And secondly, yes. I don't want any potentials to feel uncomfortable with how close Malcolm is with my family. Is that so wrong?"

I choose to ignore the subtle eye roll she gives me in response and glance around the porch at our decorating job. Red and green garlands hang from one end of the porch to the other, giant bows line the railing of her porch steps, and twinkle lights are hung all over, even covering her multitude of porch plants, the added weight of the bulbs causing them to lean slightly to the left. Poor stems could snap at any second.

My eyes travel up the door frame, noticing the chipped paint that was in the center of the door *last* week is now smooth and glossy white. Not a chip in sight.

"Your door looks nice." Suspicion lines my tone as I analyze the paint. Seriously, it looks like a brand-new door.

I've had a hunch for a while that Lola has a secret lover or something she's not telling me about. This theory wouldn't hold up in court, though. I don't have any concrete evidence, except the random little things around her house getting fixed. The chipped paint on her front door, for starters, is now glossy smooth. Leaky faucet from last week? Not a drop. Creaky step on the deck? Silent. That and the random afternoon phone calls. Either she has someone coming around being...handy. Or she's been going against doctor's orders and doing it all herself.

She glances over her shoulder at the door and shrugs, taking a sip of tea. "Your boyfriends will just have to accept that Malcolm isn't going anywhere, and they'll have to live with it."

Choosing to ignore that sentiment, I ask, "How's the hip?" just as Dolly Parton, my golden retriever, bounds through the open front door and joins me on the swing. We jostle side to side, and the loud chains grind as she nestles her head onto my lap.

"Don't change the subject," she argues, steadily rocking back and forth.

My groan sounds more like a whine as I abandon the swing and wander back into the house. If she won't tell me about her secret handyman boyfriend, I won't give her the satisfaction of stating the obvious.

I'm painfully aware that my overly attractive, burly best friend could send any possible boyfriend scrambling for his keys. Anytime we've gone out, Malcolm was practically a billboard over my head that said *do not approach*. Since I swore off men, it hasn't been an issue. It actually made those nights more fun by not having to shake off the dogs or hide in the bathroom from the drunk, handsy guys at the bar. But seeing as I want to find someone now, it might be a hindrance. Options have been heavily weighed surrounding this decision. And after the mixer fiasco, the fear of running into him at a speed-dating night had me running for the hills. It's become clear that I need to set some boundaries. But how can I tell the sweetest man alive, the man who wants nothing more than other people's happiness, that I don't know if he should be around as much? And what will my family say? They like him more than they like me most of the time.

"Have you talked to your mama?" Lola yells at me through her screen door, the rise in octave accentuating her Filipino accent.

"Not since Thanksgiving." Reality has the power to burn my tongue when I say it out loud. "You?" I call back to her.

A screech of the rocking chair is followed by the shuffling of slippers before Lola joins me in the kitchen. "No. Not even for Christmas." The sadness in her voice is heavy. Reality also has the power to break my lola's heart.

"Aye, I'm sorry, Lola." I wrap her in a hug. We don't talk about my parents often. We don't acknowledge the hard truth that my mom is so caught up in her own life that she seems to forget about *us*—her mother and only child. And don't even get me started on my dad. He's just a cowardly man who follows my mom around like a lost puppy. All her business trips, self-reflection retreats, even the personal-development seminars—most associated with one pyramid scheme or another—my dad tags along without question, even if it means missing the holidays. In the past eight years, I can count on one hand the number of times I've seen my parents, but I can't put a value on the number of times I've wished it was different.

My grandma releases me and rests her hands on my cheeks. "I'm sorry too." Her eyes are misty, squinting upward when she smiles at me. The lines of her face, a map of a life well lived, deepen. I can really see her age now, especially since her most recent hospital stay. She was always the energetic and spunky one. A bright, sparkling light in the world. My grandpa was the quiet one, beaming at her like she was his own personal shooting star, granting his wishes. Lola, being the star she is, decided to audition for the local Christmas play, breaking her hip during her reindeer solo. She ended up being on bedrest for two months, forcing her to change her lifestyle. Lola had to give up some of her hobbies—you know, the ones that require your arms and legs flailing about. Ever since, that sparkle of hers has started to dull bit by bit.

Lola shuffles into the living room, her slippers almost sliding off her feet as she does. She traces the bottom edge of a framed photo that hangs on the wall as you enter, a black-and-white photo of my grandpa sitting on the hood of a vintage car—thick, dark hair windblown, wearing a cutoff shirt, with a cigarette hanging out of his mouth, a vibrant look of love in his eyes as he peered at Lola as she took the photo.

Wishing for what they had seems silly. It seems so far out of grasp sometimes, and waiting so long to get back out there has done me no favors. Not everyone was lucky enough to witness a love like theirs like I did. It was pure and generous and raw. It made the feelings of emptiness fade when Mom wasn't around. Knowing I had Lola and Grandpa helped cover that open wound. But now that Grandpa is gone, no matter how much she tries to hide it, I know Lola is lonely.

And you'd think her daughter would sense the loneliness too.

Like mother-daughter telepathy. *That's a thing, right?*

I shove down the gnawing feeling that bubbles up anytime I dwell too long on my mother and glance at the rooster clock that hangs above the oven. It's been off center for a year, and every time I look at it, I tell myself to straighten it.

It's almost four. No time to do it today. "I have to run." I kiss the top of Lola's head, grab my bag off the counter, and rush out of her house. "I'll see you tonight!" I say, screen door slamming abruptly behind me.

Chapter Four

Kate

"Do I have to wear this the entire time?" Nick, my newest online dating candidate, groans as he pulls at the scratchy wool fabric currently strangling his neck.

Matching Christmas sweaters. With a guy I barely know.

Somehow, I convinced myself it was completely normal to bring a stranger to my family's holiday party and jokingly mentioned matching sweaters. Much to my surprise, Nick was game. Part of me feels flattered that I found a guy willing to go along with my quirky ideas, but another part of me is concerned about my mental state. Truly. I feel like I have no filter lately, just making decisions willy-nilly and seeing what happens. My last relationship was so controlled, giving me no room to truly be myself. Maybe some subconscious part of me is reveling in the unknown, the hot mess that is dating altogether. I don't know. But I do know I should probably be a little more cautious, maybe have a serious talk with Ellie. She'll probably have some psychological term for what I'm doing.

"Yes." I stealthily roll my eyes as he continuously stretches the neck of his sweater—a bright-red turtleneck with a snowman in the center. "And if I recall, you said you were 'all in with the Christmas mumbo jumbo.'" I use air quotes to emphasize the exact words he used to invite himself to my family's Christmas party. If he felt the need to come with me, I felt the need to make it worth his while. Enter the five-dollar sweaters I found at Super Thrift.

Why I decided to unload my desperation about not wanting to attend another family party without a date while perusing the produce aisle, I will never know. The site of paired tomatoes drew it out of me, I guess. But that seems to be my track record lately. So far, the online dates have gone kerplunk because I can't *shut up*. So yes, out of desperation, when Nick invited himself to this party, I just said, "Well alright, then."

"I know. I just didn't think you'd choose the cheapest sweaters possible." He stretches the neck again. "I think it's giving me a rash." His voice comes out whiny, and I curse myself for following through with this.

I pull down the road that leads to Lola's house as he proceeds to scratch his neck like a maniac. This boy is about to grate my last nerve. I screech to a halt, biting back a cackle when he almost flies through my windshield. Pulling into the driveway, I park behind Benny's silver pickup truck and inhale a deep breath. Just about everybody and their dog is already here...waiting for me.

Of course I'm one of the last to arrive.

With a date.

I pinch my eyes shut at the image of everyone watching us walk up the porch steps through the living room window. I can see Benny wearing a Santa hat, which is very on-brand for him. The theme is Christmas in March. The idea sounds absurd, but after Lola was in the hospital over the holidays, Benny decided we should have a family Christmas as soon as she recovered. Recovery took almost three months. The woman's pride got the best of her when she refused to participate in therapy.

My grandma is sitting on the couch, laughing at Benny conducting our aunts and uncles in a Christmas carol. Her gray hair is pinned back and hidden under an elf hat. She's sporting the Christmas sweater I embroidered for her last year, and her legs are propped up on the ottoman, feet wiggling along with the music.

A few other family members come in and out of the living room, including Ellie, who is filling drinks and providing appetizers. She and Benny embrace and begin conducting the carol together. Deep-seated envy starts to creep in. The envy that comes every time I see the gleam of true love in their eyes. It's not their fault, obviously. But can you blame a girl for wanting what other people have? It's human nature.

Sweat starts to build up on my forehead and neck as I watch the party from inside my car. *It's a billion degrees outside.* I dab the droplets away with the sleeve of my sweater, resisting the urge to itch every part of me that the scratchy fabric touches. Yes, the sweaters were cheap, but this girl is on a budget. And I refuse to spend my coffee money on matching sweaters that failed to fill the void my annoying, hopeless-romantic self desires.

"Are we doing this or what?" Nick asks. The redness of his neck peeks out from the top of his sweater as he gives it one final scratch.

"Yes, yeah," I stammer my words, pulling my purse from the backseat before exiting the car. My chunky Doc Martens crunch in the fake snow that covers the front lawn. Ellie must've done this after I left earlier. I fluff my sweater, hoping the humid air will dry the sweat that's accumulating on my lower back, then walk around to open the trunk of my car.

"Cute place." Nick assesses his surroundings, the passenger door screeching like nails on a chalkboard as he closes it.

I sift through my trunk, organizing my contributions to the party—dairy-free eggnog, dairy-free cookies, wine, and two Dirty Santa presents—before piling them into my arms.

"Did you bring anything good?" He looks over my shoulder at the containers I have labeled. For a second, I swear his face contorts like he sniffed a gallon of old milk. He probably realizes I *saw* his reaction, because he forces a smile and reaches for the sacks. "Here, I got that."

Nick grabs the gifts and wine, clearly leaving the items that disgust him for me to carry. *Such a gentleman you are, Nicholas.* A loud honk startles me, and I turn to see a giant orange truck whipping into the yard, headed for the spot right next to my beat-up Subaru. My cheeks sting instantly from my smile as I see Malcolm climb out of the truck, sporting the Christmas sweater I bought him last year.

"Who's that?" Nick whispers to me as Malcolm walks behind the tall bed of his truck.

Heat sizzles deep inside my stomach as Malcolm approaches, making me sweat even more.

"Malcolm!" I reach out to him then snap my arms back to my sides, remembering the need for better boundaries. I clear my throat and gesture between the guys. "Malcolm, this is Nick. Nick, this is Malcolm." I pause for an appropriate amount of time before wrapping my arms around Malcolm's waist and squeezing him tight. Even when I wear my platform boots, he towers over me. It allows my head to nuzzle perfectly into the center of his chest where his heartbeat does that skippy thing it always does under my ear. I wonder if he's seen a doctor for it yet.

"Malcolm Geer." Malcolm reaches over me to shake Nick's hand.

"Nick Harlon," he returns. "Kate's date."

My arms go limp at Malcolm's waist, whipping my eyes up to his. Dread swims in my gut at Nick's response. The excitement I felt from seeing my best friend quickly fizzles as I see the smile on his face shift into a scowl. He nods at Nick, refusing to meet my eyes. *Crap.*

His shock is no surprise. I've blindsided him. I was going to tell him as soon as I saw him. I was going to spill the truth that I'm so tired of feeling lonely and desperate for love that instead of attending this party with him, like I've done for every party for the last two years, I brought a stranger.

But stupid Nick beat me to the punch.

"Nice to meet you," Malcolm says through gritted teeth before reaching into my trunk to collect the rest of the containers.

"I'd be careful with those. They're dairy free." Nick chuckles as he walks toward the house. Malcolm draws in a quick breath as he puts the containers under one arm and shuts my rickety trunk with the other.

"He's a catch," Malcolm grumbles as we round the side of my car.

"We're still getting to know each other." I bite my nail, nervous jitters jolting their way across my arms and legs.

"So...a date." It's not a question as Malcolm clenches his jaw. The edge in his tone lingers in the air as we shuffle our way through the lawn.

"I just... I dunno. I figured I'd try to find an actual date this year." I choke on the word *date*, the humid air doing its darndest to suffocate me.

"Is it because we lost at Jingle Shots last year?" he jokes, and I feel relieved at his effort. I know he's upset with me for not telling him about Nick, but the man never dwells on piddly nonsense. And he seems to never get mad at me. I love him for it. I hate when people are mad at me. Especially him.

"Last year was rigged, and everyone knows it. We should've won!" I yell toward the people in the house. Not that anyone will hear me over the sporadic caroling and clinking of drinks happening, but I stomp my foot in protest anyway, driving my point home.

"Why, then?" He stays by my side as he asks, walking in step with me, his long legs forcing themselves to take smaller strides, always matching mine. He does that, no matter where we go. He's always keeping his steps in tune with mine—probably because he knows I can't keep up with his nine-foot-long legs.

"Why what?" I trail off, taking in the splendor of holiday cheer before me.

Laughter and chatter mixed with Christmas tunes flow from the open door of the house as Nick lets himself inside. I roll my eyes as he points back at me and Malcolm as we make our way slowly to the house. A few aunties' and uncles' heads poke out in the door frame, looking at Nick, then at me, followed by whispers, gasps, and shaking of heads. Nick has for sure told them he's my date, and now I have to answer to my entire family. *Why did I do this to myself?*

"Why the date?" His voice is a timid whisper as he halts at the bottom of the porch steps, just a few feet to go before we reach the mini North Pole that awaits us. I stop next to him.

The question of the century: *Why did I bring a date?*

This is the perfect scenario to lie. Right here, right now. Just do it, Kate. Lie to your best friend. Tell him you just felt like bringing a date. Don't tell him that you're sad and alone and feeling so desperate to find someone that you started online dating a month ago. Don't tell him you hit rock bottom and threw all your standards out the window by bringing Nick. All just to avoid telling your family at "Christmas" that yes, you are still single, and no, you don't foresee grandbabies in the future. *Again.* Not that I want tons of babies. I don't even know what I want a year from now. But the reality that I am as single as my

Aunt Edna, after vowing her life to celibacy at the age of fifty, is enough to make me want to curl up and die.

"I don't know." I shrug and kick at the fake snow on the steps in front of me. "I'm just...tired of being alone." I guess the truth is happening.

Malcolm grabs my elbow. "You're not alone." His eyes go a shade darker, if that's even possible with how crystal blue they are. "You have me."

Something in his voice weighs on me. Is he...*hurt?* I expected him to be disappointed that I kept this dating thing a secret, but this feels different.

"I— You— Yes, I do. But..." Words are hard. "You know what I mean," I whisper.

His throat bobs as he watches me, eyes twinkling under the Christmas lights. But it's not a happy twinkle. I don't know what to say. I don't know what to do. A part of me feels like I'm abandoning him in this weird and cruel world to go find my happily ever after. I want him to find his too.

"We could—"

"If you kids don't hurry it up, I'll die before this party is over!" Lola's voice booms from the doorway, cutting me off.

"Sorry, Lola." Malcolm beams at my grandma. She blows him a kiss before pointing her finger at me, an unspoken *hurry up* if I ever did see one.

"We're coming." I can't help but roll my eyes at her. She doesn't like that. She waves me off as she shuffles away, mumbling curse words under her breath.

I turn back to face Malcolm. "Look, I—" But he's already walking up the steps.

"Come on. I don't wanna be on the naughty list," he calls over his shoulder before stepping into the house.

My entire family swarms him. Kisses, hugs, cheek pinches, the works. He'll never be on their naughty list.

Chapter Five
Malcolm

"You knew about this?" Benny's eyes are about to bug out of his skull at his fiancée. They herded me into the kitchen the minute I walked in here. No, *'Hello, thanks for coming.'* Just snatched my phone like the meddling vultures they are, and they have been glued to it since.

"She just told me today! I swear!" Ellie defends her friend, giving me those pity eyes I despise. *Don't pity me.*

"She likes a clean-shaven man?" Benny lets out a whistle as Ellie snatches the phone and scans it even more. Kate's dating profile. Yeah, I may have made a fake profile to scope out the situation. It took less than five minutes to figure out which app she is using and answer the *About Me* questions. Someone had to. "How do you feel about this?" Benny's bug eyes are on me now, gesturing a hand around his jaw. This behavior, paired with his Santa hat, is making it real difficult to take him seriously.

"I don't know. She's an adult. She makes her own choices." I shrug and take a sip of brandy from my reindeer cup. I don't need to tell them how I feel or about my new impulsive urge to shave. *Clean-shaven men.* Four years of pristine patience gone in seconds.

"Are you okay?" Ellie asks. The worry in her voice makes my skin crawl.

"I'm fine." I down the last sip of my brandy before popping the cork of the bottle and filling up again. "Can we drop it?"

Benny and Ellie glance at each other then back at me. Probably some weird, engaged-couple telepathy thing they're doing. I stare at them, unblinking and huddled in the corner of the kitchen, away from the cheerful festivities. The awkward silence builds, and their anticipation is palpable and infuriating. Benny sips on his cider loudly. Ellie taps her fingers on the counter slowly. Both of them are chomping at the bit to keep talking about this situation.

The situation where I, an almost forty-year-old chump, have had a crush on my best friend for five years. Someone so polar opposite of me that the idea of us being together is laughable. The friend that has finally decided to start dating again after three years. Before that? I had to endure the trainwreck of a relationship unfold between her and Eric.

Picturing him makes me want to gouge my eyes out.

Everyone with a brain knows I have feelings for Kate. On some level, I think Kate does too. And when Eric left, everyone—and I do mean everyone—leapt at the chance to get us together, meddling their way into a complex friendship. Lucky for me, Kate swore off dating, and I didn't have to put up with our librarian, Margaret's, wooing tactics. Apparently, all it would take to get Kate to give me a chance is the right moves. I grimace at the memory of Margaret shaking her hips and puckering her lips.

Now, Kate is back on the market. So much so that she's bringing strangers to her lola's house. And if the darting eyes from the family are any indication, it's clear what everyone here thinks. They think I should just ask her out. It's that simple.

To them.

But to me, not so much. I don't like most people. I don't like feelings. And I definitely don't like my friends knowing about my feelings. If I could gag myself and get run over by my own truck, I would if it meant not having to endure this conversation.

"So you're really not going to tell her?" Ellie whispers. "Don't you want to know if she feels the same way?"

"Nope."

"Apo, don't you lie to your friends." Lola limps into the kitchen to join us, the bells on her sweater jingling with each step, her elf hat abandoned on the couch.

Benny and Ellie rush to find her a chair and help her sit down steadily. The woman had hip surgery, was told by her doctor to take it easy, yet here she is, forcing us all to have a Christmas party in March.

"I'm not lying," I grumble at the scoffs and eye rolls I get in response.

"Don't you lie to me either." She shoves her knuckle into my thigh. They sat her next to me and just vanished. Of course they did.

"Lola ..." I squat down, getting eye level with this fragile woman—basically my surrogate grandmother. "I don't think it's a good idea." I rub the back of my neck when her eyes shift downward. I can't stand seeing her sad. It's like seeing Kate sad in forty years. It guts me.

Laughter and clinking of drinks come from the other side of the kitchen counter. Even when I'm squatting, I'm still tall enough to see they're all playing Christmas charades. Kate sits on the armrest of the couch, a solid five feet from Nick. Her *date*. I can tell she's uncomfortable by the way she's white-knuckling her cup and looking over at the kitchen every few seconds.

"Go rescue her," Lola says.

"Why? She brought him here. She should suffer the consequences."

Lola chuckles at me then proceeds to jam her knuckle into my arm this time. "She's just ready to find happiness. She'll learn where and who to find that with soon enough." She gives me a wink.

I blow all the air out of my lungs and smooth out my beard. I want her to be right. I *want* to be Kate's happiness. But what if I'm not what she wants? Am I really going to jeopardize our friendship just to put myself out there?

"I can't lose her," I breathe.

"You won't." She pats me on the shoulder then uses me as a brace as she stands on wobbly legs. "You can't lose someone you're destined to be with."

Destiny. Fate. The universe. Kate and her lola are the quirky kind of people who believe in that stuff. For a long time, I thought it was idiotic. But there's something about their faith in the future that sends a flutter through my chest.

Hope. They have hope for things unseen. And as crazy as that sounds to some, over time I've realized that all we can do is hope. Plotting and planning gets us nowhere when things go wrong. A vague picture of desert sand and orange flames flashes across my mind, mixing with the colored lights on the Christmas tree. Planning can get us killed.

I shake off the memory and help Lola make her way around the kitchen counter where Benny can lead her to the couch. The family bickers at her for walking too much, an uncle mimics her slow pace, an aunt swats at him, and a few cousins giggle. I scan over the group, noting who's here and who's missing, reminding myself to call Uncle Jerry back and find time to fix Auntie Dawn's faucet.

My eyes land on a set of dark-brown ones with hints of auburn. Eyes swirling like a fresh cup of coffee, sparkling with warmth under the Christmas lights. Eyes that dance when they laugh at her own jokes, twitch in the corners when they're angry, and squint to hold back tears when they're sad. Eyes I would die for.

Kate's eyes stay pinned on me as she mouths, *"Help me."* I shrug at her and take another drink. A silent plea with a pout is shot my way. I hold up my finger, *just a minute,* and take an extra-long and slow chug of my drink. I watch her groan out at my snail's pace, a dribble of brandy leaving my mouth as I laugh. *"Fine,"* I mouth.

I finish my glass and make my way into the living room. Christmas charades has morphed into another game about a bowl or something. I take a seat on the floor near the couch. Lola is on the far end, winking at me. Aunt Edna is next to her, talking Nick's ear off, who is seated right next to Kate. The proximity of his knee to hers sends a jolt up my spine. He's practically in her lap.

Kate waves at the open spot on the floor next to her feet.

I pat the seat on the floor next to me.

She waves again.

I pat again.

Then we stare at each other in a standoff, her date completely oblivious to what's happening a foot away from him. Kate caves, huffing as she scoots her feet across the carpet to where I'm sitting.

"Care to join me?" I rest my arms behind my head and lean against the wall.

Kate towers over me, her small frame swallowed by a colossal Christmas sweater. It's hideous. It looks like she lost a fight with an elf in a tinsel factory. I wonder why she wore something so ugly when underneath that sweater is a figure so beautiful it could send a man to the moon. Is it possible Kate didn't want Nick to gawk at her? Because I'm confident if she was wearing something else, ole Nicky Poo wouldn't be so engrossed in his conversation with Edna.

Kate groans, plopping down on the carpet beside me. We watch everyone play games in silence. She taps her fingers against her thigh to the Christmas music, each nail a different shade of red, looking at everyone in the room but me.

"You're off beat." I chuckle.

She stops tapping then puffs her cheeks out, red splotches forming like they always do when she does that.

I lean over and whisper, "What's wrong?"

"Hmm?" She leans in, a piece of her curly hair getting caught on my beard. "Oh, nothing. I don't know. I just..." Taking a breath, she finally looks at me. "Are you mad?"

"About what?"

"This whole"—she waves a hand as if to present the living room on *The Price is Right*—"dating situation."

"Dating situation?" I muse.

"I just don't want you upset that I didn't tell you."

"Why didn't you?"

She doesn't respond right away. Instead, we watch the chatter across the room. Holiday cheer in all its glory. I used to hate this holiday—growing up in a broken home with separate holidays and all. The holidays at the Divata home are always a highlight for me. Kate's family has been nothing but welcoming to me the last five years.

A part of me, much bigger than I will admit to anyone, hopes I never lose it.

"I didn't want you to feel alone." Her voice is a whisper. "We've been buddies for so long, and eventually, I'll have someone, and I won't be able to be just *your* buddy anymore."

"Because you'll have two buddies." I nod in understanding.

"Not what I mean!" Shoving me in the shoulder, she giggles. It's a sweet sound, and I hate myself for how I let it make me feel. All warm and fuzzy and ridiculous. "I just mean…" Nick turns around and waves at us. She pauses and waves back. I don't. "I just mean—" She focuses back on me, but her face is sadder than when her dog Hilda died. "I won't see you as much if I'm dating someone. You'll have to…share me."

Her words hit me like a blow in the stomach. *Share* her. I try to not focus on the sentiment sounding like she's a possession and focus on the reality that she won't just be my curly-headed firecracker anymore. She could become someone else's.

Everything around me goes silent as the reality of the situation starts to sink in. The moment slows as I watch a slow breath leave her lips. They start to draw me into a serene mental space when, out of nowhere, a deafening clang shatters the silence, reverberating up my spine and into my ears.

Terrified and on instinct, I brace for bullet fire and turn my body into Kate's, shielding both of us from the impact. My entire body goes instantly rigid and shaky as I hover over her on all fours. Her eyes lock onto mine. Her mouth moves, but I can't hear what she says through the ringing in my ears. My heart pounds viciously in my chest, and my vision blurs. Everything about this says I should run for cover, but keeping Kate safe is my priority.

I stay pinned above her.

Placing her hand on my chest and splaying her fingers wide over my heart, she mouths, "*It's okay.*" I don't budge. My chest is heaving, and my arms are trembling. Images of the desert flash across my mind. The heat, the dirt, the blood. Everything around me feels fuzzy. Voices are muffled and distant. Kate's eyes are focused on mine as her fear fades slowly as I stay planted in place. My shoulders pull tight, panic prickling at my neck as I try to focus.

Her eyes. Her cheeks. Her lips.

I catalog them one by one, confirming she's in one piece.

A drop of water lands on her cheek. She blinks, wiping it away, then she reaches up to my cheek to wipe mine. *Am I crying?* She wipes again, this time on my forehead. *Sweat.*

"Malcolm, it's okay." Her voice sounds far away, but the ringing starts to subside. "Malcolm, we're okay." She grabs my cheeks and rubs her thumbs back and forth, wiping away more sweat. Her pupils dilate and constrict as they stay locked on me. I focus on them, the shade of coppery red on the outer edge, the dark swirl of chocolate brown in the center. I can see myself in them. A reflection of a man, pitiful and afraid.

"Malcolm, you alright, buddy?" A hand grabs my shoulder, momentarily jolting my gaze away from Kate. Benny is at my side, shaking my shoulders and pulling me up. "Sorry, man. Jerry dropped the punch bowl."

"Darn thing sliced my pinky!" Jerry yells from the kitchen sink, a pile of broken glass laying on the counter next to him.

Kate sits up, her gaze shifting into a sympathetic frown as I straighten.

"Kate, I'm sorry," I stutter my words. "The noise, it just—"

Her hand finds my cheek. "Shh, don't. It's okay." She brushes her fingers down the side of my beard, and my body shivers in response. Her slender arms wrap around my waist and squeeze. "Are you alright?"

Resting my chin on her head, I nod. Her curls tangle in my beard again. For a moment, I don't pull away. I can't. I let her soft hair cushion my face as I slow my breathing. She squeezes one more time before letting go, hands grazing slowly across my lower back. What the feeling of her hands on me does to my insides is too embarrassing to admit.

"Here, drink some water." Ellie hands me a glass as Kate steps back. The room is staring at me. Us. And the big fiasco that just happened under the Christmas tree. Jerry is at the back of the room, mouthing his apologies. Fantastic.

If it were possible for awkward silence to be heard, this would be that time. I can hear it loud and clear. Smoothing out my beard, I chug the water and take a bow. "Merry Christmas, everyone." Might as well make light of something awkward, or they'll all keep staring at me.

Kate eyes me guardedly before sitting on the couch. "Bravo." She forces a smile and single clap at this absurd situation. Nick joins her on the couch, two drinks in hand as he wraps his arm around her and whispers something in her ear.

The reindeer cup in my hand crumples.

Kate's and Nick's heads snap to me, her eyes widening at Dasher's face squished in my palm. "I'm gonna go," I grit out.

"'Night, everyone." I wave, hug, and shake my way through the house. "Goodnight, Lola." I kiss Kate's grandma on the cheek then nod to Benny and Ellie as I reach the front door.

"Malcolm, wait!" The warmth of her voice threatens to swallow me up. Kate weaves through the family and meets me at the front door. "Will you be—"

"I'm fine, Stanley," I snip unintentionally, and she recoils at my tone. Deep breath. "I'll be okay. I promise." I pull her by the hem of her ugly sweater and wrap her in a hug. Her body relaxes under mine, and I follow suit. The power this woman has on my nerves is strong enough to power a nuke. "I'm sorry if I scared you."

She speaks into my chest. "Don't apologize. I'm just sorry you're still going through this."

"It's not like it used to be."

"Good." She looks up at me, resting her chin on my chest, arms still around me. I could stay here, in this moment, forever. "I need to know you're going to be okay."

A small ringlet of hair falls across her face. I pull it away and tuck it behind her ear. "Don't worry about me," I say, then kiss the top of her head.

"You're gonna have to move that a few inches south, Geer!" Paul, one of Lola's cousins, but not an uncle, calls to us from the kitchen.

Kate and I release our hug and look at him. My confusion is clear when he laughs and points above us. I look up, and my soul leaves my body.

Mistletoe.

Kate chokes out a laugh then grabs my arm and starts to laugh even harder. A wheezy chortle leaves her throat as she points at me and then the mistletoe. The girl has tears running down her face, for God's sake.

"What's so funny, Stanley?"

"It's just—" She gives a breathless laugh. "Of course that would happen—" *Another* laugh. "When I'm here with a date." She grabs her side and bends at the waist, losing control as she spirals into a fit of giggles. The entire house is watching her now—including her *date*.

"We can opt out, then."

"No, you cannot!" Ellie yells from the couch. "My house, my rules."

"Not your house, ma'am," I retort, looking at Lola and Benny and give them my best pleading look.

Benny whispers something to Lola then faces me with a smug grin. He rubs his chin, *pretending* to give it thought. His grin widens when he says, "Mistletoe is binding!"

The house cheers and claps at my misery. I groan and run my hand down my face. This is not how I want my first kiss with Kate to go.

"Kiss her already!" Lola yells from next to Edna. Nick, on the other side, is glowering at her then at us. He's too chicken to oppose the family. Smart man.

I pinch the bridge of my nose and look back down at Kate. She's biting her lip, with her arms behind her back, bouncing on the balls of her feet. Is she *nervous?* That's interesting.

"Well..." I drop my hands to my sides. "What do you want to do?"

She glances at the room then back to me. "What do you—"

"No." I stop her. "None of that. I asked first."

"Dang it," she mumbles under her breath. Still biting her lip, her eyes flicker as she contemplates. Then a slow, devilish smile moves across her face. "Mistletoe is binding, I guess." She shrugs one shoulder, a coy look on her face as she steps closer.

She's enjoying this.

"You think you can handle me?" She bats her eyelashes.

"Why are you tormenting me?" I grumble.

"I just think it's good for you to embrace some spontaneity." She giggles, stepping closer.

We're toe to toe...under the mistletoe... Alright, I need Jerry to come punch me in the face for thinking that.

"I can be spontaneous," I whisper, my breath blowing a stray hair away from her face.

"I've never seen you be spontaneous." She gives me a smirk.

"Stanley, are you *flirting* with me?" I can't fight the smile that escapes me when Kate gives me a sneaky wink, biting her glossy lip again. *Distracting.*

"Just trying to make it worth your while." Her cheeks flush pink with her words.

I lean down, letting my breath hit the soft spot on her neck. Goosebumps form instantly as I whisper against her ear. "What about your date?"

She glances over at Nick, who's chatting it up with Edna again, ignoring the scene in the doorway. "I don't think he's very concerned." Her eyes meet mine again, serious this time. "This won't ruin anything, right?"

"Only if we let it."

"Will you...let it?" Her words come out in a quivering whisper.

I take her hand, holding it in mine against my chest. "Never."

A deep sigh leaves Kate's mouth. "How do you want to do this, then?"

"I thought you wanted me to be spontaneous?" I smirk.

Her cheeks are red now, eyes expectant as she looks up at me. Everything I want in this life is right here. Everything I've missed out on. The girl that has had my heart on a string for the last five years is within my grasp.

But it can't start like this.

I want Kate Stanley more than I want air to breathe. It's almost pathetic how gone I am for this woman. I've dreamt of this moment in ways I can't admit. But it can't be like this...with an audience. It can't be because of some fake, stupid house rule. If I'm going to get Kate Stanley to give me a shot—a *real* shot—I need it to be perfect.

Cradling her face in my hands, I stare at her full lips. They part slightly as my breath trembles out of me. Her eyes widen at my gaze before she quickly shuts them and presses her lips back together. They're a raspberry pink tonight with a light shimmer. So distracting. So tempting. "I'll give you spontaneous."

In an instant, I wrap an arm around her waist, dipping her low underneath the mistletoe. Her face is stunned at the swift motion. The house is giggling and gasping all around us.

Then...I kiss her on the cheek.

Chapter Six

Kate

"The cheek? What's so wrong with that?" Emma shrugs at this mind-boggling information, setting up her paints and brushes for the class day, waving her paintbrush in the air as if to tell me I'm *freaking out for nothing*.

"Um, nothing. I just thought it was interesting." I shrug back. Maybe I am freaking out for nothing.

"Interesting?" She muses, crossing her arms over her chest, accentuating that little bump underneath her paint-splattered apron.

"Not interesting," I deflect. "Weird. I thought it was weird." *Just play it cool, Kate. You're probably overthinking this like you do everything else.*

"Did you want him to kiss you on the lips?" The paintbrushes in her hands swish toward me, pointing at me. Accusing me.

"No!" I yell abruptly. I don't sound convincing at all. Did I want him to kiss me? Surely not. This is Malcolm we're talking about.

"Are you sure about that?" Planting her hands on her hips, the brushes stick out like a tail on one side.

"Yes, yeah. I'm sure. Totally."

"Well then, there's nothing to worry about. Maybe he was just trying to be a gentleman." She waves me off, brushes now being placed in their appropriate cups on the table.

Nothing to worry about. *Perfect.*

I just spilled every single detail surrounding the mistletoe fiasco the other night, and this is what I get? I knew I should've had this conversation with Margaret. At least with our eighty-year-old librarian an aloof response wouldn't be as baffling. But Emma here is supposed to be my friend. Malcolm's friend too! Yes, I came to her because I need someone level-headed to discuss this with. But I half-expected her to at least ask me what his breath smelled like. *Mint-infused brandy.* Refreshing and spicy swirled together in an invigorating concoction. My mouth waters at the thought of it.

"What is it?" She eyes the thumbnail I'm now biting.

I yank my hand away from my mouth and wipe the dampness from the corners of my lips. *What is going on with me?* "Nothing."

"Are you sure you didn't want more than a cheeker?" She raises an eyebrow at me. It's just as accusatory as the brushes. I might as well have a spotlight on me in the middle of an interrogation room.

"I'm sure." My words linger in the air, like my thought is incomplete. I wrap my arms around my waist and squeeze. A hug would be really nice right now. "I'm sure," I repeat. I have no idea what I wanted to happen. I just know that, since that moment under the mistletoe, my feelings toward Malcolm and everything that has to do with him has changed, and I have no idea what to do with them. My brain keeps getting flooded with Malcolm in ways I've never thought before. Excitement and confusion are battling it out inside my chest like a 90's film dance-off, pulling out wild, unrealistic moves with me caught in the middle, stunned and sometimes breathless.

I don't know whether to embrace these thoughts or shove them deep down inside me. Heat flushes my neck and cheeks at the recent change in my daydreams. When I used to imagine a paramedic jumping out of a moving ambulance to rescue me from a car wreck, the person always wore sunglasses, and the sun was so bright I could never make out their features. But we'd kiss, as if my rescuer was the Prince Charming I was waiting for. It was an odd dream, but I grew attached to it, savoring it every time it happened. But then two days ago, the rescuer was no longer wearing a medic uniform. No, he was wearing a fishing shirt and khakis, sliding on his knees across the grass to pull me out of the broken window. And instead of sunglasses, it was a set of piercing blue eyes gazing down at me. Eyes I see every day. And just as I was preparing to *kiss* my rescuer, I woke up in a puddle of sweat and gasping for air. Blood was coursing through my veins like it needed to revive all my organs.

There's no denying that the rescuer was Malcolm. And the effects it had on me physically were jarring. Every part of me twisted and burned, making me feel almost uncontrollable. I've never had such an episode like *that* before. And I've never had an episode over Malcolm, for crying out loud!

"Well, there you go." Emma pulls me out of my thoughts just in time. Any longer and I might've spontaneously combusted in the middle of her classroom. "It happened. It's over."

"And *cheeker* is weird. Please don't ever say that again."

Emma snorts and unties her apron, the sweet baby bump no longer hidden by paint splatter. She has that sweet glow about her, but I'm not allowed to mention it. Apparently, it's sweat, and it's annoying, so it's better left unmentioned. "Sorry," she laughs. "Come on, I'm starving."

We make our way down the hall to the break room as students shove their way around each other, almost knocking us down as they race to the cafeteria. Gertrude, the cafeteria lady, only bakes one large batch of the good brownies on Mondays. They're basically crack. If you don't get there in time, you're stuck with a fruit bar. Why even get dessert at that point?

We're the first ones to snag a table for lunch in our break room. Half of the faculty stays in the building for lunch, and the other half tends to be as antisocial as they possibly can by going to a coffee shop or eating in their cars.

"Is Sarah Kim joining you for camp?" Emma takes a seat at the big, round table in the center of the room.

"She is. She's our *team assistant*. It's pretty adorable, honestly. She'll do anything she can for a chance to include sports in her college admissions packet." I shake my head and join Emma at the table.

"The girl is ambitious." She smiles, biting into her sandwich.

"The girl is a headache," Malcolm's deep, warm voice fills the room, and it makes my cheeks heat. We still haven't talked about the other night. We've never been *that* close to kissing before. Actually kissing. And being that close to him has never left me so stunned that I lost sleep over it. I just think the fact that we were basically breathing the same oxygen for a solid thirty seconds might need to be addressed. You know, for peace of mind. But by the looks of it, no one is freaking out about it but me.

This is the kind of situation that could drive me mad.

It will drive me mad.

"She just wants to succeed," Emma says with her mouth full of potato chips. Crumbs fly as she tilts the bag upside down to get every last piece into her mouth. Remember when I said she was glowing? The glow seems to dull a bit here.

"Okay." Malcolm's face is pinched as he watches Emma and sits in the empty seat next to me. We both watch her inhale the rest of the bag. Her table manners disappeared around the second trimester. "You get 'em all?" he asks with a sly grin.

Emma's eyes whip to his face. They aren't the sweet eyes of our friend and colleague. Nope. They're the eyes of a ravenous mama bear about to rip Malcolm to shreds.

"Dude, don't anger it," I whisper behind my hand, slouching as far down into my seat as possible. Emma crumples up the bag and stands from the table, tossing it in the trash. Completely ignoring Malcolm's comment, she collects papers from her binder for today's meeting and starts passing them out to the faculty that is slowly migrating into the break room.

"Are we covering camp today or not?" Malcolm asks without looking at the agenda Emma just handed him. I elbow his ribs and point at the first point.

Camp Coming Up.

For the past five years, Malcolm and I have been partners in coaching tactics, tag-teaming our practices and schedules. It's created a sense of comradery they hadn't had at Glendale in a long time, breathing new life into the school.

Volleyball and football aren't your typical buddy sports, but we've made it work, and it's always made Athlete Camp that much more exciting. We both take a group of athletes from different sports and spend an entire week running drills, scrimmages, and attending seminars. It's a high school coach's dream! Or maybe just my dream—whatever, it's fun. And for the last five years, I've been able to go with Malcolm and a few of the other coaches.

"Yes, Athlete Camp is our big topic today," Benny announces as he walks into the break room, holding two cups of iced coffee. One cup has a large heart drawn on the center. Envy bubbles in my chest at the sweet gesture as he hands the cup to Ellie, who walks in behind him. They share sweet smiles and part ways as Benny begins today's meeting.

"Do they make you want to vomit or what?" Malcolm leans over, whispering to me behind his coffee mug.

Correction: *my* coffee mug.

My pink mug with a picture of Hilda, my pug that lived to be fourteen, on it. The first secret Santa gift Malcolm gave me four years ago, when Hilda was still alive. Poor thing had a heart attack and died in her sleep a month later.

"Maybe not vomit, but they definitely make me want to throw something at them," I whisper back. He gives me a soft pinch in the arm before repositioning back into his usual pose, leaned over the table with an arm resting perpendicular to me, the other holding his mug in the air, his back taut and rigid. It doesn't ever look natural, how he sits. But that's what he does, every day. The one time I asked him why he didn't just relax in his chair, he stiffened even further then cracked his neck like I scratched my nails on a chalkboard. I never mentioned it again.

"Throw something at who?" Ellie asks, taking the vacant seat Emma just left.

"Um, no one." I gnaw on my lip and swivel around in my seat to face Benny.

"She said you guys are gross," Malcolm mumbles.

Ellie tosses her sticky note pad at my head and whispers, "Rude!"

"I still love you," I whisper over my shoulder and glare at Malcolm. Benny clears his throat and stares at us as if we're the hoodlums in the classroom. I mumble under my breath, "Ellie started it."

Another pack of sticky notes flies over my shoulder, and Benny continues staring at all of us, as well as the rest of the faculty. They're annoyed. We're cutting into their lunch break. "May I finish?" He clears his throat, forcing a seriousness to spread across his boyish face.

"Please hurry," Malcolm answers over his shoulder. He's still facing away from Benny, drinking his coffee. It might come off as rude, not facing your boss in a meeting, but everyone has realized two very important things about Malcolm in the last five years:

He's never rude intentionally.

And we should never question him about it.

"As I was saying, Athlete Camp is next week. Unfortunately, Bill can't attend anymore."

Wait, what? Bill isn't going to camp?

"So, unless we get one more volunteer," Benny continues, "there will only be two faculty members attending, which makes it very difficult to manage the students as well as the coaching seminars."

"We need help!" I yell, startling the entire room—and myself a little bit—the projection of my voice practically throwing me out of my chair.

"Um, yes," Benny says hesitantly, telepathic questions being thrown at me through his gaze. *What was that for? Why do you look crazy right now?*

That's what I'm assuming he's thinking because there is no doubt I look like a maniac.

Gripping the back of my seat, my eyes feel twice their size. The truth is, *I* need help. The thought of spending an entire week alone with Malcolm right now is freaking me out for some reason. I've never had any concerns about this the last few years. It's always been one of the best weeks of my year. But after *mistle-gate*...with his steamy breath rippling across my face and his oaky cologne tingling my nostrils... I don't know what to think about any of this. My mind can't seem to land on one certain point.

Why was he nervous? Why were his lips trembling? And why did the idea of kissing him seem so appealing?

These are not the typical buddy-bro-bestie thoughts I usually have pertaining to Malcolm, and I can't bring myself to ask him about it. I'm too chicken. And being alone with him in seminars and coach dinners will inevitably force the conversation to happen.

I don't know if I'm ready.

"Do we have any volunteers?" Benny asks the room.

Please, somebody volunteer. My forearms burn from the death grip I have on my chair.

"Is it me, or are you afraid of going to camp with me, Stanley?" Malcolm whispers. My grip tightens as I glance at him. His eyes are still fixed on the big break room window behind me, creasing in the corners as he fights a smirk.

"N–no," I stutter. "I just don't want us drowning, trying to juggle all the kids on our own." He nods an *ah* in response, still looking out the window, coffee cup at his lips. "We really need assistance to ensure the athletes are fully supported," I say to the room, clearing my throat.

A few head nods in agreement, but no volunteers. Of course not.

"I'll go," Ellie offers cheerily.

"Yay!" I whip around in my chair, reach across the table, and squeeze her.

"Honey, er...future Mrs. Divata, you will be unavailable." Benny's voice is pinched, like he's trying to remind Ellie of their pre-established plans. I groan loudly into her shoulder then slide across the table back into my chair. Ellie mouths an apologetic, *"I tried."*

"Alright, then it seems like we will just have the two faculty members attend. Now, let's focus on end-of-term evaluations," Emma says as she takes over the meeting.

Defeated, I rest my head in my hands and press my palms into my eyes. Somehow, not seeing anyone in this moment is comforting.

I hear Emma's footsteps and the rustling of paper around me. The chair next to Ellie slides out, and Benny sits next to her. I know it's him because I hear their whispered hellos and flirty giggles, all followed by Malcolm's muttered, *"God, help me."*

I smile into my hands at his voice. The disdain he has for the idea of love in general has always been amusing—another reason why the other night has me baffled. His eyes under the mistletoe weren't that of disdain. They were something deeper. *Intimate.* A deep sea of unspoken thoughts swirled inside of them, threatening to overflow. Even after he pretty much barricaded me from open fire in the living room, the most surprising moment of the entire night was under that dang mistletoe.

"That's all for today, everyone." Emma concludes the meeting, and people shuffle out quicker than they came in.

"Well...looks like it's just you and me." Malcolm tugs on one of my curls tied on the top of my head as he scoots his chair out.

I stay seated and stare into my palms as I hear Malcolm's boots move across the floor to the sink then the running water and clanging of his mug as he gently places it back in the cabinet. His footsteps fade until there's silence. I blink and adjust to the bright sun shining in through the break room window and peer out at the football field. The green turf is freshly cut, the goal lines painted a crisp white. A few students lounge on the bleachers for their lunch. A few others stretch and run drills down the red track that circles the field. I give myself a second to collect my thoughts before heading to fourth period and go to stand.

"You gonna tell me what's up?"

"Cheese and rice! I thought you were gone!" I screech as I grip my chest and lean against the table, Malcolm's voice just about throwing me into palpitations.

He chuckles, "Sorry."

He stares at me as he leans against the doorframe, waiting for a response. What am I supposed to say? *I'm freaking out about the other night, and I don't know how to act around you?* Yeah, no. Then it would seem like the other night means something, and what if he was just joking? What if I'm the one making this more than it needs to be? The possibility of that sends erratic flutters through my chest.

Oh great, now I'm giving myself palpitations.

"Spill it, Stanley." His eyes glisten at me like the ocean. A sea of wonder—and concern, based on the crease forming between his eyebrows. They've always been so captivating, drawing me in and filling me with this sense of calm I can't get anywhere else. Like God Himself said, "I have these eyes capable of making someone feel both calm and exhilarated, and I'm going to attach them to a man so surly and grumpy that it will confuse the heck out of people." They defy all logic.

I open my mouth to speak, like normal people should do, but nothing comes out. My throat makes a raspy, bubbly noise instead. I clamp my mouth shut because it's clearly useless.

A ding comes from my pocket.

You've scored! pops up on my screen.

I gnaw on my lip as I stare at the screen, afraid to open it in front of Malcolm.

Another ding. I stare down at my phone, torn between the man in the doorway and the app blowing up my phone.

"See you later, Kate," Malcolm whispers, rubbing the back of his neck and backing out of the room like he's interrupted something.

Dread coils itself around my heart and throat and squeezes as I watch him walk away, making it near impossible to call after him. My limbs feel like they're tied to bricks, heavy and useless. The *need* to have a conversation with Malcolm is becoming clearer and clearer, but the mere thought is clearly affecting my sanity. I feel like a lunatic. Every part of me is sirening off to abandon ship before it's too late.

Another ding in my pocket sends a surge of frustration through me. I open my phone to a slew of matches. It's as if the universe has unleashed havoc at the most inconvenient time for these men to find my profile all at the same time.

I open the first match and am met with, *Yo, drinks at Mariachi's tonight?* No flatteries or introductions, just straight to the point. The message from *JusticeBeaver3000* isn't my ideal choice for evening plans, but if I go, maybe it'll distract me from the Malcolm situation.

It probably won't, though, if his username and the fact that the one solitary photo on his profile is of half his face is any indication, this guy is not the best option for a distraction.

If only I were a dragonfly.

Why, Kate? Because, Kate, dragonflies play dead to prevent mating with unwanted males. Play dead, and *JusticeBeaver3000* will fly off to some other insect.

Seems like a logical plan. Yes, I'll go to this date and play dead.

Chapter Seven
Malcolm

When I accepted the job at Glendale, I was told I would never be forced to assist with extracurricular activities. I could focus on math. That's it. But of course, my coworkers weaseled their way into my personal life and convinced me to lend a helping hand. Hence, the head coaching job for the football team. A temporary fill-in of sorts. And I was told I'd have help. I wouldn't have to lift a finger except to point and yell at the players. A selling point for me.

Benny promised it would be an easy job until they found a permanent replacement. Just a few short months of staying at school late and spending my weekends on the field. Not my first choice of extracurriculars, but it would, *"be over before you know it."*

I'm not a lazy person.

Or a selfish person.

I'd rather just spend my time doing what I want. And I'd rather do it alone.

But today, my time is being spent racing around in the pouring rain to pick up the fifty orange cones scattered across my football field. Getting soaked while my *help* cowers away underneath the roof of the team's golf cart again is not my first choice of activities. She's also using my jacket as a shield.

"Can we do this later?" Sarah Kim yells at me through the rain. I can't even see her face underneath the pile of nonsense she's thrown on top of herself.

"I'm sorry, are you cold?" I growl through the rain that pelts my face, swiping up the final cone and racing back to the cart. "You didn't have to come out here, ya know."

"What else was I supposed to do? You think I want to watch the team work out?" Her half-hidden face is unreadable to me when she asks this. Honestly, I'd rather not know what a seventeen-year-old girl is thinking—about anything.

"Don't you have books you can read or something?" I start the golf cart and pull off the track toward the team building.

"That wouldn't make a very good team manager, now would it?" She sticks her hand outside of the cart, the rain soaking her sleeve as we pull into the gravel parking lot. The girl was practically on the floor, hiding from the rain, a moment ago, and now she's throwing her arm out in it? I will never understand teenagers.

"You're not the team manager."

"Assistant. Manager. Same thing in my mind." She hops off the cart before I come to a complete stop. My heart jolts over the thought of a student injuring themselves on my watch, let alone a clutz like Sarah Kim, who couldn't even catch a beach ball tossed to her.

She hoists up the stack of orange cones, dropping a few in the process, before sprinting inside the football gym and leaving me alone in the rain. A moment of solitude.

Indoor workouts are never ideal. The team gets stir crazy and about fifty percent of the time, I have to break up a fight. I can hear the yelling and grunting through the closed metal door and take a slow breath before heading inside.

Half of the guys are standing on their heads while a few others hurl wadded up socks at them. We're supposed to be getting ready for camp, but today's weather has put a damper on the week's plans, and now I'm stuck inside with *this.*

My assistant coach for the spring, Bill the Janitor, is plopped inside the coach's office, playing on his phone. He's useless. The boys are acting rambunctious and childish, completely disregarding the workout I wrote for them to do on the board. I let out a sharp whistle, and they line up in formation in response.

"Alright, seeing as we can't be trusted to follow instructions in my absence," I project, "we'll have to add a morning workout tomorrow to make up for lost time."

The entire team groans in unison, with a few choice words said under their breath.

"Do you wanna make it two?" I bellow so loudly I feel my gut shake, and the room goes silent. "Bill, could you get out here, please?"

Without looking back over to Bill, I can hear him topple out of the swivel chair and race into the gym area with the rest of the team. "Hey, Coach. I was just letting the boys have some free time." His grin is chummy and proud, and I have to remind myself that I don't have the privilege of firing him.

"Ms. Kim!" I holler over my shoulder. Sarah rushes to my side. "Please set up the cones for sprints."

Groans again.

"We do this, and we go home. Got it?"

The team nods in agreement and walks slowly over to the end of the indoor turf patch to line up for their turn. They look pitiful, and their enthusiasm from a few moments ago is gone. It almost bums me out. The gym has been an immense help with strength training and conditioning, especially during the off season, but there are days

I want nothing more than to stay on the field for hours and watch the boys pummel each other.

The team begrudgingly starts sprinting back and forth in the normal sprint sequence as Bill shouts at them to run faster. I walk into the coach's office and pull up the team roster and my work email when my phone buzzes in my pocket.

> **Kate:** Can we talk?

I reread her text multiple times, waiting for a second text to come through. When it doesn't, my throat starts to dry out and constrict. I can usually read Kate like a book, but after her behavior at our lunch meeting today, anxiety has been whirling in my gut like a bad burrito. I probably pushed her too far at the party.

My thumbs feel shaky as I type out a response.

> Is everything alright?

Reasons to have a talk are swimming in my head. The probability that she wants to talk about the other night and the mistletoe is super high. I'm not as smooth as I want to be, so it's quite possible she saw right through me. It's possible Kate could tell how much it killed me to hold myself back in that doorway and not kiss her the way I've dreamt of kissing her for the last five years.

It's also possible she has another date set up, and she wants to continue discussing it with me, as if I'm her gal pal and she needs to spill the tea regarding her dating life to me instead of her actual gal pals. If that's the case, someone needs to come bust my kneecaps right now.

If it's the latter, we have a problem. I finally have my chance to get out of this friend-zone vortex I've been sucked into. The best way I can do that is if Kate is single at camp.

She responds.

Kate: Not really ☒

I crack my thumbs and respond.

Wafflin' at 5?

Kate: Yes! I'll see you there!

A knock at my door jolts my attention.

"Coach?" Garrett Connors is leaning into the doorframe for support as he heaves for air. He grips his bad knee and winces as he attempts to shake off the pain. The kid finally got cleared to join in conditioning after being benched for eight months after his injury last year, but it's clear he needs to take it easy.

"Take a breather, Connors. End with some band work," I tell him before returning my attention to my computer.

"Thanks, Coach," he says through gasps.

Out of the corner of my eye, I watch him walk unsteadily to the opposite side of the gym. Free weights, bands, and benches line the wall. A state-of-the-art weight rack is bolted to the wall perpendicular to where Connors sits.

"Yo, Coach! Why does he get a break?" Ethan Blake yells at me mid-sprint.

"Get your leg snapped, then come talk to me, Blake," I bellow at him without looking up from my screen. I have twenty-eight exams to grade and a roster to finalize for camp. I check the time, 3:15, and calculate the amount of time I have to complete everything before I need to meet Kate.

Being a math teacher is boring on paper, but it's the only thing that makes sense to me. You can solve almost anything with math. Hungry? Add food. Tired? Add sleep. Angry? Subtract whatever the hell makes you angry.

Over the top of my computer screen, I see a few guys cutting their sprints short and hopping to the back of the line.

Lazy? Add more sprints.

"Everyone starts from zero!" I shout through my glass window. A collection of groans, yells, and curses are said in response. "Thank your teammates!"

Everyone gasps and stumbles back to the starting line, plowing through the sprints faster than the first time. I join Bill on the side of the turf and watch the boys sprint back and forth. Devon Johnson finishes first and throws himself on the ground at the far end.

He's followed by Zane, my starting receiver, Marshall, our kicker, and Travis Van, my running back. One by one, they plow through the last sprint, cheering on their slower teammates and hounding the ones who should've finished faster.

Being the head coach for three years can be the bane of my existence some days, even if I do enjoy torturing some of these hotheads. But this team pulls me down memory lane far too often because, as much as I hate to admit it, they remind me of myself. I was a hothead not too long ago. And the only family I had were the guys in my unit. For years, nothing else mattered to me but the mission and those guys. When you're young, it's easy to forget that life can end in a moment.

Until you actually lose someone. Then it all changes.

One of the hardest damn lessons I've had to learn is accepting that life has to go on without some people.

The final player heaves himself past the rest of the team and hurls into the trash can. "Shake it off, Tim!" I yell, reviewing the roster from the doorway. "Strong work, but tomorrow let's try to do what I have planned, alright?"

Mumbled responses agree, and I dismiss them with a wave.

"Yo, Coach! When will the camp roster be out?" Travis Van runs up to me, his crooked nose from the brawl he had with Devon last fall still an eyesore.

"End of the week. Camp is in three. You have plenty of time to prepare if that's what you're asking." I head toward the door, leaving the mess for tomorrow and flipping the lights.

"So I actually get to—"

"Mr. Van," I cut him off, "you are my top running back. The best in this district, according to some people. And I told you if you made improvements in your grades and stayed consistent with practice, the likelihood of attending this year was probable, correct?" He nods.

"Have you missed any practices?"

"No, sir."

"Have your grades improved?"

"Yes, sir," he says with pride.

"And those were the stipulations, correct?" He nods emphatically. "Without the roster being made, I cannot confirm nor deny your attendance." His eyes begin to fall at this. "But..." I say quickly, and he perks back up, "seeing that I am a man of my word, maybe you can put two and two together, huh?" I meet his eyes, a hopeful gleam to them. "Now please, go home."

He smiles and races out the front door, hopping into a bright-red sports car blaring some derogatory music as he peels out of the parking lot. Gravel sprays at my feet from the spin of his tires.

I sure hope I don't regret this decision.

I get to the diner at the worst possible time—peak after-school hours. Everyone is here, stuffing their faces with waffles, the post-class rush of students swarming the counter to order and hogging the good seats by the window. I rub the sore spot between my neck and shoulder as I scope out a place to sit when a soft, delicate hand bursts into the air, beckoning me.

"Had to fight off a pack of wildlings for our spot, but I got it." Kate beams at me with pride as I make my way into the booth seat across from her, a mug of black coffee on the table waiting for me. It's these little deeds Kate does that tug at my heart. I wish I could hate it.

"My hero," I say, chugging the coffee when a waiter I haven't seen before approaches the table with two plates loaded with food.

"Vegan special. And pancakes." His voice lingers on his words in confusion. Yes, I'm a freak for wanting pancakes from their waffle establishment. He stares at my plate, and I clear my throat. I have been ordering pancakes from this place for five years, and I refuse to fall into peer pressure to order their waffle special. Pancakes are superior, end of discussion.

"I got your usual," she says behind fluffy lashes, fighting back a fit of giggles as the waiter finally leaves the table.

"You are too kind." Her cheeks go pink as I hold her gaze.

She breaks eye contact first and focuses on her food. I resist the urge to keep staring at her like some kind of psychopath. I don't know what it is about Kate Stanley that has me so damn fixated, but since the first day I laid eyes on her, I've been nothing but a fool.

Clearing my throat, I start working on my pancakes, doing my best to pretend I don't notice her fidgeting fingers as she attempts to cut into her waffle.

My pancakes are practically gone by the time she meets my eyes again. "So..." she begins confidently, but then, as if someone just whispered in her ear to be quiet, she cuts herself off and presses her lips into a thin line. A pulse trembles up her jaw as she fights the urge to talk.

"Yes?" I ask with a mouth full of pancakes.

"I'm sorry about earlier." She says it so fast I almost miss it. Fidgeting, she plucks at the prongs on her fork, and it sends a faint ringing reverberating in my ears. I roll my neck at the chill it sends down my spine.

"It's alright." Wiping my jaw and beard with my napkin, I smile. It really is alright. Was her behavior in our meeting weird? Yes. But that's Kate in a nutshell: weird. I watch as her shoulders deflate in relief, then she straightens the salt and pepper shakers, hums a soft tune, and waves the fork around like she's conducting a concert. She is lost in her own magical thoughts for a moment, one of those momentary daydreams she tends to fall into. I think they happen more often than she realizes. Another weird quirk of hers. Blinking back to the conversation, she blushes when she realizes I'm still watching her, and the pink of her cheeks sends a spark right into the center of my chest.

She's weird in all the best ways.

"Are you sure? I acted like a crazy person! I don't know why I did that."

"It wouldn't have anything to do with the other night, would it?"

Her fork clatters against her plate, sending bits of waffle flying toward the window. Kate's eyes go wide as she chokes on her bite. She pounds the center of her chest in a poor attempt to suppress the choking. The struggle escalates when she starts gasping for air, and her face turns beet red. I hand her a glass of water, but her eyes avoid mine as she chugs. Once the water is drained, she fans herself and nervously bites her lip, embarrassment now the reason she's as red as a tomato.

She lets out a soft, defeated breath, giving in. A defeated, *you-got-me* sigh that finally gives me my answer. It *is* about the other night.

"We don't have to talk about it if you don't want to," I reassure her.

"Do you want to talk about it?" she asks in a whisper, still not meeting my eyes.

"Only if you want to." Sipping my coffee, I refuse to smile back at the eye roll she gives me. "No pressure here, just an awkward mistletoe moment. Those tend to happen at parties, ya know."

Leaning over across the table, she fixes her dark eyes on me, as if she's looking into my brain for information. "We almost kissed, though." She whispers it like she's in a confessional, and she's admitting her deepest, darkest offense.

"But we didn't," I whisper back dramatically. "Did you want me to kiss you?" If she says yes, I might jump across this table.

I have sat on the sidelines, witnessing the most perfect girl be just out of arm's reach, patiently waiting for the moment she decides to give dating a go again so I could shoot my shot. When her chump of an ex broke her heart, I did the respectable thing and waited. That plan failed when she decided to "swear off men" and announced "all men who tried dating her after a three-year relationship were impatient pigs." Clearly, I didn't want to be labeled as a pig in her mind, so I bided my time. I endured the friend zone in some of the most humiliating ways, attending a Taylor Swift concert being the worst. I went from having zero chickens to having thirty-six chickens because of this dang woman. I went from enjoying medium-rare steak three times a week to only eating steak on Thursdays because that apparently makes sense to her. I never even questioned her reasoning.

I've worked on myself and gone to therapy to work on my *issues*, finally coming to the conclusion that maybe being in a relationship isn't the worst possible thing that could happen to me.

And it all started with Kate Stanley.

Seems pathetic, doesn't it? That a woman like Kate, so quirky and opinionated, can sway a guy like me. But damn if she isn't one of the most irritatingly motivating people I have ever met. I'd probably be holed up like a hermit, struggling with my demons until I keeled over in my recliner at the age of eighty-seven, if she hadn't pestered me so much. Sure, her constant pushing can be a tad overbearing—grating your nerves, even—but you get used to it.

She still hasn't answered my question. "Well? Did you?"

"What? No!" My words fluster her even more as she waves her fork in the air and gives me a nonchalant *pft* sound that is less than convincing. "I don't— Did *you*?" she stutters then points her fork at me accusingly. *A tad jittery about this, Kate.*

I give her a wink, and I swear I see her hold her breath. "Maybe."

A mixture of noises and breaths sputter out of her like a backfiring engine. "I didn't ..." Her words hang in the air, trailing off as she releases a shaky breath.

Didn't what?

She anxiously gnaws on her bottom lip, lingering on a potential *I didn't want to kiss you.* The thought of her rejecting me, right here in the middle of Wafflin', sends warning signals blaring in my head. Even when she has the power to gut me from the inside out, I can't look away from her. A pitiful and borderline desperate feeling of hope pulses in my chest.

As if some higher power out there knows I need saving, a ping on my phone grabs my attention. Checking it, I let out a groan. "Dammit."

"What's wrong?" Kate asks, the awkward tension in the air floating away as she leans across to eye my phone.

I rub my temple at the nuisance of a companion I have waiting for me at home. I need to get rid of this damn chicken. Disgruntled, I say, "Nugget got out again."

Chapter Eight
Malcolm

"Could you for once behave like a normal chicken?" I grumble, more to myself because this thing definitely doesn't understand me, as I scoop Nugget out of the front seat and shove her under my arm.

Fine, I don't shove her. I could never.

As pesky and frustrating as she can be, I have to admit that I have a soft spot for her in my heart. Can't believe I've had her for five years. Who would've thought chickens would live so long?

Nugget chirps up at me, as if to say she will live forever, as we head inside to the hardware store.

"Aye, glad to hear you got that thing contained!" Uncle Jerry hollers at me from the checkout counter. The guy retired from this place two years ago, but he can't stay away.

"Glad to hear you still have nothing better to do than pester me," I mutter under my breath as I mosey to the back of the store. Gary, the shop owner, greets me with a scraggly grin and slight belch as he sets down his grimy coffee mug.

"What do we need today, Geer?" Another belch.

"I'm out of feed." I scan the back corner of the store, eyeing the empty crate that usually houses baby chicks, before returning my gaze back to him.

"You bought the last load three days ago. No innocent poultry to rescue today." Gary winks at me.

"That's not why I—"

"Whatever you say." Another wink.

"Quit lying to yourself," Jerry chuckles, inserting himself into the conversation. "We know why you empty the place out every two weeks."

"Can it, old man." I snip, rubbing my neck. Nugget chirps to join the discussion as well. "You, hush it." I direct my attention to her, immediately softening at the runt of a chicken and scratch her on the head.

"Seriously boy, when you gonna tell her—"

"I said, can it." I cut Jerry off before he can keep blabbing. Gary chuckles, giving Jerry an all-knowing wink before rounding the counter to the bags of chicken feed.

I'm very aware my feelings for a certain someone aren't that secret, at least not to the people who don't matter in the situation. But I don't really care to be pestered about my love life by two elderly men with missing teeth. I'm pretty sure it's been since before I was born that either of them had a serious relationship.

"You're just wasting time, ya know?" Jerry mumbles.

"I have a plan, alright?" I heave the bags of chicken feed onto a rolling cart housed by the counter and hand Gary some cash. I wave him off to keep the change, like I always do, even if I think I should get a discount with how often they bug me about my personal life at this place.

Wheeling the cart out, with Nugget snuggled under my arm, my phone goes off. This encourages Jerry to hightail it behind me and "assist" me. Assist being code for butting deeper into my business. *Who could be calling Geer? Is it Kate? What gossip can I spread at Wafflin' later?* The man is the beginning and the end of the make believe phone tree around here.

My phone continues to ring and I pull it out, silencing it immediately. Not without Jerry clocking who is calling.

"You're not—"

"I'll call her later." No need chatting it up with my sister in front of Uncle Jerry. He doesn't believe she exists anyway, since he's never met her. And I'd like to keep it that way. Jerry can be a lot for some people. And my sister is not in a place to deal with a lot.

"Aye! Boys!"

Aunt Edna, who is also *a lot*, peels into the parking lot of the hardware store, whipping into the first handicap parking spot she can find. We'll just ignore the fact that her sticker expired three years ago and she refuses to park anywhere else. Without missing a beat, she hops out of her green station wagon and barrels over to Jerry and me.

"Are you coming to fix my sink this week or not?" She eyes me with her hands firmly on her hips. It's as if she thinks this stance will speed the process along.

"Yes ma'am, I'll come by tomorrow." I heave the bag of feed into the bed of my truck, with Nugget still firmly tucked in place. "Unless you need it done sooner?"

"No, tomorrow is fine." She waves me off as she turns back to her car, flippant and unbothered, then yells over her shoulder, "Kate will be there!"

I watch her climb back into her car, shutting the door on the hem of her long skirt—the one with dancing kittens scattered across the fabric—before she peels out of the parking lot.

"That woman is loco," Jerry mumbles on an exhale, "so really, why don't you talk to your sister?"

"I do talk to her, Jerry. I'm just busy."

He eyes me, fully aware that I'm lying. Talking to my sister is hard enough, and I have no interest in explaining why to anyone, least of all

Uncle Jerry, who wouldn't recognize his own business if it hit him in the face.

"Don't give me that look. I'll call her later."

Mumbling under his breath as he heads back towards the store, he says, "I don't get this generation. Avoid each other. Avoid feelings. Being stupid."

"Bye, Jerry," I wave over my shoulder and climb into the truck.

Much to my dismay, my mind bounces off of Jerry's words the entire drive home, the entire time I feed the rest of the chickens, and the entire time I brush out Nugget's feathers, who will squawk all night if I don't. He's right.

I do avoid people. I don't talk. And maybe I can be a bit stupid.

Especially when it comes to Kate.

There's something about this woman that sweeps away all my common sense, leaving my mind spinning like I'm stuck on a never-ending rollercoaster ride. I know I can't avoid this situation, especially with camp coming up. And knowing she's putting herself out there for some internet weirdos to deliver her pathetic one-liners when I haven't even put my hat in the ring is stupid. Unfortunately, I have no idea what I'm doing when it comes to dating—being single for almost six years, with two awkward blind dates dispersed in there somewhere doesn't bode well for me in this department. And as much as I hate to admit it, I need help.

Help I don't want to ask for.

Help I know will drive me crazy.

While cooking dinner, I make a phone call and it's answered on the first ring.

"Don't ask me about the scrimmage this year, it's out of my hands." I hear clanging of dishes and a heavy exhale as Benny continues, "they've done it for ten years, that's just how it is."

"That's not why I'm calling." Even though it is something I should think about. The fact that this camp puts on a huge coaches vs athletes football scrimmage at the end of the week *for fun*. That *fun* being the reason we lost Garrett last season.

"Oh okay, what's up?" Benny asks. More clanging and a sizzling skillet happen in the background. I hesitate to respond, and because Benny can be more intuitive than his therapist fiancée, he quickly asks, "what's wrong?"

A beat passes and I still don't say anything. This was a bad idea.

"Malcolm ..." Benny's voice is stern, but calm. That typical approach he gives the students when they're about to admit to egging the soccer field.

I blow out the air in my lungs, and steady myself. *You need help, Malcolm, just tell him.* With all of the air out of my lungs, I say weakly, "I need Ellie's help."

"Oh man." He chuckles, probably aware how much this pains me. Asking anyone for help, let alone the woman who lives for helping others. It wouldn't be so bad if she could stay calm about it, but whenever I ask Ellie for anything, she acts like she's had ten cups of coffee—giddy and buzzing, *nothing* like the Eleanor Bailey I met a year ago.

Benny calls for Ellie in the background and all I hear is the word help, followed by a small squeal and pounding footsteps.

"Hi!" Ellie practically screams through the phone, "what do you need?"

Like pulling off a Band-Aid, I talk fast and in one breath, "I need a plan to get Kate to see me as more than a friend and I don't think I can do it on my own. I can't avoid her at camp so we need to come up with something fast. I need your help."

"Eeeeee!" Ellie shrieks so loud my phone speaker crackles, "let me get my notepad!"

It's time to get your girl, Malcolm.

Chapter Nine

Kate

"Are we getting a suite?" Tessa is practically crawling out of her skin with excitement as we announce the location for camp this year.

"Will we get a night out like last year?" Chloe squeals next to her.

The girls continue giggling, planning their *vacation* on the beach instead of the camp that is meant to help them with college scouting. I can't blame them entirely, though—we're going to the beach.

Sunny Florida.

The thought of sand in my toes, water splashing my ankles, my skin sizzling under the sun... If I'm being honest, I have to contain my own excitement. I've never been to Florida, or to the beach before, actually—not for lack of trying, of course. Unless we count the hole-in-the-wall restaurant Ellie dragged me to last summer, Tropic Burger. All the waiters wore hula skirts, and I do mean all of them. Jimmy Buffet played on repeat over the speakers. And there was sand everywhere...the ground, our seats, the tables. It was a miracle it wasn't in our food. That black bean burger special was the closest thing I've had to a beachside meal in my entire life.

"No suites. Yes, one night out. And *no* dates, so don't even ask." I force a stern look at the group.

Unified groans and moans commence at my audacity. How dare I ruin their chances of canoodling with players from other schools when they could potentially meet the long-distance partner they've been waiting for since freshman year?

"And don't even try sneaking around. I will find out!" I point my pen individually at the eight girls sitting across from me on the gymnasium floor. More painful moans and groans. You'd think I was grounding them with this behavior.

"Now, we'll have group conditioning workouts in the mornings. Then, you'll break up into your individual sport groups. Tess and Chloe, you'll represent our volleyball team, so please be on time. Birdie, you— Birdie, please focus." Her head is craned in an awkward position as she doom-scrolls on her phone.

"Huh?" It's not really a question, just a sound she makes as her eyes stay pinned to her phone.

Birdie Whitmore is my most unreliable athlete, yet the most talented. Taking the top rank in every sport she participates in, I have no choice but to take her to camp with me. Somehow, the girl can nail a brand-new routine with one eye on her screen and the other pinned on the football players. And her grades are perfect. She's like some superhuman species that I can't quite figure out.

"Can you at least *pretend* you're listening?" I roll my eyes and continue, "You, Andie, and Claire will represent cheer, but you'll be doing rhythm with color guard and pom due to the number of athletes and space. That leaves Daphne, Stella, and Jess representing softball. Everyone will be joining the baseball team for hitting practice and—"

"What?! They get to practice with the boys?" Chloe's eyes fill with rage at this information. Good gravy, somebody save me.

I let out a sigh and try to wrap up before any of these girls find out Sarah Kim will be spending almost all her time with the football boys. "We leave at 6 a.m. tomorrow. Please don't be late."

They take that as their cue to leave and scurry out of the gym, not a single glance over their shoulder to say bye. I switch the lights off and head toward the exit, the setting sun peeking in through the small square windows at the top of the bleachers. The red letters of Glendale glisten on the floor as the light bounces off them.

I take a moment to lean against the wall that sits underneath the *Volleyball State Champions* flag and slide down until I hit the hardwood floor. The soles of my shoes squeak as I pull my knees into my chest.

The smell of citrus wood cleaner and rubber hit me as I take a deep breath. So many years of my life have revolved around this little gym. From the years I played, to becoming the assistant coach, to now being the athletic director for all of Glendale. The years flash across my mind in a blur, good days and bad, swirling around and bringing me to this moment. Right here. On this gym floor. *Alone.*

Ugh, that word. Alone.

I've been saying it way too much lately. And *feeling* it even more.

I'm not sure when these feelings truly hit, but I know that, lately, the reality that I am more alone than I have ever been in my entire life has been a major downer. So much so that I've led myself to believe the only way out of it is online dating. Online dating, for crying out loud! Not that it's inherently bad to find your soulmate through an algorithm. Uncle Jerry met Sheila that way, and they're happy as clams.

I guess I just pictured myself reaching for the last bag of gluten-free flour at the store, hand colliding with another. One larger and rougher but soft in all the right places. A gentle graze of a thumb across my knuckles. Eyes landing on the man of my dreams right there in the middle of Whole Foods.

It's absurd. I'm aware. And I do grocery pick-up now, so that idea is the furthest from possible on the sheer fact that I rarely step inside the store anymore.

So here I am, putting myself out there for the internet to see. It's terrifying, being judged solely on my pictures and a 200-word limit *About Me* section—which is not near enough space to share who I am with someone. But I'm trying nonetheless, no matter how uncomfortable the swiping makes me.

The Nick thing was clearly a bust, but it was a start. Putting myself out there after Eric has been the biggest challenge of my life. And up until a few months ago, I was really enjoying my life and the people in it. The idea of trying to date wasn't near as appealing.

"It'll happen for you one day."

Benny's words are etched in my mind. I remember the crisp morning vividly. I was helping him pick out a ring, helping plan and organize the proposal, all the way down to which knee he would kneel on. The guy ended up proposing on a park bench a day early because he couldn't wait any longer, but still. A full week's planning went into it, ending with us enjoying one last cup of coffee as two single people.

I never doubted Benny would find the love of his life one day. My cousin is one of the best men I know. He was destined for happiness. I just never expected to be the last one to find happiness. I'm literally the last one. In our entire family. The last person of typical dating age that doesn't make people question if they collect doll heads or shark teeth. *I'm looking at you, Aunt Edna.*

His words were meant to be encouraging. Of course they were. I know this. But my brain decided to spiral into a toxic thought pool and practically drown in pitiful *lonely me* thoughts.

I hate feeling lonely.

I've done everything in my power to not feel lonely, ever since I was little. When my parents were so consumed in their own lives that they never noticed me, I ran down the road to Lola's. When the girls on the team would try and ignore me, I'd go hang out with Benny and the rest of the track boys. When I took the job at Glendale, I refused to feel alone among my peers and forced them to be my friends. I tend to be suffocating in relationships. I'm highly aware. But none of them seem to mind. Even Malcolm, who hates everyone and everything, has never once made me feel alone.

But for the last two years, I have been alone. Truly alone.

"There's nothing wrong with being by yourself," Lola would tell me constantly.

And that's what I've been since Eric left.

Going from seeing your boyfriend every single day, even working with him, to living on your own with your dog was jarring. It took me months to be okay with sleeping by myself. Some nights, Malcolm or Benny would sleep on my couch. Just knowing someone was there was all I needed.

Until one day, I didn't. I was finally okay with being by myself. Independent. A free spirit with no constraints to another person.

The bombshell was liberating. This revelation might have come after one too many margaritas, but it was a revelation all the same. I was going to be alone, and I was going to be okay with it. To hell with men.

A ding from my phone brings me out of the memory.

You've Matched! in bright-gold letters pops up on my phone. The dating app I signed up for has informed me numerous times today that I've "matched" with someone. This should be exciting, but the dread of actually opening up the app and seeing what awaits me has had me sliding the notification closed and not going any further.

I take a deep breath, blowing my ringlet curls out of my face, before hopping up onto my feet. I take one last glance at the gym, letting the nostalgia fill me with a sense of calm. I truly love this little place. It's my home. For a moment, I feel like, as long as I have this place, I'm not alone. Who needs an *internet boyfriend* anyway?

But can the gym hug you and kiss you and buy you ice cream when you're sad? My inner rational thoughts sound eerily like Lola. I picture her eyeing me from the stands across the floor.

"Dang it. Fine," I say to myself, pulling my phone out to check the app.

Then another ding comes with the phone in my grasp, signaling another match alert. That's five in one day. I shove the phone in my pocket, overwhelmed by it all.

Another ding. Cheese and rice, this is going to be exhausting.

"Sha-booyah! Sha-sha-sha-booyah, roll call!" the girls chant on the right side of the bus with a few reluctant boys on the left joining in. The bus driver, a Florida native, joins in to the best of his ability. Malcolm sits in the seat next to me, his head tilted back, eyes firmly shut as we bounce down the highway toward our hotel.

The rapid movement makes it near impossible for me to rest, but Malcolm has no issues snoozing away next to me. I stare at him, tracing the line of his perfectly shaped beard as it leads to his lips. Memories of mistletoe and subtle hints of brandy threaten to overtake me when we hit a pothole. I tear my eyes away from his lips, traveling my gaze downward, landing on his Adam's apple.

And an Adam's apple it is.

It bobs slightly.

My mouth dries for some odd reason. Since when has Malcolm had such an intriguing Adam's apple? *How many times am I going to say Adam's apple?*

An all-too-familiar ding snaps me out of my trance. I sigh and click my phone screen off.

"Another match, huh?" Malcolm's low voice comes out in a purr. His eyes are still closed, but the corner of his mouth twitches up when I cross my arms.

"Yes," I groan, leaning my head against the seat. "I still haven't checked any of them."

"What's stopping you?"

What is stopping me? I want to date again, so why am I refusing to check out any of my matches? And why is Malcolm's Adam's apple so dang interesting?

"You're staring." He smirks at me.

"I am not." I whip my head forward.

"You've always been a terrible liar, Stanley."

"Is that supposed to make me feel bad?" I attempt bumping my shoulder against his, which he attempts to dodge, turning his chest toward me, and at the same time, we hit another pothole. The combination of events throws me into Malcolm's huge body. *Hard.* My head smacks against his chest. He grips my shoulders to steady me, squeezing twice before sitting me up.

"Golly! Do you have body armor under there?" I growl, rubbing the side of my head.

"Nope. Just solid man." He chuckles, giving his chest a one-two pound that sounds like hitting a wall. *Solid man.* "You good?" he asks as his eyes evaluate my face with concern.

I see stars for a moment. "I'm fine. Hard to believe there isn't a sheet of rock under there with how bad this hurts."

"Would you like to see for yourself?" He gives that smirk again. Is he...*flirting?*

"What? No! I was just saying it feels like I smacked into a wall. Like you're just so hard, er...I mean, wide—no. You're just...ugh...you're just a lot."

"Again, I say, solid man." This time, his smirk is followed by a wink and wave as if to present himself as a prize to the audience. And I'm definitely staring at his chest now.

"We're here!" Birdie screeches from the back of the bus, saving me from the awkward lingering of my eyes. I'm pretty sure they are going rogue, and my brain no longer has control over what they look at. Or...gawk at.

The entire right side of the bus—the girls' side—lets out giddy screams, scrambling for their bags and barreling toward the door before we even come to a full stop. A screeching halt sends Chloe, Tess, and Birdie flying to the floor, with Claire tumbling into a seat. Charlie and Garret cackle a few rows behind us, whistling and clapping as the girls try to peel themselves off the floor. I have to bite my lip to resist cackling with them.

"She is beauty; she is grace!" Travis yells from the back of the bus. The boys hoot and holler at his quip, leading the girls to bicker at them.

Malcolm grabs my hands and presses them against my ears, his callused hands pressing firmly against the sides of my face and muffling the chaotic noise building as everyone starts to argue. Everything around me fades away, and for a solitary moment, all my senses are focused on Malcolm's hands. I can't help but lean into it, my eyes fluttering at the sensation that travels down my neck from his touch.

But then Malcolm lets out a whistle loud enough to burst an eardrum, snapping me back to reality. The bus falls silent.

He grumbles as he stands and faces the kids behind us. "Alright," he projects, using his military-coach voice, a rumble from deep inside his chest. "Get your crap, and get off the bus. You're athletes, so try not to trip over your own feet while you're at it."

The kids leave the bus in a single-file line like a group of little troops following Commander Geer's orders.

"These kids will be the death of me this week," Malcolm mumbles, pinching the bridge of his nose. "You can uncover your ears now."

My ears?

My hands are still splayed against my face, the memory of Malcolm's hands holding them firmly in place. I chuckle, flexing and twisting my hand, before stepping off the bus.

As we pile off the bus, we embody a group of chaotic toddlers barreling toward the double glass doors of the hotel. Based on their squeals, points, and touching of everything, you'd think these kids had never been out in public before. I have to do my best to be the adult in the group and not react like the rest of them, forcing myself to not get distracted by the lush, green palm trees that line the cobblestone walkway. Or the trickle of white sand tracked in by the other guests. Or the salty air whipping my curls across my face as we make our way inside to the hotel lobby. Or the fancy man in a fancy uniform, taking our bags like we're royalty.

A shiver of giddy excitement rolls up my arms, and I have to shake them out as I approach reception.

"Welcome to the Regency at Palm Beach!" The tall man standing behind the counter forces a smile at the group of teenagers hovering in front of his desk. "You all must be here for the Collegiate Scouting Camp, I presume." The group starts talking over each other in response, invading Mr. Front Desk's space even more, if that is possible.

"Alright, alright. You're embarrassing us. Sit over there and chill out." Malcolm rescues the poor front desk clerk. "Glendale High School, checking in." He leans his arms on the desk, rolling his neck and cracking his back.

The apple bobs again.

"Here you are. Thirteen athlete passes, two coach passes, and three rooms."

"Wait, what?" My gaze rips away from Malcolm's neck as I laser focus on Mr. Front Desk. "That can't be right. We reserved four rooms."

"Yes, four rooms. Two athlete suites and two coach rooms," Malcolm growls irritably. The noise is almost palpable—if a growl could be palpable, anyway.

"Oh dear, let me have a looksie." Mr. Front Desk's fingers fly across the keyboard, and a small bead of sweat builds on his temple as Malcolm and I watch him. "Well, it looks like a, uh, Mr. Bill Cummings reserved only three rooms."

"Freaking Bill," I groan. We left it up to the janitor-turned-assistant-coach to make reservations. Rookie mistake. "Could we reserve a fourth room, then?"

"I'm so sorry, but we're fully booked for the week." Mr. Front Desk's eyes go from solemn to sheer terror as I stare at him. You know those moments in cartoons where someone is so angry they have steam coming out of their ears? If that could actually happen in real life, I have no doubt it would be happening right now, steam and flames blasting out of my ears as I stare down this man. "I–I'm so sorry." He fidgets behind the counter, voice practically quaking. "We could put you on a waitlist."

"That's alright. We'll manage. Thanks, Jeremy." Malcolm takes the room keys and camp passes from *Jeremy*. A ripple of shock moves up my spine from the hand he's placed on my lower back as he steers me away from the desk. "If you stared at him any longer, Stanley, he would have burst into flames." His beard tickles my ear as he whispers, "He's innocent in all this."

"Well, Bill isn't here for me to blame, so Jeremy it is. How are we going to manage with only *three* rooms?" I grumble in a whisper. My heart is beating out of my chest as we approach our group gathered in the lobby. And I don't know if it's the Florida heat or the thought of sharing a room with Malcolm, but something is happening inside me—something I can't quite pinpoint—and my face and neck feel like they're on fire.

"Is the thought of sharing a room with me getting you all hot and bothered?" Malcolm chuckles.

"What? No. What makes you say that?" I heave a breath, trying to fill my lungs with oxygen and failing. *What is with the air in this place?*

"You're beet red." He faces me, crossing his arms over his chest. Gosh, what a chest. It's a *man's* chest. Which yes, Malcolm is clearly a man. But why is his chest so...interesting all of a sudden? Why is *Malcolm* all of a sudden so interesting? "And fanning yourself with your room key." He eyes the tiny plastic card I'm waving back and forth between us.

"I— It's— Florida is sweltering, alright? *I* am sweltering. This entire lobby is sweltering!" My words come out louder than I intend as I flail my arms out to the sides. Eyes bug out at me from our group, and

Malcolm does the thing where he pretends to smooth out his beard, but really he's just suppressing a cackle, before handing out room keys.

"You good, Ms. Stanley?" Devon asks, already unconvinced with whatever response I will conjure up.

Instead of words, I wave my hand and bow. Because that's a clear indication that I'm *good*. Totally good. All is chill in the world, and I am not bothered in the slightest about the room mishap or the inconvenience it poses. I am *chill*.

"Alright. Guys, you'll be in suite 416, and ladies, you'll be in 428."

"We get suites? Dude, yes!" Travis is elated as he holds up a hand for Malcolm to high-five. It's denied.

"Suites are just a cool way to say pull-out sofa, *dude*." Garrett pats Travis on the shoulders as a sign of support for the devastating reality. Travis is unfazed as he giddily skips to the elevators.

"Coaches rooms are between you guys, so no funny business. I'm looking at you, Jess. Save the pranks for at home." Malcolm lets his military tone seep through his words, and Jess nods erratically. *Sir, yes, sir.*

Up on the fourth floor, we accompany the kids to their rooms, waiting as the girls get settled into theirs and head toward the guys' room.

"You know I'm not going to stay in the room with you, right?" Malcolm follows me closely down the hall as we approach the suites.

"Where are you going to sleep, then?" I ask, feeling a twinge guilty at his chivalry. Of course he's already come up with a plan to make sure I'm comfortable. He's probably already made other arrangements within the fifty steps we've taken from the front desk.

"With them." Malcolm winces as Charlie knocks over a hallway table, Devon swiftly catching the lamp that nearly shattered on the ground. "On the floor."

The boys proceed to wrestle in front of their room door, desperate to be the first to open it.

I stare at the mayhem before me, thanking the universe for the lone bed and night of silence awaiting me on the other side of my door. For a millisecond, I forget about Malcolm's back problems and the fact that him sleeping on the floor will set this entire week on a path of a grumpier Mr. Geer, if that is even possible.

I can't let him suffer like that.

Malcolm has slept at my house before, on the couch, but still. I could hear his light snoring through my thin walls. It's not like this is completely uncharted territory. Why is sharing a hotel room with him freaking me out so much? There's enough space to navigate each other and avoid all awkwardness. There are two beds, and we can survive sharing a bathroom.

It's fine.

The suite door down the hall swings open and slams into the wall as the guys forcefully wedge themselves through the space. The door slams shut with a loud bang, *bros* and *dudes* hollered behind the closed door.

"You can't stay in there. Listen to them." I gape down the hall, grateful to be in charge of the quiet girls two doors down.

"It's fine. I've slept through worse." He gives me a wink, hoisting his duffel bag over his shoulder as he goes to walk away.

Grabbing his hand, I plead, "Don't."

Malcolm eyes me, the blue of them glistening under the fluorescent hallway lights, his wheels clearly turning as he ponders his decision before shoving his hands in his pockets. He lets out a slow breath and asks, "Are you sure you're comfortable with it? Because the last thing I want is to make you feel uncomfortable."

Needing to convince myself more than him, I shrug aggressively and say, "We're adults. It'll be fine." I playfully swat his arm, and his shoulders relax at the act.

It will be fine, Kate.

"Just stay with me."

Chapter Ten

Malcolm

Just stay with me.

If it were possible for Kate's words to hit me like a truck, it would be those.

The words replay in my head like a damn symphony as I make my way back down to the lobby. I just need to breathe for a second. The effect this woman has on me is downright ridiculous, and four little words have rendered me a stuttering idiot in the hallway. And the fact that we're sharing a room now has my blood pressure almost at a stroke level. This place is pretty much a resort, so I should be relaxed. I should be as relaxed as the guy in the Hawaiian shirt sitting at the bar sipping his drink with a little umbrella in it. But nope. I am feeling the most on edge I've felt in months. Maybe even years. I knew getting out of the friend zone wasn't going to be easy, but I didn't expect the universe to throw us in the same room on day one.

"Hello, Mr. Geer! How can I help you?" Benny's voice comes from the other line after one ring. He's clearly still at the school or he wouldn't sound so professional.

"We have a problem." I pace back and forth in the hotel lobby, working through the breathing exercises my therapist gave me.

I hear movement on the other line, then my phone jingles with his incoming FaceTime. I click it on and see Benny's and Ellie's faces fighting for room on my screen.

Watching their faces practically melt together does something to my heart. Most days, I'd rather get run over by a train than watch them act like a couple. Some call it adorable. I call it nauseating. It makes me want to burn down an entire Christmas tree farm. But on the rare occasion I don't get annoyed by their sickening infatuation with each other, I actually do feel happy for them.

"What happened?" Ellie asks, her face full of worry.

One last breath out and I feel better. My instincts have me checking over my shoulder before speaking. *This isn't a war zone, Geer. Just chill out.* I smooth out my beard and say under my breath, "We're sharing a room."

"WHAT?!" the squished heads yell at the same time.

"What happened to the reservation?" Benny's face is calculating. He's clearly thinking of all the scenarios that could happen if two of his faculty members *share a room*. I don't blame him. After what happened last term with him almost losing his job, he's been a headache about school policies.

"Bill messed it up."

"Freaking Bill," Benny mumbles. "Will you—"

"I will be professional," I interject, already aware of his concerns. "No funny business, Ben."

"I know, I know. I just mean—"

"It'll be fine," Ellie reassures him. "There are no policies about faculty members engaging in...things"—she waves her hand at the screen—"with each other anymore. They're free to do as they please." She gives me a supportive smirk.

"They're at camp! A camp we sent them to and paid for." Benny's grumble is almost comparable to mine.

"Nothing will happen. You know me, and you know Kate," I reassure him.

"Yes, I do. Alright." He attempts a steadying breath. "Well, then, what's the issue? You know, if you're not gonna..." He trails off, wincing at where his mind was going. I'm sure the thought of his cousin, who is practically his sister, doing anything but holding hands with another person is enough to send Benny to Crazy Town.

"The *issue*, honey," Ellie speaks through her teeth, "is Malcolm's entire plan is ruined. How can he woo her if they'll be together literally every second? The mystery and tension of romance is out the freaking window now!" Ellie seems more upset about all of this than me.

"Exactly. So what now?" I rub the back of my neck and roll it out. The plane and bus ride killed my back, and the stress of this "plan" has become an added physical pain.

"We just come up with a new plan!" Ellie answers before Benny can get a word out. "Yes. You can still do a few things, but the other things, like lingering hugs goodnight or walking away backward, gazing at her, will have to be thrown out." Ellie waves her hands around and reaches for a notebook—the infamous notebook full of doodles and secrets. She starts scribbling away like a maniac, Benny and I both watching.

"Great, you just let me know what you come up with," I murmur under my breath. Including them in these plans hasn't been very enjoyable, but I hate to admit that it's probably necessary. According to them, just asking Kate to dinner wasn't *strong* enough to pull me out of the friend zone.

A group of kids races through the lobby with beach towels and a speaker blaring some nonsense about *big energy*. I glance over, clocking each face and making sure none of them are from my group.

"Where are you at?" Benny asks, eyeing the commotion that passed behind me.

"The lobby. I told Kate I forgot toothpaste."

"Did you?"

"Of course I didn't forget toothpaste. I just needed to calm down," I snip. Benny's eyebrows furrow as he watches me. Ellie stops writing and eyes me too.

"Are you alright?" Her voice is therapist-y.

I take a slow inhale, looking away from their pity eyes, and watch Hawaiian Shirt order another drink.

"Are you still having nightmares?" Ellie whispers.

Nightmares.

"I haven't had any in a month," I whisper.

"Good, good." Benny nods.

"What if I—"

"Just try to stay calm and manage your stress the best you can," Ellie interrupts my question before I can let it consume me. "You won't let the plan be ruined because of *freaking* Bill. Use the forced proximity to your advantage, alright?" She does a good job at reverting back to the conversation in an attempt to not let me dwell on my issues.

Over the years, I've been able to push the memories aside, suppressing them with every ounce of energy I have. But then I get comfortable, thinking they aren't a problem anymore. And then it creeps in again when I least expect it. It could be from lack of sleep or a familiar sound.

Hell, I had to call my therapist in a panic because the bird that flew over my house one morning reminded me of a helicopter.

But for years, I didn't have a therapist. I refused to talk to anyone about it. Detaching myself from the past seemed like the best option, until the nightmares were happening every night, and I realized it was getting me nowhere.

I've made progress.

But I can't shake the anxiety gnawing at my insides at the real possibility of having a nightmare around Kate. It's one thing to know about the nightmares—which she does—but actually seeing them is a different thing entirely. And that terrifies me.

What if it scares her away? What if she pities me? What if the fact that I cry like a baby at night over watching my friend die is too much for her to handle?

"It's going to be fine, Malcolm." Benny pulls me back to the conversation, reassuring me.

I just nod. The tiny amount of confidence I had in winning Kate over is just about gone now.

Chapter Eleven

Kate

You have got to be kidding me.

I assess the room around me, my mouth on the floor as I take it all in. The room is gorgeous, yes. Everything is white, with gold and blue accents on the curtains and the floor, and wicker accent furniture. Very coastal vibes with abstract art of the sea and sand on every wall. It's as if the interior designers of the hotel wanted an endless reminder for their guests that they are at the *beach*. It's a beautiful oasis compiled in one single 800-square-foot space.

I would be in heaven if it weren't for one teeny-tiny issue.

There's only one bed.

One. Bed.

Alright, maybe *tiny* isn't the best way to describe the severity of the crisis before me. This is a problem. A big problem.

"Katherine Stanley. There is only one bed. One. Uno. Isa. One singular bed in the center of this room." I talk like someone is with me, listening, which there isn't. I'm alone, waving my arms around manically, presenting the room to my audience of one. Me. "And talking to yourself isn't going to make this situation any less crazy, so maybe stop that. Right now."

I halt, taking a deep breath and pinning my arms to my sides. Forcing myself into submission physically is the best way to prevent a freakout, right? Of course it is. I nod confidently, feeling ready to handle this situation with a level head.

Then, as if I am screaming into the abyss, my brain decides to alarm over and over.

THERE IS ONLY ONE BED!

Adrenaline courses through me as I scramble throughout the room, looking under the bed, the couch, in the bathroom, anywhere they might store a futon or secret mattress around here. I even feel the walls for secret buttons or handles to pull down a bed from the wall. Panic starts to rise in my chest as I come up empty. Of course there's only one bed. This room was reserved for ONE person. Ugh, freaking Bill. If he didn't have such an unstable heart, I would call and give him a piece of my mind without fear of sending him into an arrhythmia.

"Alright, this is fine." Deep breath in. "Everything is going to be fineeeeeeee—"

"What is—"

"Ahhh!" I jump around, clutching my chest as Malcolm stands in the doorway.

He chuckles, the corners of his blue eyes crinkling as he stands there, all broad country-boy manliness, in the doorway of this immaculate and overly fancy resort hotel. Such a stark contrast. If he had it his way, we'd all sleep in a Super 8 this week. *"Saves money,"* he'd say. His eyes dance all around my face, probably analyzing and processing that I was just in the middle of a minor freakout. I can't help but blush under his gaze.

Why is he looking at me like that? Has he always looked at me that way?

"Is everything okay?" He laughs again, the sound soothing the tension creeping up my neck. Shutting the door behind him, he sets his bag down and walks into the kitchen nook.

He can't see the issue yet, the *one bed* is around the corner of the kitchen, blocked by a decorative wicker partition. A versatile option for privacy and aesthetics, I guess.

"Uh, yeah! Actually, no. Ugh." I rub away the sweat lining my forehead. "Did you get toothpaste?" I sit at the kitchen island as he walks to pour himself a glass of water from the complimentary pitcher we had waiting for us. I was too stressed to even notice the little amenities we have all over the place. Water in the fridge, fresh fruit on the counter, a fancy set of toiletries in a basket with a cute fluffy headband. Goodness, this place is perfect.

Well, almost perfect.

"I did. Let's see what we have here." He finishes off his water and walks around the island, slowly taking in each nook and cranny of the place. I put my head in my hands and just wait for the inevitable freakout to come. I hear him hum in either appreciation or scoff in annoyance as he makes his way through the suite. "This place is a little bow gee, isn't it?"

"It's bougie," I correct, smiling into my palms.

"Right, whatever. We could've saved if we—"

"You're joking if you think the parents would let us take their kids to a Super 8." I walk around the island to get myself some water and watch him eye everything. Shake the curtains. Shimmy the couch. Fluff the chair pillows. Do all men do this?

"I'm just saying." He shrugs as he looks out the balcony door, which overlooks the ocean—another thing I missed in my freakout. "Let's go out here." He smiles at me over his shoulder before going onto the balcony, leaving the door open. The warm, salty air beckons me.

I follow him but feel the bed staring at me, taunting me, with its pillow eyes.

We sit in the chairs nestled side by side on the balcony and take in the view overlooking the private hotel beach and vast ocean that stretches farther than I can see. It's late in the afternoon with the sun hidden by a few clouds, small beams of sunlight peeking through and glistening on the water just below us. I scan the groups of students scattered on the beach, pointing out our kids to Malcolm. Some are sunbathing, some are playing volleyball, and the others are playing football. My chest warms at the scene, the current crisis not feeling as significant as gratitude swells in my heart.

They really are good kids. And this place is beautiful. And I'm here with my best friend. Yet, I'm freaking out over something so small. Surely we can manage one king-sized bed for a few nights.

Taking a deep breath in, I taste the salt from the air and lick the corners of my mouth. The idea of sitting out here in the morning with a cup of tea sounds splendid. And to have this man drink his coffee next to me doesn't sound too bad either. The sun warms my face as I close my eyes and picture the next few days.

My involuntary smile pinches my cheeks as I ask, "Isn't this perfect?"

"So perfect," he whispers slowly.

I look over at Malcolm, who is...*staring at me?*

His smile is a different one. Soft and tender. I don't see that one very often. It's reserved for when he goes to the woodworking show, or when he watches *Saving Private Ryan*. The smile he has when he's completely engrossed in the thing he's taking in. Heat splotches my cheek as he clears his throat and turns toward the beach. "Absolutely perfect."

Something about that smile sends an unfamiliar sensation zinging through me.

"So..." he says without looking at me, "what are we going to do about the bed?"

"The bed?" I cringe, the sensation fully replaced with anxiety as it ripples itself deep down into my belly. "So you've seen it?"

"First thing I saw, Kate. But I had a feeling you were worried about it, so I figured I'd let you have some more time to process before bringing it up." He leans back in his chair, sprawling his long legs out in front of him and crossing his ankles. "So, what's the plan, Stan?"

"Leaving it up to me? Gee, thanks." I groan and pull my legs up under me on the chair.

"Of course not." His tone is steady and comforting as he reassures me. "I just know that sometimes you see something one way and can get so riddled with anxiety about how it might affect someone else." He shrugs casually, like the simple fact that this man truly knows me and just revealed my inner turmoil like he was recalling what he ate for breakfast this morning is just that—casual. Continuing, he adds, "And sometimes—and I mean no offense—those feelings can cloud the other possibilities. Right?"

"Maybe," I answer reluctantly. Giving him a side eye roll, I rest my chin against my knees and let out a big sigh. Of course he's right. I get so focused on the negative possibilities that I see right past the possible solutions. And Malcolm is usually there, patiently waiting for me to realize this.

"What has you worried?" He drums his fingers against his chest, making a light thumping noise against the solid peak of it, and I gulp. Another feature now registered in my brain for a future *episode*, I'm sure.

"We've never shared a bed before..." My words linger like the salt on my lips, my eyes pinned on the rise and fall of his chest.

His chest expands and deflates smoothly. "You are correct. We haven't."

"And I know your back will be ruined on that sofa." I poke his chest. I can't help it. He grabs my finger, sending goosebumps up my arm. I swat his hand away and retreat my arms back around my legs, hoping he didn't catch what that touch did to me. *Episode buffering.*

"It might not—"

"Oh, don't even," I cut him off. "You were debilitated for a week after crashing on my couch at Christmas, and this week is too busy for us to be walking around like crippled old people."

"Some say I *am a* crippled old person." His eyes sparkle at me as he jokes, memories of our first meeting flashing in my mind.

"Well, yes, you are," I say pointedly. "Hence, I should consider your limitations in this decision."

"You take the sofa, then."

I scoff at him. "How chivalrous of you."

"Well, what's your plan, then?" he asks, waiting for a response. When I don't say anything, he asks, "Do you want to share a bed with me, Katherine?" The words come out low and slow, like a kind of purr under his breath. It sounds...sensual. And I find myself suddenly fixated on his mouth. My body involuntarily reacts with a shiver.

I'm hallucinating. The salty air is shriveling my brain cells, that's all. I have to block out images of his lips and other things that try to push their way into my mind.

A laugh escapes him when all I do is stare at him unblinkingly. "Well? Do you want to?" He wiggles his eyebrows at me. *What is happening?*

Panic ripples through me, and I can't help but dodge the message his eyes are sending me. "You wish I did!" I shove his shoulder. I catch his smile falter for a moment in response. He's just playing, Kate.

That's all this is. He's aware you're stressed, and he's lightening the mood for you. That's what Malcolm does. He's doing what any good friend would do. No need to overthink every little thing.

"If you're comfortable with sharing, I'd feel much better if we both got to enjoy the comfy bed. But if that's weird, we can switch." I force nonchalance with my words, but the thought of me sleeping on the sofa threatens to give away the fact that I am dying to see what that mountainous plush of a bed feels like against my spine.

Waves crash under us, drawing my attention back to the beach. The tiny balcony space is filled with a soothing white noise, drowning out the pestering anxious voices in my head. If I'm being honest, the thought of sharing a bed with Malcolm and waking up to seeing his face cast in sunlight every morning makes my heart do a backflip. I'm not sure why, but I can't imagine spending this week any other way. Maybe it's just an opportunity to enjoy a beautiful place like this with a man like him.

"Can I be honest?"

Not if it's a rejection, I think.

I assess him. His eyes are closed with the late-afternoon sun casting a radiant halo around his hard features, softening them as he relaxes into his own thoughts. I'm slowly starting to feel at ease about this situation—and oddly, a little excited. I hold my breath and say, "Of course."

"Brennan would never let me live it down..." His words fade into a whisper at the mention of his friend. Malcolm's jaw ticks, as if he can tell the protective walls around his memory just cracked a tiny bit. It's rare when he talks about Brennan.

"What?" I ask softly.

"If I gave up the chance to share a bed with a woman like you."

Chapter Twelve

Kate

"You think they'll notice?" Tessa whispers to Claire.

"Yes, they will notice if you steal the entire plate of cheese," Malcolm growls under his breath.

Everyone has been overly excited about all the amenities included in camp—specifically, the fancy snacks. I can see it chipping away at Malcolm's reserve bit by bit. They're like children in a candy store—touching everything, smelling everything, gasping and pointing like they just saw a unicorn. I glance around at the things drawing the kids' attention and have to bite the inside of my cheek to resist having the same reaction. They have a watermelon carved into a volleyball at the drink station, for crying out loud! Jess lets out a quiet squeal when a waiter walks by with an onion ring tower they have shaped into a palm tree.

"Can you guys *please* keep it together, at least until tomorrow? We've been here one day." He rubs the back of his neck and waves the waitress over.

She has long blonde hair and her skintight blouse doesn't leave much to the imagination as she leans in insanely close to his face. *Whoa there, Nelly.* He whispers something in her ear, and she lets out a literal hyena laugh in response. It might have shattered glass if it went on too long. I can't fight the eye roll that overtakes me at their exchange and turn my body away so I don't get caught. Giggles and whispers continue behind me for what feels like an eternity. Doesn't she have other tables to attend to?

"Thank you," he whispers.

The waitress leaves the table but not without glancing back over her shoulder and giving Malcolm a bat of her eyelashes.

I really don't have a problem with women flirting with Malcolm, or with Malcolm flirting with other women, even though I've never actually seen him flirt with a woman—at least, not when I'm around. But after our conversation this afternoon, I've felt myself drawn to fleshing that out more.

Just the simple fact of him bringing up Brennan was enough to floor me. I can count on one hand the number of times he's brought his friend up in conversation. But *then* to add those words...those shell-shocking, orbit-disrupting words at the end...*a woman like you*.

I'm baffled.

It feels like a part of him has talked to Brennan about me, which I do believe is possible, talking to the people we've lost. I talk to my grandpa all the time—sometimes about things I don't have the guts to share with anyone else yet. Maybe Malcolm does that with Brennan, and the sheer fact that he alluded to it has me feeling more connected to him, like he's tied an invisible string around my heart and is holding the other end, tugging me to him.

"Dude, when do we eat?" Travis groans from the opposite end of our team table. He seems to have forgotten he can help himself to the hors d'oeuvres by the drink station.

The conference room is abuzz with athletes and coaches from across the country, each sitting in their respective groups. Oval-shaped tables draped with shiny white satin tablecloths, and small, colorful island plant arrangements sit in the center. Green with splashes of pink and yellow. Small ocean-blue name plates with gold foil lettering sit atop a beach-themed cloth napkin, indicating our assigned seats. The wait staff, donned in crisp white button-down tops and black ties, black aprons tied across their waists, are a striking contrast to our group's sweaty athletic wear. Glendale sticks out like a sore thumb.

We are far from extravagant as a group, I'm aware. But this seems a tad excessive for a college scouting camp, in my opinion.

As if right on cue, a group of coaches—luckily also in athletic wear—walk to center stage and stand at the microphone.

"Good evening, ladies and gentlemen. I'm Coach Dawson with MU." He smiles and nods as scattered claps come from across the conference hall. He stands a solid two inches taller than the others at his side, and by the looks of Devon, Garrett, and Travis sitting at attention at the mention of his name, this is the guy to impress.

Devon was given a full-ride to MU, with Garrett waitlisted, pending his recovery. Travis, on the other hand, was deferred. But according to Malcolm, he could have a chance to prove himself here at camp—*if* he can stay out of trouble.

Coach Dawson introduces the other college coaches on the stage with him, each representing a different sport, then proceeds to introduce each team. A surge of panic courses through my veins like acid at the thought of standing to acknowledge his introduction of us. Embarrassing, clumsy memories flood my mind. Like when I tripped over Johnnie Larson's broken leg while attempting to present the flag during our President's Day assembly in the third grade, humiliating and forever indoctrinating me into the stage-fright category.

Luckily, after three tables stay comfortably seated during their introductions, a rush of relief washes over me at the chance to avoid the spotlight altogether.

The rush comes to an abrupt halt when he reaches our table.

"And bringing the largest group of qualified athletes this year, Glendale High School." He gestures a hand toward our table, the crowd cheers, and our table roars with pride.

And then, because I'm certain the universe is out to get me...Malcolm stands.

He *stands* and waves at the room, running his other hand down his chest and torso like some stately regency man. He may as well be smoothing out his buttoned tailcoat and adjusting his top hat right now. All eyes are on us as this man, whose broad shoulders and thick chest make him look more intimidating than most of the college coaches standing on stage. He waves kindly, pivots, and waves again. And *then,* he holds his hand out for me... *To what? Take?* Please no.

The clapping gets louder. Expectant.

Claire elbows me in the ribs. "Stand up already," she whispers through the corner of her mouth, eyes wide as she motions for me with a head tilt.

Malcolm leans down and whispers in my ear, "Please don't make me stand up here alone." The scent of his soap and oaky beard oil are both soothing and unsettling, if that's even possible. His posture is calm, but his eyes are filled with dread as I stay seated.

Claire kicks my shin.

I grab Malcolm's big hand, letting it enclose entirely around mine, and stand with him. Our team whistles, hoots, and hollers, adding more attention to this already dreadful moment. Malcolm's hand finds its way to my lower back, and I lose all the air in my lungs. Sheer coincidence, I'm sure. The suffocating feeling is surely from the hundreds of eyes on us and not the graze of his thumb against the divot of my spine.

We wave and nod until the clapping slows. "I'm going to kill you," I whisper to Malcolm as we finally take our seats.

He smiles behind his water glass. "I'm sorry. But we brought the best team this year. We have to at least act like it's a big deal—for their sake." He nods toward our team, who are clapping and watching the following team coaches stand and wave. We've started a chain reaction. He's right, our kids are impressive, and I should flaunt it. It's been almost fifteen years since Glendale has brought more than five students to this camp, and the fact that half of the team are female athletes is something I should revel in.

My girls are amazing.

"I can't believe Tanner High didn't bring a single football player," Garrett whispers to the table. The boys begin murmuring over this information as Tanner's head baseball coach sits down.

"Heard half their defensive end was caught at an underage party," Birdie mumbles behind the screen of her phone, which has not left her hands since we walked into this lush conference room. Not gonna lie, I at least thought the boys from other teams would be enough to draw her attention away from her little device, but no such luck.

"You'll have to lose the phone sometime this week, Ms. Whitmore." Ignoring Malcolm's statement, Birdie doesn't miss a beat of her thumbs as she continues texting.

He gives me an *I tried* sentiment before shrugging his shoulders, like he could sense my feelings about her and the phone situation before I acknowledged them out loud. I don't know how he does it, but Malcolm is always so in tune with everyone around him. It could be his years in the military, analyzing and assessing dangerous situations. You probably need a sixth sense to be effective. He doesn't brag about this ability, though, and he definitely doesn't let anyone be in tune with him for very long either.

A familiar ding comes from my pocket.

"Is that another match, I hear?" he teases. "Let me see."

My voice comes out in a whispered shriek, "No way!"

"Why not?" Malcolm gives me his embarrassing attempt at a puppy-dog face that somehow always gets his way. Something about this strong, burly man looking soft around his eyes and lips has me losing all my willpower in an instant.

"Because this isn't the place," I whisper through gritted teeth.

"Come on, they won't even notice." He waves at the table. Our *impressive* athletes are now fully immersed in their phones or the food that has now made its way to the table, oblivious to the outside world.

"I don't want to look." I stab a lettuce leaf and shovel it in my mouth. "Plus, why are you so interested?" With the food in my mouth, it comes out *whyyeryewsewntrusted,* and Malcolm chokes out a laugh.

"I just think..." He pauses and takes a deep breath, pondering his next words. "I just don't want to see you get hurt again, Kate. I *can't* see it." His face goes serious as he turns away from me. I see his Adam's apple bob with a heavy swallow as his hand finds my knee, giving me a double squeeze.

"Thank you." I smile down at the hand encircling my thigh. I can't explain the sensation that surges up my leg at his touch...in public. I stare at his large hand covering most of my leg and feel his thumb trembling slightly. The urge to intertwine our fingers together is almost overpowering. I've held his hand before. It's not like it's new territory for us. But this moment feels different. Significant.

I fight it and elbow his arm. "Later."

The night continues with different speakers, camp goals, changes to the schedule, and the final scrimmage at the end of the week. Since football athletes make up over fifty percent of the camp's attendance, they go all out with a players vs coaches scrimmage as the final hoorah of the week.

Last year, a coach broke their arm, and two players were out for the season. You would think it would be frowned upon for coaches and students to go against each other. It's one of the most intense and stressful parts of camp. I stopped questioning it three years ago. It's a tradition. And you don't mess with tradition.

"We will see you all bright and early." Dawson wraps up the evening and gives the room a wave. "Rest up."

You would think, after a long day of travel and conference talk, the kids would be exhausted and ready for bed. *You would think.* We make our way up to our rooms, and they are anything but, giggling and whispering about their late-night plans to go to the beach. As the adult, I could remind them they're supposed to be ready for their first workout at 6 a.m. I *could.* Instead, I wander into our hotel room, assuming Malcolm will most likely handle it anyway.

Collapsing onto the bed, I roll myself up into the expensive, luxurious comforter and form a cloud cocoon around my body, melting into the coziness.

Physical and emotional exhaustion hit me at once, weighing down my eyelids. I could fall asleep right here, right now.

The muffled sounds of the door opening and closing remind me that I, indeed, cannot fall asleep right now. I probably won't fall asleep at all tonight, actually.

After a few moments, I peek out of my blanket cocoon and see Malcolm's uncovered back in front of the bed.

I hold my breath and watch as the muscles in his shoulders flex and twist as he bends forward, sending a rippling effect down the curve of his back. Heat ignites deep in my belly at the sight. He glances over his shoulder, and I know I'm caught.

"Are you *watching* me, Ms. Stanley?" His laugh is rough and gravelly, adding to the flame burning inside me. The expanse of his shoulders stretch and widen as he pulls a shirt over his head. My gut hollows out as the heated episode that was building there starts to fizzle.

Am I disappointed?

Alright, these episodes have got to stop. This is getting ridiculous.

"I just didn't want to disturb you." I climb out of the cocoon and sit up straight, smoothing out my hair, "Give you space and all." My cheeks feel warm as he tilts his head to the side and smiles at me.

"Are we getting wild tonight?"

"Wha—what?" I choke.

"Are you a wild sleeper?" His eyes travel all over me and the bed and the mess I've already made of the comforter.

"Oh." I laugh, mostly at the absurdity of where my mind landed at the word *wild* coming from his lips. "No. I am a very still sleeper. You have nothing to worry about." I will my voice steady and smooth the comforter out in front of me.

"Good." He leaps onto the bed next to me, the force of his landing bouncing me into the air, before settling into the pillows and stretching his arms above his head. "We can't both be wild." The blue in his eyes sparkles with a playful mischief I haven't seen from him as he smiles up at me.

The warmth in my cheeks travels down my neck and into my chest, settling there. A comforting yet confusing-as-heck feeling. An all-too-real description of everything going on in my head lately.

In a matter of days, my feelings for Malcolm have gone from comforting to confusing. What happened under the mistletoe set off alarms in my head that trigger anytime he does anything remotely enticing or attractive. It's not like I've never seen the man without a shirt, or that he's never *touched* me before, but for some reason, every piece of me is aware that it's Malcolm doing these things. It's Malcolm touching my thigh or my back. It's Malcolm whispering in my ear. It's freaking Malcolm in my bed. And for some unexplained reason, I keep looking for these moments to happen again.

We stare at each other for a long moment, the reality of the bed situation thickening the air around us. I don't know about Malcolm, but I am freaking out. He's always been very calm in high-stress situations—not like this even holds a candle to a war zone or anything—but I feel myself watching him, looking for signs of stress. His eyes flicker as they move all over my face. Can he sense my stress? He doesn't say anything if he can. I see his hand twitch and his jaw tick before he forces his gaze on the ceiling.

"So..." He stretches, filling out the entire length of the bed. "Let's take a look at this match."

"Ugh." I crumble into the pillows. "Can we not?"

"Oh, come on. Someone needs to point out all the bad things about these guys. Keep things realistic."

"You look, then." I toss my phone at him.

"Gladly." His eyes sparkle as he sits up, opening the app and proceeding to the unopened matches I've received today. "Let's see here." He scrolls, and I resist the urge to peek over his shoulder. A mixture of emotions moves across his face—surprise, amusement, and annoyance. He judges each match carefully before he says, "None of these will work."

"What? Why?" I snatch the phone from his hand and skim through the options. A veterinarian, a personal trainer, and a coffee shop owner grace my screen. My eyebrows pinch as I read each profile. One is my height, one hunts for a hobby, and the other hates sports. "They aren't that bad," I say, trying to convince myself more than him.

"Maybe not, but you deserve better."

"Debatable." The woman whose own mother doesn't have time for her. Or the woman that was left for a job promotion after a three-year-long relationship. Clearly, there is something wrong with me that the people I try to love can't seem to love me back for very long. "Maybe it's me." My voice is a whisper as the scary truth floats in the air like a black cloud.

"It's not. You are never the issue." His words are serious and sharp, a finality to them.

"Right," I try to agree, but my words lack confidence. I can't help but question my ability to attract someone, anyone, let alone just by a few words and photos. I've been out of the dating scene for so long I have no idea what I'm even doing anymore. It's far from riding a bike, like Emma suggested.

And the thought of opening myself up to another person after Eric makes my insides rumble. *What if they see the real me and run?*

"I'm serious. Any man who doesn't see your worth has no idea what they're missing." He sits up, wrapping his arm around my shoulders and pulling me into his chest. "You are everything a man could hope for," he whispers into my hair, letting out a heavy sigh into the wild heap on top of my head.

I reach my arms around his waist and squeeze, feeling the tension in his back relax under my arms. He always knows how to make me feel better, even when I don't know what I need. Physical touch has always been a point of contention for Malcolm, resisting hugs or pats from anyone and everyone he can. But over the last five years, we've found ourselves like this often, leaning on each other, entangled in a hug that feels so warm and safe that I never want to leave it.

We lie there in silence, listening to the waves lap against the shore and ocean air whip around the palm trees outside of our window. After a few minutes, his breathing slows, and I know he's asleep.

The awkwardness I was dreading tonight disappears as I settle into his arms and let my eyes drift closed.

See, Kate, everything is fine.

Sweat trickles down my chest as I lie on the beach, my olive skin getting dark and toasty.

The sun is so bright, distorting my view, when I notice the outline of a tall figure approaching. It gets closer, and I see the swelling outline of bulging shoulders and biceps, holding a fruity drink in one hand and a book in the other. It's a blur at first, but the vision comes into focus as well-defined abs lengthen and flex with each step closer. Drops of salty ocean water travel down ridges of muscle. The figure has a beard and is wearing sleek sunglasses. He makes his way to me and hovers at my feet, eclipsing the light from the sun as he leans down to crawl toward me. The heat that was baking my chest turns to ice, sending a trail of goosebumps up and down my body as he inches closer. A familiar minty scent hits my lips as he lets out a breath inches from my face. The bright rays start to dissipate, making his face clearer as the distance between us closes.

My dream is interrupted by a whimpering moan. My eyes flutter open as the scene around me refocuses. My head is nestled into the crook of Malcolm's arm.

He's asleep, but his face is pinched in pain, mumbling words as he dreams.

"No, stop," he whispers, shaking his head side to side. His arm is tense under my body, his other hand clenched in a fist at his chest. "Run," he whispers again. His legs bend and shake atop the comforter, his body like an oven.

"Malcolm," I whisper, placing my hand on his chest, and I feel his heart pounding. He thrashes his arms and legs, clenching his fists and hitting the mattress. Holding his breath, his cheeks go red. "Malcolm," I say urgently.

He doesn't wake up. "Malcolm, wake up," I speak calmly as I bring my hands to the sides of his face, trailing my thumbs over the dampness on his cheeks. "Please wake up."

A jarring gasp leaves him as his eyes snap open. "Kate?" Shock and confusion move across his face as he squeezes my hands at his cheeks. He trembles as he frantically asks, "What happened? Did I hurt you?"

"No, no. You just had a nightmare." I don't let go of his face. I can't.

"I'm so sorry." His voice is tender and embarrassed. The side of Malcolm I rarely ever see. The vulnerable side that makes me want to weep.

"Don't," I whisper. The sound of our thumping heartbeats fills the room. *He's okay. He's okay.* I recite it to myself as I stroke his cheeks and smooth out his hair. Misty blue eyes stare at me, searching my face for reassurance. I wipe at the corner of his eye and smile. *I'm right here.* In an instant, he pulls me across him and wraps me in his arms, a quivering sigh leaving him as he deflates at our touch.

We lie there, holding each other tighter this time. His breathing doesn't slow like it did earlier, like he's fighting sleep. My heart breaks the tiniest bit at the cracks he tries so hard to keep hidden.

I feel useless. There's nothing I can do to shut off the memories in his brain.

So, I just lie with him, hoping it's the tiniest bit comforting.

Chapter Thirteen
Malcolm

You're weak.

It's all I've heard swarming inside my head since early this morning, when I woke up with Kate hovering above me, pulling me out of my nightmare.

The desert. The bullets. My friend.

Pounding my fourth cup of coffee, I will myself to stay awake for the first of many coaching meetings today. Of course my brain would decide to rebel and throw me into a traumatizing dream the week I'm away from home, with my therapist out of town.

They were getting better. Not the nightmares themselves—they'll probably always be the same—but they were happening less and less. I thought that was good enough, but clearly I'm an idiot.

My phone buzzes in my pocket.

> **Kate:** Are you sure you're ok??

I pinch the bridge of my nose, the migraine from lack of sleep and not enough water making itself known. Of course I'm not okay. The sheer fact that I had another nightmare, the first in weeks, is answer enough. But adding in the fact that Kate *saw* me have a nightmare? I can't stomach the pity she must have felt for me.

Rolling and cracking my neck, I respond.

> Shouldn't you be paying attention, Coach Stanley?

I'm thankful our coaching meetings are separate today. I put my phone back in my pocket and try to focus. Coach Dawson reviews the year's statistics, and a feeling swells up inside of me when I see two of my guys at the top of that list.

Is that excitement I'm feeling? *Shut that down, Geer.*

I could strangle Benny for begging me to be head coach four years ago. And I could strangle myself even harder for *staying* head coach this long. This was supposed to be a temporary situation with an easy out anytime I wanted. But nope. I had to let myself get attached to these kids and this team.

My lieutenant would have my neck if he knew how mushy I was becoming because of a few teenagers. I should have my own neck.

"Geer, would you like to lead our scrimmage this afternoon?" Coach Miles, a man who definitely aged out of his role a few seasons ago, asks from the side of the room.

No, I do not want to lead the scrimmage. Everyone waits expectantly as I take a slow sip. I am a strict no-helping-hand person around here, and I will not cave. Do. Not. Cave. Geer.

"Sure."

I'm pathetic.

"Fantastic! We will see you all this afternoon," Miles announces, effectively ending our meeting. The few of us standing against the back wall pile through the door before the typical post-meeting chit-chat finds us.

"How ya doin', Geer?" a coach asks me as we make our way back to the hotel lobby. I can't remember this guy's name. "Solid turnout you guys have this go round."

Nodding in response, I sip my coffee, hoping this indicates clearly that I am a no-*chit-chat* kind of guy. He doesn't take the hint.

"How's Garrett Connors' knee? You think he'll be ready by the fall?" Mystery Man keeps in step with me.

Taking another drink, I shrug. I don't think of myself as a rude person, per se, just a quiet, would-rather-be-alone type of person. Too many interactions within a 24-hour period makes me grumpy. Is it possible that I'm always grumpy? Yes. But I'd rather focus on the situation at hand, which is—I peek at the guy's name tag—Coach Daniels being a little too chipper first thing in the morning.

"Would you like help at the scrimmage?" he asks earnestly, anticipation all over his face.

Eyeing him, I ask, "Do you have the margin?"

Clearing his throat, he hesitates, "Yeah, I only have one athlete this year." The defeat on his face is obvious at the difference in his team compared to everyone else's. To mine.

"One is better than none," I say.

My first year at this camp, I was just the assistant, feeling overwhelmed and out of place with only two athletes. Daniels looks around the lobby as we make our way to the communal area, taking in the view. He's young—compared to me, anyway. His eyes sparkle with excitement, and I let myself feel it too. Being here can be daunting and grueling. This year feels more so than the last. I have a pack of parents awaiting my daily updates and some faculty members awaiting *personal* updates. We sit at the bar in comfortable silence, taking in the patrons of the hotel, some athletes and some typical vacationers, the hot Florida sun shining through big front windows.

Daniels shifts in his seat. The awkward silence must be making him uncomfortable. I have no idea why. I could sit in this awkward silence all day and not bat an eye. He lets out a hefty breath, tapping his fingers on the top of his knee.

"This your first year, huh?" I ask.

"Is it that obvious?" He chuckles, waving down the bartender.

"A bit."

The bartender takes his order, and we sit in silence again until he returns with two bright-pink *mocktails*. My face is probably twisted in disgust based on Daniels' reaction. He laughs and shrugs, embracing the fruity drink with an umbrella in his hand and taking a long sip.

I cheers his drink with my coffee and disregard the pink slush on the counter.

"Malcolm Geer!"

Kate's all-too-familiar voice booms across the lobby, followed by pounding footsteps. Tension rises in my shoulders as I brace for impact. Daniels' eyes go wide as he looks from me, to the sound, then back at me. The steps get closer behind me, and it's no surprise that everyone in the area is watching to see what is about to unfold as this tiny fireball approaches us.

"Kate Stanley," I say behind my coffee cup, turning slowly on the barstool to face her. The trick here is not to let her know she's riled you up. It spurs her on, and then you're trying to contain the Energizer Bunny. Remain calm, and she will stay calm, *feeding off your energy*—or some other nonsense my therapist told me.

"Why haven't you responded? Are you—"

Cutting off the spiral of worry she's about to embark on, I direct her attention to the person seated to my left. "This is Coach Daniels. Daniels, this is Coach Stanley."

Standing abruptly, he almost knocks the barstool over as he reaches out for Kate's hand. "Pleasure to meet you, Ms. Stanley." His eyes dance around her face, and his smile is unnaturally wide as they shake hands. I don't like *that*.

"Nice to meet you, Daniels. Nice drink you have there," she jokes. My gaze is pinned on the slow release of their hands and the twitch of Daniels' fingers as they make their way back to the counter. Definitely don't like *that*.

"Pretty manly, huh?" He gives her a smirk, and I'm immediately regretting letting this man sit with me.

"Very. I see you haven't touched your pink drink, Mr. Geer." She nods to the sad drink next to me. The fancy whipped topping has started to melt, with the umbrella drowning in it.

"Come on, Geer. Drink this manly drink with me." Daniels laughs, slurping down the last drop of his.

"Maybe another time," I lie, having no intention anytime soon on partaking in fruity drinks.

"Daniels, I'll see you this afternoon." Shaking his hand, I tip the bartender and give Kate a glare. "Stanley," I say before heading toward the elevators.

Kate's little steps scurry after me, I have to bite my lip from chuckling at the sound of her pardoning and excusing herself to people as we pass. It's a shame I can't ignore this woman like I can other people. She's kind of a meddler. And a heckler at times. With the best of intentions.

I know they say most people do it because they care, but it's really not that hard to worry about yourself and let other people's lives unfold how they're meant to. Everyone has to be in everyone's business. It's exhausting to witness and infuriating to experience.

But with Kate, I find her meddling endearing. I find everything she does endearing, which shows how far gone I am. There's just something about Katherine Stanley that penetrated deep inside me the moment I laid eyes on her, and no amount of her incessant meddling can push me away.

An elderly couple in nothing but towels emerges from the elevator, leaving behind a trail of water as they shuffle past. Kate's mumbles fill the space as I hold the door open for her before pressing our floor.

"I just don't understand why you won't talk to me about it—or anyone, for that matter." She doesn't take a breath. "Not just your therapist either. I think people who truly know you can help you more than someone with a fancy degree." Crossing her arms over her chest, she blows a curl out of her face and stares at me.

"Isn't your best friend someone with a fancy degree?" I air quote with one hand, mostly because I refuse to use both hands, and I'm still holding my empty coffee cup.

"Technicalities." She waves me off then proceeds to huff dramatically at the millisecond of silence that follows.

I love silence. I thrive in it. But silence with Kate is maddening because I know what's going on in her head. She's either overthinking or spiraling. Either way, it's not fun for the person witnessing her silence. "Kate." I rest my head against the elevator wall. "I'm not going to talk about this right now."

"Why? Why not?" Her tone is a cross between a scold and a plea.

"Because we have a busy day, and it's more than just a five-minute conversation. You know that."

We make our way down the hall toward our room, dodging the maid cart and a rather large family racing past us to catch the elevator we just exited. Our room has already been turned over, with fresh linens and towels placed neatly on top of the comforter.

The comforter.

I rustle my hair and rush off to the bathroom. My face feels hot thinking about it, what I did, how weak and vulnerable I must have looked to her.

"You're going to have to talk to me about it eventually," she calls after me as I shut the bathroom door.

I will, but definitely not today, and probably not this week. This week is about me turning on the charm and being irresistible. Last I checked, having bad dreams is not an irresistible quality.

I freshen up and splash water on my face, reminding myself of my goal.

Get out of the friend zone.

"Let it go. It happened. You can't change it," I whisper to myself. "Focus on the mission. Be charming, witty, irresistible." *Get your girl, Malcolm.*

"I'll just force it out of you, you know!" Kate bellows from across the hotel room.

I open the bathroom door slowly, and Kate eyes me suspiciously. Kate's pestering is also maddening, but dammit, I'm still hooked on her. There is only one way to get her to drop this conversation, and I have to act fast. I inhale slowly, building up to do one of the most annoying things I could ever do, solely because anytime Kate has seen this in a movie or read about it in a book, she gets so flustered she forgets to breathe. It seems a little ridiculous, if you ask me, but this simple move seems to work wonders on her.

So, to test if *I* can make her flustered too, I do it.

I rest my arms above my head and lean against the doorframe, flashing her a mischievous smile. "A little force might be fun," I tease.

Sure enough, she sucks in a breath, cheeks splotching red as her eyes stay pinned on my arms overhead.

Flustered.

Chapter Fourteen

Kate

> We need to talk
>
> Like right now

On the second ring, I say, "We have a problem."

"What's wrong?" Ellie's voice is a frantic whisper on the other end.

The Florida heat bakes the tops of my shoulders as I pace in front of the hotel's valet port. "Everything! Something happened, and I don't know what to do!" My whispers are borderline hysterical, catching the attention of the valet attendant, who has conveniently craned his neck to listen in on my conversation.

"Is everyone okay? Did anyone get hurt?" Ellie is no longer whispering, and I can hear the slamming of a door in the background.

"Ugh, no. Listen, listen. It's me...and..."—I clear my throat, containing my hysterics—"Malcolm." I hear her mumble my name, but I continue, "He leaned against a door. A door, Eleanor! Which usually isn't that big of a deal, right? People lean on things. It's totally normal. But this time..." I pause and swallow the air that is now clogging my throat again. "I gasped." The words come out like a secret I have been harboring for years.

Ellie's laughter reverberates through the phone. "You what?"

"I gasped, Ellie, like the image of Malcolm leaning against a doorframe was so enticing that it just took the breath right out of me." I throw my head back and listen to her cackle at my crisis. I stop pacing and plop down on a bench near the valet entrance, waiting patiently for her to collect herself.

I hear her suck in a breath and exhale slowly in a measly attempt. She forces her words out, "Why is this a bad thing?" I can hear her biting back her laughter for my sake. I guess I can appreciate her efforts.

"Because it's Malcolm! What is going on with me?" I groan.

"Does this have anything to do with the Christmas party?"

I refuse to justify her question with a response because of course it does. It has everything to do with that Christmas party and that freaking mistletoe. Blocking the sun with my arm, I close my eyes, and memories of spicy breath and beard stubble take center stage in my mind.

"Well..." She pauses. "Are you starting to have feelings for Malcolm?"

"What?" I snap up, the sun blinding me as I reposition my arm for shade again. "I—no—I don't think that's what's going on. I think I'm just out of my element. This whole dating thing has me confused and uncomfortable and scared. Maybe he's just ..." My words trail off as I watch the waves splash against the shore across the way.

"Comfortable," she says matter-of-factly. It's more of a statement than a question. "Malcolm is just comfortable and not at all scary. Maybe deep down you're wanting something like that?"

"Hmm." I let her words resonate. *Comfortable*. Maybe that's what I'm missing. It's not about the dramatic gestures, or the sparks, or the gold shimmering light shining around the man, clearly pointing out that *he's the one*. It's about having someone I'm familiar with, someone I have a history with.

"I know this would take a lot of convincing, but...have you thought about talking to him?"

"Absolutely not!" I have a strict policy on what I do and don't share with my friend, and my emotional, romantic feelings are firmly in the *don't* category. Malcolm is a wonderful listener and problem solver, but one thing I have come to learn about the man is that he is *not* a touchy-feely-emotions kind of guy. Getting him to share about his childhood was like pulling teeth. Granted, I quickly learned why he keeps those things under lock and key, and I don't foresee him being up for a chat about feelings with me anytime soon. The man is anti-feelings. "He would never be up for that kind of conversation anyway. He'd just shut down," I tell her.

"He could surprise you. Who knows?" Her sing-songy tone makes me think she *might* know. "Just give it a chance and see where these feelings go."

"I—I don't know. What if it goes wrong? What if that's not what I'm meant to do?" I rub my temple and wince at the sweltering heat that has already baked the side of my face. "I just need the universe to tell me what to do. I'm too wishy-washy on my own to just decide to have that kind of conversation."

"You need the universe to tell you if you should give a hot guy with a beard a chance?"

"I heard that!" Benny yells from the background. That poor guy can't grow a beard to save his life. Muffled giggles and movement happen on the other line as they whisper back and forth.

"I would just feel better if there was a sign—with clear instructions. It doesn't even have to be a sign. A letter would be fine. Delivered by a seagull. Preferably right now!" I exaggerate loudly, speaking directly to the universe.

"Kate?" a deep voice beckons me from the entrance of the hotel. "Kate Stanley?"

My eyes strain in the sun as I search for the voice. And then I see him, the owner of the eerily familiar and all-too-real voice, walking my direction with a blaze of shimmery sunlight hitting his face like a spotlight.

"I hate you," I mumble to the universe.

"What?" Ellie asks.

"You're not going to believe this," I whisper to Ellie as the man approaches, standing mere feet away. "Eric, hiiiiiii!" The greeting comes out in a painful stretch, and so does my arm, in a reluctant wave, as my ex-boyfriend approaches.

Ellie's gasp on the other end rings in my ears, and I instinctively keep her on the line as Eric towers above my bench in the Florida sun. His dark skin glistens with sweat, and his arms are on display underneath a tight muscle shirt. My eyes snap up to his eyes, refusing to remember how those arms felt around me or anything remotely memorable about the man that broke my heart into a million pieces.

"Well, if this isn't my lucky day. It's good to see you." His white teeth practically sparkle as he beams down at me.

I try not to gawk in awe, because the man is absolutely beautiful, and stand up to maintain a sliver of dignity. All my words are dried up from shock. "What're—" I try to clear my throat, but it's pointless. "What are you doing here?" I ask, sounding like a sixty-year-old smoker.

"I'm assisting Coach Dawson this year." He points over his shoulder at a group of coaches standing inside the lobby. "He's retiring in a few years, so I'm here to learn the ropes of running the camp." He blushes at this, a sense of pride swelling in his eyes at his accomplishments.

At what he left Glendale for.

What he left me for.

"That's great. I'm happy for you." The way his smile fades tells me he knows I'm lying. Why would I be happy for him? He took the job at MU without telling anyone—even me.

Someone from the coaches group calls out to Eric and waves him back. Holding up a finger to give him a minute, Eric turns back to me. "I gotta get back, but hey, would you like to get coffee and catch up later?"

Another failed attempt at clearing my throat. "Sure." *Why? Why did you say sure?*

"Great! I'll get with you later!" His award-winning smile is back, and it fills me with nothing but memories. Memories I wish didn't still affect me the way they do.

I watch him walk away as shock courses its way through my veins like an electric current. Sounds around me are a muffled buzz, and I almost don't hear Ellie screaming at me through the phone.

"Katherine Stanley! Hello!"

Gosh, I forgot about her. Whipping the phone back to my ear, I whine, "The universe hates me!" Then I storm back into the hotel and race up to my room.

After filling Ellie—and Benny, because he decided to be fully invested in our conversation after the mention of Eric—in on what happened and listening to their advice that I *did not* ask for, I rush around to get ready for the afternoon scrimmages.

The cool shower soothes my burnt shoulders and my shocked nervous system.

Eric is here.

At camp.

I haven't spoken to him in two years, the last conversation we had replaying in my head like a broken record.

"What are you trying to tell me?" I mumble to the universe in the steamy air as I exit the shower.

I have an hour to get to scrimmage, just enough time to lather in sunscreen and scream into a pillow.

Wrapping myself in a towel, I step out of the bathroom and find a sweaty back pushed up into a cobra pose at the foot of the bed. "Uh, hello," I say, startled but also instantly entranced at the sight of Malcolm stretching, noting the faint freckles on the tops of his shoulders and the little dimples on his lower back, ripples of muscle and smooth skin stretching every which way.

Rolling off the bed, he reaches above his head and finishes stretching. "You done in there?" He eyes the bathroom behind me.

Nodding, I step to the side of the small doorway to the bathroom. I cling my towel tight against my chest, holding my breath as his chest brushes up against my arm when he makes his way through the door. I hear him turn on the water and rustle in his bag behind me, then his strong hand encircles my arm. His fingers send goosebumps down my arm and up into my neck, and words fail me as I look at his hand then up to his face just a few inches away from mine.

"I need to shut the door, Kate." He smirks at me blocking the doorway. I feel almost unmovable, like his muscles have their own gravitational pull, and all I can do is stay planted in place so I don't get lost in their orbit. I nod in agreement, taking a small shuffling step forward. His hand retreats from my arm, leaving it mush as I melt onto the bed.

What is happening to me?

It takes every ounce of mental energy to get dressed, but I do it. Then, sprawling out like a starfish, I groan into the comforter and question life. All of its twists and turns run amuck through my head. I replay the events of last night and this morning for fifteen minutes, all while Malcolm has been...showering? The man takes the longest showers in existence.

"Why so gloomy, Stanley?" he asks, emerging from the bathroom, a billow of steam flowing out around him like a cloud.

"I just had the weirdest morning." I roll over and throw a pillow over my face, more for protecting my wandering eyes from what could be just a towel-covered body at the moment.

The bed moves as Malcolm sits next to me, tugging on my untied tennis shoes that dangle off the side of the bed. I feel the gentle pull of him tying my laces and tapping for the other foot. "Talk to me." The earnest care of his voice takes root deep in my chest. I have to tell him. Even if I didn't feel the simple obligation to warn him about who he is definitely going to run into this week, it's more just the feeling of wanting to tell him everything—which I feel constantly. It's frustrating, especially around his birthday when I inevitably give him his gifts a week early.

Peeking out from underneath the pillow, I confirm he's fully dressed. No distracting muscle or bare skin visible. I proceed to rip the Band-Aid off. "I ran into Eric."

Silence. Dreadful, unsettling silence fills the room.

I sit up on my elbows. "Did you—"

"Where?" he says through gritted teeth.

"Downstairs. He's..." I pause, sitting up and pulling my feet under me. "He's here for camp." I sound like I'm in denial, refusing to accept what I saw. Malcolm runs his hands through his wet hair, gripping the back of his neck as he nods. "And he wants..." I chew on my thumbnail. I can't bring myself to say it.

"What?" His voice is harsh as he asks over his shoulder. "What could he possibly want?"

I pull my hair out of my face and hold it tightly behind my head before I say, "He wants to catch up."

Malcolm lets out a singular *ha* before pressing a closed fist deep into the mattress and standing up. "He's got some nerve, doesn't he?" he snaps out, not at me per se, but at the situation. "The man wrecks you and then wants to just catch up like nothing happened?" he growls, red staining his neck and cheeks as fury burns deep within his icy-blue eyes.

I stare at him, mouth agape. Malcolm rarely gets riled up, and if he does, he usually maintains his composure until he's alone to process through it. The only time I've really ever seen him lose his cool was a few years ago after a phone call with his mom. I found him hours later, chopping wood like a serial killer at the back of his property.

Rubbing the back of his neck, he storms off into the bathroom, looking around for something, not finding whatever it is, and coming back out to the room. Closing his eyes and inhaling slowly, my eyes snag on his chest expanding the Glendale logo in the center of his shirt. Such a sculpted physique hidden behind a thin piece of fabric.

A trembling exhale leaves him as he opens his eyes. In an instant, I see rage wash away as his gaze lands on me. "Are you gonna go?"

Gnawing on my bottom lip, I hesitate to respond. Am I going to go? What would it mean? Why would I even want to?

"You know what"—he grabs his wallet and room key from the bedside table—"you don't have to tell me. It's fine."

"Mal—"

"Just..." He steps toward me, gripping my shoulders with a firm gentleness only he could provide. "Be careful, okay?" His eyes search mine, solemn and serious, with small specks of silver sparkling within the crystal blue. A heavy feeling settles in my gut when I realize what that look is. *Fear.*

I don't have a chance to ask what he's afraid of before he rushes out the door without another word.

Chapter Fifteen
Malcolm

Just tackle him.

It takes me less than a minute to decide what I'm going to do—tackle Eric Sanders, right here in the middle of this game. My pads feel heavier than they usually do, and my helmet is constrictive, but I focus. As if in slow motion, we head to the ten-yard line, only four seconds left, ball in our possession. I don't have to tackle him. It would be redundant at this point in the play and would probably look too obvious. But this is my only chance.

I get into position and feel the rough turf against my fingers as I steady myself. Sweat stings my eyes as I scan the defensive line in front of me, eyes landing on my target. A rush of heat builds up under my sternum, pulsing down to my hands and feet as we wait for the snap.

Everyone is in position, and my foot twitches in anticipation.

A whistle sounds, blasting my eardrum into the back of my head.

I'm catapulted out of my daydream and back to reality, where Coach Daniels stands next to me, the students making their way onto the practice field. I snatch the whistle out of Daniels' hand and make my way to center field. With him on my heels, I take a deep breath and try to let the disappointment from my unfinished daydream fizzle away.

Eric is here. Of course he is. And of course he wants to see Kate. Apparently, every romantically available coach wants to see Kate, based on the cringey small talk I had to endure with Daniels earlier.

"Is she seeing anyone? You think she'd be up for getting dinner?" he asked me like I was her relationship bouncer, as if I held the control over her romantic life. Trust me, Daniels, if I had the control, I wouldn't be here running this scrimmage right now. I'd be with her. Alone.

"Alright, everyone, huddle up!" A sea of padded-up students follows us out to the fifty-yard line, splitting up into their respective teams. "We'll start with basic formation drills, green and red going first. Blue team, start on special skills and tackles."

The teams separate, getting into position, with Daniels stepping to the red team side, and I stay with the green. The afternoon goes by in a blur as we run through play after play.

"Coach?" Devon is slouched over on all fours, heaving breaths in between his words. "You tryna kill us?" He attempts a smile, but it quickly fades as he winces and rolls onto his back.

A few other Glendale students follow suit, buckling to their knees and hitting the ground one by one. Students from other schools take note of this, assuming it as permission to collapse onto the turf for a break, and join them. Their faces are a mix of pain and despair as they look at me expectantly. A part of me wants to revel in it, the feeling of bringing them to a breaking point swelling me with pride. But I shake it, reminding myself they're just kids, and this isn't boot camp. Just football.

"Alright, alright." Sweat builds underneath my hat, and my neck stings from the sun, reminding me how long we've been out here. "Let's call it a day!" My voice carries across the field as I wave my hands at them, submitting to their pleas.

"Don't forget dinner tonight! It's luau themed!" Daniels calls out to them as they trickle their way to the locker rooms. He's reviewing the camp schedule on his phone as we follow behind.

"Thanks for your help this afternoon." I rake the sweat through my hair.

"No, thank you. I've already learned so much. Your coaching style is really something to be admired, Geer."

I wince at the compliment and mumble, "Thanks." Daniels is a nice guy, and it would really suck to have to hate him because he has a crush on the woman of my dreams. I might be having a heat stroke, but I feel a sudden urge to be honest with this guy I've known for less than twenty-four hours. "Listen..." I pause as we stand outside the locker room door. "About Ms. Stanley... I know you're interested in her, but she—"

"Don't worry about it, man." Holding his hand up, he says, "I didn't realize you were into her, or I wouldn't have even asked."

"I'm not—"

"Geer." He gives me an incredulous look.

I let out a sigh, the weight of my feelings forcing themselves out of me like a blast.

His eyes are curious as he asks the age-old question, "Does she know?"

"I don't know. Or she does and wants to let me down easy." I bite back the sound of defeat in my voice and stand up straighter. "Either way, I plan on telling her after camp."

"Why after camp? Why put something like this off?" he asks.

I shake my head. Sharing with people makes me uncomfortable. And sharing about this? I'd rather listen to Bill tell me about his hip surgery a thousand times than talk about this. But if I can't share, what makes me think I can tell Kate how I feel about her?

Daniels pockets his phone and patiently waits for me to continue. He's young and seems fairly innocent, so I can't assume he would understand my response, but I say it anyway. I have to put it out there so maybe I don't feel as crazy. "It's pathetic." I let out a breath. *Just say it, Geer.* "Of all the things in my life, Kate Stanley is the one that makes the most sense. For some hairball reason, that woman is it for me. It has to be perfect." My expectations weigh on me like a brick, threatening to crush my windpipe. I stutter a whisper, "I—I can't mess it up."

"That's not pathetic, man." He pats my back and leads the way past the locker room and back toward the hotel. "That's real." His face twists for a moment before regaining his composure. Are real feelings a painful topic for this guy too?

"You don't want to miss your chance, do you?" He nods in the direction north of us, toward a group of coaches and assistants heading in the same direction. Adjusting my hat to shade my eyes, I focus my gaze on a head of dark, bouncy curls in the center. The sun hits her olive skin perfectly, creating a glow of honey around her in a unique blend of color. It makes me sick, all this poetic nonsense I think when it comes to her. She's just so damn beautiful my thoughts get sappy. She laughs at something, and her smile lights up her face more than the sun does. Seeing it sends a stabbing pain right into the center of my chest.

"Coach Geer!" Dawson waves us over to join the group as they migrate toward the hotel. We walk their way, and I try not to indulge myself too much in witnessing the whiplash Kate has at the mention of my name. *Eyes on me, Kate.*

"Dawson"—I shake his hand—"this is Coach Daniels. He's with East Central." They make pleasantries as we join the group and head inside.

A familiar hand grips my wrist, tugging me closer to her. "How was your scrimmage?" Kate asks, moving her sunglasses to the top of her head. Her brown eyes always turn a hint of auburn in the sun, and something about that squeezes my insides so tight that it's hard to breathe. Hell, it's hard to breathe around her most of the time anyway. It's like I'm just waiting for her to find her way to me, and the longer it takes, parts of me start to wither away. Again, sappy. But if I'm being honest, it's like these major parts of me are slowly being crushed under the weight of longing for her.

"It was brutal!" Daniels answers her, snapping me out of my sappy trance. "I'm telling ya, this guy is hardcore. I've already learned so much from him." He pats me on the back, a small smirk playing on the side of his face at his *nonchalance*.

"Malcolm is a great coach!" Kate links her arm around mine as we walk. "He's also such a good sport—" Her words halt as she accidentally distracts herself with my bicep, tracing it with her fingers for a moment then pulling back as if I've burned her. Staring at my arm, her eyes widen a tiny bit before she hesitantly rests her hand back down to her side. *Real subtle, Kate.* Clearing her throat, she forces her eyes back up to me and Daniels, "He's, um, dressing up for the luau tonight."

"I'm what?" I eye her, clearly confused. This is news to me.

"Dressing up. We all are!" She beams up at me.

"Please don't make me," I groan.

"I would never *make* you. I would just..." She bites her lip, a smile threatening to break through.

"Guilt me until I cave."

Batting her eyes and puffing out her bottom lip, she stops us midstep. "Is it working?"

"Oh, it's working alright!" Daniels calls over his shoulder with a wave. Just when I thought I could like that guy.

Kate tilts her chin up at me as pride billows off her in waves. She thinks she's already won this argument. I still haven't agreed to anything. She nods toward Daniels' silhouette as he walks through the glass door. "So, is that your new best friend? I mean, I don't mind." She shrugs. "I just want two weeks' notice if I'm going to lose my spot as your right-hand lady." She gives me a playful wink, but I see right through it. A flicker of concern flashes in her eyes at the possibility of her being replaced.

I reach for the waistband of her shorts, tugging her toward me by the belt loop until we're inches apart, face to face. Her curls that are tied in two knots on the top of her head loosen at the momentum. "You are irreplaceable, Kate." I decide to grow a pair and make a move—a small one, but a move nonetheless. With her belt loop still in hand, I graze my thumb under the hem of her shirt and trace a line across the curve of her hip. She doesn't swat me away. That's a good sign. "I will never find anyone as good as you."

She lets out a slow, shaky breath and says, "Me neither."

"But I'm *not* dressing up."

Chapter Sixteen

Kate

"Do we really have to wear these?" Sarah groans as she ruffles her grass skirt for the tenth time. We pile into the elevator with the rest of the girls and head down to the lobby.

"Yes! It's on theme!" Claire points then puckers her lips at her reflection on the door before adjusting the flower crown tied across her forehead. The girls decided to skip their afternoon conference to craft their luau outfits. Grass skirts and wristlets, assorted flower clips and crowns, and a few multicolored clay earrings that are apparently *too easy* to make.

I was so impressed by their craft skills that I forgot to lecture them about skipping their meetings. Now, two hours later, I think it's a little too late to reprimand them.

Sarah huffs as she pulls at the skirt one more time. The others give themselves a final onceover—smacks of lips, tosses of hair, and other adjustments are done before the elevator doors open.

"Wow." Sarah and I gawk as we walk into a completely different hotel lobby than what we saw this morning.

It's been transformed into a tropical oasis. Bulb lights cover every inch of the ceiling and drape down the walls. The staff members are dressed in traditional luau attire, handing out flower leis and umbrella drinks, and a group of hula dancers stand near the front doors, waving and swaying along to the music playing overhead.

"It's like a real vacation now!" Sarah's smile stretches across her face as we make our way down the sand path that now leads to the front doors. The rest of the team is all squeals and giggles as they rush out toward the party.

We file behind a line of athletes and coaches all standing in line to get their leis before entering the party. Lit tiki torches line the path leading to the entrance. Electric island music gets louder and livelier the closer we get, the beat pulsing through my veins. The last party I was at—a real party, anyway—was Halloween. Emma's parties are always a blast, but this last year was full of so much drama and tension that I found myself cowering in the corner with Malcolm until it was all over. It did, however, end in a literal pumpkin smashing, which seemed very cathartic from afar. Maybe that's the key to a successful party—smashing something.

"Hello, ladies," Garrett Connors says as he joins us in line, blocking my view of the expensive tiki face at the front of the line. His knee is wrapped in an Ace bandage underneath his bright-pink shorts. He's paired them with a banana-yellow button-up shirt and bright-orange Crocs. The kid glows like a neon sign underneath the lights, and he certainly has no qualms about it.

"Nice getup, Connors!" I wave at his attire, my voice muffled by the loud music.

"Just wait until you see the rest!" he yells over the music, wiggling his eyebrows.

Sarah and Garrett link arms as they receive their leis and make their way into the party. I take mine from the receptionist and compliment her outfit, even though she probably can't hear me over the music. It's the thought that counts. Clutching the flowers to my chest, I weave through the crowd, being careful not to step on feet or my own grass skirt the girls made for me.

I finally find my kids, but no Malcolm.

"Where's Coach Geer?" I ask Devon. He shrugs in response, sipping out of a red cup with an umbrella. "No alcohol, correct?" I eye the cup suspiciously. He salutes me and points to the *All Drinks Are Non-Alcoholic* sign hanging over the bar.

He must notice the sigh of relief I have when he says, "Chill, Coach. We all respect you too much to drink under your watch." Hearing him say this stings my eyes, because for some reason, at this moment, they were words I needed to hear.

I nod at him in thanks, then continue scanning the party for a familiar set of blue eyes. After a few minutes of searching, I give up and sit with the kids on the pillows neatly placed around a small cinderblock table nestled in a pit of sand. The party continues around us, with coaches and athletes from other schools approaching our group, making pleasantries, and giving introductions. As time passes incredibly slowly, the lonely pit in my stomach starts to move up into my throat at the possibility of Malcolm skipping this thing.

Parties aren't his forte.

And themed parties? We've had better luck dressing Benny's cat, Frankie, up as a penguin and teaching her how to swim.

An annoyingly familiar blonde waitress approaches our table, her face mirroring mine at the realization that Malcolm is not with us. She forces a smile to take our orders.

"Did you get the, uh...thing handled?" Travis asks the waitress. His face is uncomfortable and cautious as she gives him a nod.

"Are you sure?" Charlie snips at her, equally on edge.

"Yes." She scowls at both of them. "It is being handled right now." She rolls her eyes and looks at me, clearly exasperated at the teenagers. I shrug, a twinge of comradery building between us as she takes the rest of our orders.

"What is going on?" I direct my suspicions to Travis because he is usually the center of any and all trouble at parties. He refuses to meet my eyes, taking a sip of his drink before whispering to Devon. I push my curls away from my face, frustrated at the thought of them trying to pull some prank or spike the punch at the party. Summoning my intimidating-teacher voice, I say, "Someone better tell me what's going on. Now."

A whirl of whispers, hesitant responses, and wandering eyes ripple across the table. Feeling outnumbered and unmotivated to discipline these kids, I pull my phone out. Maybe it's the music or the fact that I haven't eaten anything, but I start to feel grouchy as I start typing a text message:

> I didn't think wearing a Hawaiian shirt was such a big deal. You could've worn whatever you wanted, you know!! But to not come to the party at all?? Super low, dude.

I type and erase the word *dude* five times before committing to it and pressing send. I look back at the group, irritation clear on my face as they sit silently. "Please don't make me end this party early," I grumble out the words.

The idea of threatening my kids has never been my favorite tactic. Helping them choose the right decision with positive reinforcement has always been my route. It seems too gentle to some, but these kids trust me—or so I thought before they all decided to rally together and whisper around the table right now. But still. I value their trust more than their fear.

No one caves under my death stare, and we all sit in awkward silence for another thirty seconds—I know because I count *one, two, three* ten times in my head.

"Hey, dudes," Malcolm's deep voice swirls around me, extra emphasis on dude.

He towers over me, dressed in his over-the-top bright-blue tropical shirt that accentuates the hue of his eyes, tacky boat shorts with palm trees on them, and a necklace of orchid flowers draped around his neck. There's a playful annoyance in his eyes as he takes the empty seat next to me.

"Did you get it—"

"Yes, Connors. It's handled." He winks at the guys, and with that, the tension around the table dissipates, a relaxed flow of laughs and conversations make their way through the group.

"*Dude*," he whispers in my ear, mocking me. The word is the bane of his existence. "Are you mad at me, *dude*?" His question is a mixed bag of sincere sarcasm. I can see it physically pains him to say the word.

Elbowing him, I say, "I almost was, *duuuuuude.*"

He laughs at me before snatching and taking a sip of *my* drink. "I'm sorry. I had to handle something in the kitchen."

"What happened in the kitchen?" I snatch my drink back from him and sip on it, hints of coffee and mint hitting my tongue from where his lips just were. Finding it oddly addicting, I keep the edge of the cup at the tip of my mouth until the taste fades.

"Here are those appetizers!" The perky waitress returns, her eyes lighting up like fireworks at seeing Malcolm. Our mutual comradery is obliterated in an instant.

"It's nothing, just some accommodations that needed to be addressed," he whispers to me then glances up at the waitress and says, "I'll have the vegetarian plate, please." He gives a quick, cordial nod before turning back to me.

"I've told you, you don't have to do that," I say, lightly swatting at his arm. He dodges and proceeds to poke me in my arm. I rest my chin in my hand and soak up the crisp blue that sparkles at me. "You can eat meat around me."

Shrugging, he sneaks a sip of my drink again. I pretend to be annoyed at this, but the taste of his lips lingering on my cup beckons me as I take a drink quickly after him. After a few moments, I look at the table and realize there are only vegetarian plates on our table.

No meat anywhere.

"What is happening?" I ask as everyone digs into their food, sans animal products.

I'm ignored, either intentionally by refusal to respond or unintentionally because the food is really that good, and they can't stop shoveling it into their mouths. I suspect the latter when I take a bite of the grilled pineapple rice and am transported to another planet, piloted by my tastebuds. I moan and groan in delight as I shovel food in, all my childhood table etiquette lessons thrown out the window.

Sorry, Mom.

Actually, no, not sorry. Call me back, and maybe I'll care a little more.

"Do you and that dish need some privacy?" Malcolm's voice is almost a growl as his hot breath hits my cheek.

I blush at the sight he must see—my cheeks stuffed like a chipmunk's—before slowing down and maintaining my composure with a light thump of my chest.

"Please...don't stop." His words stop me dead in my tracks. They're like a seductive whisper, sending a wave of heat down my body.

I can't look away from him, the sensuality in his eyes and playful twitch of his lips pulling me in like a magnet. And as if he feels it too, his body heat starts to hit me as he leans in closer, our thighs resting against each other. I can't tell if I've fallen into a food coma and am now hallucinating, or if this is really happening, but he leans in so close that we're breathing the same air, planting his hand on the ground directly behind me. His other hand slides slowly across the table toward me, and I feel myself wanting him to wrap it around me and pull me against him. *What am I thinking?* My heart beats sporadically in my chest, and my breath hitches as his body gets closer, everything around us slowing to a stop. Even the music. All I see is Malcolm, and for a tiny moment, he's all I want to see. I involuntarily close my eyes in preparation for something, anything. Whatever he's going to do, my body wants it.

A crowd behind us erupts, ripping me away from the moment. Malcolm's eyes beam at me, and before I know it, he snatches a big piece of charred pineapple from my plate and retreats back to his seat to eat it.

"How dare you!" My attempt at snatching the piece back is thwarted by the shielding of his massive arm. "Get your own," I whine in defeat and scoot my plate farther away from his grabby hands.

His big, strong, grabby hands.

The grabby hands I was just wishing were all over me.

If I don't stop, I'll keep envisioning my best friend's hands as little playthings all over my body. I can't go there.

This might not be the best solution, but if I want to maintain my friendship with Malcolm, I need to get out there and go on some dates. I need to accept a few of these matches. Surely, then the confusing thoughts about Malcolm will fade with time. If not, these daydreams will manifest themselves, and I'll lose all control.

I can't lose control. Not with him.

The only way I can avoid ruining my friendship with Malcolm is if I find other grabby hands. But not too grabby. No creepy clingers around these parts. No.

"What is going on in that curious brain of yours?" Malcolm asks as he eats the last of my pineapple.

"Oh, just everything. You know me." I chuckle uncomfortably, taking another bite of rice.

"I do." He says it like he's proud, like knowing me is such a great thing. I instinctively roll my eyes at his tone, internally guffawing at the wonder that is me. "It brings me great joy knowing you, Katherine Stanley." His eyes are honest as he says this, and I have to look away. He's the most kind and honest man I know—sometimes painfully honest—and I wish I could believe him when he says kind things to me. I just...can't.

Maybe there's a root cause to this self-doubt.

My mind quickly detours down a path that is my mom, and I shove the thoughts deep inside a box and lock it up tight. Letting Malcolm's words replay like a symphony in my head—*great joy*—I let it play as I stuff the locked box in the corner of my mind.

"One of these days," he says around a mouthful of rice, "you'll believe the compliments I give you."

"Quit reading my mind."

"Never." He smiles.

The group of hula dancers make their way to the center of the party, going through their routine effortlessly. The party erupts in applause as they finish and saunter off toward the kitchen. Hoots and hollers follow as the staff carries out a limbo stick, corralling groups of people to start the line. Garrett and Claire are the first from our table to join.

We laugh at the many failed attempts by coaches to break their backs then applaud at the ease of the athletes as the stick lowers inch by inch. An array of colors flows like a chain of dominos as each person makes it closer and closer to the ground. I chuckle as we're waved at by Jess and Chloe. The ludicrous idea of either of us partaking in such an activity is downright hilarious. I decline the chance to embarrass myself in front of everyone—until Malcolm's thick hand is taking mine and dragging me toward the line.

"What are you doing?" I squeal, giggling when he mimes the technique he plans to use. "You're going to ruin your back." I can't help but laugh at the determination in his eyes as we approach the front of the line. He waves me forward, like the gentleman he is, and I bend backward with ease, barely missing the bottom of the pole with my hair, which is starting to frizz at the edges from the sticky humidity.

"He's going to kill himself," Garrett laughs as he joins me to watch Malcolm attempt to conquer this gauntlet.

Malcolm stretches side to side, twisting at the waist and rolling his neck. He squats a few times, pausing for a moment to evaluate the height, then straightens and stretches his hips and legs, for good measure. I cover my mouth to hide the smile stinging my cheeks at the scene—this beast of a man going to battle with a stick. And then, as if the man has turned into the infamous *Flubber* from the 1997 Robin Williams' movie, he does it. He contorts himself into a shape resembling a beanbag chair and practically glides underneath the stick with ease.

The crowd goes wild, erupting into applause as Malcolm stands up straight, saluting the limbo stick and giving a gracious bow in all directions. He does all of this with the same serious, surly look that has a permanent residence on his face. But a slight twitch of his eyebrow tells me he's delighted with himself.

The boys high-five him and each other as their coach proves, yet again, he is full of surprises.

"That was impressive." The joy I felt watching the victory is suddenly gone as my ex appears with a drink in each hand, a wave of awkwardness following him. "I don't remember him being so..." Eric pauses, and I reluctantly look at him, feeling immediately defensive as I wait for him to finish his statement. "Happy."

I let out a singular laugh. "That's because you never got to know him."

"Maybe not." He takes a sip from his fruity concoction and offers me the other cup, and because my parents didn't raise me to be rude, I accept. "He's really made something out of the team, hasn't he?"

"He really has." The pride that swells in me manifests itself across my face as I watch Malcolm fight the smile tugging at the corners of his lips. "Even if he denies it."

"He always was a humble guy." Eric's words are earnest, and for a moment, I'm grateful he's speaking. It's nice to agree on something with him when we never could before. "Are you still up for coffee?"

Freaking heck. I almost forgot.

Coffee. With my ex.

Using the cup to shield the nervous gnawing of my lip, I reluctantly agree with a nod. *Why, why, why?* Why is he so insistent? I don't want to get coffee with him, do I? I keep my eyes on Malcolm, the pillar of peace in this detrimental storm of emotions I'm feeling. When his eyes meet mine, they go stormy, like what he's seeing is enough to send him into a rage. Guilt whirls in my gut like acid as he approaches us.

"Coach Geer," Eric greets him with a genuine smile and an outstretched hand.

"Sanders," Malcolm's voice clips out the word. Anyone with a brain cell can gather he doesn't mean it when he says, "Nice to see you."

"You've still got it in you." Eric nods at the limbo stick now sticking upright out of the ground like a symbolic victory flag stabbed into the dirt on the battlefield.

Malcolm's jaw clenches as he forces a smile in response. His eyes are cold and laser-focused on Eric.

Then, Eric leans in closer to me and says, "I'll see you in the morning."

Eric leaves us, the silence palpable as Malcolm tries not to impose. He's always been that way, never forcing a conversation with anyone, no matter how bad he wants to. Last year, when Benny knew months in advance that we were hiring Ellie, he didn't tell Malcolm anything, and Malcolm refused to ask on the sheer principle of *"if he wants to tell us, he will."* But that didn't suppress the fact that the idea of Malcolm working with someone without any prior knowledge of who they were, where they came from, what their reason for taking the job was, drove him bonkers. I had to take him out for a steak dinner just to get him to quit moping around about it.

"You can ask me, you know." I gnaw on my thumbnail and slosh the fruity drink around in the other hand.

"You don't have to tell me." He rakes both of his hands through his hair, and a small piece falls forward, calling attention to itself. He lets out a weak, defeated sigh. "If you don't want to."

"We're just getting coffee. I don't know why he wants to. I just...couldn't say no."

Another singular laugh escapes Malcolm as he throws his head back. The thickness of his neck and bob of his Adam's apple would be hypnotic if the situation wasn't what it currently is. Awkward. He shoves his hands in his pockets, irritated, and walks over to the bar.

Leaning over to the bartender, he asks for two of something. I watch as he waits for his drinks, moving his weight from one leg to the other, kicking sand off his shoe, raking a hand through his hair again, then proceeding to take one of the extra drink umbrellas and break it.

Is Malcolm throwing a...*temper tantrum?*

Approaching him like he's a baby deer, I slide into the barstool next to him. "Are you mad?"

"Yes." He breaks another umbrella.

Sliding the supply of drink decor out of his reach, I rest my hand on top of his. My voice is a wavering whisper when I ask, "Are you mad at *me?*"

His head hangs for a moment before he wraps an arm around me. "No." He kisses the top of my head, some of my curly hair getting entangled in the scruff of his beard, and whispers into my hair, "Just the situation. I don't want to see you get hurt."

I wrap my arms around him. His muscles flex at my touch, and it takes everything in my power not to hyperfixate on the feel of him as I rub soothing circles on his back. But I can't blame what my hands want to do when Malcolm's muscles have their own magnetic force. The taut ridges on each side pull together, forming some kind of road map to a small divot above his waistband. My fingers tremble as he lets out a long, gravely sigh against me.

Focus, Kate.

Shaking myself out of the trance of his body is near impossible, but I overcome. Retreating my hands back to my sides, I weakly clear my throat. "I'll be alright."

Chapter Seventeen
Malcolm

Ice-cold water.

It's the only thing that can shock me out of this daydream. It stings my skin as it runs down my face and chest. I'm half tempted to splash soap in my eyes for the extra burn. It's a punishment for being stupid, for getting too close. The freezing water jolts my system and sends painful goosebumps down my legs.

"Idiot," I mumble as the water hits me. I really am the most pathetic man.

Since seeing her this morning, practically glowing in the sun, I was done. She was in her typical coaching outfit—black collared tank top, black shorts, and bright-red tennis shoes. It had only been an hour since I saw her, and I was going through withdrawals. I've known Kate for over five years. We've gone weeks without seeing each other. But all of a sudden, I'm some pitiful lost puppy when she isn't around. So, the moment she was in arm's reach, I couldn't *not* touch her. And now it's all I want to do.

Even at ten o'clock at night, the Florida heat seeps through the crack of the bathroom door, warming me the moment I step out of the shower. The slicing pain of cold is just about gone. I splash one last bit of water on my face for good measure, though. I deserve it.

"What are those?" Kate's eyes and smile are unnaturally wide as I walk out of the bathroom. She's perched on the corner of the bed, wrapped in a hotel robe. Of course she is.

My gaze dips to the small divot of her collarbone and trails over the tiny, but extremely visible, part of her shoulder uncovered by the robe. Her creamy, olive skin torments me.

"Malcolm?" she asks again, and I blink back to her face, responding with a grunt. "What. Are. You. Wearing?" I picture her words like her texts, intentional punctuations for dramatic effect.

"Pajamas?" I deadpan.

"Yes, but..." She giggles at me when I cross my arms at her. "Why do they have little pigs on them?" She bites her lip, and it's another nail in my coffin.

Raking my hands through my wet hair, I ignore her laughs. "These are very manly and very comfortable pajamas. And they were a gift, so hush."

I've always been a man of discipline. I had to be. Being in the military forces you to build up a tank of perseverance, enduring whatever is thrown your way. But my reserve is depleting little by little every time Kate looks at me that way. Her brown eyes twinkle as she stares at my pants, gnawing at her lip. I imagine releasing it from her teeth with a gentle tug of my thumb, and it sends a twitch up my hand.

"Oh my gosh, are those the ones from Aunt Edna?" She cackles, answering her own question. Yes, my light-blue fleece pajama pants, with little piglets dancing in all directions, are from her aunt. They are obscene to look at but surprisingly comfortable. And they were the first gift I had received from anyone after moving to Glendale. Something about the notion stuck with me, and I have yet to part with them.

"Don't be jealous." I pull the covers back and climb into bed. "You wish you had pig pajamas."

"I do, actually." She climbs out of bed, one eye still on the pants, as she gathers her bathroom items. Walking around the bed, she stops on my side, standing over me with her items clutched against her chest. She clumsily maneuvers them to one hand, taking her free hand to feel the fabric of my pants. The tension that started in my shoulders stretches down to my calf, where she has the hem of my pants between two fingers. "They do look comfy," she says with a wink before sauntering into the bathroom.

I collapse further into the bed and listen as she turns on the water. The sounds of zipping, rustling, and clanking happen on the other side of the door. It should distract me. It should take away this rigid pull happening inside my body. But it doesn't. Nothing does. I feel like a bungee strap being pulled to its max. One wrong move, and I'll snap.

"So, I wanted to ask your opinion," she yells from the other side of the door, as if the bathroom isn't five feet from the bed.

"Oh yeah?" I yell just as loud. I decide to distract myself with a stretch, loosen up the tension from travel and from Kate. I swing my legs off the side of the bed, landing in a squat position, twisting and letting the motion pop my spine. "You can't pull off piggie pajamas, so don't even ask."

Her laugh is whimsical, flowing through the door like it can't be contained. I close my eyes and picture the smile that happens with that sound, the brightness of her eyes and the pinching of her cheeks as she laughs again. It has me so weak my knees wobble as I transition to a hamstring stretch, almost falling over when she lets out a musical sigh to tie the sounds together. God, I am a putz.

"You believe in fate, right?" she speaks through the door again, softer this time. I don't hear any secondary noises, as if she's standing still, waiting for my response.

"I guess so." I shrug, not taking the question too much to heart. Kate has always been a *if the fates align* type of girl, and it's always been over the simplest of things. If the moon is full, then we're going to have a terrible night at the game. If we can't find a front parking spot, then we're meant to go somewhere else first. If she doesn't get chosen to read some early edition of a book she's been brainwashed over, then it's not meant to be read. I tend to go with the flow and just listen to her work these things out verbally. That's how she processes. But there are times where she really wants my input, and most of the time, it's already hand in hand with the conclusion she's come to. "Why? Are you doubting the power of the universe again?" I laugh and slide to stretch my other leg.

The bathroom door creaks open as she steps out wearing a matching red pajama set that I'm assuming is silk based on how it shimmers against her skin. Dancing flamingos are scattered all over the fabric. She twirls to show off another Aunt Edna purchase then curtsies.

I give her a single thumbs up, using my other hand to prop myself up for the stretch. "She has a certain taste, doesn't she?"

"Oh, definitely. I don't think she owns anything that doesn't have either a cartoon animal or some sort of inspirational quote embroidered into it." Kate smiles at the thought of her aunt. Edna is a sixty-year-old single cat lady. Four cats and a parrot, to be exact. Living her best life, as some would say. I respect the woman.

"Sounds like Edna." Transitioning to a back stretch, my spine cracks at least ten times as I move. I let out a groan of relief at the sound. The travel and lack of activity over the past few days are starting to make themselves known in every inch of my body. Limbo probably wasn't the best choice. "So, what's up? What's with the fate talk?"

"Well..." She chews on her thumbnail, leaning against the bathroom doorway. "With the whole Eric thing..." She trails off.

Irritation settles in my core, and I have to force myself to do one of those absurd breathing exercises my therapist taught me to do when I feel any negative emotion. I try to *center* myself. "What about it?" I ask, already knowing where this conversation is headed.

"What if the universe is trying to tell me something?" Her voice is a timid whisper.

I finish my stretch and stand, leaning against the side of the bed and crossing my arms. "What do you think it's trying to tell you?"

She lets out an exasperated sigh, blowing a curl out of her face. Her eyes dance around the room as she fidgets with the hem of her pajama shorts and shifts on her feet. "I don't know...never mind, it's stupid." Waving off the conversation, she rushes around me and the bed, grabs a blanket off the sofa, and lets herself out onto the balcony.

She leaves the door open, an invitation clearly saying *please follow me* in Kate language.

Giving her a second to herself, I turn the lights down inside then join her. The warm, sticky air is surprisingly pleasant against my face as I take the empty seat. Her face is fixed on the dark ocean as small waves slowly approach the shore and disappear. The palm trees lining the pathway from the hotel move in the wind, a small whisper of a noise mixing with the waves and lulling us into a comfortable silence. Extensive silence used to be debilitating to me, triggering involuntary memories I tried to suppress. Memories of Brennan. The helicopter. The flames. Things I prayed could be extracted from my brain. But over time, the silence has become comforting, and the memories have faded or been replaced with happier ones.

Silence with Kate is rare, which is probably why I don't struggle as much when she's around. She keeps my mind busy, in all the good and happy ways, leaving no room for anything but that. Good and happy.

I wrap my arm around her, assuming she's had enough time to process whatever is going on in her mind, and whisper, "Talk to me."

She glances at me then back to the ocean, embarrassment heating her cheeks. "It's silly."

"I promise"—I take a breath—"I will only laugh a little bit."

Elbowing me in the ribs, she settles into her chair and leans back into my hold. She fits perfectly in the crook of my arm—so perfectly that I want to barf at the mushy thoughts that consume me about it. Us, old and gray, and a little senile, with her nestled under my arthritic shoulder.

"What if the universe is trying to tell me something?" She shimmies herself deeper into my side, like a small creature nuzzling itself into its nest. "Look," she continues, "I know you don't like him. I don't even know if I've forgiven him or not. But what...ugh. What if the universe is telling me to be open to it? To be open to something I didn't expect?"

I rest my head against the paneled wood behind me, but I'd rather slam it through the wall to end this conversation before I fall victim to telling her to *follow her heart,* like a moron. "If it was"—I pinch the bridge of my nose—"emphasis on the if...would you want to?"

She's silent for a moment as she ponders the question, then she exhales forcefully. Her lips flutter and distract me like it's their superpower. "I just don't want to feel like this anymore."

"Like what?" I tug at one of her loose curls and place it behind her ear, my fingers trailing hesitantly down her neck before resting on her shoulder and squeezing gently.

"Lonely." The admission makes her voice crack, sounding like it could break her in two as she deflates under me. "I know that's pathetic, but I am. I'm so happy for Ellie and Benny. Emma and Steven. Even freaking Bill and Margaret." She lets out a whine, burying her face into my chest.

Yes, Bill and Margaret are officially an item—a little too much fun punch at the Halloween party. Margaret was hysterically happy for weeks, acting like she had just won the lottery. With Bill. The man who wears a toupée to church on Sundays. I'm still wrapping my head around it.

"Like, I know I have you. I have Lola. And our kids. Life is great in almost every aspect. But at the end of the day, I'm alone. I'm ready to share my time with someone, to have that person who understands me more than anyone, who doesn't mind just sitting at home watching reruns of *Friends* until we both fall asleep on the couch."

"We do that sometimes." It's a laughable attempt at casually saying *pick me.*

"We do." She looks up at me, and the moonlight illuminates her face as a soft smile spreads across her face. "But you know what I mean. There's just something about sharing a life with someone. Someone who won't leave you for a new job or a business trip..." Trailing off again, she looks back out over the balcony, her face changing from relaxed to tense before finally landing on flat and empty. Kate doesn't get this way often, letting her memories consume her. She's been burned too many times in the past—by her parents, by Eric. It's the biggest reason I've never pressed the idea of being more than her friend. I couldn't risk being one of the reasons she feels the way she does. And I sure as hell won't be lumped in with the people who have left her feeling this way. Empty.

Smoothing her hair under my chin, I tug her closer and wrap both of my arms around her. "I'm sorry." It's the only thing I can think of to say. I hate that she feels this way. And selfishly, I hate it even more when I'm right here. My jaw pops from clenching so hard at the thought of it. "I don't want you to feel this way." I kiss the top of her head, which is normal because I've done it a thousand times. And then, because I have lost all control, I take a deep inhale and smell her hair. The lavender hits me like a brick, pulling a soft moan out of me like I'm taking a drag of something addicting. "Ugh, your hair is distracting."

Giggling, Kate sits up and turns to face me. The emptiness in her eyes is gone as she smirks, tousling her hair in my direction. She flips it back and forth dramatically, like she's auditioning for a 90's shampoo commercial. "You're obsessed."

I don't argue because maybe I am. I just shrug and settle deeper into the chair, pulling a leg over my knee.

The momentary silence is broken when she asks, "Are you lonely?"

"I don't have time to be lonely," I joke. It's a partial truth. My time is split evenly between the school, the field, Kate, and the animals. Any spare time I have is spent recharging from expending so much social energy elsewhere. But the other side of that truth is...yes, I feel lonely sometimes. I'm lonely at night when my mind wanders back to the desert or to Brennan. Or when I get the once-a-quarter text check-in from my mother. More than that, I'm lonely when I'm not with Kate. I'm a miserable man when I'm not around her. Kate crosses her arms, clearly unamused by my answer, so I say, "I can be, yes."

"Is that why you beg me to stay with you past your bedtime?" she jokes playfully.

"I do not beg." I lift my chin like the distinguished gentleman I am. "I simply present it as an option, and you comply rather quickly."

Kate lets out a belly laugh that echoes out toward the beach. "You practically grovel at my feet the moment I head for the door. 'Stay, Kate. Don't go, Kate,'" she says, a poor attempt at mimicking as she clasps her hands together at her chest.

"You could easily leave, no problem. You, *ma'am,* only have yourself to blame." Her cheeks pinch at the small bit of Southern accent I let slip out. She gives me a heck of a time any chance she gets when the Texas twang slips out. But she has two accents: her *wannabe-Southern* Oklahoma accent, as she calls it, and the feisty Filipino accent that happens when she bickers with her aunts and uncles.

Wrapping the blanket tightly around her, she rests her head against her raised knees and settles her eyes on my hands resting on my chest. Her blinks are slow but focused, sleep beckoning her as we sit. "I'm sorry you feel lonely too."

Tilting my head toward her, I smile. "I don't feel lonely right now."

Her sleepy eyes brighten as a smile stretches across her face—a beautiful, unabashed smile—as she shyly asks, "Really?"

"I'm never lonely with you, Kate."

She closes her eyes and gives a hum in response, the smile still firmly in place.

"You know..." My words stretch as I sprawl my legs out and roll my neck, easing the tension in my joints. "I could spend every moment with you, and that's all I'd ever need," I say matter-of-factly, like I'm telling her the time, keeping my gaze fixed on the black sky ahead.

A beat of silence passes before I look back to her for a response. Her head is cocked at an unnatural angle as she stares at me, still hugging her knees. Her smile has been replaced with the classic deer-in-headlights face.

"What?" I ask, concerned about the immovable expression she's giving me.

"Every moment." Her words are robotic, like it's a statement she is still processing.

I replay what I said, realizing how crazy it must sound to her. Every moment with her. *Slow your roll, Geer.* Sitting up, I run my hand down my face and smooth out my beard. I twist uncomfortably in my seat, the words weighing me down like they come with their own gravitational pull. I roll my neck and arch my back, fighting the tightness moving all over me.

You said it, Malcolm. You can't take it back.

"Look, I just…" I groan and drop my head. Kate hasn't moved from her perched position. Taking a deep breath, I face the music. "I'm just saying that I'm not lonely when I'm with you. I'm actually happy. And I guess if spending time with you is what makes me feel this way, then I don't want to stop doing it." Giving another shrug, I lean over and rest my arms on my knees. I've never been one to lie. But I've also never been one to throw my feelings out there like they're candy at a parade. I just did both—withheld the full truth while simultaneously telling her how I feel about her.

What is wrong with me?

My common sense is shriveling up like a prune from the lack of routine and reality since being here. We're here for work, but my brain isn't registering. It must be operating under some vacation-mode umbrella. That is the only explanation for my erratic actions lately.

Kate clears her throat—the first noise she's made in about five minutes—adjusting herself in the chair to a more relaxed position. "You know I feel the same way, right?"

It's a whisper, but it hits my ears like a siren.

Some instinctive part of me is triggered by her words, and the smile she gives with them, like it's only meant for me. Without hesitation, I pull her blanket back and take her hand. I could shake it. I could just hold it. But no, I take her small, delicate hand and press it against my chest, covering it with mine. For some reason, right now, I need her to feel my heart stutter at her touch. I need her to feel my shaky breath as she rubs her thumb across my sternum. I need her to believe me when I tell her that I'm not lonely when I'm with her. That I am the happiest I have ever been, and it's because of her.

I keep our hands firmly against my chest as I lean closer to her, cataloging each intricately woven detail. The pink in her cheeks is more prominent the closer I get, the small freckle just underneath her nose is clearer, and the parting of her lips is evident when we're inches apart.

My throat bobs, and a gust of wind blows her hair in my direction, the lavender intoxicating. "Kate..." I hesitate.

"Yes?" Her warm breath hits my lips as her dark eyes dance all over my face.

"I've been wanting to—"

BEEP! BEEP! BEEP!

I'm interrupted by a blaring alarm and flashing lights from inside our hotel room.

"Is that the fire alarm?" Kate's yell is muffled by the constant screech overhead.

I nod, knowing full well my words won't be heard over the noise, and pull her behind me as we race out of the room. Piggy pajamas are on full display as we rush down the stairwell. The sound is jarring the entire way, sending a creeping ripple of distress up my spine as we make it out of the lobby.

Just about everyone and their dog tumbles out of the doors like their lives depend on it. We find our group, and I immediately do a head count. "Where is Johnson?" I snap at the guys.

"Over here," Devon groans, lounging on an outside bench by the street. His arms are slung over his face. He looks like hell.

"What's wrong with him?" Kate asks.

"Sleeping beauty gets cranky when he's awoken." Travis chuckles, leaning against one of the palm trees that welcome us to the front of the hotel. The rest of the group laughs as Devon moans and rolls onto his side, leaving no room for anyone else to sit as he takes up the entire bench.

The alarms continue inside as the staff starts to file out of the hotel. Multiple fire trucks and law enforcement pull up, exiting their vehicles with purpose. I hear the girls whisper to each other, commenting on the different firefighters, comparing them, and pointing out the "*cute ones.*" If I roll my eyes any harder, they will roll out of my head and roll across the ground, which might not be a bad thing. Maybe it would shut them up about the *"arms on that one."*

"I'm sure you were just as passionate as a teenager," Kate whispers to me, giggling at the irritation plastered on my face. "Just be patient with them. They'll grow out of it." She beams at the girls, probably thinking their heart eyes are adorable or something ridiculous.

"These teenage hormones are a plague to the inner well of my patience," I grumble to her.

Kate lets out an exuberant laugh that lights up her face and startles the peanut gallery from their creepy ogling. Her eyes gleam under the streetlamps that line the parking lot as she grabs onto my arm, laughter rolling out of her in a rush, leaving her out of breath. When she bends at the waist, I have a deja vu moment.

The mistletoe.

The same bashful glee from that night overtakes her. This tends to happen when she's starstruck, like when she met Kevin Jonas at a concert a few years ago. Her entire demeanor becomes giddy and exposed, which usually results in her responding hysterically, like she can't believe what is happening to her.

It's adorable.

And it's never happened with me. Until the mistletoe. Now it's happening again, and I can't help but hope it's because I'm the one making her giddy. I can't fight the smile that stretches across my face as she clings to my arm, sheer joy pouring out of her.

"You guys seem to be having too much fun over here."

That voice.

My back goes taut, and Kate goes quiet as Eric approaches us.

"Usually, a fire alarm results in fear or anxiety, not belly laughs," he speaks again.

I clench my jaw so hard it threatens to snap in two, which might go in my favor, because then Kate can rush me to the hospital and not let go of my arm to go talk to her ex like she's doing right now.

"Have to have fun somehow," she tells him, crossing her arms over her chest. He eyes her pajamas, giving her a slow smile that makes me want to hang him by his toes from the top of the palm tree hovering above us.

"Well, lucky for you guys, it was a false alarm," Eric says to the group, and a few heads look up at him, uninterested. "Someone thought pulling the alarm would make for a good prank." He laughs, and I want to rip my ears off.

"It wouldn't be camp without the kids trying something," she jokes.

The sirens and alarms shut off simultaneously with the firefighters giving the crowd of guests a thumbs up to go back inside. Our group scurries inside, but Kate and Eric don't budge, feet firmly planted as they continue talking.

Instead of sticking around to hear their poor attempts at chit-chat, I graze my hand across Kate's back and turn back toward the hotel, only acknowledging them with a wave over my shoulder.

I let the echoes of the alarms drown out my thoughts as I make my way back to the room. I see Kate's phone still sitting on the bed and send her a text.

> Sleeping on the couch tonight. You hogged the covers last night ;)

I move the coffee table so it's out of reach and cocoon myself securely in a blanket, fully preparing myself for a nightmare. Knowing the chaos from the evening is trigger enough, I sabotage myself even more by letting the overstimulation of my brain fuse with the overstimulation of my body and fall asleep replaying what happened on the balcony.

Or...almost happened.

Chapter Eighteen

Kate

"Would you like that hot or iced?" the young cashier, *Chad*, asks in a monotone voice, eyes glazed over with boredom. Like me, he is probably less than overjoyed to be at a coffee shop before 7 a.m. But lucky for him, he's getting paid to be here. I am not.

"Iced," I say, my response equally monotone. It's almost 90 degrees outside, and the sun is barely up. Of course I want it iced, *Chad*. I blink away my cynicism and force a smile, leaving him a five-dollar bill in his tip jar. My generosity is met with an eye roll and a crumpled-up receipt. I mouth, *"Thank you,"* and quickly turn to find a seat.

The coffee shop is housed in a tiny cottage a block from the beach. It's quiet, with a few early risers reading the paper, scrolling their phones, or sitting in silence. The place is filled to the brim with old-fashioned black-and-white photos, vintage knickknacks, and retro-styled posters. Nostalgia oozes from the walls, slightly calming the pinball nerves that are bouncing in my gut.

I check my watch a tenth time in a matter of thirty seconds. It's only 6:43. Eric said we could meet *around seven*, and because I am a chronically punctual person, I got here the moment the open sign was faced out. The ever-so-lively Chad calls out my order, making it sound even more boring than it already is.

Coffee with a splash of oat milk.

I collect my mug and scoot back into my seat. The farthest corner in the back seems like an appropriate choice for an early morning coffee date with my ex-boyfriend. I check the time again—only 6:47.

I try to make myself busy, but scrolling my phone is boring, checking my email is useless since I checked it before bed last night, and checking my text messages just bums me out.

> **Malcolm:** Sleeping on the couch tonight. You hogged the covers last night ;)

> No I did not! And please don't, you'll ruin your back! I can take the couch.

Malcolm was already sound asleep on the couch by the time I got back up to the room last night. And he was long gone when I woke up this morning. I texted, asking if he had an early morning workout, and the only response I got was *yep*. Those same pinball nerves migrate up into my throat at the thought of him being mad at me. There's no question how he feels about Eric and me, and I don't blame him. If I were to see someone break his heart, I would probably develop a full-proof kidnapping plan, leaving them stranded in the desert with only a pint of water to hold them over. And I'd feel only a fraction of remorse for my decisions.

With Malcolm's background, I'm sure his plans for revenge would be much more elaborate and covert, probably borderline torture if it wasn't illegal—or as he puts it, "strongly frowned upon."

My thumb hovers over our text thread for a moment before chickening out. I could easily ask if he's upset, but I already know that answer. But I don't know the other answers—to the questions I'm refusing to ask myself.

What am I doing here?

Why did I agree to this date?

It's not a date—is this a date?

My head throbs as I question every life decision that has led me to this point. When this happens, I tend to let everyone in on the questioning, sabotaging myself.

I sip my coffee then send a regretful text. I know it will not be received well, and I don't even know if what's about to happen is something worth sharing yet, let alone getting people in a tizzy over. Common sense and logical thinking don't start operating in my brain until after 7 a.m.

> **I'm getting coffee with Eric...**

Text bubbles pop up immediately, and I wince at the influx of responses.

Ellie: WHY?!

Benny: Good luck

Ellie: DON'T LISTEN TO HIM. NO GOOD LUCK!

> **Emma:** ☒
>
> **Ellie:** Is he there yet?? Did he at least buy your coffee??
>
> **Benny:** Knowing Kate, she's there early and already finished her first cup
>
> **Ellie:** Ugh!! I don't like this!
>
> **Lola:** did malcolm go with you…
>
> **Emma:** We will support you no matter what ☒
>
> **Ellie:** As a therapist, I must advise against this
>
> **Lola:** i am a grown woman… I don't do what emma says…

I bite my lip and hold back a laugh, their responses momentarily calming me. The squeaky coffee shop door opens, and I look up from my phone to see Eric walk in, wearing a slim-cut black polo, light-brown board shorts, and a backward baseball hat. The view is enough to send a woman into cardiac arrest. He really is a sight to behold. Dark, creamy skin shimmers under the rising sun, and his crisp white smile sparkles like he's a toothpaste spokesperson. His big arms threaten to rip the sleeves of his shirt to shreds as he lifts a hand to wave at me. Eric has always been the pretty boy, and when he showed interest in me, I was starstruck. Growing up, I was never the one to date the popular guy or thought to be worth the time for that crowd. I wasn't worth most people's time. So, when the pretty, popular guy at work asked me to dinner, I said yes. Nowadays, the pretty, popular guys are less appealing, especially when one of them shatters your heart.

My phone buzzes about ten more times on the table as my family continues to blow up our thread. I shove it under my thigh when Eric reaches the table.

"Good morning," he says, leaning over to give me an awkward side hug. His wristwatch gets caught in my hair, and his chest presses into the side of my face, nearly smothering me.

"Hi." I hug him back then untangle my hair from his watch, completely ignoring the lingering of his hand on my shoulder as he sits down. Nope. Nothing to overthink. Nothing to drive me into the pit of spiraling thoughts. "How is your morning?" I ask, wrapping my hands around my mug.

"Good, preparing for our scrimmage tomorrow. It's nice to have a late morning for once." I choke on my coffee at that statement, blinking the tired out of my eyes as the clock on the wall strikes 7:03 a.m. He waves the two cashiers down at the counter. Luckily, the girl who seems much more vibrant than Chad practically bounces over to our table. Her breath hitches as she approaches the table, eyeing Eric with thirsty eyes as he takes up a rather large portion of the table with his broad shoulders and thick arms.

"Wha— what can I get you?" she stutters and fumbles with her notepad, her eyes locked on Eric's arms. They really are distracting. I'm pretty sure his muscles have muscles. I avert my eyes from the slopes of his arms and focus on the lopsided wind chime that dangles on the deck of the shop outside. It jingles a mesmerizing tune in the breeze.

"Kate?"

I blink out of the hypnotic clutch the chime has on me and turn back to Eric. He looks at me expectantly. "Yes?" I ask.

"How have you been?"

"Good, good. Camp has been great." I nod erratically and take another sip of coffee.

"It has, huh?"

I nod, unsure how to carry this conversation forward. The big question of, *Why are we here?* weighs on my chest. His coffee appears on the table, and he takes a sip, awkward silence filling the space. I tap the rim of my mug, willing the universe to bless me with the gift of gab, like my lola, but I come up short. By how skittery Eric's eyes are, I can tell he's struggling too.

Another moment of silence passes. "So..." we say in unison.

A smile tugs at the corner of his mouth, and the sight warms my chest. It's almost enough to dissipate the heavy weight settling there—unsure if it's the awkward tension or a little bit of indigestion from the heavy taste of whole milk swirling within my coffee. *Oat milk, Chad. I asked for oat milk.* I force another gulp down my throat, wincing at the ache it leaves behind.

"What's been new with you?" Eric asks, draining his iced latte and slurping the empty cup aggressively. The noise is loud and obnoxious, drawing attention to our table. A few patrons, including the waitress, glance at us as annoyance fills their eyes. Eric then proceeds to shake his cup full of ice at the waitress, mouthing the word, *"Refill."* The scene plays in slow motion, a rerun I've seen one too many times. It sends a chill of discomfort down my spine. His table manners were always maddening, making me wish I could morph into a turtle and retract into my shell, or a chameleon so I can blend into my surroundings.

Instead, I just cover half of my face and look out the window, waiting for the exchange of glasses to happen without internally combusting from embarrassment.

"Thanks," Eric says as the waitress drops off his drink, topped with extra whipped topping. Clearly, she is too infatuated with his charm to be offended by table manners. An elderly couple at the table in front of us, however, is not, as they stare daggers at him above their crossword puzzles. "So, what's new?" he asks me again as he shifts his weight onto the two back legs of his chair.

I try not to gawk at him as the chair legs scrape the floor, reminding myself that I am no longer tied to this behemoth caveman. "Not much." I try to clear the remains of my coffee from the inside of my throat. "We placed second at state last year. The kids have done great with their standardized tests since we changed our format. Emma stepped in to coach cheer when Maddie left, and Benny is currently interviewing to fill the vacant history position."

"Sounds about the same." He gives a courtesy kind of smile. "What about Malcolm?"

Malcolm.

I hesitate to respond, unsure of where to begin in regard to my friend and current room buddy. My phone buzzes a one, two, three pattern underneath my thigh—the pattern designated for Malcolm. And then another one.

Either he has me bugged and is currently listening in on this conversation, or the universe is playing me right now.

I shimmy my leg over and pull my phone out casually. "Oh, you know, Malcolm is Malcolm." I wave my words away, as if it will be enough for me to not drift off into thinking about him in the middle of this coffee date.

Eric chuckles but says nothing, just watches me as he slurps his latte, letting the painful silence drag on.

"What are we doing here, Eric?" I finally ask on an exhale.

He takes another slow sip before responding, almost to the end of his second drink. I can't endure another slurping debacle, so I rush the conversation along. "Look, if there isn't a purpose to this meeting, I should really be getting back."

I go to stand from the table, and he stops me with his big hand wrapping around my elbow. "Wait, I just..." He looks around, embarrassment pinking his cheeks, and whispers, "I wanted to catch up. I've missed you." Releasing my elbow, he watches me, his dark eyes misty and weighted. Something about his admission draws me in, not because I want him to have been missing me—although it feels nice to be missed by someone—but because I know Eric. We had a life together, and that history doesn't just go away. In some ways, I've missed him too. I sit back down and gesture for him to continue.

"Life has been crazy, Kate. Dawson is running me ragged. We've lost three scholarship donors, and my replacement backed out for next season. I haven't been home to see my family in almost a year." He pinches the bridge of his nose and takes a breath.

His sweet family—the family I thought I would call my own one day. They live less than an hour from me, and the desire to run up to see them has always been in the back of my mind since we broke up. Tricia, his mom, was always so loving and supportive, filling the void my own mother left. I can remember the first time meeting her. Her curly hair was pinned back, and she was wearing a light-blue polka-dot dress with a linen apron hanging around her shoulders, untied in the back. It was covered in chocolate frosting. Vegan frosting. From the chocolate cake she made for me. Before even meeting me, she was baking for me. I can't tell you the last time my own mother did anything remotely generous like that for me.

"Poor Trish, I bet she misses you terribly."

"She does. And she likes to remind me every day how long it's been since I've seen her," he groans, pulling out his phone and opening up the text thread between them. The last text she sent reads, *'286 days since I've seen my son.'*"

I choke out a laugh. "She was never one for subtlety."

We both laugh, sharing a fondness for his mom. "I was just..." He pauses, exhaling a slow breath. "I was just so pumped when Dawson said I could come to camp. I knew you'd be here. I've wanted to reach out, see how you were. I figured you hated me, so I haven't, and I thought this was the perfect opportunity to bump into you." His words flow out of him at record speed, like he's been holding them back for days. He leans back in his chair and looks out the coffee shop window. I follow his gaze. People are starting to venture out to the shops or toward the beach to start their morning. The coffee shop sits at the top of a hill that overlooks the beach, and a walking path sits on the edge of their small parking lot. A bright, crisp blue coats the sky now with streaks of orange scattered along the lower edge that meets the shore, the sun in the midst of rising above the ocean.

"It's beautiful, isn't it?" Eric asks, his eyes softening as he watches the sun.

"Do you get many views like this in Michigan?" I ask, watching a family of five pile out of their minivan and race each other down the walking path.

"I think we have better ones." He winks at me, his competitive nature glazing his eyes as he downs the rest of his drink. To my pleasant surprise, he refrains from his aggressive slurpage and slides the cup to the edge of the table. Eric was always ruthless on the field and in every aspect of life, so I'm not surprised that he's mentally cataloging and comparing sunsets. Something universally beautiful is still fair game in his mind.

"Always the competitive one." I smile, leaning back in my chair to face him.

"Doesn't beat an Oklahoma one, though."

"Oh?" I look at him, surprised.

"Yeah, just something about the sunrise over our field before class started…can't beat it." He lets out another sigh, this one sounding more defeated than the last.

"Eric…" I pause as his daydream eyes refocus on me. "Have you talked to Dawson about this? About feeling stretched thin? Maybe you need to mention that you need to go home every once in a while."

He rakes his hand down his face and over his chest, rubbing a circle in the center of his sternum—his tell when he's uncomfortable. "I know. I'm just afraid to piss him off. I don't want to ruffle feathers by being upfront about what I want."

"That's never stopped you before." I grin at him. He returns it and checks his watch.

"Listen, I gotta run. Do you want to have dinner tonight? There's this really nice Italian place a block from the hotel." He sounds so hopeful and sincere, and my heart breaks at the thought of turning him down.

And then the thought of telling Malcolm hits me, making my stomach churn, threatening to send my coffee traveling up my esophagus and onto this table. No matter how many times he denies it or simply avoids the question when I ask if he's okay with this, his sleeping on the couch last night was answer enough. Malcolm is not okay with me seeing Eric.

But I know Eric. He was all I ever knew for three years, and I can tell he needs someone right now. What exactly I have to offer him, I don't know. But I've had more than enough time to heal from our breakup, so surely a simple dinner, chatting about our jobs and our families, will be harmless enough.

"Dinner sounds great."

Chapter Nineteen
Malcolm

I spent years in the desert with only a bar of soap and a three-pronged comb for maintenance. We'd go days without a shower because we were so exhausted that we'd just collapse onto our cots, still fully dressed in our combat uniforms. My beard resembled a tumbleweed most of the time. So, it's understood that my morning appearance shouldn't faze me. But when I woke up this morning with my face plastered to the side of the leather sofa, looking like I stuck my fingers in an electrical outlet, it became clear I need to reassess what I let bother me.

Especially with Kate in the same room.

I don't need her seeing the disheveled version of me. The version that probably whimpered into their pillow all night because they were having nightmares like a child. When I brushed my teeth, I barely recognized myself.

Adding that to the searing pain settling deep into my spine from the couch has now made me unfit to tackle any normal conversation.

"Another?" the waitress asks me.

I grumble a nod as she fills my coffee mug again. She just stands there, staring at me. I try to make it clear that I'm not interested in the polite morning chit-chat and migrate my gaze to the empty tables in the opposite corner of the room. The hotel restaurant is a fraction of the size of their fancy conference room. Dining tables are lined neatly in rows with weird seashell salt and pepper shakers in the center. The room is more outdated than the rest of the hotel, with brown leather seats and geometrical carpet to match, like they didn't care to update this little corner of the place, letting it live its days out as an eyesore.

This room is comfortable.

And it's empty, which makes it even better.

Mostly empty, anyway.

The eager waitress looks like she is going to crawl out of her skin if I don't say something. So, I won't.

I give her a nod of thanks for topping off my coffee. I don't have the mental capacity for small talk, especially with a woman who has ogling eyes similar to my students. Don't get me wrong, she's attractive. I just can't humor the idea of chatting it up with a woman that isn't Kate, even if it is harmless weather conversation.

Especially not when I know Kate is on a coffee date with another guy.

At this very moment probably. I check my watch. Yes, this very moment.

The waitress takes my silence as a hint and finally leaves the table. I can breathe. Pulling my phone out to check today's camp schedule, I ignore the slew of text check-ins sitting in my inbox from Benny and Ellie. I haven't updated them on my Kate progress, and I sure as hell haven't told them about her morning plans. But I know Ellie will combust if I don't give her something.

As if right on cue, the woman texts me.

Ellie: *SHE'S HAVING COFFEE WITH HIM?*
Ellie: *WHAT ARE YOU GOING TO DO?*

I clench my jaw, my teeth screaming in protest under the pressure, as I click my phone off. What am I going to do? She's a grown woman. I can't just crash her coffee date.

"Mornin', Geer," Daniels interrupts me just as I begin to imagine *bumping into Kate* at the exact coffee shop she texted me she was going to. "May I?" He nods to the empty seat at my table.

As if my raised eyebrow is answer enough, he takes the seat, coffee in hand. "You ready for the big game tomorrow?"

"It's a scrimmage," I correct. Shouldn't have to. He's a coach too, but whatever.

The big *game*.

The final event of camp before we all leave on Friday. Every year, the coaches and athletes split into teams to have one final brawl before we head back home. From what I was told when I first came to camp, it was meant to be a touch game to limit injuries, but over the years, it's become the biggest scouting event of the week. If the kids can take down some of their college counterparts, they think they're proving themselves worthy. The last three years have ended with at least one season-ending injury or suspension—or both. Now they have waivers for everyone to sign at the beginning of camp, releasing the football association from any liability, and it's because of this *game*, which is really a scrimmage.

I grunt into my coffee mug. I'm less than excited about a potentially brutal game, especially when it almost ended one of my athlete's careers last year. Garrett Connors has taken an entire year to get back to a place where he feels confident running again, let alone practicing.

"It's just a pissing contest," I grumble under my breath.

"Not a morning person, huh?" he asks with a genuine smile on his face, as if he's actually happy to be awake and sitting across from me, a grumpy bear as some would say. I shrug. Alright, maybe I'm just being a jerk now, but I kind of want to see how far he'll go with the one-sided conversation.

"Geer just isn't a *person* person," Travis Van says from behind me, making it clear that we are not alone.

"A *person* person?" Devon, who is also behind me, questions Travis' quip attempt. "He just doesn't like people...of any kind."

I look over my shoulder to see most of my team squishing themselves into a booth—a four-seater busting with six large, hungry teenagers. They're sitting on top of each other as they try to eat from the heaping piles of food they've carried over from the buffet.

"It's nice to see a team spend so much time together. My guy has only been interested in the girls from other schools or playing his Xbox." Daniels scoffs, sipping his iced coffee. It has whipped topping with caramel and chocolate drizzle down the inside of the cup. This man really has no shame.

Memories of Brennan and the coffee machine his wife mailed to him when we were on tour plow through my mind. He was always concocting different drinks with way too many flavors in them. Different sauces, sprinkles, and way too much whipped cream on top to make the *perfect* drink. Some were a hit, and others were better off as tank fuel.

Brennan's face fades as I focus on Daniels. The similarities between the two are unsettling, and I have to look away to collect myself for a moment.

"Don't worry. We're here for the girls too," Charlie says through a mouthful of food.

The guys all give a variety of responses—whistles, cat-calling, and the like. As ridiculous as they are, I can't bite back my smile and shrug at Daniels—*what're ya gonna do?*

We share a laugh as he finishes off his latte. "So, how're things on the Stanley front?"

"Dude, put a muzzle on it," I practically hiss at the man, trying to shut him up, darting my gaze in every direction to make sure no one heard his question.

"What's up with Coach Stanley?" Garrett, the kid with ultrasonic hearing, pipes in.

If my looks could burn someone to a pile of ash, Daniels would be on the floor being swept up by housekeeping right now. His eyes widen in terror as he whispers, "Shoot, sorry." He glances over my shoulder and winces. They're probably burning a hole in the back of my head with their bug eyes right now.

"Nothing, Connors." I try to roll away the tension crawling up my back and refuse to look at the table behind me. "Eat your food."

In a blur, chairs tumble, feet scurry, and dishes clank as the guys rush from their table and pile into our table. I refuse to acknowledge what's about to come, so I pull my cap further down onto my head, shadowing most of them from my site, and stare at the brown ring of coffee grounds at the bottom of my mug.

"What's up with Stanley?" Charlie asks.

"Is she sick?" Travis asks.

"Nah, she probably got fired," Ethan adds.

"Dude, shut up. She'll never get fired," Devon snaps.

"Is it Coach Sanders?" Garrett whispers to me, but everyone else hears, and the speculation worsens.

"Oh, that's gotta be it. She was obsessed with him," Travis says.

"He crushed her, man," Devon snips. He is like a nephew to Kate and Benny, and I would bet he feels the same way I do about the guy that broke Kate's heart. He and I had to endure a vegan baking class for a weekend because Benny was out of town. I sure as hell wasn't going to go alone, so I bribed him with a week of hall passes so he'd go with us. It was equally the most ridiculous and intriguing thing I ever did. *Baking*. Who would have thought there was so much math that went into vegan cinnamon rolls?

"Will they let it go?" Daniels leans over the table to ask me. The guy can already tell these kids are resilient.

I eye him, making my answer clear. *No, they will not.*

"Should you just tell them?" he attempts to whisper, but the rest of the table has silenced themselves to listen to us. Just when I was starting to like Daniels, he goes and spouts my business off like he can't control himself. I make a mental note to try to pay someone off to accidentally stumble into him at the scrimmage tomorrow.

"Dude, just tell us, and we'll leave you alone," Ethan pipes in.

"No, you won't." I scratch my chin with both hands before interlocking my fingers at the base of my neck, tense pressure spreading down into my shoulders. The impending gossip that's sure to follow if I reveal what's going on will get me found out. There's no way these guys can keep something like this to themselves.

"We won't tell," Garrett says like he just read my mind. He's been really good at reading a room since meeting with Ellie regularly. Damn that woman.

The rest of the table nods in agreement, gesturing their fingers across their lips like a zipper, or holding a finger over their mouth. Silent. They're trying to promise me they will keep it silent. But I know them, too well, and even when something as small as, '*I'm buying her a new clock for her classroom,*' was shared, it spread like wildfire.

If I admit my unrequited love for my best friend to this table of goons, I'm basically lighting the match myself.

"Maybe we can help," Devon offers.

"Yeah, maybe they can," Daniels adds, as if he knows us all well enough to confidently say yeah, let these hormonally crazed teenagers help you with your love life.

"How about no?" I say flatly.

More whispers and speculation occur.

They're never going to leave this table. I'm never going to get a moment's peace. The only chance I have to get out of this conversation is if I make a break for it.

I shove myself out from the table, almost tripping over Travis's feet in the process. Protests follow me as I grab my room key and mug.

"Hey, guys!" Kate's voice stuns my senses, a ricocheting ball of fire moving down my throat and into my chest. My shoulders tense, and my gaze whips to Daniels, who has made himself practically invisible as he slides so far down into his chair he blends in with the kids.

"Hey, Coach!" Charlie blurts it out unnaturally and high-pitched. It's a miracle Kate doesn't stop dead in her tracks. The table looks visibly uncomfortable, giving small waves.

She eyes them, suspiciously, before turning to me. "Good morning," she speaks like there is no one else around. Or maybe that's how I hear it. Sure. Either way, I want nothing more than to wrap her up in my arms and take her upstairs with me.

I give her a nod when she's beckoned by the group of girls standing in the doorway to the dining room. She waves at them before waving bye to the table. "See you guys this afternoon!"

Her smile is bright and unfaltering when she looks at the guys, and they all look like they've seen a ghost, staring wildly at her with mouths forced into creepy smiles and hands still held up in frozen waves. "Okayyyyyyy," she says, clearly unsure how to take the scene. I can't blame her. They look like they're accomplices to a crime. Turning to me, her eyes soften as they move all over me, the corner of her mouth twitching up as she gives me her secret smile. "I'll see you guys later," she says again, still watching me. Gripping my forearm with a double squeeze, she lingers there for a solitary moment before retreating down the hall with the girls.

I let out the breath I didn't realize I was holding and feel my cheeks burn as I stare at the empty space she just left.

"Dayuuuuuuuuuum," Ethan laughs, drawing my attention to the peanut gallery.

"Geer has the hots for Stanley." Travis gives a sly smirk, and I immediately regret letting him come to camp.

"Atta boy, Geer!" Charlie claps.

Dread fills my gut as I reluctantly sit back down. They'll just hunt me down if I try to retreat upstairs.

"Dude, how long has this been going on?" Devon asks. His tone is calm amidst the rowdy whispers moving around the table.

"Does she—"

"No. She doesn't know," I interrupt Garrett and moan into my hands. "And I'd like to keep it that way." They all protest, typical moans and groans threatening to overpower my own thoughts. "At least until I figure out what I'm going to do," I whisper more to myself than to them.

"Dude, this is sick. First, Mr. Divata and Ms. B. Now, you guys." Charlie's excitement is comparable to a child at Christmas, which is expected. The kid is always meddling in people's love lives. I swear he was the one who sent Margaret flowers to light a fire under Bill's tail. "What are we gonna do about Sanders?" he asks the group.

"We could slash—"

"No. No committing felonies—in any form." I run my hand down my face and stare at Ethan, painfully aware of his tendencies. I'm also pretty certain he had something to do with the fire alarm last night. "And you guys need to get to your morning workouts. Quit bothering me."

A ding from my back pocket draws their attention, eyes darting back and forth expectantly, as if I am going to read my messages to them out loud for a little story time.

Their stares bore into me, and I relent, pulling my phone out to see Kate's name light up on my phone.

"It's her," Devon whispers as he looks over my shoulder.

"Thanks," I snarl at him and open the message then immediately click my phone off and shove it back into my pocket. "Alright, time to end this."

"Come on, what'd she say?" Travis whines.

"Let us help." Daniels finally joins in with the brigade. My disappointment in him to fall under this teenage peer pressure is clear when he gives me an innocent shrug.

A silent beat passes as they all wait patiently. Again, I can just leave anytime I want and go back up to my room, but alas, I sit. "She's going out with him again," I say through clenched teeth.

A low, demeaning whistle is shared by a few guys, along with a few winces—winces, yes, because the truth of the situation is painful. Kate is going on a date with her ex, and she just sees me as her friend, yet I continue sitting at this damn table with these kids whispering all around me.

"We need the girls' help on this," Charlie says, pulling out his phone.

I abruptly slam my hand down on top of his phone, his childlike hand twitching under mine. "No!" I yell, startling the table out of their scheming. "It will get back to her."

"They'll be discreet," Travis tries to reassure me.

"Nah, Geer is right. We can't risk it. We gotta handle this on our own," Devon says, nodding for Charlie to put his phone away. He does so reluctantly. "We all got game. We don't need their help."

Ethan and Garrett guffaw at that as Devon gives them a sly smile. The only *game* these kids have is on the field. I really should be talking to my adult friends about my very adult dating-life situation, but I am *still* sitting here. I shake my legs to make sure they have feeling in them, readjust in my seat, checking for any new gravitational pull that has overpowered me, and find nothing. Yep, I am sitting here by my own free will.

"So what are we gonna do?" Daniels asks the table. He's fully invested in this now.

"I got it!" Garrett yells, his excitement is evident as he tries to wipe the smile off his face. Leaning halfway over the table, he lowers his voice to a whisper, and I find myself clenching the edge of my seat. I don't have time for this. Using plots and schemes to win a girl over has never been my way. But I lean in, waiting for Garrett's master plan, fear and excitement sticking to my skin like the salty air. The sliver of self-respect I was maintaining after waking up this morning is completely gone by the hands of six rambunctious teenagers when he says...

"We're gonna crash their date."

Chapter Twenty

Kate

"Are you trying to torture yourself?"

Emma is the least-encouraging person right now as I pace up and down the side of the gymnasium floor, filling her in on my morning coffee date. I'm still not sure if we're calling it a date—he didn't even buy my drink.

"Three more laps, ladies!" I yell as the girls make their way around the running track on the second level of the gymnasium. I'm really enjoying this setup, sitting in the middle of the floor, directing my little puppets through stair sprints from my lawn-chair throne in the center of the gym. Well, it's a fancy fold-out chair from the hotel. It has three different reclining positions that I have taken full advantage of.

"I'm not torturing myself. I'm just weighing my options." I recline to the farthest setting, practically lying flat as the footrest pops out. "Plus, the guy looked pitiful. I think he just needs a friend."

"Kate, y'all dated for three years. You can't just chum it up like old pals from camp over a fancy Italian dinner," she snips over the sounds of wild children increasing in the background. "Boys! I'm on the phone!"

She has a point. It's almost impossible to look at Eric and not remember our life together and not let those feelings resurface a tiny bit. But I wouldn't call Tony's Pizza a *fancy* Italian dinner. By the looks of their outdated website, people can show up in beach towels and get their greasy slices on paper plates.

The girls round the corner on their final lap, each speeding up as they see the finish line.

"It'll be fine." My words sound painful as they leave my lips, tension crawling up my arms and legs as I try to stretch out in the chair. "It. Will. Be. Fine."

"Are you trying to convince me? Or yourself?"

Emma laughs as I stutter and whine, "Sh–shut up."

Passing the finish line, the girls barrel down the steps and rush onto the shiny wood floor. It glistens under the massive fluorescent lights that hang on the ceiling. This building is huge, with spotless, cream-colored walls and black cushioned stadium seats on every side. The college campus is ten minutes from our hotel, which means this is theirs, and they have relinquished use during their spring break for our camp. Coach Lawson has worked so hard the last ten years, arranging and organizing this camp to be a sought-after opportunity by students, and it shows. I bask in the fluorescent glow another moment before turning to the pile of gasping, red-faced teens plastered to the clean floor. Someone named James was in here this morning, pushing one of those floor scrubbers up and down, getting the perfect shine and clean lines. Him realizing the nice girl with curly hair that brought him a cup of coffee would be the reason he has to mop twice today is questionable.

"Good work, ladies!" I sit up in my chair, my legs still propped up on the leg rest.

Claire glares at me before falling flat on her back, her stomach rippling with her gasping breaths. Birdie groans into her arms that are stretched across her face, and Tess lies on her stomach with the cold hardwood floor aggressively squishing her cheek, attempting to blow her sweaty fringe bangs off her face. *Hard work.* These girls are the definition of it.

"Have you told Malcolm?" Emma redirects me back to the phone pressed against my ear. "About the second date, I mean."

I hum in response, glancing around to make sure the question wasn't heard through the tiny speaker squished against my ear—unlikely, but you can't be too sure. Teenagers have an otherworldly knack for finding out hidden secrets—especially *these* teenagers. And trying to be discreet around the girls is becoming painfully challenging the longer we are here.

Close proximity to Malcolm has never been an issue. But the last few days, I have been drawn to him more and more. I don't know what to make of it. I just know resisting him or not thinking about him is becoming near impossible.

It's like my dog, Dolly Parton, with any new squeaky toy. She doesn't have a clue what makes it squeak, but she can't contain herself when she sees it, tail wagging furiously, chasing it like there's no tomorrow.

That's who I'm acting like. Dolly Parton.

And Malcolm is my squeaky toy.

And just like Dolly, I have no idea what's making him *squeak* to me. But he is.

"What did he say?" she asks as a loud bang happens in the background followed by a whispered curse word and shuffling footsteps.

Gnawing at my thumbnail, I think back to the very short and unenthused response I received when I told Malcolm about my dinner plans this evening.

"Good luck," I deadpan.

The hasty shuffling stops on the other end of the phone. "That's it?" she asks, just as dumbfounded as I was when I received his text. I give another hum, not as lively as the last, sounding more like a *humph*. "Well, then..." She pauses contemplatively. "That's very grown up of him." Her words are unconvincing.

"Uh-huh, very." Another deadpan because I don't know what to make of it. And based on Emma's hesitation, she doesn't either. We all know how Malcolm feels about Eric. Even when he had to work with him, they never got along, which was awful for me. My boyfriend and best friend tolerating each other at family gatherings was less than ideal.

"Coach, can we get out of here now?" The floor squishes Tess's cheeks so much her words morph together, sounding like *cahweegetouttahurrnow*.

"Yes. Go get cleaned up, and we'll head to the beach!"

The mention of the beach is enough to resurrect the dead as the girls squeal, jump up from the floor, and race out of the gym.

"I guess he isn't too worried about it," I say to Emma once I'm alone. "I mean, I don't want him to be worried. I guess I was just expecting more than a two-word response. Something more than just *good luck*." Emma snorts on the other end of the phone when I mimic Malcolm's deep voice.

I walk out of the gym into the sweltering sun and struggle to adjust my eyes to the bright light. The hotel is just a few minutes' walk from the gym, and seeing as I don't have time to get a good run in this week, I try to get my steps in when I can. The girls are already out of sight as I make my way down the small walkway. Palm trees line one side of the path, blocking half of my body from the blazing sun, and the other side meets the road where a variety of vehicles weave in and out of parking lots on their way to the beach. Little shops sit neatly across the road, their doors ajar, allowing the hot air to whip in and out of their establishments. Odd but comforting similarities spring up as I walk past—little nods that remind me of Glendale.

The smell of fried food catches my attention when I'm a block from the hotel. My stomach growls in protest when I try to ignore the smells of fried dough, cinnamon sugar, and coffee—with a hint of garlic, which is...interesting.

Coming to a halt at the stop sign near the hotel, I turn to face the smells. A small sign hangs outside of a shop, *half off all pastries,* and I'm immediately sold.

"Ms. Stanley!" Sarah Kim sits at a table outside of the glorious little shop—another sign to venture in there and eat my weight in buttery goodness—a pile of books sitting in the chair opposite her.

"Hi, Sarah!" I motion to her, waiting for my moment to cross the street safely. That's just what I need, to get hit by a car in front of my student, traumatizing her for life. Reaching for the shop door, I notice she doesn't have anything to pair with her pile of books. No coffee, no croissant, not even water. An interesting little duck, she is.

"Care to join me?" I gesture toward the door.

She beams at the invitation, scooping up her books and following me inside. The cold air jolts me awake, shivers traveling down my arms and legs. By her shaking, I can tell Sarah regrets leaving her warm seat outside. A couple snags the only empty table, sending her into a mini frenzy as she huffs, circles around, and gives up in finding another seat.

"I'll wait for you outside." Her teeth chatter and arms shake like we're in the Arctic. "Can you get me a hot chocolate?" she asks over her shoulder as she hoists her books closer to her chest and pries the door open with her free hand.

My phone buzzes as I place our order. A text from my mom moves across my screen, and my gut swirls, nausea moving up my throat. She's probably asking for something. Last time I heard from her was after four months of radio silence, and she needed me to pick up something from the post office before it was returned to the sender. Apparently, the knock-off Manolo Blahnik shoes just had to be purchased while she was out of the country.

> **Mom:** Spoke to Lola, I'm sorry I missed the party. I'll try to make the next one!

I chew on my thumbnail, down to the bit almost, before responding.

> It's alright, maybe next time.

Bubbles pop up and disappear for a few seconds—an impending request, I'm sure. I have half a heart to put my phone away and ignore her follow up. But the other half is still hopelessly holding out for an *I miss you* text. Or even a simple *saw this and thought of you,* with a picture of a chicken in hot-pink Converse. Doubtful, but one can hope.

Seconds before giving up completely, her response comes in, sending an ache deep into my belly.

> **Mom:** Could you do me a favor and check my plants next time you're around?

My order is called from the counter, and I shove my phone in my bag instead of responding. Clearly, she's forgotten that I already check on her plants.

Every two weeks.

For the last four years.

I grab the drinks a little too aggressively, cracking the side of one, and rush out the door. Sarah snagged a table catty-corner to the shop on a patch of sand. Her nose is in a book, barely noticing me when I set her hot chocolate down, sans crack. Mine, however, leaks iced coffee down my hand and onto the table. I swat my hand against my thigh to dry it off erratically and toss my cup in the trash against the side of the building with a grunt.

"You good?" Sarah asks, her eyes still pinned on her book.

"Fine," I lie. I'm *not* good. Anytime I hear from my mom, I'm as far from good as anyone could get. I shake off the irritation and focus on the book in Sarah's hand. "What are you reading?"

I crank my head to the side to try to read the title, but she shuts the book and quickly folds her arms on top of it, pinning me with a glowering stare. Don't ask about the book with kissing cartoon characters on it. Got it.

"So, I hear you have a date tonight." The hot chocolate steam rises from her cup, and she winces when she attempts to take a drink. She fans herself and hangs her tongue out of her mouth like a puppy. It's still halfway out when she says, "With that one buff guy."

I snort because Eric is the epitome of buff. Borderline too muscle-y if we're being honest. My mind trips over the images of his muscles—the flex of his arms as he leaned against the chair this morning.

As if the tape in my brain was tampered with, the film skitters, and the image changes to a pair of arms that are slightly softer but just as strong. Arms with chiseled forearms and taut biceps being hugged by a trim light-blue polo. They're crossed over a chest that is broad and solid, accentuating the divot in the center that directs you up to his neck. I trace the curve of his neck up to a soft beard hugging the edges of a perfect jaw. A jaw I know to house a small cheek dimple on one side and a freckle on the other. A rasp of air leaves me when my imagination lingers on a set of lips, soft and somewhat tempting as they smirk at me, hitching up on one corner. A silent laugh escapes his tantalizing mouth, and a rave happens in my chest as palpitations skitter rapidly followed by a suffocating flash of heat shooting up my neck and settling deep into my cheeks. My lungs protest their duties as the heat threatens to smother me.

Another *episode*.

"Earth to Stanley." Sarah waves her hand in my face, snapping me out of my thoughts, sending a swish of hot air against my face. My lungs relent, inhaling the air deeply and settling the nerves that were building up.

Words are hard when I blink back to reality and give a mumble in response.

Sarah laughs and gathers her books. "Well, I hope it goes well!" She stands from the table and heads toward the crosswalk, stack of books—five, to be exact—in one hand, hot chocolate in the other.

"Wait." I shake my head to banish the smoldering and borderline restricted images of Malcolm I've been having lately, refusing to accept they are the root cause of these *episodes,* then follow her. "How did you know about my date?"

She gives me an incredulous look, like it's a universal fact that no one's love life is secret around Glendale, which is understandable. After everything with Ellie and Benny, the kids have been having a field day with any and all information they can get their hands on regarding our love lives. You would think they would be more focused on their own, but nope. I'm convinced they view us as old spinsters, and they believe when any of us find love, it's the work of wizards.

"You think Coach Geer is okay with it?" She gives me a wary side-eye as we make our way back to the hotel.

I groan. "Why is everyone so worried about Malcolm?" I unintentionally yell, startling a few valet workers across the parking lot, as the aggravating unfairness threatens to swallow me. "Everyone is so worried about that ole grump's opinion, but what about me?" I stop abruptly in the middle of the lot, Sarah slowing to a stop next to me. Panic covers her face as her eyes dart around, watching for moving vehicles. "What about what *I'm* okay with? Coach Geer is a grown man. Surely he can manage his friend going on a date with someone! He could go on a date too, and I would be fine." I bellow the rhetorical question in Sarah's direction, and she nods rapidly, side-stepping closer to the parked cars. My feelings about Malcolm are lumped into the crazy that is the rest of my life. I feel myself boiling over in confusion and seem to be reacting the only way I know how—loudly and erratically. "Why are we so concerned? If he's not okay with it, then he needs to come talk to me, right? Right! Malcolm Geer is a grown man. A man that is so annoyingly honest all the freaking time. So, if he has an issue, he can come talk to me about it!"

"Talk to you about what?" Jolting me forward in surprise, Malcolm lets out a soft chuckle behind me. Sarah's face is a tight line as she glances from me to over my shoulder, where he's probably standing.

My body tenses from the nape of my neck down to my tailbone, like my spine has been replaced with a metal rod. Awareness surges through me as my erratic behavior replays in my head. Why did I just act like that? I'm irritated, yes. But I'm not irritated with him. Malcolm is innocent in all of this, but dang it, everyone needs to chill.

He is fine.

I am fine.

Everything. Is. Fine.

Taking rigid baby steps, I slowly turn around to face him. It's awkward and unnatural—and a bit amusing based on the face Malcolm makes as he watches me. His backward hat is an alarmingly pleasant sight, snapping the tension in me like a rubber band. Tingling sensations reverberate deep into my stomach and down my legs, hitting every nook and cranny of my body with the alert of *BACKWARD HAT! BACKWARD HAT!* He removes his sunglasses, and I swear it happens in slow motion, blinking at me with eyes that make today's blue sky look gray and dull.

There's intentionality in his gaze as he pins me with a stare. "What do you need to talk to me about?" He steps closer, so close that only the smallest of molecules could pass through the space left between his chest and mine. The proximity draws a heavy gulp out of my throat.

Heat swells inside me and courses through my veins like rapid-fire missiles, speeding up my heart, constricting my lungs, and tingling my fingers and toes as his breath touches the side of my face. It feels like a caress, so soft and slow that my eyes shudder in response. I open my mouth to answer his lingering question, but words do not come. Failing. My brain is failing to operate.

"She said if you have a problem about her date, you can talk to her about it." Sarah is clearly proud of herself as she snickers this information. I glare back at her, but she's already racing up to the hotel.

"Oh, did you now?" He plucks at one of my loose curls, sending it bouncing near my ear. "You think I have a problem with your date?"

Heat is still all over me, and I have to clutch my neck for comfort. "N—no. I was just stating"—I clear my throat—"that, um...*if* you had a problem, that we could talk about it. You know, like adults." I force a cough, dislodging the heat that's blocking my airway. Adults. We are adults. And whatever is happening to me physically is just a manifestation of guilt. That's all these recent *episodes* are.

"Ahh, yes." He gives a chuckle and a nod, instantly relieving the nerves that were working their way through me. "Well..." he says as he lingers, leaning in ever so slightly, "do you want to talk about it, Ms. Stanley?" The smell of coffee on his breath and the oakiness of his body wash swirls around me. A comforting smell.

I take a step back to collect myself—enough room for a small child or a puppy to pass through, a reasonable amount of room. "Do we need to?" Dropping my hands into fists at my sides, my fingers dig into my palms when I see his face falter, a hint of discomfort lining his mouth and eyes.

"Look." He lets out an exhausted sigh, removing his cap to scratch the top of his head. His hair is wild and untamed underneath, a stark contrast to his entire demeanor in life. My fingers dig deeper, sending a shooting pain down my palms, as I fight the urge to run my hands through his dirty-blond locks. "You're right. We're adults. And you know how I feel about Eric. But..." Looking up at the sky and readjusting the cap back on his head, he pauses for a moment.

Malcolm has never been a man of many words. Deep conversations have always been difficult for him. I've always assumed it was because he didn't care to expend the energy on things like that. *"Just say how you feel and move on,"* he used to say. Irking me more than it should, I would pry for more and drive him mad. Vulnerable conversations are essential in relationships, and there were times I would feel like it was his excuse to avoid them altogether. Eventually, I realized it's just how he is and grew to accept it—most of the time. But eventually, he started to get deeper with me.

In his own ways. In his own time.

His singular cheek dimple deepens when his jaw tightens—a sign he's trying to muster the courage to keep talking.

Taking one of my hands with both of his, it stings my chest. The gesture is so intimate and tender I don't think he realizes how this would look to someone else. The slow, easy touch. A gesture I crave from someone. Something to show me I'm the one they want to have moments like this with. In the middle of a parking lot. Malcolm is the least physical-touch person I have ever met, but over the past five years, he's become so comfortable in our friendship that these soft, easy touches happen all the time. A hand on my lower back, an arm over my shoulder, a pinch at my waist. These little acts, that are so incredibly personal and intimate, he does with me because we're friends and he trusts me. But one day, he'll give them to someone else. Someone he'll trust more than me. Someone he chooses to live this life with. He does it so naturally with me, and my eyes sting at the thought of losing it to another person.

Don't be selfish, Kate.

"I want you to be happy," he says, giving my hand his typical double squeeze. "That's all I want. And if going out with Eric again makes you happy, then that's what matters." He drops my hand slowly, leaving it feeling cold and empty. "I'll just keep my plan to kidnap him and dump him in the wilderness to myself, unless it's needed." A deep, rumbling laugh leaves him as he turns back toward the hotel.

Chapter Twenty-One

Kate

"Is that what you're wearing?"

Malcolm stifles his laugh behind his fist when I glare at his reflection in the mirror. He has draped himself across the bed in the most effortless, *I don't care that you're going on a date,* posture I have ever seen. Maybe a little too effortless. Ever since this afternoon, he's been a little forceful with his, *'It'll be great,'* chit-chat. And if there is one thing I know about Malcolm, it's his inability to lie. Anytime he's caught in the thick of some scheme or dishonest venture, he becomes this overly cheerful, sunshiny person, asking you how the weather is or how your cat is. Last summer, when I forced him to lie to Uncle Jerry about who really smashed his back window out with a football (*me*), Malcolm was so cheerful that Jerry invited him on a family cruise—the yearly family cruise I have yet to be invited to. According to Benny, the lie continued for the entire vacation. Malcolm was in so deep he ended up doing karaoke, charades, and a belly flop competition.

He was instantly the family favorite.

All because I made him tell Jerry it was him who decided to kick a football in high heels in the middle of the night after three margaritas.

"What's wrong with it?" I smooth out the pink blouse I've tucked into a pair of black jeans. My pink Converse, with a tiny speck of turf stain on the outside of the left foot, ties the outfit together.

"It seems a little casual, don't you think?" Stretching himself across the bed, his shirt rides up and reveals a faint diagonal line of muscle that travels along his waistband. It peeks out like a road map for your eyes.

I force my eyes back up to my face in the mirror and roll on a layer of Chapstick. "We're going to some hole-in-the-wall pizza place." I shrug, content with what I've put together. "Plus, it's camp. I didn't really pack for a date this week."

"Right, because why would you?" He winks at me, leaning back farther until his upper body is against the headboard. The motion jostles the entire bed, sending a tingling awareness down the front of my body. His arms flex as he rests them on top of his head, that line near his waist taunting me even more. My heart flutters into my throat, and I have to turn away from the mirror to rid myself of the distraction behind me.

Hyperfixating on his outfit comment, I look down and re-evaluate my entire wardrobe in a matter of milliseconds. "Do I look alright, though?" I ask, fixing my gaze on the turf stain.

The bed squeaks and ruffles as Malcolm rolls out of it ungracefully. A thud sounds when his feet hit the floor. "You look fine," he says, leaning against the bed in front of me. He's within arm's reach, and for a moment, I want him to wrap me up and tell me it will be okay. That what I'm doing is okay.

"Just fine?" I huff out a laugh.

"Kate, you look great. You always do." The smile he gives is sincere, and it's all I need.

Tousling my hair one final time, I grab my purse and stand up straighter. Confident. Confident that this is the right thing to do. The universe wants me to do this, to go on this date, or I wouldn't keep running into Eric, right?

Right?

I gulp, swallowing the doubt trying to creep up my throat, and squeeze my fists around the strap of my purse. "Great, then let's do this."

Malcolm's neck tightens, his Adam's apple bobbing as he pins his eyes on my crazy curls. The humid air has made it pointless to bother straightening them, so all week they have been a wild mess atop my head, ringlets every which way. Pain is etched on his face as he stares at them, like what he sees offends him.

"I can't get them to calm down, okay?" I whimper, trying to smooth down the top of my hair. "This weather is the bane of my existence," I whine some more, erratically trying to flatten curls, licking my fingers and running them through the strands. "Maybe I should tie it back?" I try to pull my hair back, but he stops me by gripping my elbows.

"Do. Not." His words come out forced, one syllable at a time. The pain on his face is still there, but his eyes soften as he pulls my arms down. "Your hair is perfect."

The familiar stoney look on his face finally registers when I feel a twitch on my arms, resistance fighting at his fingertips. It's the same look he has when I tempt him with mint-chocolate-chip ice cream—his greatest weakness.

My greatest weakness is cream cheese, which is a problem for a vegan, both physically and ethically.

I dip my eyes to the slope of Malcolm's bicep and clock a light-blue vein stretching up the inside of his arm. I can't resist the urge to graze my fingers down the line of it, feeling the pulsing of his blood under my touch. It's quite possible his arms are becoming one of my weaknesses. "Thank you."

We both watch as I trail my fingers up and down his arm, like I'm committing it to memory or something. Malcolm clears his throat and whispers, "You're gonna be late." He keeps watching my fingers, my sparkly nail polish flickering with the motion. Lowering his arms away from mine, he gives me one last double squeeze. "Have fun." His forced smile wavers as his voice cracks ever so slightly.

"Are you sure you—"

"Kate," he stops me before I can finish. "Quit."

In a moment, my life flashes before my eyes. Dramatic? Maybe. But when Malcolm reaches up, brushing the sides of my neck with his knuckles and drawing small lines along the edge of my jaw with his thumb, the only thing to do is think dramatically.

All the air leaves my body, and I feel like I'm floating as his fingers rest against my face, like I'm a balloon, and he's the one tethering me to the ground. Again, dramatic, but our faces are so close. His grip is a tender control that sends an ache down to my core.

"Quit doubting me. Quit doubting yourself. Go, eat your weight in pizza, and come back here to tell me all about it." The line of silver that circles the bright blue of his eyes flickers once, growing larger the longer he stares at me.

I simply nod, and he releases my face.

He releases the balloon.

I still feel like I'm floating when I walk up to the address Eric sent me for dinner. The outside of the building is *not* what I saw online. Rod iron sconces sit on each side of a rather large, antique door, which opens as I approach, and a short gentleman wearing all black waves me in. The walkway of the restaurant is dimly lit with deep maroon walls and an antique couch sitting perpendicular to the host stand. Sounds of Europe play in a soft symphony overhead. A couple waiting to be seated is wearing what I would call church attire, the man's button-up jacket matching the woman's dark-blue floor-length dress. My mouth goes dry as my underdressed self follows the host to our table.

The tables have place settings with small candles sitting in the center and fancy glass decanters of water. Eric is waiting for me, wearing a button-up that is oddly similar to the man at the front, his eyes widening at the rips over my knees and the bright-pink Converse squeaking across the tile floor as I approach.

"You look nice." He gestures to me, clearly sarcastic and proud of this little mishap.

"You said Tony's Pizza," I snip at him then smile gracefully at the host as he pulls my chair out for me. "Not Rome, Italy."

"Antonio's Pizzeria," he corrects. "Tony's Pizza is on *South* Main. This is *North* Main." Laughing, he drapes a cloth napkin in his lap and begins pouring us water.

I gape at him then quickly snap my jaw shut and glare. He continues to snicker as he hands me a menu, getting a kick out of my blunder. *Hilarious.* "At least I made it." I snatch the menu from his hand and flip it open.

We go about the usual dinner steps—ordering an appetizer, then our meal, discussing how the day went, etc. It's pleasant, but I feel distracted and uninterested. A pair of blue eyes and bulging biceps force their way into my vision every few minutes. I start to think I'm hallucinating when I mistake someone for Malcolm sitting in the back corner of the restaurant. I realize it can't be him when the man has a pair of orange-tinted creeper glasses on, a fedora, and tinsel strands entwined in his beard. He's also hunched over a plate of lettuce, eating with leather gloves on. Definitely not Malcolm.

I finish my part of the appetizer and notice the guy is *staring* at me. Weirdo.

The waiter brings our orders, and Eric excuses himself to the restroom. In a rare moment of bravery, I shift in my seat and stare at the creeper, stating with my eyes, *Got a problem, pal?* He cowers further down into his bowl of lettuce, pinning his eyes on the dessert menu.

Quiet laughter grows louder behind me.

A partition in the center of the seating area with lush greenery separates one side of the room from the other. The dim lighting makes it difficult to make out faces, but a head of spiky black hair catches my attention. Glancing back at the creeper for a moment, at ease when I see he's more focused on ordering his dessert than me, I slide out of my chair and walk over in a crouch to the partition, catching a few concerned glances along the way.

The laughter fizzles, followed by whispers that sound all too familiar the closer I get.

Reaching up to the top of the partition, I stay bent over as I grip the edges of the fake ferns. Shoving the greenery to the side, I jump up and yell, "Aha!" Five familiar faces stare at me in terror as I stand on my tiptoes to scold them over the partition. "Not very sneaky, are we, boys?" I catalog each person in attendance: Garrett Connors, Devon Johnson, Travis Van, Charlie Henders, and—I gasp in betrayal. "Sarah?"

She cowers down and pulls the furry hat she thought was a good disguise farther down in front of her face. "They made me come," she says behind Garrett's shoulder.

"What gave us away?" Devon asks, pushing his ridiculous disguise glasses to the top of his head.

"Travis's hair." I shrug and rest my arms on the partition, my calves aching as I stay firmly on my toes.

The table groans, throwing their napkins and swatting at Travis. Charlie tries to flatten the spikes down, but Travis waves him off, smoothing the edges and tips with his fingers.

"What are you guys doing here?" I ask the table.

Excuses erupt simultaneously, all different from the other.

"We wanted Italian."

"Sarah's mom is paying."

"We went to the wrong place!"

Devon tosses the glasses off his head in defeat. "We were spying, alright?" He's the first to cave under pressure. He was never the best at keeping secrets, especially under my penetrating stare. Naomi, his mom, helped me master it my first year of teaching. "We heard you were going on a date and wanted to scope it out." He throws his hands up in surrender. The glasses, a brown wired pair with orange-tinted bifocal lenses, clink as they topple to the center of the table. They look exactly like Creepy Fedora's glasses.

I gasp, whipping around to see Malcolm watching me, wide-eyed, in the corner, an equal mix of terror and embarrassment in his eyes as he bolts for the front door.

"Hey!" I yell, startling a few people in the middle of their meal, and race after him.

Chapter Twenty-Two

Malcolm

"Hey!"

She yells it about a million times before she catches up to me in the parking lot. The keys to our rented van fumble to the ground as I try to climb in.

Plowing her body into the front of the van, she yells, "What are you doing here?" Her chest heaves rapidly from her sprint.

No sudden movements, minimal eye contact. That's what I do as I retrieve the keys and climb in. Maybe she'll go away if I pretend she isn't there. Like a bear in the wild. Which is what Kate resembles when I make the mistake of glancing at her. She plants her hands on her hips, irritation marking her face as her eyebrows furrow deeper and deeper.

"Excuse me!" Throwing her arms out, she accentuates each word with force, "What. Are. You. Doing. Here?"

"Coach! Coach!"

The guys come racing toward us, looking like they just robbed a bank. I haven't seen them run that fast since their timed evaluations last spring. Ripping the sliding door of the van open, they pile in, one on top of another.

"She's pissed," Devon whispers the obvious as he climbs in the passenger seat.

Kate slams her hand on the hood of the van, standing as if she, herself, can stop the vehicle from moving forward if I were to step on the gas. "Malcolm Eugene Geer!" she bellows out in her disciplinary tone.

"Eugene?" Garrett cackles in the back.

I roll the window down and yell back, "That's not my name! Now move!"

"I will move when you tell me what the heck you guys are doing here, crashing my date!" Slamming the other hand down, her nostrils flare, and a vein in her forehead starts to bulge. I haven't seen her this mad in a long time. The last time was when the seniors Saran-wrapped her car the night of an ice storm. It was stuck in the parking lot for days, paint chipping away with each frozen, plastic layer we had to break off.

"Wait, so Eugene isn't your middle name?" Sarah asks, squished between Travis and Charlie.

"No," I growl, "now be quiet."

"Can we just tell her the truth?" Charlie asks, fear lining his tone. He's always tested his limits with Kate. You'd think being on the end of this stare-down on a regular basis would build some fortitude in the kid, but nope. He cowers down and whispers a prayer.

The truth. These kids don't even know the full truth. They just think I was concerned for my friend going on a date with her ex, not that some part of me wanted to sabotage the date because I'm head over heels in love with her. I'm a crazy man. This whole idea was ridiculous, and I let my jealousy get the best of me.

"Devon!" Kate yells, her stare now pinned on the passenger seat. Devon winces and reaches for the door handle.

"I got it," I grumble, climbing out of the van and pulling out the weird butterfly clips and tinsel Sarah put in my beard to destroy any last ounce of dignity I have.

Kate crosses her arms and taps her foot on the pavement. "What are you doing here, Malcolm?"

"I'm sorry," I say, holding my hands up in surrender, the streetlamp shining on me like I'm under interrogation. "They roped me into spying on your date."

"They roped you in?" she asks in disbelief. "You? The man who couldn't even be swayed to give up his parking spot for a disabled employee?"

"Bill had hip surgery, alright? He could walk just fine!" I throw my hands out to the side, refusing to lose that argument again. "His normal spot was closer to the ramp anyway." I point at her, and she shoots her hands up to indicate her innocence. "Whatever." I wave at her in defeat. "We were just checking up on you. Them because they're bored teenagers, and me because—"

"Because why, Malcolm? Tell me, honestly." Her voice is sharp and annoyed, and I want to punch myself.

I flinch at the tone, afraid to speak. It's rare that I can't speak my mind, but with her, the fear I have of ever upsetting her trumps every ounce of internal pride that usually prevents me from keeping my mouth shut. Her feelings are a sounding board to my thoughts, filtering out any blunt thoughts that might come out. I can't tell her why I'm here, because honestly, I'm embarrassed to admit it—even to myself. To admit I'm jealous of her going on a date is childish. I pride myself on my careless approach to life. Letting stuff slide off my shoulders when things don't go my way is my signature.

"Malcolm..." her voice cuts through the air like a blade on glass.

I kick at a piece of trash abandoned in the parking lot, avoiding her laser-beam eyes like my life depends on it. This woman is intimidating as hell when she wants to be, and it's not often that I'm on the other end of that terrifying stare.

Rubbing the back of my neck, still fully craned down toward the crumpled-up wrapper I have busied myself with, I say, "I, uh...we"—I wave to the van behind me—"were concerned..."

"Concerned," she repeats in disbelief.

Clearing my throat, I force myself to look at her and the now flattened paper under my boot. "Concerned. We just don't want to see you get hurt."

"You don't think I can handle myself?"

"No." The word slips out before I can stop it, and her face twists uncomfortably. "I mean, yes. Of course you can handle yourself. I just..." Impatience ripples inside me, trickling down my spine like icy water. I can't keep it in any longer.

"I just think you're making a poor decision, alright?" I snap. "Going on a date with your ex? After what he did to you? Because you think the universe is telling you something?" My questions come out hard and fast, accusations thick in my throat. Kate's eyes waver for a moment before going cold again, a forceful effort to keep her composure. "You don't need the universe to tell you what to do, Kate."

"Hey, guys." Eric weaves his way through the parked cars to join us under the flickering streetlight. "Is everything okay?" He places his hand on Kate's back, and everything inside me threatens to rage. I shove my fists in my pockets to restrain myself, or they'll be hanging him from the streetlamp, shading us all with his upside-down silhouette.

Kate's eyes remain fixed on mine. "We're fine. Just ran into these guys," she says, waving at the group, who hesitantly returns the gesture. Devon ducks down in his seat to avoid being recognized by his future coach. Eric nods to Kate in understanding and leans in to whisper something in her ear, his lips dangerously close to the spot I've imagined nipping at a million times. The spot she lets brush against my beard when she hugs me. The spot that I know makes her eyes flutter and roll back when it's gently grazed by a thumb. The spot he has no right being near anymore. He shoots me a friendly wave before turning back toward the restaurant.

I hate him.

I manage a nod in return, my teeth clenched and eyes burning. I can't hide how his touch on her makes me feel. I might snap his hand if he lingers too long.

I wait for what feels like an eternity for Eric to be out of earshot. The man stalks around like a bear but has the speed of a turtle. Closing the distance between us, I give Kate an apologetic smile. "I didn't mean to ruin the date."

She rolls her eyes, the harshness of her gaze fading when she focuses on me. "I can take care of myself, you know."

A ringlet falls across her face, and I catch it with my fingers. Pushing it behind her ear, I let my thumb brush the spot and watch her eyes flutter closed. A small sound only I can hear leaves her mouth. The sound is almost enough to send me to my knees right here in this parking lot.

Pulling my hand back and shoving it under my arm, I whisper, "I know you can."

I take a small step back. Adding more space between us is the best option right now. For me. For her. For her date. And for the nosey teenagers watching our every move. She notes the motion and does the same, giving me a nod of understanding.

"Just know that I will always want to take care of you, Kate. Even when you think you can do it on your own, I'm still going to try to do it for you. You're stuck with me."

A smile lights up every inch of her face at that. "Good."

"Mint chocolate chip?" Sarah asks, disgust marking her face like I've committed a crime.

"Yeah," I say with my mouth half full of ice cream.

She fakes a gag before taking a bite of her birthday-cake ice cream. "You're eating toothpaste, pretty much."

"Toothpaste-covered Oreos," Garrett adds, inhaling his double chocolate scoop like it's his last supper.

The group heckles me for my dessert choice the entire walk back to the hotel. I endure it for three blocks before speed-walking past them to create some distance. I wasn't planning to join them on their late-night munchie run, but it beats wallowing alone in my hotel room. The sheer fact that I've been choosing company over being alone in any form over the last few years is evidence enough for what Glendale has done to me. For years, after losing Brennan, I was content with being alone—living my life, tending my garden, doing the crossword by myself. But somewhere along the way, I've desired companionship more and more, like a dull ache in my chest that never goes away. It doesn't hurt, but I know it's there.

"Coach, wait up!" Charlie catches up to me, the rest of the group a block behind.

"What, Henders?" My tone does not convey the companionship my heart desires—an ongoing issue I'm working on.

"With the scrimmage tomorrow, I was wondering if I could play?" He tosses his empty cone in a nearby trash can.

"Play?" Henders is the only baseball player we brought to camp this year, and it wasn't even necessary that he come. He has a scholarship lined up at Northwestern next year, so camp wasn't a requirement for him. "When was the last time you were on the field?" I ask, curious about what spurred this desire on.

"Three years." He winces.

"Well, I can't start you ahead of some of the others. They're here for scouting opportunities. That wouldn't be—"

"I know, I know," he interrupts, grabbing the back of his neck with both hands as discomfort pinches his eyebrows. "I just want to try—if there's a chance."

"This isn't some prank to ruin the game?" I wouldn't put it past him to pull something like that. Usually, I wouldn't care, but something in me has me refusing to lose tomorrow. It could be the Eric situation. It could be pent-up frustration. Either way, I'm not risking a loss because one of my guys wants to have a little fun.

"No, no. I just want to go out with a bang. This is my last hoorah before college." His face falls.

I stop walking to face him, his words hitting me like a brick to the throat.

Last hoorah.

Brennan's last words to me before his helicopter went down ring in my ears. Charlie's eyes flicker with a hint of sadness as he looks back at the rowdy group approaching, and I feel it, deep in my gut. The sadness he must feel about having to leave Glendale, having to grow up and move on, mixes with my own. Sadness over growing up. Sadness over last hoorahs. Sadness over losing my friend.

The group catches up to us, loud and unfiltered from their sugar high.

"Last hoorah, huh?" I ask Charlie in a whisper. He nods, his face melancholy and eyes hazy. "Captain?"

Devon perks up. "Yes, Coach?"

"What do you say we get Henders fitted with some pads?"

Gleeful eyes surround me, fist-bumping and high-fiving Henders as if they just won the lottery. It was the answer they had all been waiting for. Putting him in tomorrow must have been a dinner conversation I missed.

"Thanks, Coach!" Charlie reaches out to hug me then thinks better of it and pins his arms back down to his sides. Garrett, however, has no sense of personal boundaries and wraps his arms around both of us. My repulsed groan is shushed as everyone joins in on the weird thing people call a group hug. The desire to crawl out of my skin fades when I hear someone whisper, "You guys are the best."

I'm still riding a subtle high from the endorphins that betrayed me from that hug when we part ways in the hallway. The room is dark when I get back with no sign of Kate. It's past ten.

They're probably enjoying their night. Holding hands. *Kissing*.

My chest hollows out at the thought.

Dread follows me around like a shadow, clinging to every part of me as I rush to get ready for bed. Having a conversation with Kate about the events of this evening will end in one of two ways: me admitting my feelings, or me going to bed a liar. Neither of them can happen. The only choice I have is to hurry up and get to bed before she gets back—a temporary fix, of course. We will have to talk about things eventually. We're only here for another day and a half. If I can just put this potentially friendship-ending conversation off until we get back, I'll be fine. I'd rather get rejected in the comfort of my own yard. My office would suffice, even. Somewhere I'm comfortable and safe, not a thousand miles away with nowhere to run.

I crawl into the bed as the softness of the cream sheets clings to my damp post-shower skin. The whistling of wind moves through the crack in the balcony door. I curse myself for not shutting it, climb out of bed, and shuffle over to close it.

The click of the balcony door shutting and the latch of the front door opening happen simultaneously. For a moment, I pray the room is so dark she can't see me standing twenty feet in front of her, in my boxers.

My prayers are unanswered when she whispers, "Hi."

The brassy doorknob is cold against my lower back as I back as far away from her as possible. Kate's face is hidden in shadows, making her expression unreadable and a thousand times scarier than in the light of day. I can usually read her like a book, having the home advantage.

"Hello." I sound like I missed puberty when my voice cracks out the second half of my greeting. "How was—"

"Don't even think about it." She's a foot away from me now, moonlight revealing half of her face to me. Her light-pink lipstick is worn off, and her hair is pulled back in a tie. Curiosity races through me at why she looks so undone. It hurts. "Now spill." Crossing her arms in that cute, defiant way, she waits.

"Do you want to get cleaned up first?"

"Nope. Now talk."

"Kate," I groan, sliding my body out from against the door, the knob leaving an awkward imprint on my skin. "I don't know what you want me to say."

"I want you to start being honest." Her words sting as guilt settles itself on my shoulders.

Pulling my hoodie on over my head, I feel it's important to be semi-dressed for this kind of conversation. I slide onto the bed and gesture to the open space beside me. The internal struggle of her decision to join me is written all over her face.

She watches me, a battle of patience and impatience shifting in her eyes. Letting out a sigh, she leans back on her hands and kicks off her shoes—laces still tied, like a maniac. "What scares you, Malcolm?"

"Wh—what?" I choke out, stunned by her question.

"What scares you?" Turning to face me, she pulls her feet underneath her and sits on her knees.

"Um. Spiders?"

She shoves my arm, and a smile pulls at the corner of her mouth. "You know, I've known you for five years now, and I don't know what scares you. I don't know what shakes you to your core. Do you even know what scares me?" She places her hand on her chest, one of her bright-pink straps sliding off her shoulder as she does.

"I think so." My eyes are pinned on the hollow of her collarbone and the softness of her freshly bronzed skin. She waits, again, eyes heavy lidded from the night's events. "You're scared of elephants. You're scared of your Aunt Edna's lumpia." Her eyes dance as her one-sided grin stretches to a mind-blowing smile. "You're scared of Lola's one-word texts. I think you might be a little scared of Emma, especially on Mondays." She lets out a single *ha,* the smile still firmly in place. "But most of all, I think..." I suck in a breath, hoping I don't eat my words. "You're scared of not being wanted." Her eyes widen at this, unease swarming within them. She looks away and bites at her thumbnail. I tug her hand away from her mouth and encircle her wrist with my hand, and her pulse pounds in my palm. "Am I close?"

She scoffs at me, pinching my thigh with her free hand. "You're kind of close." Smiling, she rests her hand next to my bent leg, her thumb tracing the small scar at the top of my knee. Her dark skin is striking against the pale color of mine. It's almost laughable. "What about you?" Her eyes stay locked on my leg, thumb moving carefully back and forth over the rigid scar.

Relaxing back onto my hands, I look up at the pendant light fixture directly above us. "I'm not sure." A half truth. I know what I'm scared to lose—who I'm scared to lose. But what I'm scared of is a different thing entirely. It used to be death, the fear of leaving this Earth sooner than expected, leaving behind everyone and everything you've ever known to end up in the sky for eternity. That was what scared me. But the older I got, the more death I started to witness, and after losing Brennan, it became clear to me that it's unavoidable. "I guess I'm scared of feeling helpless." I shrug, the truth lingering like the warm air between us.

"Is that why you keep helping Uncle Jerry with his pool?" She snorts.

"It's a luxury pool with jets, Kate. That's reason enough." I scoot back to the top of the bed, resting my head against the thick pillows. Kate joins me, pulling the comforter over her legs and nuzzling deep into the plush. "But yes, I guess I help people because I want to feel useful."

Turning her body toward me, she flattens the comforter so I can see her face. "Is that the reason you help me?" Her eyes are expectant, anticipating my answer.

"One of them," I lie. "It's my duty to help the damsels of this world."

She swats at me then rests her hand on the peak of my chest, a sting pinching where she hit too hard. The pain subsides as she rubs soothing circles on the swell of my chest. It's enough to put me in a deep, pleasurable sleep. The noise that leaves me is almost obscene. My cheeks flush as she giggles into the comforter.

"It's not because I'm a damsel, and you know it."

"Uh-huh, whatever makes you sleep at night."

My heart pounds loud and fast in my ears as she splays her fingers, pressing firmly into my chest. My eyes flutter shut. Her touch is enough to ignite the burning passion stuck in my chest and set it ablaze.

"Just admit it," she whispers.

"Admit what?" I ask, my eyelids heavy with want.

"Everything you do for me..." Her hand moves lower, tracing the ridges of my abdomen. My breath shakes in response as her fingers dance down the center of my stomach, marking the valley that travels from my chest down to my belly button. "You do it..." She lets out a big yawn, sleep disrupting her thought.

Taking her curious hand and pulling it up to my jaw, I kiss the bed of her palm. Her eyes flutter shut as she lets out a soft, gratifying hum. Her dark, thick lashes dance as she fights sleep.

Another big yawn and her body slumps, succumbing to the late hour. Her words are a sleepy whisper, "...because you're crazy about me."

"You have no idea."

Chapter Twenty-Three

Kate

A dream. It feels like I woke up, left one dream, and entered into another one. My dainty arms are tangled around a much thicker and burly one, dark skin wrapping around a trunk of muscle with a faint pink line cutting across the bicep. A farmer's tan. My ankle is crossed over his, like they found each other in the night.

Drool is slithered down my cheek and neck, caking pieces of my hair to the side of my face in the process. Malcolm stretches, his body lengthening against mine, and lets out a soft hum as he continues sleeping. His mouth twitches up in a smile. It's comforting to see him having a peaceful sleep after the other night.

I let myself soak in the sight of him in the morning, in the bed, lying next to me, for a moment before slowly releasing his arm and sliding out of bed. Everything about the scene is comforting. Even if Malcolm sleeps like a Victorian child on his deathbed, limbs straight and head pointed up to the ceiling, it's peaceful in the most adorable way. The sight sends a warm fuzzy deep down my center. Goosebumps cover his legs from where the air conditioner blasted him all night. I cover him with my half of the comforter and slide into the bathroom.

I spend a dramatic amount of time in the shower, replaying the events of last night. Seeing Eric. Seeing Malcolm in disguise. The attempted kiss goodnight from my ex. Falling asleep next to Malcolm.

I feel dizzy from the emotional roller coaster I've put myself through. Maybe Emma was right: I am torturing myself.

A knock sounds on the bathroom door. "You alright in there?" Malcolm's voice, rough and gravelly from the morning, sends a tickle down my spine.

"I'm done now!" I rush around, throwing on my clothes for the day, and swing the door open. He's leaning against the doorframe, wrapped in a towel with droplets of water gliding down his arms and ribs. They taunt me as they travel down farther and farther. I snap my eyes up to his, a pool of blue so hypnotizing it's hard to think straight.

"I showered down the hall. You were taking so long." A borderline psychotic laugh bubbles out of me when he gives me a wink. My limbs feel like rubber when he slides past me into the bathroom, the heat from my shower not holding a candle to the scalding tension I feel from his closeness. "May I?" He touches my elbow and tries to direct me out of the way, but all I can do is wobble my way to the door frame for balance, letting incoherent sounds come out of my mouth as a response. He watches me, concern and amusement lining his face, as he closes the door.

I throw myself onto the bed and let out a muffled moan. *What is happening to me?* One night touching the man's arm and I'm falling apart.

Another knock on the door disorients me when I realize it's not from Malcolm. I roll off the bed and check the peephole of our hotel room.

Eric stands on the other side. I press my head against the door and wait, hoping he will assume I'm not here and leave.

He doesn't.

Reluctantly, I open the door to the uncomfortable man holding two cups of coffee, one with an *I'm sorry* scribbled on the side. Eyeing the cup, I ask, "What's up?"

He holds out the apology cup, a small frown pulling at his lips.

"It's alright." I take the cup.

"It's not." He rubs the back of his neck and stares at our feet. "I shouldn't have kissed you. I didn't mean to make things awkward."

Well, you did, buddy.

"It's fine." It's not. But I don't need to prove my point when he's figured out what he did was wrong and inappropriate on so many levels. "Is there anything else?" I ask curtly.

"I just want to make sure we're alright." He finally looks up at me, eyes filled with regret.

"We're fine. It's in the past." I wave the situation off, mentally and physically. What else can I do? Yeah, the guy tried kissing me, *twice*, but I can't change it. He made a poor decision. There's no need to let it ruin the final days of camp with weird, awkward tension. I just have to make it through tomorrow, and I won't see Eric Sanders again for a long time. A part of me feels at peace with that, and I don't know if it's the universe giving me the okay, or if it's just the realization that I've outgrown someone, and I don't need to feel wanted by them anymore.

"Thanks, Kate." His face is sincere as he turns and walks away.

I let out a sigh of relief when I click the door shut.

"He kissed you?"

I whip around toward Malcolm's clipped tone. He's standing at the edge of the bed with his fists clenched at his sides and back ramrod straight—the military stance he slips into when he's either angry or anxious. Fury blazes in his eyes.

"He *tried* to kiss me," I correct.

He doesn't move. He's a statue. I watch as his eyebrows pinch and the lines on his forehead deepen with his thoughts.

"Did you want—"

"Ugh, no!" I throw my arms out to the sides. "Absolutely not." Feeling defensive, I say, "I turned it down." Every part of me wants to reassure Malcolm that nothing happened with Eric. Malcolm ponders this, fists unclenching ever so slightly.

Malcolm relaxes, his eyes softening as I step closer to him. "Good." His words are a hot whisper on my chin as I look up at him.

"Why?" I raise a dramatic eyebrow, my heart pounding in my ears when I get the guts to ask, "You jealous?"

That distracting Adam's apple bobs. The muscles of his neck tighten, and the vein that drags along the side pulses rapidly. His mouth parts, and mint tingles my lips. My mouth parts in response—of its own accord, I might add. We're so close, and something about it feels different, like I *want* to get closer. I want him to close the gap. Some primal part of me wants Malcolm to press his lips to mine so I can taste his mint toothpaste and feel the prickle of his beard around my lips. The rational part of me is missing. Every logical cell in my brain that would tell me why I can't kiss my best friend seems to be on a hiatus at the moment.

"Yes," he says.

"Yes?" Our conversation is now lost in my mind as I bite my bottom lip to keep myself from tugging his face against mine.

"Yes, I was jealous." He leans in closer, his voice a seductive whisper.

"Oh?" My breath quivers. It's all I can manage when he steps closer, pressing his chest into mine, his fingers grazing the tips of mine, sending a heat wave washing over me. It pulses through my chest, my stomach, every inch of me until all I see is red. My body is no longer just experiencing mild episodes about this man. It's downright malfunctioning.

And I can only think of one fix. *Which is ridiculous, Katherine!* He is your friend. He is not one of your dating options. This is a man who prefers life alone, with chickens and steak dinners. A man with a life so different from mine it's baffling how we get along. I cannot keep letting my mind wander down this *what if* road.

"I am jealous." It's a husky murmur as he moves in closer, his mouth just an inch from mine. A borderline obscene noise leaves me as he moves his hand up my arm, goosebumps following in its wake. "Insanely jealous." His eyes soften as conflicting emotions swirl in them like a whirlpool until they settle on something intense and unmistakable.

Need.

His gentle caress moves up my arm, past my shoulder, and settles at my neck. My eyes flutter closed when he touches a spot behind my ear, the pad of his thumb stroking my cheek for a moment before he moves it across my bottom lip. My entire body shivers as he tugs at it, need stirring within me now.

A knock at the door jolts Malcolm out of our trance first. Resting his forehead against mine, he sighs, "We gotta go." The chatter of our teenagers bellows out in the hall, and I find myself wishing they would get locked in a stalled elevator.

A lingering kiss on the forehead is all I get before Malcolm releases my arm and heads for the door. I stay planted, feeling as if I've had an out-of-body experience, before shaking out every limb individually.

Arm. Arm. Leg. Leg.

Just like Ellie taught me.

I collect my things, and my thoughts, and follow Malcolm.

The chivalrous man holds the door open for me as the rest of the team races to the elevator. He runs a hand across my lower back, my wrist, my elbow—touching any part of me he can get away with as I pass him. "After you, Ms. Stanley."

"You almost kissed?" Ellie just about busts my ear drum as she squeals on the other line. A slur of shrieks, yips, and the sound of a cat getting stepped on blare through my phone as I wait in the hotel lobby.

"I think we did...I don't know," I groan and slouch to an almost parallel position to the floor in my chair, receiving a few glares from the group of high-profile elderly ladies sitting at the bar. My lack of lady-like etiquette is probably offensive to their judgy eyes.

"What do you mean?" Ellie's question is followed by some faraway whispers. Benny. Probably listening in, per usual.

"It all happened so fast! One minute we were talking about Eric, and the next we were practically Velcroed together!" I exclaim, my manic voice drawing more eye rolls. "El, I could *smell* his breath."

"Okay, ew."

I ignore her. "It was, like, pre-kiss vibes out the wazoo!" I place my fingers on my throat, feeling my pulse ratchet up at the memory of Malcolm's lips.

"Would you have kissed him? Ya know…" Ellie pauses. "…if he initiated." She sounds giddy, her words coming out in a high-pitch whistle.

"I don't know." I pinch the bridge of my nose, the weight of everything filling my head with a buzzy pressure.

"Don't lie to us," Benny pipes in.

"Excuse me, I don't remember dialing *your* number." The pressure moves to my temples. I let out a gruff moan and rub one side.

"It's my job to check on my employees." His voice is smug on the other line.

"Don't you have other faculty to harass?"

"Nah, no one has anything interesting going on." A gush of air rushes out of him followed by the squeak of leather. "So, really, what are you going to do?"

"I. Don't. Know. Bayani." He gasps in fake offense as I call him by his Filipino name. "Can you give the phone back to my friend now?"

"Am I not your friend?"

"No." The biggest lie I could tell anyone. Benny is the closest person I have in my life, edging out Malcolm and Ellie most days. After his parents died and he started living with Lola, we spent almost every weekend together until I was eleven, when I officially moved in with them. Even in the absence of my parents, having Lola and Benny made it bearable. Family dinners on Saturday nights were sitting on the floor around a coffee table, whooping Benny at Bananagrams, and Sundays were fighting over what movie to watch until Lola broke it up by making us watch *General Hospital* reruns. It was a simple upbringing, but I loved every moment of it. I felt loved and wanted every single day. Some days, it was almost enough to forget about the parents uninterested in raising their only child.

"Liar," Ellie says in the background. They share whispers and giggles, their bliss palpable through the line.

For the past few months, the reality that my family is growing apart has been forcing itself into my thoughts like a tiny weed growing through a crack in the middle of a concrete slab—tiny and fickle but persistent as heck, and not even an entire can of RoundUp can get rid of it. Their laughing blends with the noises in the lobby as I wait, picturing their coziness on the couch that sits in the corner of Ellie's office. Happy—that's what I feel for them. Truly. But it doesn't hide the desire that I want that too. I want the giggles that make others cringe. I want the soft whispers like no one else is around.

I couldn't be happier that Benny's new family is Ellie. And Lola has her secret handyman boyfriend. Everyone has their person, that someone who makes them feel wanted. I just want that. And I think the closeness with Malcolm lately has started to cloud my overall goal to get that.

I can't deny the chemistry with Malcolm, the ease of it. But being with Malcolm isn't an option. He's my best friend. He has his life, and I have mine. We've forced it to mesh overtime, tolerating each other's quirks, like his incessant need to quote the entire *Lord of the Rings* films, or his borderline neurotic fascination with naming each of his chickens. The man has almost thirty chickens now, with no intention of stopping, and he remembers them by name. He gave each of them personalized saddles to tell them apart, because Sparkles and Cowgirl are both black and speckled, but, "they're their own chicken and need their own identity." Malcolm's deep voice replays in my head at the memory.

"I think I'm just going to let the rest of this week play out, and then, when we get home, maybe discuss expectations. I have no idea what's going on in his head, but if I want to find someone, I can't let myself get distracted with my best friend."

"Second best friend," Ellie corrects.

"My *guy* best friend," I continue, annoyed at the interruption. "As I was saying…I can't get distracted, even if it's with a hot man that has been giving me intense vibes ever since the Christmas party. I can't focus on that. I have to focus on the endgame."

"Which is what exactly?" Ellie poses the question, some underlying reason hiding in her tone.

"To find someone," I say, dragging the words out in a growl, irritation evident as I readjust in the lobby chair. I check my watch. "Where the heck is your sister, by the way?"

As if she was a genie and that question was the act of rubbing her lamp, Emma glides through the front door of the hotel lobby. Steven, her husband, follows behind, carrying three different suitcases. I try not to eye the load, seeing as they're only here for two nights, but he catches me and gives me a swift nod. *Don't mention the bags* is written all over his face.

"Hello, Ms. Stanley!" Emma rushes over to me, looking like she just ran a marathon—face red, sweat lining her forehead, heavy gasps occurring with each stride she takes across the lobby. Somehow, in a matter of days, her belly looks twice the size that it was when I last saw her. I pin my gaze on her face, resisting the urge to touch the sweet bump she's failing at hiding with the oversized tunic she's sporting. She snags the phone from my hand. "We've got it from here," she informs Ellie then proceeds to disconnect the line.

Handing my phone to Steven, she walks over to the front desk to check in. Steven hands me my phone back, equally confused as to why he has it. "How's the week been?" He forces a smile, the kind that is trying too hard to communicate that he knows absolutely nothing about what's going on in my personal life, and he hasn't listened to Ellie and Emma discuss it at length for the entirety of their travel.

I glare at him. "Fine," I say through my teeth. He pats me on the shoulder before joining Emma at the desk. His dark skin puts my sun-kissed glow to shame and makes Emma's ivory skin look like she hasn't seen the sun in years. He wraps his hand around her waist and rubs her belly as they wait for their room keys. Another ping of jealousy stings my chest at the sight of someone else's happiness. "It's fine," I whisper to myself.

Emma thanks the concierge, leaving the giant bags for Steven, which he gathers without hesitation. "Shall we?" She directs me to the elevators, I follow, taking one of the bags off Steven's hands. He gives a grateful nod as exhaustion lines his face and posture. Ever since they found out they were pregnant, Steven has been working extra shifts to build a bigger nest egg so he can work less when the baby gets here, all so Emma can start as Glendale's principal next year. It's sweet, but the weight of stress is clinging to Steven like chains, dulling his usually perky demeanor.

We climb into the open elevator, the bags taking up half the empty space. "Steven, thanks for doing this. Dr. Reynolds had a last-minute schedule change and had to leave camp early. Without you, we wouldn't be able to have the scrimmage today." Steven smiles at me, pressing the floor for our rooms. Dr. Reynolds, the orthopedic doctor that takes a week off every year to be the onsite doctor for our athletes, free of charge, left yesterday afternoon on short notice. For liability purposes, we can't have strenuous workouts or scrimmages without some type of medical professional on staff. One phone call to Emma, and Steven was loading their car. Of course, it probably wasn't fully up to Steven to be here. I'm sure he'd rather have stayed home and slept than left the airport at 5 a.m. to get here and stand on the side of a football field in 90-degree weather all day.

As we drop off our bags, I sense a shift in the air. Silence. Weird, awkward silence. We meander back to the elevator—in silence. Suspicion creeps in as I begin to glance between the two of them leaning against the back wall of the elevator, me on the side wall. We hit the second floor when a small group of senior citizens piles on, half naked with their revealing swimsuits on. Emma's gaze snaps to the ceiling when the only gentleman in the group, wearing a bright-orange Speedo leaving nothing to the imagination, gives her a wink and saddles up directly in front of her. Steven shoves his fist up to his mouth and bites his finger as he restrains his laugh. The older man shimmies his hips left and right, offbeat to the elevator music, while the older women in the group spur him on with whistles and catcalls.

"You've still got it, Herb," one of the ladies says as she claps.

Herb glances over his shoulder at Emma, shimmying his shoulders at her, before shuffling off the elevator. Silently, we exit behind the group, and differing expressions mar our faces from the experience. Steven belts out a laugh, and his bright teeth shine against his dewy dark skin. Emma erratically brushes off the front of herself—shirt, arms, belly—essentially brushing off the old-man aura that must have clung to her. Steven's laughter continues when she lets out a repulsed sigh before leading us out of the hotel. She leads like she's the one who has been here all week.

We find our way to the field where preparation for the scrimmage has begun. "So..." I drag out, breaking the endless silence, "what's up?" My face is apprehensive as I glare at them from the backseat when we find a parking spot.

Emma unclicks her seatbelt from the passenger seat, twisting to face me. Ungracefully, the belly is an obstacle. "Why are you kissing Malcolm but you won't date him?"

"We didn't kiss!" I throw myself face down into the backseat, my damp skin sticking to the leather. "We. Almost. Kissed." The seat muffles my words as I glance out of the corner of my eye. Emma looks at me incredulously. Unconvinced.

"Semantics." She waves me off, climbing out of the car. Steven follows suit, opening the back door for me. Emma waits for me as I peel myself off the sticky material and stumble out of the car. "The point is"—she points at me for emphasis—"why are you getting so cozy with him if you're not even interested in dating him?"

"I'm not—"

"Yes, you are," she interrupts. "Malcolm is a good man, and he deserves honesty. If you don't like him more than a friend, then this flirty nonsense"—she waves a circle around me, indicating it is *me* that is causing the flirty nonsense—"needs to stop."

"But he—"

"I don't care who started it," she interrupts again. Very much like her sister, she can just about read my mind. "It's about who stops it."

We make our way toward the gym that sits catty-corner to the field, the sun oppressive at our backs. "If you care about him or yourself, you will stop what you're doing. Or one of you is going to get hurt. Or worse..." Emma trails off as she enters the gym without us. Steven holds the door for me as I follow.

"What's worse than that?" I murmur to myself.

"Both of you will," Steven says.

Chapter Twenty-Four

Kate

Steven's words ring in my ears as we spend the next hour setting up for the scrimmage. I glance around every few minutes, looking for Malcolm, but he's nowhere to be found. He's probably pacing the locker room in his surly, nobody-talk-to-me, pre-game mode.

Refusing to get distracted.

Not wondering where I am.

Why does that even matter, Kate?

People start to arrive twenty minutes before the game starts, filling the bleacher seats one by one. The place is almost packed when we add the finishing touches to the medical tent. Steven has changed into bright-blue scrubs, and Emma and I sport matching t-shirts that say *Medic Team*. We are less than qualified for the position, but my athletic background is enough to assist with passing out water and taping up twists and sprains. Emma busies herself with organizing the medical supplies and repositioning the A-frame sign a thousand different times before deciding it looks fine in the original spot Steven put it.

"Have they had a lot of injuries at any of these things?" Steven asks, placing a piece of paper on the exam table lining the tent wall.

"A couple." I glance out of the tent entrance—*again*. "A few concussions, the occasional broken bone. Nothing you can't handle, I'm sure." I give him finger guns, my eyes still searching the entrance, bleachers, and field for any sign of Malcolm.

"Let's hope for none of that today!" Emma chirps. "Safety first!" The woman is a beacon of hazard prevention. She once forced my classes to wear tinted glasses during a *Big Bang Theory* presentation. She was convinced the bright flashing of light could cause optic nerve injuries—from the tiny three-foot box television with a permanent black circle in one corner. "Who did their safety debriefing?" Emma joins me under the tent opening, the area of shade around us disappearing as the noon sun starts to come out.

"Uh, I don't know." Still no sign of Malcolm. "Maybe the coaches." I stand on my toes and see the first group of players making their way toward the field.

"Hello! Earth to Stanley!" Emma waves her hands in my face, the yellow sun hat she's wearing is folded up in the front, resembling a sunflower.

I blink back to her, slightly distracted by the beam of yellow surrounding her head. "Hmm?"

"Tell me what is going on in that curly head"—she trickles her fingers through the air between us—"of yours."

"I'm just ready for the scrimmage to start." My eyes dart between her and the field, still searching. The second team starts to file onto the turf with the coaches following close behind.

"Kate..." Emma eyes me warily. Her patience has always been calming, that motherly patience I missed out on. "Talk to me." Her voice is tranquil and almost hypnotizing as she waits for me to respond—another motherly tactic she has mastered.

I focus on her and the horrendous hat. "I just...ugh..." I gnaw on my thumbnail and speak around my hand. "I need to talk to Malcolm. I need to clear things up."

"I agree. You should. But you can't do that anytime soon. He has to focus on the team, and you do too." She hands me a sideline duffel bag full of tape, Band-Aids, and other essentials. "That's why you're here." She turns me to face the field and bleachers, my group of girls lining the front rail that overlooks the guys, sporting team shirts and cheering on their counterparts. My heart swells at the team spirit. "Worry about the game right now. You have time to talk to Malcolm. He's not going anywhere."

Her reassurance powers my steps as I head to the field, duffel and enormous water bottle in tow. I find the group of coaches for the first team with Coach Lawson giving his usual pep talk. The players and younger coaches listen so intently a missile strike wouldn't distract them. Eric waves at me from the field, stretching as he prepares to play. Nausea burns my throat at the weirdness between us. The friendly dinner I had hoped for, the closure I needed, gone in the blink of an eye—all because he had a surge of testosterone after a couple glasses of wine.

I spot Coach Daniels across the field, standing with a few coaches I don't recognize. I peer over them, looking for the one I do, with no luck.

"Hello, Ms. Stanley," Daniels greets me behind his orange framed sunglasses.

"Daniels, hi! Where's Malcolm?" There is no way I don't look like a lunatic with how fast my head whips back and forth as I look around for him.

"He's letting me—"

Coach Lawson blows the whistle, cutting off Daniels, as four players take the field, each wearing a band wrapped around their biceps with the letter C stitched on it. Team captains. The sun bakes us, and I shade my face with the giant water bottle, my gaze distorted from the rays of light as I watch the coin flip. The sun makes it hard to tell who from our team is out there until my eyes land on a familiar set of forearms and farmer's tan. The red-tinged, pale skin and light-colored hair that trickles up the chiseled arms is hard to mistake. He turns around, adjusting his helmet strap as he makes his way back to the sidelines. Bright-blue eyes meet mine, and my jaw feels like it could dislocate from how hard it drops.

"What. Are. You. Doing?" I bellow at Malcolm as he joins the pre-play huddle. He smiles at me, ignoring my question. Oh, heck no. I stomp across the sidelines, shoving my way into the huddle. A few familiar faces smile at me, and a few stare at me like the mad woman I am. "Malcolm, what are you doing? You can't—"

They clap once, the huddle breaking up, and they take the field. Malcolm attempts to follow, but I grab him by the collar of his jersey and drag him backward a few steps.

"Whoa, ma'am! What was that for?" He readjusts his shoulder pads, rolling his neck and arms.

"What are you thinking? You can't go out there!" I gape at him.

"It's just one game, Stanley." He squeezes my elbow.

I grab his wrist. "What if you get hurt?" I'm too concerned for Malcolm. I don't even try to hide the whimper in my voice.

He stops mid-step to turn back to me and grips my shoulders, leveling his gaze with mine. His eyes soften as his smile stretches across his face, a thousand unspoken words passing through the thick air between us. "I'll be fine. Don't worry about me."

"You know that's impossible for me."

He belts out a boisterous laugh as he tilts his face up to the sky. The sound would be contagious, causing me to laugh with him, if I wasn't on pins and needles. He pulls his helmet up to the top of his head, and sweat glistens on the edges of his face and tip of his beard. "It's not even a full game, Kate."

My eyes sting, either from sweat or the sheer idea of my friend getting plowed over by some teenagers. As if he can sense the worry boiling inside me, Malcolm cups my jaw with both hands and squeezes my cheeks. From afar, the motion would look silly, but something about the slow way his calloused thumbs graze down my face makes all the air leave my body. "Everything will be fine."

I blink back the moisture swelling in my eyes. "You promise?"

"I promise." His smile falters for a moment before he forces it into a wide grin and heads back out to the field, like he, too, can sense the conversation coming, the boundaries we have to set. He's telling me, and himself, that everything will be fine.

"He'll be fine," Daniels reassures me when I join him on the sidelines. "I've heard the guy is a tank out there."

Tank is an understatement.

Malcolm is a powerhouse on the field when he needs to be. Just last summer, he outran half the team for a forty-yard touchdown just to prove to them they weren't trying hard enough—or to show off.

Only he knows.

But it was fun to see the kids grovel at his feet like he was God when they realized how athletic he still is. It was odd to watch him strip off his work boots and socks like he was unwinding after a hard day. Malcolm stood in the center of the field, grounding himself with bare feet on the turf, sizing up the competition. The kids never stood a chance.

I size up his competition this time, noting the older players right off. One of them is Coach Foust, who is a fossil in human form. I don't think I've seen someone so old attempt to crouch down to the starting position. It's very possible I heard his hips pop all the way from here.

Another coach, Coach Taylor, weighs about three hundred pounds and towers over everyone. His breathing is so labored he looks like he could collapse at any moment. Yet, he makes it onto the field and into the starting position as well.

Malcolm takes his position on the far left of the line, closest to me. My eyes widen when he glances over, giving me a wink. This kind of thing would usually send me crawling on my hands and knees to a man—tight pants accentuating curves, arms flexing as they grip the turf, then adding in a wink just for me... But the stress of watching Malcolm take the position of tight end, one he rarely plays, sends the nausea from earlier crawling back up my throat, leaving the taste of acid in my mouth.

"Red Team, are you ready?" The defense nods at the referee's question. "Blue Team?" he asks us, the offense. They nod, settling into their starting positions with fervor.

"Red and blue team?" I ask Daniels, recalling that they're allowed to come up with their own names. Daniels gives me a shrug like *what're ya gonna do?* "That's...original."

The snap happens. The ball is pitched back to Coach Stent from South. Malcolm blocks, allowing Stent to cover almost thirty yards in the first play. Devon, Ethan, and Travis yelp in celebration from the sidelines in their makeshift coaching attire. I release the breath I didn't realize I was holding and glare at Malcolm's backside as they huddle up around Daniels. Knowing Malcolm, he's being humble and letting Daniels call the shots for the game, staying in his lane as a player and not letting the duty of coach bleed over into his role as a teammate. He's always been skilled at keeping things separate, whether it's his work and home life balance, or simply maintaining a neutral position for the sake of peace.

Another play happens, and I bite my thumbnail the entire time. Coach Taylor goes down like a tree, needing extra hands to help him limp off the field. Our team scores a touchdown in the first few minutes of the quarter, and the crowd goes wild. They're riding the high when they race to the sidelines, and the defensive line swaps out.

Malcolm sits on the bench next to me, his dampened hair shining in the sun like gold. He pants slightly and gazes up at me with a cocky grin. "See, it's going to be fine."

I roll my eyes, refusing to believe that until the final second on the clock ticks off. These kids are ruthless, and I wouldn't put it past them to try to pummel the strongest coach on that field.

"Are you mad?" He squirts his water bottle in his face and wipes the wetness with his palm. It feels obscene almost, like it should be happening behind closed doors, him stretching and raking his hands fully through his hair and shaking it out. I feel myself staring—no, gawking. Gah, what is so irresistible about this man now? Has he always been this attractive? Stupid question, Kate. Yes, he has. But why am I feeling attracted to his attractiveness all of a sudden?

I blame the slew of poor dates recently, getting dolled up in hopes of a connection, only to be left sitting on my couch at the end of the night, alone, with the pit of yearning deepening more and more. It's almost a bottomless pit at this point. That and the tubs of ice cream that come with the couch sitting.

Maybe that's what's wrong.

Not the ice cream, but that I'm so ready to find someone that my hormonal instincts are drawn to the closest option I have, which is absolutely absurd and pathetic. If I let myself yearn over something I can't have, then who's to say I will keep my standards when I go on the next date when we get back?

The first half of the game goes by quicker than Coach Foust's ankles being swept from underneath him. It was a sneaky move on our part, but the trick juke made Foust collide with the turf with a force you only see in the movies. The crowd gasped, the teams stopped, and Foust screamed like a toddler—like Emma's twins when they weren't allowed to eat a second cupcake at Henry's birthday. He bounced back up quickly but tumbled again, giving in to the pain and benching himself.

Steven is delighted when I help wheel Foust into the tent during halftime, going full doctor mode while Emma questions his understanding of the safety briefing and if he had signed a waiver.

Clouds have started to cover the sky, making it more humid than hot but less scorching overall. I wince as I rub sunscreen on my neck and arms, cooling the sting of my darkened skin.

"Hold still," Steven instructs Foust as he whimpers and flinches away from Steven's touch. A double sprain is all he has, but you'd think he just received a terminal diagnosis based on the tears streaming down his cheeks.

"Heading back out!" I call over my shoulder as I head back to the field. The second half starts in a few minutes, and I didn't get a chance to check if Malcolm was feeling alright before they barreled off the field.

I make it to my post as the Red Team makes their way out, Eric bringing up the rear with their head coach for the game. He spots me and jogs over, my entire body going rigid in response, like he's a bear and all I know to do is get into the fetal position.

Before I can get to the ground, he's at my feet, winded and sweating. "Man, your guys are good!" he exclaims. "Johnson is fast for his size."

"He's worked really hard to get to this point. You won't be disappointed when he's with you next term." I keep my eyes on the field to avoid Eric's heavy gaze.

"For sure, for sure. And that Malcolm..." His words stall when my head whips to him, and Eric's lip twitch up in a devilish grin. "He's—"

"He's what?" I snip, my thumb tingling at my side with the urge to be gnawed on. Clearing my throat, I adjust my tone to a more well-mannered one. "He's what?"

"A strong athlete..." Eric pauses to evaluate my face, infuriating me more. I force it into a line, a nonchalant, I-couldn't-care-less-what-you-have-to-say-about-my-best-friend line. "Is there something going on with you two?" His eyes light up with gleeful anticipation.

"There's nothing going on with us," I groan, throwing my head back, the overcast sky still bright enough to temporarily blind me.

"Alright, alright." He holds his hands up in surrender. "Just asking."

Pressing my palm into the center of my head, I blink the sun out of my eyes and look at him. "It's fine. It's just..." My words linger in the air, like my thoughts, itching to get out in the open. Eric waits expectantly. "I don't know what's going on with Malcolm. He's wonderful and my best friend. I would honestly die if I lost him, which is why I am currently trying to decide how to tell him we need better boundaries. Ya know, friend boundaries. Lately, things have gotten out of hand, like so out of hand I don't even know how to go back to normal. I think about him all the time and wonder if he's thinking about me. I wake up missing him. And I'm not sure when these feelings started, really." I throw my arms out, my voice picking up at the relief of getting everything out. "I started dating again, about a month ago, right?" Eric's face doesn't change as he continues to listen.

"I'd sworn off men for a while, didn't want to deal with their nonsense. I mean, who does, right? But then Benny and Ellie got engaged and started planning their wedding, and everything was perfect. Except for me. I was lonely, I guess. I'm no spring chicken anymore—

"Kate, you're only thir—"

"Old enough," I cut him off, "to start evaluating my life and figure out what I want. I have the best job, the best friends. Really, everything in my life is perfect. But I still feel myself searching for something. Searching for a missing piece. A piece that I *think* was missing well before you even left. I figured why not start by putting myself out there again and seeing if the missing piece was just finding my person. Instead, I've gone on about eight horrendous dates. Like, so bad I need Dr. Phil to psychoanalyze some of these dudes. And all I'm left with is this feeling that I might never find what I'm missing." Eric gapes at me as I suck in a breath, and embarrassment stings my cheeks at the word-vomit I just unleashed. "I don't know why I told you all of that."

"That was a lot of info." He rubs the back of his neck, looking uncomfortable and at a loss for words, which is rare for the chatterbox.

We stand there in silence for a beat as his team runs through their warm-up when the Blue Team starts to file out of the locker room. Daniels and Malcolm walk out together, hunched over a clipboard. Malcolm nods enthusiastically, patting Daniels on the back before jogging after the other players. His pace falters a few steps when he sees me and Eric standing side by side, but he quickly corrects himself and sends a timid wave in our direction.

"I will say this..." Eric puts his helmet on, gripping the mouthguard attached to the face mask. "Malcolm is a good guy who clearly cares about you. And aside from your occasional bouts of verbal diarrhea"—he chuckles at his own joke—"you, Kate Stanley, deserve a good guy." He gives me a soft and accepting smile before he walks over to his side of the field.

Malcolm makes himself busy with pretend stretches, circling his arms around like Lola does in Jazzercise, waiting until Eric is a good distance away before he trots over to me, a mix of emotions marking his face. He moves his helmet to the top of his head, revealing his golden locks plastered to his forehead and red marks on his temples from the pressure of his helmet. He uses his tongue to push his blue mouthguard out of his mouth. Teeth, tongue, lips. He makes a slight smacking noise as he pulls the rest of the piece from his lips, licking the extra moisture away with a slow swipe.

It's a dangerous sight.

"Are you just stringing ole Sanders along, Stanley?" He gives another wink, and I feel it in my bones.

"Uh, no," I defend. "He keeps coming up to me!" I press my hand against my chest dramatically.

"Oh yeah?" He reaches back to grab his ankle and stretches his quad. The line of his leg muscle presses against the tight sheen fabric of his pants, threatening to burst free. "Want me to beat him up?" he jokes, stretching the other leg. I gulp audibly at the smoothness of his movements.

"Calm down, Rocky."

"Kidnapping?"

"Stop it." I laugh and try to give him a playful shove in the arm, but he catches my wrist and rubs the inside with his thumb.

He lets out a slow breath, staring at my arm and the movement of his thumb. "Look, I want to—"

"Geer, huddle up!" Devon calls out from center field.

"Dang it," he mutters to himself then asks, "can we talk later?" He slides his mouthguard back into place and walks backward onto the field.

I nod. "After?"

"Yeah, after the next game!" His words and smile are so distorted from his mouthguard that I almost miss the information that was tossed at me.

"Alright—wait, what?" I'm confused. "*Next* game?"

Chapter Twenty-Five

Malcolm

"First game was cake, dude."

"Fo sho, the next one will be easy!"

"You never know. They could have a secret weapon. Don't sell them short just yet!"

Charlie, Travis, and Garrett are huddled up, discussing game play and the odds of a double win. I try to focus on them and not the rank, acid locker room smell singeing my nose hairs. It's almost worse than Bill's leftovers.

I retape my wrists, ankles, and left knee, stretching and flexing each appendage to test the stability. I can't believe I agreed to do this. These kids are on a different planet than me with their energy, acting like this is their Super Bowl. But I could honestly not care less about the outcome. I rarely ever do. If my team can just not make a fool of themselves or waste my time out there, I'm content. But when Sarah told me Kate brags about my skill on the field, it flipped something inside of me. All of a sudden, I needed to care, and I needed to play.

Field advantage, as Garrett would say.

I'm feeling out of sorts with everything lately, but I need any advantage I can get.

I roll my neck and shoulders, deep aches spreading faster than my sunburn. I stand up and feel the chronic twinge in my back fire, jolting a spark of pain up my spine. I curse under my breath and sit back down.

"You good, Coach?" Garrett asks me from over by the lockers.

"Just old," I grumble back, rubbing my neck and jaw. Might as well check their stability too.

The guys let out quiet snickers when I stand, slow and cautious. I don't have any plans to go down like Taylor or Foust today.

One minute I was sideswiping a coach from Central State, the next I saw Taylor face down on the thirty-yard line, not moving. I thought he got knocked out. Nope, he just felt like catching his breath, and the ground was the best place to do that.

"Let's get out there!" Daniels calls out from the entrance to the garbage pit of a locker room.

I take small breaths as we file out, the smell just near strong enough to knock me out. Lockers are slapped, high-fives shared, and chanting noises bellow as we head to the field. Halfway out the door, a thunderous bang jolts me, sending panic creeping into my bones as I look around for the cause. Similar to crunching metal, my head starts to buzz at the memory, and heat rushes through me, restricting my oxygen.

"They dropped some metal chairs back there," Devon squeezes my shoulder. His eyes are calm and sympathetic, and a part of me hates it.

I give him a grateful nod, almost forgetting his dad struggled with PTSD after his tour in Iraq. Devon idolizes the man, striving to impress him in everything he does. It's a shame for a kid to witness their role model feel weak and vulnerable—even worse when it's their dad. But over time, it's helped Devon learn acceptance and patience in ways I never would have at his age.

He taps me on the shoulder pad with his fist before jogging behind the rest of the team and through the makeshift tunnel they now have standing. After the first game, the entire camp staff had a field day with the PR opportunity that could come from a televised game. I am less than enthused about the idea. Why film a bunch of has-beens? Especially when half of them should be put on stretchers. It'll be underwhelming, but I committed to playing and to impressing Kate. So here we are.

The sun is starting to set, a mixture of orange and pink shimmering above the turf. A different look than this morning's game entirely. The splashing of ocean waves is almost too far away to hear, but I register it, focusing on the soothing motions as I put one foot in front of the other. The sound of the metal chairs clanging is almost gone when I make it to the sidelines.

Kate isn't there.

Disappointment deflates my puffed up, pre-game energy. She'll be here eventually, but talking to her beforehand will calm my nerves. I've been nervous ever since this morning, when I decided I was going to tell her how I feel about her, tell her she should stop this dating-strangers-and-getting-coffee-with-exes nonsense and be with me. The game this morning was the perfect distraction. And I would say deciding to wear the extra-tight pants played in my favor, but the heat rash forming on my groin indicates otherwise. Either way, I saw her glancing my way one too many times, and it surged me with this charged intensity I haven't felt in years.

We're officially past the ridiculous stage when it comes to my feelings for Kate. They're a mess of emotions I can't ignore any longer. I have to tell her. Forget the fact that she can crush my heart like a tomato if she wants. I've been dodging my feelings with people for far too long out of fear of losing another person I love. And all those boundaries have done is turn me into this cold, distant gorilla that people cower away from. The few brave souls that haven't cowered away either love the challenge or can see who I am at my core and accept the mess inside.

I start my very long and specific stretching routine while the younglings jump straight into warm-up tackles and sprints. The wonderful parts of aging—needing an additional ten minutes before I can even start warming up.

Setting my helmet down on a shaded part of turf, I sit and begin. Stretch, breathe, reset. I get through five passes of the combination when a white, plush hand towel lands on my head, blocking my sight.

Whipping the towel off my head, I use it to wipe the sweat pooling on my chest and collarbone. "Thanks, Stanley."

"How'd you know it was me?" Kate takes a seat next to me, crossing her legs and splaying her fingers out in the turf in front of her. The motion is slow and mesmerizing, and the thought of her doing that up my back sends a hot sensation deep inside me.

"Your shadow." I smile, hiding the lie. I knew she was close. Her lavender shampoo is hard to miss.

Reaching farther, she swishes her arms back and forth on the ground, smiling like a kid in the snow. "It's so soft." She lets out a hum, laying her face flat against the feathery green blades. That hot sensation intensifies as I watch her. Something must be seriously wrong with me if her simply lying on the grass does me in. "How are you feeling?" Her eyes are closed, restful and serene, when she asks.

"I feel fine."

She opens one eye to assess me, cheek still firmly pressed against the grass as her one eye moves up and down. "You sure?"

"Yes." I finish my stretches, ignoring the partial truth I'm reluctant to share. I feel fine physically, but mentally, I'm what the teenagers would call *unwell*. I still have no idea what I'm going to say to her later, or if I'll even be able to without having an aneurysm. It could go one of two ways, and the dread that comes with a possible poor outcome has burrowed itself so deep into my stomach I think it's become an actual ulcer. I let out a shaky breath, the panic clawing at the back of my throat.

"Well…" Rolling over, she takes in a slow breath, the sun shining on her like a beacon. "I'm glad." She lies there for a moment, her honey darkened skin glowing under the setting sun. She has no idea how beautiful she is, just lying here in her sweaty work clothes, hair tangled in a heap above her head with a small piece of turf dangling from a loose curl. She could stop a train dead in its tracks, especially if I was the one operating it. I'd go off the rails with just one look at her. "Let's survive this next game so we can get food. I'm starving."

Starving.

The sentiment rings differently in my head. I'm hungry alright. Hungry for Kate. I'm a caveman. A lovesick brute, with this primitive nature inside of me barking at my woman as she walks away. Me make words to speak now.

"Tony's Pizza?" I joke.

She lets out a sarcastic laugh followed by a thumbs up over her shoulder, her side profile revealing a wide smile and bright eyes. Happiness looks good on Kate, and I'm begging this big universe she relies so heavily on to let the fates fall in my favor tonight.

Please let this go well.

Please give me the balls to tell her how I feel.

Please let Kate be happy.

Let her be happy…with me.

I finish up my warm-up with very little time left before kickoff. The Red Team takes the field with about half of their team on the sidelines, injured or refusing to play anymore. Daniels claps his hands together and gestures for the guys to circle him. We huddle up and review our first few plays, the cool summer air stilling around us. "Ready?" Daniels calls to the team.

"Break!" Charlie belts out, and the circle claps once and breaks apart.

We take the field, and I quickly realize there are only three of us coaches left uninjured. Even if we're a bunch of has-beens playing a third of a real game, some of these guys are taking it too seriously. The panic from earlier finds its way back into my throat. I gulp, feeling the thick moisture clinging to my tongue as we get into our starting positions. I may have some minor abilities left, but some of these guys are barbarians. I wouldn't put it past them to try to whittle out those of us left standing just because they can.

The pressure of my tape job restricts my wrists as I press my fingers into the turf. Daylight is almost completely gone now with the bright stadium lights illuminating the field. The bleachers are barely visible underneath the striking white that shines on us. I glance to my left, catching one last look at Kate. She beams at me, like I'm the only one she sees out here in the sea. For a moment, she's all I see. Cast in moonlight, she glows like something out of a dream. Her smile is soft and intimate, brown eyes speckled with auburn and gold. Even from thirty feet away and clouded in dim evening light, I can see them perfectly.

It's just me and her, and all the unease I've felt swimming inside me since this morning starts to fade, like the sun behind her, being replaced by the calm stillness of the moon and stars. A wave of confidence fills me, igniting my adrenaline like a gas fire. It could be comparable to the kids surrounding me, like some unstoppable force of nature. A meteor plummeting toward Earth couldn't stop me now. I'm doing it.

I'm telling her everything. Tonight.

I'm telling her that I am crazy about her. That I have been for five years, and I can't imagine my life without her.

I'm telling Kate that I'm in love with her.

And then...everything goes black.

Chapter Twenty-Six

Kate

"Keep him awake for a little bit longer. I think he's safe to shower, but don't let him be alone too long."

Steven's instructions are loose marbles in my head, thrashing every which way. Watch for vomiting. Watch for seizures. Slurred speech, agitation, more vomiting. He communicates this to me like I'm not sitting here stunned and traumatized from what I just witnessed.

One second I'm giving Malcolm one last thumbs up, and the next I see him lifted into the air and taken to the ground with blunt force. The biggest senior from South blazed a path across the field and tackled Malcolm so hard I could hear the impact from the sidelines. I had to watch as the giant climbed off his limp body as he lay flattened out on the turf.

Steven and Daniels rushed the field in seconds, but I couldn't move. My body was in shock. Seeing him lie unconscious did something to me that I've never experienced before. My fight-or-flight response was paralyzed at the sight of Malcolm's unmoving body. Relief washed over me when I saw him move his legs.

"Call me if you need anything." Steven gives Malcolm one final look over, shining his fancy pen light in each eye for good measure. "I think he's going to be fine."

"You bet I'm fine, buddy!" Malcolm sounds half-drunk, and the giddy laughter he lets out every few seconds really adds to the effect.

His obscure behavior eases some of the pent-up anxiety squeezing my chest. I sniffle and wipe the wetness from my cheeks. I haven't stopped crying since they helped him off the field an hour ago. Steven presses a hand on my shoulder, giving a reassuring squeeze as he leaves our room. Malcolm waves at him manically with both hands high in the air. His shoulders dip as he lets out a happy hum, his blue eyes glazed over with innocence. Another tear escapes the corner of my eye. They are acting of their own volition. I have no control.

"Knock, knock." Malcolm presses his hands against his cheeks as he giggles. With his concussed glee, he keeps whispering jokes to try and *cheer me up*. I look at him expectantly, forcing a smile. "Orange..." His smile stretches so far it might jump off his face. "Orange you glad I didn't say yellow?" Hysterics take over, leaving him breathless and cackling at himself as he continues to squish his cheeks.

Another dang tear slithers its way down my face. Malcolm stops laughing and watches it drip off my jaw and onto my leg. His eyes are solemn as he wipes up the wet trail with his thumb. "Why are you sad?" This is the tenth time he's asked me, his memory still wonky from the hit.

"I'm not sad." I force another smile, wiping my cheeks and sitting up straighter.

"But you're leaking." He points at my cheek.

There's a childlike curiosity in his voice, and it only adds more to my confusing emotions. I was terrified for him, and something nearly broke inside me at the image of him lying there helpless. It feels pathetic to think a big guy like Malcolm getting tackled was enough to undo me. He played football for years. He's been trampled over in practice so many times I've lost count. This shouldn't be any different. But it is, and I have no idea how to process it right now.

"I'm just emotional. I was so worried about you." My words come out shaky, and I have to shove my palms into my eyes to block the tears from flowing. Again. It's embarrassing how much I've cried over a concussion.

"You were worried about me?"

The more the event replays in my head and the turning of my insides that follows, it's becoming clear to me that *worried* is an understatement.

He bats his eyes at me playfully. The guy is out of his wits. This is the most lax I've ever seen him, even after the accidental drink mix-up at the New Year's party two years ago. He sang "Piano Man" on top of a toy piano he found in Emma's coat closet, a cappella and off-key. It was a miracle he didn't snap the thing in two. Even then, he wasn't nearly as befuddled as he is right now—giggling, blushing, and stumbling on every second word. It's adorable, yes. But it's not Malcolm. And I keep getting choked up watching him wander aimlessly around our room, gazing into the abyss like he's pondering life from a different point of view.

Malcolm stumbles toward the bathroom, gripping his lower back with both hands. "My back," he mutters.

"You were hit pretty hard." I reach for his anti-inflammatories on the bedside table. "Maybe you should take a hot bath."

"Oh yeah?" He stands up a little straighter. "A bath, you say?" He wiggles his eyebrows as a sly smirk pulls at his lips. "Care to join?"

"Malcolm. Geer." I toss the medicine bottle at him, which he catches with ease. Glad to see his motor skills are still intact.

"I'm just kiiidding." He stretches the word out as he draws his head back and stumbles back a step into me.

"Careful now."

"What if I fall?" he pouts, whispering over his shoulder to me.

"You'll be fine."

"Alriiight..." Stretching his words again, he lets his shoulders fall then whispers, "I'll take one...all alone." The swell of his bottom lip juts out with force as he stares at me. I instinctively push it back in with my finger, which I realize is a mistake when he nips at it.

I yank my hand away, guarding the bitten appendage. "You are a crazy man!"

"Crazy about you. *Boop.*"

He actually boops my nose before scurrying away and shutting the bathroom door. This six-foot-two, surly man, who thinks any physical touch outside of a handshake is asinine, just booped me on the nose.

Crazy about you.

His words cling to my brain like syrup, thick and sticky. A sweet satisfaction trickles through my senses and leaves a freaking mess of everything. We were supposed to talk tonight. I was supposed to set boundaries and tell him all this flirting—or whatever the Florida heat has done to our brain cells—needs to simmer down so we can go back to normal before we go home. I had it all worked out in my head. An easy, simple conversation about the importance of our friendship, and my goal to find someone, and how it's become clear that the two very separate aspects of my life are now bubbling over into each other. I have always considered myself a flexible person, going with the flow of things like it's my job. And being a high school teacher, sometimes that's all I can do. But something about this situation with Malcolm has me all over the place emotionally, and going with the flow is just not going to cut it. I can't let myself get worked up over his face or his lips anymore. I can't be having emotional breakdowns when he gets plowed over by a group of teenagers. Putting myself back out there requires a level head and a well-oiled wheel of emotions.

But my cogs are all out of sorts because of this man, and I clearly can't have a conversation with him when he's *booping* me on the nose.

I hear a small thud followed by a slew of curse words, and I jump to the bathroom. Swinging the door open, I find Malcolm wrapped in a towel on the floor, his long legs stretched out in front of him as he holds the tub stopper over his head like a trophy.

"Are you alright?" I ask behind a stifling laugh.

"I need help." His pout seems to be permanent at this point.

I let out a sigh and reach around him to turn on the water. Filling the tub is a test of self-discipline as I try to focus on the temperature of the water and not the bare chest and arms sitting at my feet. I sidle past him once it's ready. "All set. Be careful, please." He salutes me then giggles again as he pulls himself up.

Time passes in slow motion as I listen to the splashing of water, hums, and snickers that happen on the other side of the bathroom door. The last few days' events replay in my head, adding to the pressure forming behind my eyes. I press my palms into my forehead, resisting the urge to ask myself, *What are you doing?* The entire Eric situation, the Malcolm situation, not to mention the dating app notifications that have been silenced since we landed in Florida. My brain hurts from all of this confusion, and I've done it to myself. The chaos is my own doing.

A loud slosh of water happens, and I can hear Malcolm getting out of the tub. Clearly, tonight won't be productive in solving one of my issues. But I can rest confidently knowing that one of them is put to bed—Eric. It doesn't always take the universe to tell me when a door is meant to close, and that one closed a long time ago. Sitting up against the headboard and letting the tension in my limbs release, I feel something in my chest release as well. A tight knot unravels—one that's needed to for years, but I was pulling in the wrong direction, tightening it. The weight of holding a grudge against my ex, and refusing to date because of him, starts to dissipate.

The bathroom door creaks open, and Malcolm emerges, fully clothed, with a towel draped around his neck. Steam rolls off him in waves.

"How was your bath?" I ask.

"Good." He nods, and I half-expect him to be back to his normal self until he says, "But very lonely." He gives me a pitiful pout and a wink, solidifying that Malcolm is still completely out of it.

"Well, you're going to have to deal with it." My tone is an eye roll enough, which causes him to pout even harder. "You are Mr. Lone Wolf tonight, sir."

"Aww," he whimpers, "Kitty Kat…"

"Ew, absolutely not." I rejected that horrendous nickname long ago, banning it from every name scenario that I might ever find myself in.

"What? You don't like it?" He puts his hands on his hips, one eyebrow raised. I should blame his injured brain cells for his lack of common sense right now, but the way he stands there, confident that *he* is the one who should be offended when *he* was the first person to boycott the nickname, just about pushes me past the edge of sanity.

"We should get some sleep." I fear we are both headed for hysterics if this continues.

His eyes widen and eyebrows twitch, itching to wiggle suggestively. "Together?"

"Yes, Geer. We've shared this bed already. Slow your roll."

"Oooh, goodie." Clasping his hands together, he bounces once on the balls of his feet, delight swimming in his eyes. He dives onto the bed, Superman style, with a wide grin plastered on his face, landing so hard he has to reach out to grab my arm so I don't fly off the bed. He winces in pain and rubs his forehead, settling on top of the comforter.

Brushing a strand of gold hair away from his face, I ask, "How bad does it hurt?"

"Meh." He presses deeper in the center of his forehead with his thumb. "I'm fine."

We sit there for a moment, silence passing between us slowly as he releases his finger from his head. A small red blotch marks the pressure point he was holding, directly in the middle of his eyebrows. He lets out a breath, blinking his eyes open and squinting at the ceiling. The lights around the bed are dimmed, a thin ray of moonlight coming through the crack in the curtains, the rest of the hotel room hidden by shadows. If I weren't next to him in this bed, I wouldn't be able to make out his face. His blue eyes are almost icy when he turns to face me, the moonlight flickering across his face as the curtains sway next to us.

"Am I acting different?" he asks, his voice still light like before, but there's a twinge of speculation underneath, as if he's starting to feel more like himself and can tell that he is acting *cuckoo*.

"A little." I smirk. "But it's kind of adorable."

"You're kind of adorable."

"You keep saying things like that."

"I mean them."

"You're concussed."

"Am I?" he asks contemplatively.

I bark out a laugh. "Yes. You are the epitome of concussed. I hardly recognize you."

"Weird. I feel like myself." He shrugs, turning to face the ceiling again.

"You are definitely not yourself. You're saying the most off-the-wall things, probably thinking them too." I laugh again, watching him watch the ceiling. He stays upright against the headboard, his usual metal rod posture on display against the wood of the bed. Not everything about him is different, that's for sure.

"I'm not thinking anything out of the ordinary."

"You sure about that?" I pose the question, twisting to face him better. "Earlier you called Steven *Stevie Poo*."

"What?" He looks mortified, wide blue eyes crystalizing with terror. "You're lying."

"Scout's honor. You said, and I quote, 'I think you're the best, Dr. Stevie Poo.'"

Malcolm throws his hands up to his face, pressing his palms into his eyes, and lets out a humiliated groan. I can't help the laughter that bubbles out of me. It flows out faster than the waves at high tide on the beach, one on top of the other. I laugh for who knows how long before I collect myself and take a deep breath. When I look back at Malcolm, he's watching me. A smile pulls at the corner of his mouth, but his eyes are serious—and fixed on me.

"What?" I ask around a gaspy breath.

"You're beautiful, Kate."

"You're delirious." I try to shove his arm, but he catches my wrist, pulling a swift maneuver that drapes my arms around his shoulders and my torso across his chest. The movement makes me dizzy. *That* and the smell of his soap. A splendid kind of dizziness that makes me breathless, clinging to him like my life depends on it.

"I mean it." He strokes a piece of hair away from my face, grazing his thumb down the side of my cheek. Wild tremors move all over me at the motion. His eyes are heated as they scan me, feeling like a warm caress on my face. "You are the most beautiful woman I have ever laid eyes on." He rests his hand on my collarbone, and my chest heaves under his fingers as they trickle back and forth. His touch is tender and slow, but the intensity in his eyes is blazing.

"I think..." my voice trembles and eyes flutter, fighting to stay open and focused. "I think you need sleep."

"I need you." He continues stroking, moving up my neck and down my shoulders with both hands.

My voice is a weak whisper in response, "Malcolm..."

I don't know what to say. I can't get my brain to focus on anything but his hands and the slight parting of his lips. For a moment, I feel lost in the sensations, the burning in my chest, the tingling in my arms and legs, the tremble in my lips, my body reacting to him in a way it never has. My mind and body feel fragile, vulnerable, like they're far from one another, in places they've never been, being held together by Malcolm's touch.

I reach for any sense I have left floating around me, but before I can pull away, his hands are gripping my face and pulling me flush against him. His lips crash into mine with a soft hunger, slow at first, then growing in intensity. Before I know it, I'm kissing him back, surrendering to the decadence of his mouth on mine. The taste of sweet mint tingles my lips, and the scruff on his face nips me in all the right places. The fragility of myself tethers to him like a lifeline, my emotions swirling around in a chaotic whirl around us.

I feel greedy, gripping at his face, his shirt, his arms. Anything I can touch, I reach for. I rake my hands through his damp hair, and his lips tremble in response. Need rushes through me, like a jolt of lightning from my head to my toes, reaching every end of me. His heart hammers in his chest against mine, his breathing rapid and uneven. His hands move from my face, down my spine, and around my waist.

I can feel the resistance in his squeeze, the urge he's fighting to pull me closer. I want him to.

Then he stops.

Pressing his forehead against mine, lips swollen and breath heaving, his eyebrows are furrowed with pain etched on his face. "I'm sorry," he breathes.

"Your head?"

He nods slowly, the motion worsening his pain. I slide over next to him and pull him to me, letting him rest his head on my chest. He lets out a sigh of relief and relaxes under my arms. I squeeze him tight against me, and he follows suit, wrapping his arm around my waist as he settles into the mattress. The pounding in my chest starts to slow.

"I'm sorry," he whispers again.

"Don't be." I run my fingers along his hairline and down his neck, and he smiles under my touch. "That was poor timing, kissing with a head injury." I laugh softly, and his smile widens.

Head injury. The stupidity of my decision to kiss him back plows its way into my brain, destroying any post-kiss elation I was feeling. He's concussed. Did I just take advantage of him? Does he realize what just happened? Will he even remember this tomorrow?

As my mind begins to spiral, Malcolm reaches up to stroke my cheek. His eyes are heavy-lidded and ready for sleep. One stroke, then he pulls back his finger, pointing at me. *Boop.*

He lets out a half-giggle with a snore following quickly after.

Yep, this was a mistake.

Chapter Twenty-Seven
Malcolm

I'm hungover.

At least, that's how it feels. The pounding in my head feels like someone is shoving my face into a wall while hitting me with a purse full of coins repeatedly. It's also what I want to do to the gentleman behind the counter.

"Alright," he says slower than what should be allowed in the human language, "you're all checked out." The receptionist hands me my receipt in slow motion. I reach to take it and miss it by a few inches, the room tilting on its axis as I do.

I can't believe I got a concussion.

"Thank you." I squeeze my eyes shut, leaving the handful of room keys on the counter. I walk away, the pounding reverberating so hard I lose balance and miss a step. I think I hear him say, *"Come again,"* but I can't be sure. I slow my steps, shuffling my boots against the tile to avoid stumbling into the giant palm leaves by the doors.

"Shotgun!" Travis yells over everyone as the valet pulls the shuttle around.

"Coaches get shotgun," Kate's soothing voice comes from my left, "especially those with head injuries." She steps to my side, grabbing my elbow. This time, I can't tell if it's my concussion or her touch buckling my knees.

"You good?" She eyes me warily, fingers leaving a trail down the back of my forearm.

I nod, the motion making me nauseated with the pain. Seeing her eases it, but not enough to keep my eyes open. I feel like I haven't seen her in days. The last thing I remember was seeing her wave from the sidelines, the stadium light shining over her like a spotlight. We've been going nonstop, trying to get to the airport this morning to fly back home, and I've barely spoken to her. In the midst of the rushed packing this morning, all she's been able to ask me about yesterday was if I remembered anything. My answer was not what she wanted to hear for some reason.

Bits and pieces of the night come and go.

Steven shining a light in my eyes.

Emma crying like she was at my funeral, which is not that uncommon in her state.

Daniels helping me to the couch.

And *Kate*. Her fingers in my hair or on my arm. I feel like I dreamt it. Her touches were so intense and focused. It didn't feel like the soothing touches of a caregiver, which is why I'm confident it was a dream. You can guess my disappointment when I woke up and she wasn't there—and I had a headache from hell.

If they could weaponize headache-inducing methods, torturing for information would be a lot less messy. And a lot less frowned upon probably.

We file onto the shuttle, and Kate ushers me into the front seat like I'm a crippled grandpa. I grumble in protest but refrain from speaking. Any motion created with my neck or jaw sends a jolt up into my eyes. I glance at the clock, 5:45 a.m., before shutting my eyes. Either everyone is wiped, or Kate has threatened them to stay quiet for my benefit. Either way, I'm grateful for the silence as we head toward the airport.

My gaze flutters open with each turn, the streets still dark with streetlamps guiding our path. No one is on the road either, and it looks abandoned compared to the past few days. No vacationers trotting down to the beach or shop-goers crowding the street corners. Most businesses aren't open, and the gaudy signs used for marketing aren't blocking the walkways yet.

We get to the airport quickly, filing off the shuttle in a haphazard fashion. The guys are half asleep, whining about having to carry their bags. The girls are rushing to get checked in so they can get to Starbucks before the line gets too long. And Kate stays at my side like my own personal care assistant. I hate it. But also, I love it. Her concern is evoking emotions in me that I don't know how to process. Is it her just being a friend? Is it just her kindness? Is it a liability thing, and Benny has instructed her to watch me? The questions roil themselves in my head, pain upticking with each thought.

I try to focus on her arm linked in mine, her hand rubbing smoothly up and down my arm. Focusing on that only worsens the pain as I'm reminded of my thwarted plans from last night.

We were supposed to talk.

But nope. I got distracted and got pummeled for it.

"Alright, everyone," Kate calls to the group, halting the girls in their tracks on the way to their iced lattes. I sit in the closest seat I can find, dropping my bag with a painful thud at my side. Sounds from all around me throb in my temples—suitcases toppling, doors opening, gate change announcements on the overhead. The sounds overtake one another, sounding more and more like gunfire. And explosions. And helicopter crashes...

I grip the armrests of my chair, my knuckles going white and palms burning from my hold, praying for another black-out episode Steven warned me about. An unnerving lump forms in the back of my throat, blocking the air I'm trying to breathe.

My chest gets tight, and my breaths are ragged. Just when I'm about to bolt for the door, Devon towers over me, handing me a set of headphones.

"They're noise-canceling." He smiles and pats me on the shoulder.

Taking the seat next to me, he helps adjust them on my head. Silence surrounds me instantly. Relief washes over me, and I focus on the movement of Kate's mouth as she talks. She hands out flight tickets and reads aloud from her phone. She drives the girls mad as they attempt to inch away. Pointing at them, she makes them come back. My lips twitch with a smile at their slumped shoulders and eye rolling. The coffee will be there in a few minutes, ladies.

Mid-discussion, something on Kate's phone draws her attention away from the conversation. Concern mars her face as she steps away to answer it. The girls use this as their moment to race to the tiny, innocent woman manning the coffee shop register. Gray eyes bulge at the stampede of messy buns and clunky slippers. I'm honestly amazed, and slightly disappointed, that none of them ate it in their scurry over. I can sense the tiny woman's overwhelm from here.

She's halfway through pouring the second drink when Kate rushes into my view, gripping me by both shoulders. Fear in her eyes.

"What's wrong?" I rip the headphones off my head, and a plethora of sounds hit me at once.

"It's Lola..."

I'm on my feet in an instant. She lets out a terrified sob into my chest. "Stay here," I say to Devon before guiding Kate toward the ticket counter. "Excuse me, ma'am?"

The woman behind the counter startles from behind her crossword puzzle. "May I—"

"Do you have any earlier flights to OKC?" I set my wallet on the counter, keeping one arm around Kate's waist, her back rising and falling rapidly as tears soak her face. I squeeze her tight and pull her into my shoulder, letting the tears soak me instead. "Please?" my voice cracks.

The attendant grasps the severity of the situation and begins to move fast on the other side of the counter. I watch as her fingers type on the keyboard rapidly, eyes scanning the screen in a blur. "Yes, we have two seats that leave in twenty minutes."

"Perfect, we'll take them." Handing her my debit card, I pull Kate's wallet out of her back pocket and hand the woman her license.

"Can you come with me?" she whispers into my shoulder, throat thick with trepidation.

"You won't go alone," I whisper back. Over her head, I wave Devon over, who's been standing watch, worry etched on his face. She's practically his lola too. When he sidles up next to me, I motion for him to hand over his ID, and the woman books their flights.

In moments, we are at the new gate with the new flight boarding its last group. Devon rushes ahead, carrying his and Kate's bags. Kate, still clinging to my side like a life raft, squeezes me against her. "What if she—"

"Shhhh, don't think like that." I wipe the tears from her cheeks and hug her into my chest. "Hurry." I give her a double squeeze on her shoulders and turn her toward the boarding door. The smile she leaves me with is both beautiful and excruciating as I see terror settle on her face. It's almost too much to bear.

A sea of people rush around me as they head to their own destinations as I watch the attendant close the bay door to the plane. I grip my jaw, feeling a lack of control when a small sob breaks through me. *Please let Lola be okay.*

The flight home is grueling. Not knowing what's going on and not being with Kate when she needs me feels a thousand times worse than my concussed headache. I welcome the nausea the turbulence causes, giving me something to focus on.

When we land, my phone pings with a message.

Benny: *Mild heart attack, they're taking her to surgery. Kate is with her.*

She can't have any more visitors until after 3 p.m. :(

Benny knew I would hightail it to the hospital the moment we landed if I could. I text Kate, letting her know we made it back, and I will be there as soon as she needs me.

I take the kids back to the school and wait until they all head home, then I lock up the supplies we brought with us and climb into my truck. The orange glistens in the late-morning sun, freshly washed. No sign of life marks its doors, no dirt or grime on the tires. It's clean and shiny and nothing like how I left it. I fear for how the inside of my house looks after letting Ellie and Benny have my key to *keep an eye on things*.

As expected, when I get home, I find everything out of place—dishes organized by color, couch cushions fluffed, and a *Welcome* mat at the front door. Why am I friends with these people? Remind me to get my key back immediately.

Five hours go by before I hear anything else about Lola. Enough time for me to pace my land a hundred times, move the chicken coop out of the sun, and weed around my tomato plants. My hands are caked with dirt when my phone rings in my front pocket.

"Lola is going to be fine," Kate says on the other line, "for now at least. I'm going to kill her when we get home."

I hear Lola arguing with someone in the background, probably the doctor, as Kate explains what happened. Lola had a minor heart attack during a fitness class—something she is forbidden to do, according to Kate and Benny, because she gets too competitive and hostile. It's clear where Kate gets her feistiness from. I bite back a laugh as Lola begins arguing with Kate.

"Do you ladies need anything?"

"You're a saint. Food and clothes would be perfect." Kate's voice sounds lighter on the other end.

"Tell him to bring me some pancit!" Lola yells in the background.

"Absolutely not! Do you know how much salt is in that?"

I listen to them bicker back and forth for a moment, letting their voices still the worry that was building in my chest. *Lola is fine*—for now, anyway. Apparently, Kate heckled the doctor to force Lola to stay in the hospital through the weekend so they can make arrangements. Babysitters, if we're being honest.

I rush around, almost forgetting to wash the dirt off my hands, as I get to Kate's place to collect her things. Something about packing the woman you love's clothes feels intimate—probably because I felt like a creep tossing certain things into a bag. Who knows what kind of coverage she's going to have, but I know there are at least five pairs.

The hospital is quiet when I get there, hallways empty and the light of day starting to fade outside the large windows. It's almost enough to soothe the ache still lingering in the back of my head. A few nurses weave up and down the hall as I make my way to Lola's room. Kate is leaning against the wall, waiting for me. Her eyes are tired and shoulders pulled down, the stress of the day all over her. But when she sees me, the spark in her eyes is back, and I feel my pathetic, sappy self inflate with hope.

I let out a sigh of relief when she wraps her arms around me, and I feel her shoulders relax with relief as I squeeze her. The bag of food I brought crinkles loudly at her back, which makes her laugh against my shoulder. "You're a lifesaver."

"Just doing my duty."

"Aye! Katherine Joy, hurry it up!" Lola yells from inside her room. Even from twenty feet away, it's loud enough to send a pulse of pain down the back of my head. Kate groans pitifully and leads me into the room. Lola is set up in bed, pillows cascading around her in a sheet of white with her blue fluffy robe draped over her tiny frame. Her speckled hair is in two knots on the top of her head. "Malcolm! My apo!" She just about jumps out of the bed to greet me, and I have to rush to her side to keep her feet from hitting the ground.

"Lola, stay," I urge her and sit on the edge of the bed. My head threatens to burst from the quick motion, but I fight it and focus on her.

"Are you here to rescue me?"

"No, he is not," Kate snips, sitting in the recliner in the corner of the room.

Lola mumbles in Tagalog under her breath, "You are not the boss of me."

"Seeing as you had a heart attack, I believe yes, I am the boss of you now. No more absurd fitness classes. No more wandering off by yourself for hours." She shoves a bite of food in her mouth. "And no more secret handyman boyfriend visits!"

"Handyman boyfriend? What are you— Katherine Stanley! Are you tracking my love life?" Lola gasps and bores her eyes into Kate over my shoulder. The look makes me shudder.

"Don't think I haven't noticed all the updates happening at your house. I know *you* aren't the one fixing the shingles on your roof." Kate talks with her mouth half full, taking another bite and wiping the corner of her mouth with a tissue. "Don't deny it!"

"Uh, Kate—"

"Don't bother." Lola rests her hand on my wrist, cutting me off.

I assumed it was obvious that I'm the one fixing up Lola's house. I wasn't looking for recognition, but the idea of Lola having a man—friend? partner? whatever a woman her age tends to have—spending their time painting and fixing leaks is absurd. I glance over my shoulder and see Kate eyeing her, a duel happening over my head. Maybe I can let her think what she wants. It's quite hilarious seeing Kate's face when she figures out how wrong she is about something.

Last year, she was confident Ross from night school was stealing her pens, seeing as he shares her classroom. She was irate one day that her favorite purple gel pen with a fuzzy cap was gone. Her treasured Secret Santa gift was now missing, and the only possible culprit was Ross, the man who carries one folder to class every evening and grades every piece of parchment with the same black pen since he started years ago. A creature of habit was surely the one who stole her prized possession, right? Wrong. It turned out, Emma's twins had been making themselves busy during their Saturday morning visits, stashing the pens, paper clips, and crayons they hijacked from the art room in the bottom desk drawer of Kate's desk—the drawer she refuses to organize. It took me all of two minutes to open it, pull out the junk, and reveal hundreds of pens sitting on the bottom. Kate's cheeks were red for hours with embarrassment.

"Exactly. Don't bother." Kate directs her attention to me. "I'll figure out who soon enough."

Our phones buzz and ding simultaneously—a group chat from the faculty.

> **EJones:** *Is Lola doing alright? - Emma*

The urge to remind Emma that she doesn't have to sign her messages is strong, but I resist. As I type a response, Benny beats me to it.

> **BDivata:** *Yes, should be released tomorrow :)*
> **KStanley:** *You say released as if she's a free woman now... WHICH SHE IS NOT*
> **EJones:** *I won't ask what that's about, then. - Emma*
> **EJones:** *Anyway! URGENT STAFF MEETING IN ONE HOUR! (Minus you, Kate. Stay with Lola) -Emma*
> **MGeer:** *I'll fill her in later.*

Glancing back at Kate, she gives me a small, grateful smile. The smile doesn't reach her cheeks. It's tired and defeated, and something in my chest constricts at the sight of it. Seeing Kate be anything but happy is enough to suffocate me from the inside out.

"Lola, I have to go. I'll come see you tomorrow." Leaning in to give her a kiss on the cheek, Lola wraps her slender arms around my shoulders and squeezes, restricting the oxygen to my damaged brain. For just having a heart attack, the woman still packs a punch.

"I'll walk you out. *You!*"—she directs an accusatory pointer finger at Lola—"Don't you move a muscle." Lola mumbles Tagalog insults under her breath as Kate leads me into the hallway. "Thank you for coming by. She loves seeing you."

"You know..." I say as we walk past the nurses' station, "I didn't come just for her." In front of the opening elevator, I turn to face her and shove my hands in my pockets.

Kate's eyes flicker to me then to the elevator, then at her shoes, the ceiling, down the hall—everywhere but me. Blowing air through her tight lips, she rests her hands on the top of her hair. Something's off.

"What's wrong?" I ask.

"Malcolm..." She halts and begins to chew on her thumbnail—the universal sign that Kate is uncomfortable. Did I make her uncomfortable with what I said? Was it that bad?

"I'm sor—"

Stopping me with a hand in the air between us, she asks, "Do you really not remember?" She drops her hand to her side, waiting. I don't know what she's referring to, and her eyes tell me I *need* to remember whatever it is. I rack my brain, desperate for an answer, but nothing. Her shoulders sink, my silence clear that I don't know what she's asking. "You don't remember what happened last night?" Her gaze hits the floor, and mine follows, her bright-pink shoes stark against the scuffed-up, cream-colored tile.

Bits and pieces of last night have slowly come back over the day: my weird remarks to Steven, me offering a job to Daniels, telling Emma she was glowing like the moon. I acted like a fool, so who knows what I said to Kate to make her so uncomfortable. I pinch the bridge of my nose and squeeze my eyes shut, the pounding in my head a dull ache compared to earlier.

Forcing myself to relive memories never goes well.

My throat tightens as painful flashes try to tear their way through my mind. The desert heat, dirt caked to my face, the weight of my gun slung over my shoulder. The dirt residue from this afternoon feels thick on my hands, seeping deep into my knuckles. I scrub them against my jeans and try to shake the crawling sensation moving up my neck at my thoughts.

"Kate, I—I'm sorry." I scratch my head aggressively, feeling the specks of dirt clinging to my skin like a heavy shadow. "I don't." My voice feels thick.

"That's alright. I just wanted to check. Hey…" She lingers, tugging on the hem of my arm sleeve. "It's fine. It's probably for the best anyway."

"What do you mean?" I look at her.

"I just mean this week was kind of crazy. You know, with seeing Eric, and your concussion…it was just a lot." Her face is stern, focused. It feels like she's looking straight through me. "I just want to make sure we're good."

I eye her, a thousand questions written on my face. She bites her thumbnail again, clearly questioning if she should continue. I'm not going anywhere until she says what she needs to.

She relents. "Malcolm, you're my best friend. And I would die if I lost that—if I lost you. I've just had a lot of time to think this past week, and I want to make sure we're good, that you and I will always stay friends, and nothing will change that." Fear and hope morph her face, the auburn tint of her eyes shifting as she focuses on me.

Stay friends. Just...friends.

It's a punch to the gut. It's a harder hit than yesterday.

My behavior led to this. The intentional flirting, the soft touches, the compliments. God, the compliments. I scared her. I tried too hard, and now I've ruined my chances.

"Right," I say, quickly pressing the down button on the elevator. It opens instantly, thank God. "Friends." Stepping in, I give Kate a wave before the doors shut between us. The fear of reality stings my eyes as I descend to the ground floor.

Embarrassment is a tricky thing. It either grazes past you, barely touching the surface, or it penetrates deep within, reaching every small space that holds you together, nearly pulverizing you down to nothing. And sometimes, it's a moment with someone who means everything to you that leaves you thinking you might never come back from it.

Lucky for me, I don't think anything crazy has happened to pulverize me yet—nothing I can remember, anyway. Now, I just have to make Kate forget everything that happened this past week so we can go back to normal. I scoff to myself as I stand outside my truck. *Normal.* The word feels heavy and disjointed. Nothing about this is normal. Things shifted this week. But if all Kate wants is to be friends, maybe that's her way of saying, *I know how you feel, but I don't feel the same.*

The pulsing in my head thumps so hard I feel dizzy. Gripping my door handle, I breathe slowly and fight off the panic trying to claw its way through my chest. I can't lose her. And I can't let my feelings scare her away.

The panic slows to a small tremble deep in my gut, and I steady myself. If all she wants is my friendship, then I will be the best damn friend she's ever had.

And maybe, over time, I will get over her.

Chapter Twenty-Eight

Kate

"Impossible," I say, throwing myself onto the couch.

"So then why are you still swiping right on these randos?" Ellie glares at me from the other end of the couch, wrapped in my fuzzy polka-dot blanket.

"I just can't risk what we have based off one kiss—especially one *concussed* kiss. He doesn't even remember it! He's already back to his usual broody self and everything."

I skim the most recent match that graces my screen.

Glen.

An accountant with a pet guinea pig and a weird collection of Russian nesting dolls. I assumed it was a photo of his grandmother's house, but he was eager to confirm that they are, indeed, his dolls. Vintage. Timeless. Dolls. With orange-painted hair and thick triangle-shaped eyebrows.

"Did I tell you about the first time Benny kissed me?" Ellie swoons dramatically as she remembers her first kiss with my cousin.

"Ugh, yes, Eleanor. You've told me many a time how perfect, and wonderful, and majestic it was," I say, a damsel-like, high-pitched emphasis to my words, "giving you these feelings you didn't even realize you could feel." I flutter my lashes and fake faint, just for her benefit. She's unamused, with her lips pursed, as she gives me an I-hate-you-sometimes face.

"Anyway..." She sits up straighter as Frankie, the disgusting naked cat my cousin loves with every fiber of his being, readjusts in her arms to present me with a rather unwelcome display of her wrinkly, bare backside. "That kiss was impossible to forget too. And it's hard to imagine having that with anyone else. Just think about this Glen guy." She waves at my phone dismissively. "How would he feel if he went to kiss you, and you're over there thinking about kissing Malcolm?"

She has a point.

But I can't worry about it. It was one kiss, and half of the participants were disoriented and a tad unhinged. The thoughts of Malcolm's playfulness and *flirting* come flooding into my mind, sending a tingle of excitement up my spine.

"I'll forget it eventually—"

"You just said it was impossible to forget."

"Ellie! Can you not recall every little detail for once? We're forgetting it happened."

"We?" she asks, offended. Knowing her, she will cling to this information like it's her source of oxygen, waiting for any moment she has to ask about it. I love her, but she's the worst little meddler that's ever existed. And she's a therapist? I feel bad for her patients.

"Yes, *we*. Now drop it."

Just when I think Ellie is going to press me again, she lets out a small sigh of defeat and strokes the feline in her lap. "Let's watch something."

The first commercial shows a group of girls skipping down the street—probably an advertisement for some beverage or tampon. One of the girls is wearing a miniature veil in her hair and a white sash that says *Miss to Mrs.* in silver glitter. The girls with her are all wearing different colored wigs, snapping photos of the bride-to-be doing a plethora of poses by the traffic light. My gut twists at the sight, the sheer joy she must be feeling as her big day approaches.

The pit of loneliness starts to stretch in my stomach, emptying me out from head to toe, physical effects of *bleh* washing over me as the commercial fades.

I have no idea what's wrong with me. For years, I was content with where I was at in life. The desire to be with someone was so far out of my mind I was starting to think it would never come back to focus, and I was fine with that. But then, like the flip of a switch, everything changed. Watching my friends get engaged was my undoing.

The universe clearly wants me to avoid this downward spiral by redirecting my attention to a slew of faculty messages, all revolving around the biggest event of the term…prom. Emma has been on a scary level of party planner lately. Maybe it's the pregnancy hormones. Instead of nesting, she's planning. Ellie groans as she reads through the list of messages from her side of the couch. We don't speak of the tyrant Emma has been lately. It's an unspoken fact that she's been a tad exhausting.

EJones: *Decorating starts tomorrow!!! One week, people!! - Emma*

She has had four "urgent faculty meetings" since last week, all revolving around prom.

Ugh, *prom.*

Every year, we're required to stand around in a humid gymnasium, guarding the punch bowls, watching the bathrooms, and separating the grinding Neanderthals from one another in the middle of the dance floor. I once called it our final battle of the year. Teachers versus students. Malcolm just balked at me the first year, telling me I didn't know how to be intimidating. Let's just say he was painfully surprised at the work we put in to keep the kids sober and abstinent the entire night.

After an evening full of rom-coms and wedding planning, I head to Lola's so I can relieve her sitter. Helping plan Ellie's wedding has been a mixed bag of emotions, adding in her constant, *"We don't have to do this,"* interruptions, and I am spent. My duty as a bridesmaid is to help, even if it threatens to swallow me whole in the process. It comes with the territory.

I pull up to Lola's house just as Malcolm is taking out the trash. He gives a small nod before pinning his eyes to the ground. "How was wedding planning?" he asks as he beelines for his truck, not giving any indication that he really wants to hear how it went.

"It, uh…went well." I stand in the middle of the yard. "How was Lola?"

Looking over the roof of his truck, he laughs. "She kept asking me to take her to the casino. I compromised and let her beat me at blackjack." His laugh is short, restricted, like he's restraining himself around me. The thought of Malcolm not being himself around me sends a sharp pain down into my stomach. He's felt so far away since we got back from camp, and that was the exact opposite of what I wanted. I just wanted things to go back to the way they were, where he was my best friend, the person I shared everything with and went to for pity parties over shared tubs of coconut ice cream. These last few days have sucked. Lola's health, being back in class, and now this weird, stand-offish interaction has been enough to send me crawling to the nearest grocery store to empty out their supply.

I grip my elbows, the distance from him feeling almost unbearable, and hug myself. The loneliness ignites in my chest even more as he forces himself to keep from looking at me. "Well, thank you. For everything." I ignore the stinging in my eyes and force a smile.

"Always."

I watch him climb into his truck, giving me a small wave before he pulls out of the drive. Dirt stirs up around his tires, leaving a cloudy trail behind.

Tears are streaming down my face before he's fully out of sight. The distance he's left in his truck feels more than just physical. I think it's safe to say I've done what I didn't want to do and made things weird with Malcolm. A small breeze tickles my ear as I stand on the front porch, staring into the darkness, a quiet whisper of, *"Don't lose him."*

Blaming him for kissing me in such a way that I can't think straight might seem like the obvious choice, but the concussion speaks for itself. He doesn't even remember it. He doesn't remember the feeling of his lips on mine, and he probably never will. But I do, and that's the issue. That kiss is burned into my brain, obliterating everything in its path. I can't let something like this come between us. I won't let it. So, I have to backtrack and make things right before I lose my best friend.

Over a kiss.

An impossible-to-forget kiss.

"Alright, people! We have five days, and this place looks horrendous!" Emma projects across the gymnasium floor with her hands on her hips, stewing over our lackluster attempt at decorating. The theme is *A Night Books Are Written About*—a theme I'm still trying to wrap my head around as I glue old book pages to the inside of vintage picture frames.

"So, this theme…" I trail off, trying desperately to rid myself of the glue residue that encases my fingers. "What does it mean?"

Emma scoffs at me. Not just a light scoff, but a forceful, how-dare-you-not-get-it type of exhale that has me wishing I had kept my mouth shut. "Books are tangible representations of life, and love, and stories you dream of." She waves her arms overhead, as though giving a world-changing speech, and I wince in regret even more. Emma on an artistic, life-is-better-with-art tangent is my least favorite version of her. She gets very pompous, and it takes her a long time to come back to Earth. "Books are art in the simplest of forms," she continues, "speaking to us in a thousand different ways. You know George R.R. Martin said he has lived a thousand lives because—"

"He reads," we all say in a monotone unison before she can finish.

She jabs a finger in the air at us individually—first at Benny on top of the eight-foot ladder, weaving string lights around the basketball hoop, then at Ellie who is knee deep in glitter and hot glue, then at me with my plastered page fingers, and then behind me.

"Don't shove that finger at me. I just got here," Malcolm grumbles.

I turn and see him carrying a giant wooden sign—probably something Emma forced him to make by hand—as he sets it down and presents it to our dictator.

It's a huge carved, wooden sign, standing just a few inches taller than him, painted cream with intricate vines and small books engraved around the border, with the words *Glendale Prom 2024* in deep red painted script at the top. It's beautiful.

Emma gasps and clasps her hands at her chest, then sniffles, "It's perfect." Her tyrant aura fades as she gives Malcolm a hug, easing the tension in all of us. He winces at the affection, trying to avoid colliding with her growing belly before conceding and hugging her back. I catch his eyes for a moment, the icy blue warms at me for a moment before freezing over again.

Don't lose him.

It's probably just me overthinking, but this whole going-back-to-normal thing is starting to feel less and less friendly than before. Maybe I became so engrossed in his closeness that anything besides that is jarring. Or maybe it's the fact that I can't get the thought of his lips out of my head. Or his hands. Or his scruffy jaw rubbing against my cheek.

I press my fingers to my pulse point, the beat erratic and bounding, as I watch the corners of his lips twitch up in conversation as he focuses on Emma and not me. Why is this bothering me so much? He's allowed to have friends other than me. He's allowed to talk to other people and not immediately come up to me. *Get over yourself, Katherine.*

"Dude, it looks so good!" Benny says, climbing down from the ladder.

Malcolm nods. "Well, I still have to finish the banners—"

"I thought I was in charge of the banners?" Ellie asks from the floor, insult pinching her eyebrows.

"Well..." Emma gnaws on her lip. "His are back-ups. In case yours..." She trails off as she gestures to the unsightly crinkled banner at Ellie's knees. The letters are different sizes and off center, angling toward the corner. A huge blob of glitter from where she dropped the bottle earlier has now been turned into a lumpy moon, with a Sharpie border encircling it.

She gazes up at all of us. "Is it bad?" I have to bite my lip to keep from giggling at the sincerity in her voice.

"It's beautiful, babe," Benny says, rubbing her back. "We will definitely use it, won't we?" He eyes Emma and me for support. I look away. His puppy-dog eyes are unbearable sometimes.

"We. Will. Use. It." Emma says through gritted teeth.

"Maybe in the bathroom," Malcolm mumbles quietly to me.

The response is startling. I look around to see if anyone else heard him or if it was really just for my ears only. I turn to face him and watch as his smile deepens before he gives me a wink and focuses on the banner at our feet. The glitter reflects the sunlight and shimmers under us, accentuating the silver in his eyes.

"Hi," I breathe. I feel my heart hammer in my chest as his smile widens, his perfect teeth on display.

"Hey," he whispers softly, still eyeing the banner.

I've missed you. It's all I can think and all I want to say. Even standing a foot away from him, he feels so far away. He scratches his jaw, and it sends a jolt through me, the memory of that scruff rubbing against my face and neck plowing through my mind with force. It threatens to throw me into hysterics right here in the middle of the gym. I can't deny that I want to kiss him again, that I can't stop thinking about it. But I'd be kissing my best friend. A man older than me, a man with a different life than me, and different interests. I can't imagine Malcolm wanting to be with someone like me. A girl so flippant and erratic at times. A girl who can't commit to a paint color in her kitchen because her mood changes like the seasons. I have eight different colored brush strokes in the center of my island, welcoming guests. Malcolm has one color throughout his entire house—white.

"Where is your brain at right now?" he whispers to me, leaning so close that his minty coffee breath tingles the corners of my mouth. I blink away from his lips and watch him rake his fingers through his tousled hair. "Do you need some food?"

My stomach growls in response.

"Come on, let's get out of here." He tugs on the hem of my shirt.

I feel elated for the chance to spend time together, hope swelling inside me at the chance to make things right. We can get back to normal. Maybe we just need more time—pending the universe ridding me of the lingering memory of his tongue gliding over mine, of course.

That's all we need. Time. Time to get back to the way things were, hanging out like the pals we are.

Just the two of us.

"We'll join you!" Benny says.

Or not.

Chapter Twenty-Nine

Malcolm

"Henders, if I see you put gum on the underside of your desk again, I will make you eat the pieces that have been there for the last thirty years." Charlie halts the gum sticking then quickly rushes to the trash and tosses it.

"Good choice. Five more minutes, then we move on to statistical equations."

The class groans in misery, which is oddly motivating to me.

"Mr. Geer, can we end early today?" Birdie asks behind the screen of her cell phone. She finished the pop quiz first and proceeded to pull out the device and scroll. It would usually drive me nuts, but she's my top student. And she graduates in a month, so my tank for caring is just about empty.

"And why would we do that, Ms. Wilson?"

Setting the phone down, she levels me with a look of contempt. "Prom is in three days, sir. Some of us have very important responsibilities to focus on."

"More important than statistical equations and probability fractions?"

The look of disgust on her face answers my question.

I check the time. With only fifteen minutes left in class, what's the harm in them leaving early? It's not like I'll be reprimanded by my boss. Benny is currently drowning in prom nonsense. I'm sure he'd be more than happy to hear I let these rascals out early to tackle the never-ending to-do list Emma and Birdie seem to be creating together.

"What do the rest of you think?" I ask the class, half of them nodding in agreement and the other half shrugging like they don't care. Typical response. "Fine," I concede to the request. "Finish your quizzes, then get out of here."

My school year always ends up this way—lack of interest or ambition, from me and my students. I get it. It's been a long year, and with my B average overall, I should be pleased with how it's all turned out. But this year has been a whirlwind, especially the last few weeks. I'm usually really good at keeping my work and home life separate, keeping my feelings under lock and key. It's my specialty. But clearly, I have been doing a piss-poor job as of late, because my work life and home life have a rather addicting common denominator.

And that denominator has somehow grown infinitely. As hard as I try, everything is bleeding together, and I can't stop myself from thinking about her all the damn time. I come to work thinking about Kate. I go home thinking about Kate. I fall asleep and dream about Kate. I dream about holding her, kissing her, being with her.

Just last night, I had a dream that we went to prom together and kissed. It felt so real, almost like deja vu. The feel of her skin against mine, her soft lips caressing my neck and jaw, was exhilarating and familiar. I woke up frantically searching for her in my empty bed. Again, piss poor at keeping things in check.

As the kids rush out of the classroom, I can't help but think about my life before Glendale. It was perfectly quiet and peaceful. Being alone was my favorite thing. But the people here seem to have ruined me. They've ruined my quiet, lone-wolf life, making me desire their company like the annoying good people they are.

My phone buzzes as I journey out into the hall, dodging groups of kids shuffling by, most of whom are looking at their phones and not where they're walking.

Benny: *See you in 15! :)*

The text is followed by a GIF of three men dancing around in tuxedos.

Yep, we're shopping for tuxedos today. Apparently, this is prime time to buy with prom-season sales. A bone-chilling cold seeps into my skin, leaving me feeling on edge as I make my way through the sea of people.

"Coach! Coach Geer!" Sarah Kim waves at me over the other kids' heads as she timidly pushes her way around her classmates. No one budges to let her by.

Knowing this will take forever, I sigh and turn toward her. The blockade of bodies splits like the Red Sea when I approach. I hate admitting how much I enjoy the impact I have on these kids. One look from me and mouths shut. Change in my direction, and entire bodies shift or disappear completely.

The seas have parted when I reach Sarah, her head covered with what could only be described as cat ears. But they aren't regular cat ears you see at Halloween. They have feathers on them and some sort of spiky attachments down the band. I force my eyes away from the atrocity. "Yes, Ms. Kim?"

"I need your help!" Her eyes are bugging out of her skull, darting in every direction as we make our way down the hall.

"With?"

She halts and faces me. Her neck and cheeks go bright red as she glances around. Leaning in to whisper, she says, "With my prom dress."

"Nope." Absolutely not. I turn on my heel and speed away. There is no way in hell I'm partaking in any extra prom activities. I've done enough. I don't even want to go to this stupid thing. Last night at Wafflin', we ended up reliving our prom memories, and I had to endure telling my traumatizing memory—how Tracy Dilbeck agreed to be my date and then ditched me after two songs to make out with Georgie Hall. Then, she had the audacity to ask me for a ride home when Georgie decided he wanted to take Piper Holmes to the after-party and not her. It was the most humiliating night of my transformative years—more humiliating than when I tried frosted tips.

"Please, Coach!" Sarah pleads, tailing me into the break room. "Benny said you guys would be there today, and my mom won't be back in time!"

Ellie, who is working tirelessly on the prom banners that will never see the light of day, looks up from the center of the break room, eyes filled with concern. "What's going on?"

"Mr. Geer won't help me!" Sarah points an accusatory finger at me and pouts. Ellie shoots a deadly gaze in my direction. I know Sarah is her favorite student, no matter how much she denies it. Sarah gives me a disgruntled sigh and bats her sad lashes at Ellie, which makes Ellie cross her arms at me like I'm some kind of delinquent.

Thanks a lot, kid.

"Why won't you help her?" Ellie asks, a twinkle of manipulation in her eyes as she waits for my response. I know this song and dance too well. She'll ask me a thousand questions, cornering me into a self-reflective whirlpool, then I'll start to drown in my defenses, swirling around and around in my head until I realize she's right and I'm wrong, succumbing to her advice, letting her reach out her metaphorical hand, and taking it before I die on the wrong hill. Which doesn't make sense, I know. How could there be a whirlpool on top of a hill?

I don't know. I just know that Ellie is too damn good at her job, and I hate it.

And I can already see what's about to happen. Somehow, someway, Ellie is going to convince me that helping Sarah is a normal aspect of my job description, and I should accept it. So, instead of answering her question and risking that, I back away from the pile of glitter and glue at our feet and head toward the door.

"Mr. Geer," Ellie snaps, trying to draw me back in.

Stay strong, Malcolm. Do not let this woman and her guilt-ridden eyes suck you back in. You are a man. A man with principles. And those principles will not waver over some teenager drama.

I make it to the doorway, my boot halfway into the hall, when she says again, "Mr. Geer," more pointedly this time.

"No, dammit. I will not help her with her prom dress issue. There is a line I will not cross, Ms. Bailey, and that line is made up of thread and tulle." I hate myself for knowing what tulle is.

"Oh." Ellie's arms drop to her sides, realization moving across her face. Ha, I won. I beat that little minx. "Sarah…" She turns toward her, face filled with solemn understanding. "How about I help you with your dress?"

"No, *he* has to!" She points in my direction. I take another step out into the hall. They're like bears. If I back away slowly, I won't get attacked.

"Can you tell me why Mr. Geer has to be the one to help you?"

"Because!" Sarah groans, covering her face with her hands, cat ears toppling forward slightly. She speaks into her hands when she says, "Because he was a football player, which means he knows what football players like." Her words come out high-pitched and whiney, which grates me even more. I have to get out of here.

"Oh boy." Ellie looks at me sympathetically, eyebrows arching skyward as if to tell me I should consider helping her.

"Please don't make me," I whisper pathetically.

"Hi!" Kate startles me, walking up to me in the hallway. "Whatcha doin'?"

"I'm getting bombarded by these two, that's what!" I am now the one pointing accusatory fingers with both hands, like it's a stick-up in an old western.

"Mr. Geer has been requested to assist Sarah Kim with a prom task," Ellie sing-songs, as if this entire situation is a normal occurrence for an almost forty-year-old.

"Of course he'll help you, Sarah!" Kate sing-songs right back, hugging my arm as unrelenting pride sparks in her eyes at me. "What do you need?" Kate directs her attention back to Sarah with her arms still wrapped around mine like a koala bear clinging to its branch.

"I need help deciding what dress to wear."

"Oh..." Kate's shock loosens her grip, hands sliding down and away from my arm. She looks at me warily, and I give her a confirming nod. Yep, that's what you just signed me up for. "Well, that's, um...maybe that isn't—"

"You just said he could help!" Sarah's defiance shakes the cat ears again, this time the other direction, and they just about slide off her head and hit the floor.

"I— I did," Kate stutters.

"And Benny—er, Principal Divata, whatever"—she corrects herself with a half-hearted wave—"said you were already going to be there today anyway, so it's not like it's an inconvenience!"

"You have a point," Kate whispers contemplatively.

"Great! So I'll meet you there!" Sarah skips toward the door, clearly proud of herself for winning this little battle.

"Way to go," I grumble through the side of my mouth.

"We can both help you." Kate's prideful tone is back, brassier than ever. She beams at me, as if she has found the perfect solution. I can't help but smile at the happy in her eyes, even at the cost of myself. "Right?" she asks me. Her eyes are so full of hope it practically guts me.

They all stare at me. Waiting. Motionless. I still have a chance to bolt for the door. Run for the hills. Hell, I could run into the trees behind the football field and let Mother Nature take me. My boot squeaks on the tile floor as I shift my body, and Kate's eyes bore deeper into me, the hope slowly turning into desperation.

God help me. "I guess we're going dress shopping."

The girls squeal in excitement, and I wish the Earth would split in two and swallow me whole this very moment.

***

"Why did you drag me into this?" I grumble in Kate's ear. She's scouring the racks, dresses slung over her arms and a pair of shoes in one hand. Her dark curls are pulled up into a half braid, small wispy pieces grazing her bare neck. I haven't been this close to her in almost two weeks. Keeping my distance has been excruciating, worse than when I had to swim ten miles with a fifty-pound rucksack on my person.

Kate laughs at my misery, eyes dancing with delight at the current situation. "You can't deny that this might be more fun than trying on tuxedos."

"The jury is still out."

I glance up from the racks of dresses to the other side of the store where Benny is being measured. The last time I went tuxedo shopping was nine years ago.

For Brennan's wedding.

A rigid tightness crawls up my neck and into my jaw as the memory of the one he wore that day flood my mind, blending with the haunting image of him lying in his casket, wearing that same black tuxedo. My chest tightens, heat rising in my throat as I try to blink away the scene and focus on the sparkles and tulle in my hands.

"All you have to do is give a thumbs up or down," Kate interrupts my thoughts, her voice pulling me back to the present. "Give your honest opinion, and it'll be over before you know it!" She plucks another dress off the rack—a purple one with lace on the shoulders—and adds it to the growing pile. Hideous.

"That means I have to actually *look*." The idea sends a crawling feeling down my back, and I have to shake it off, knocking one of the dresses off a hanger.

Kate rolls her lips. They tremble in the corners under the resistance, but a small bubble of a laugh slips through. "Just follow my lead. Look at me the entire time." She waves these instructions off, completely unaware of how often I already do that. I wonder if she'll ever be aware of how often I look at her. How often my eyes are drawn to her like magnets.

I'm constantly amazed at the things she's never noticed.

She slips away with the pile of dresses, and I'm left alone in the clearance aisle, a plethora of prom hopefuls scouring the options around me. Fluff, puff, and glitter threaten to suffocate me as I find my way to our reserved booth. Yes, there are designated seating areas we have to *book ahead of time* in a place like this. A specified selection of chairs faces a mirror in the center of the store. My hope for subtlety on being here goes straight out the window when I see myself in said mirror. Linen button-up, scuffed work boots, and my Glendale baseball cap are an eyesore compared to the peppy moms and grannies accompanying their teenagers. Aside from Benny, I'm the only male in this place, except for Sebastian, who works here and is currently telling Sarah that orange is *not* her color.

The girls make their way to the seating area, flute glasses filled with cider in hand. I would know because I've downed five of them sitting here.

"Alright, ladies. Let's get this thing started!" Sebastian booms from the back, clapping his hands and gesturing Sarah to the room behind the mirror. I slouch down into the cushioned chair I'm currently residing in and lean my head against the back. Sebastian hovers over me with a tape measure draped around his neck and a pencil behind his ear. "Are you having fun?"

"A blast," I say, closing my eyes as he gives me a twitchy smirk.

"It'll be over before you know it," Kate whispers from my right. "She's going to pick the purple one."

I moan into my hands, sliding even farther down until the chair tips my hat off my head, blocking my eyes. This is perfect, actually. I'll just stay right here.

I hear a small gasp leave Kate and the rustling of movement in front of me. Peeking through a hole in my hat, I see Sarah glide out of the dressing room wearing a green number with puffy sleeves. It's almost as bad as the purple one. I glance over to Kate, who is giving it a thumbs up, a giddy smile stretched across her face.

She looks over at me expectantly, thumb still raised. Sarah is preoccupied with assessing the back of the dress when I finally sit up. I readjust my hat to see more clearly and confirm my original thoughts. Awful. It's so awful I wouldn't bury my worst enemy in it. The material is shiny, the sleeves are almost as big as her head, and there's a huge bow in the back, drawing a little too much attention to that specific area. Sarah's not my kid, and I don't have any feelings about what she does and doesn't wear out in the world, but I do respect her enough as a young lady to be honest.

"It's awful." I give a thumbs down.

"Malcolm." Kate scoffs at me, her smile changing from joy to horror, her cheeks screaming for relief the longer she holds it in place.

"I'm not gonna lie to the kid. Sarah, it's bad."

"Thank goodness, because I hate it." Sarah rushes off behind the partition.

Kate gapes at me, a mixture of impressed and confused distorting her features. "How did..." She trails off, turning to face the mirror again. I watch as she ponders, her nose wiggling side to side when she does. You can confirm Kate is in deep thought by one of two things: wiggling her nose or sticking out her tongue to one side. Both are adorable to witness but impossible to take seriously. I watch as her nose slowly stops moving, her gaze shifting back to me. "Is there anything you can't do?"

The question catches me off guard. How I left that impression with a dress vote is beyond me. I chuckle and scratch my jaw with both hands. "I don't know what you mean."

"Oh, come on." She sighs. "There isn't anything you can't do, Malcolm! For heaven's sake, you hand-carved a massive prom sign in less than a week!"

"I just had a lot of time on my hands," I say softly, hoping it doesn't come across as a jab. The truth is, I agreed to do it to keep myself busy. Going from spending almost every moment with Kate before camp then coming back and barely seeing her has been eating me alive. My hands were burning at the sight of her, longing to touch her. Hold her. Kiss her until my vision went hazy. I had to do something to get rid of the pent-up energy.

"Ah, I see." I can sense by her tone that she knows exactly what I mean by the extra time. Unease settles on her face, pulling her lips and eyebrows down slightly. "Regardless, you're a man of many talents."

"Thank you." I attempt a wink at her, but she's back to focusing on the mirror, her fingers tracing a line around her lips. She's lost in thought again, and I desperately want to know what she's thinking.

Sarah comes out in the purple dress, and Kate perks up, her feet tapping with excitement. I stand corrected. It's not as bad as the puke-green one. But it's not great either. It looks like something a mother would wear to a wedding. The lace sleeves poke out in the corners, making her look much wider than she really is.

"Well?" Sarah asks, holding her breath.

Kate goes to throw a thumbs up then resists, looking to me for confirmation. Of course this entire situation has turned into me being the deciding vote. Somebody kill me now. I shake my head once, hoping that's finality enough for this decision. But with Kate, I should stop assuming she will do what I expect, especially when she turns to face me, trying her hardest to speak to me telepathically, based on her creepy eyebrow movement.

"Just say it," Sarah groans, watching us through the mirror.

"I think it's ugly," I say.

Kate throws her head in her hands and groans my name. "Malcolm!"

I have to clench the arms of my chair to keep from jumping toward her. The sound of her muffled voice groaning my name sends a deep sensation throughout my body, coursing through my veins like its own blood supply.

"You have to be nice," she reprimands me through a forced smile.

"No, no. This is what I need. Thank you, Coach!" She steps off the tiny pedestal, the Barney tail of a dress rustling as she walks back to her dressing room.

"I am being nice," I say when Sarah is out of sight. "Honesty is nice. No one likes a liar."

"Are you calling me a liar?"

A chuckle builds in my chest as Kate's cheeks burn with fury. "Of course not. I'm just saying honesty is the best policy." I shrug and fill my tiny glass with more cider.

"Yeah...it is." Kate disappears into her thoughts again, staring blankly at the glass in my hand. I wish I could know what's going on in that head of hers, but she doesn't want that with me. And it's probably better if I just ignore it, even if it fills my stomach with acid. The potential for an ulcer is high the more I dwell on anything Kate-related.

She pulls her phone out, giggling at the screen. Knowing my luck, it's another online dater delivering some pathetic one-liner. I down the cider and fill my glass again like it's alcohol, but really, it's straight sugar.

"Are you honest with me?"

I choke on the cider at her question then clear my throat twice to get words out. "What?"

"Are you always honest with me?" she asks sternly, raising an eyebrow in suspicion. I'm no genius, but I know Kate Stanley, and I know when she has a motive. Her face goes rigid as she focuses on the inevitable result she's waiting for, shoulders tense and jaw ticking. I catalog each body part's movements, confirming my own suspicions.

I scratch my head and reposition my hat before resting my hands on my chest. "No. I'm not."

The gasp that leaves her body is enough to fill a thousand balloons. I smirk at her and give a light shrug. Of course I'm not always honest with her. When she asks if I like her movie choice when it's about lovesick vampires, or if I want to help with a classroom project instead of going home on time, or even when she asks if I'd rather go with her to that new vegan restaurant downtown than eat the steak I have marinating at home, I'm not honest. She asks, thinking it's the activity that will sway me, but really, it's just the chance for more time with her. Technically, it's lying, but I'd rather make the choice that I know makes her happy than indulge myself. Why miss out on watching her smile slowly grow into a cheek-stinging grin from sheer joy when I can easily just cook the steak another time?

"So, you're a liar, then?" She crosses her arms with no intention of letting the topic go.

"No, I'm not. I'm just saying that I'm not always honest."

She gives a humph in response to this, throwing her shoulders back into the chair—eyebrows pinched in the center, jaw clenching, feet bouncing up and down rapidly—a tiny tantrum fighting to break through. I've seen a few of them. The worst one was when someone ate the last everything bagel the morning after she finished her carb fast. The poor girl was miserable for two weeks, eating nothing but salad and tofu. I thought she might waste away at any moment. So, when she was told Margaret brought fresh bagels, she half sprinted down the hall in heels to get to them. Devastation and horror ripped across her face as she tore through the bags to find there was only plain wheat bagels left.

"Are you always honest with me?" I ask her.

"Yes!"

"Really?" I rest my chin in my hand and eye her, well aware that's not true. No one is completely honest, no matter how hard they try to be. There are just things in life that are better left unsaid. If the truth isn't beneficial or edifying, it's unnecessary to share it. Simple as that. "So, last month, when I asked if you wanted to go with me to an outdoor expo, and you said, and I quote, 'That sounds so fun. I'd love to,' you were being honest?"

She gapes at me, her right thumb twitching as it rests on her arm. Pink moves across her cheeks, and her eyes slowly move into a squint at the realization that she's been checkmated.

She stays silent, so I ask, "Why are you asking, anyway?"

Kate doesn't answer as she looks straight ahead, crossing her arms deeper across her chest. Sarah comes out in a black dress that is more subtle than the rest, and I feel proud of the direction she's going—until she pulls out hot-pink leopard-print gloves to pair with it. Kate sits up straighter, eagerness moving up her spine as she gives Sarah a soft clap.

Sarah looks at me through the mirror, a pleading look on her face. "Better," I say. "Are the gloves necessary?"

"The gloves are adorable!" Kate interjects. "They're fun, and they fit her personality!"

"Yeah." Sarah crosses her arms at me. "I like them."

"Well, you don't need any man's approval, especially mine. So, if that's what you want to wear..." I rein it in, letting my words trail off. It hits me then how fatherly I sound, and that was far from my intention when agreeing to this. Sarah twirls in front of the mirror as Kate jumps up to take photos for her. "Let's send some to your mom!"

"Who are you going with, anyway?" That fatherly feeling gnaws at me a tiny bit more. For some reason, I need to know who her date is.

Sarah hesitates, posing for another photo, mouth opening and closing as she twiddles with the gloves. Kate lowers her phone slowly, no longer taking pictures. Sarah's face goes ghost white as realization washes over all of us.

"Are you going with Ethan?" Kate asks, wincing, like the answer will physically pain her.

Sarah doesn't respond.

That's answer enough for me. "Well," I say, pushing up from the armrest of the chair, "in that case, you need something with sleeves and a turtleneck."

Kate giggles, while Sarah puts her hands on her hips. "I can handle myself, thank you."

"I'm just saying"—I toss my hands up in surrender—"the kid has a mind of his own."

"I'll have you know"—Sarah whips around to face me—"Ethan can be very kind! He has been nothing but a gentleman to me and has respected my wishes." She starts to ramp up, jabbing her gloved thumb into her chest. "Anytime I've asked him to slow down, he has! And when we ki—"

"Nope. La la la. I don't need to hear it." I shove my hands over my ears. I see Benny's reflection behind me as he waves me over to him. Thank God. I turn to him, throwing my arms over his shoulders and whispering, "My hero."

"I tried to hurry." He chuckles.

"You're weak, Geer." Kate rolls her eyes, slouching back into her chair and topping off her cider.

"Ah, hush, this takes precedence." I wave her off and focus back on Sarah. "Stick with black, red, or white. Animal prints or animal ears are fine in moderation. You want to be yourself, yes, but you still want to look classy, right?" I wave a hand at her for understanding, and she nods. "Good, now don't ever ask me for a favor again."

"So bossy." Kate giggles after downing her drink, a bit of a haze in her voice. Maybe the sugary drink does have an effect.

"Now, let's continue on with this tortuous day." I redirect to Benny.

"It won't be that bad," he says, draping an arm over my shoulder.

"We'll see about that."

Benny guides me over to the tailor, and they begin discussing colors and fabrics. Their voices fade into a soft muffled sound as I continue watching Kate fluff Sarah's dress and hair for another picture. It's little glimpses of Kate's goodness that tighten the grip she has on my heart. Her generosity, her joy, even her tiny tantrums. I want all of it, and something tells me she does too, but I need to be sure. Figuring out what Kate wants has always been a challenge—one I accept regardless of the outcome—but I can't with this. I can't spook her with my own feelings.

"What do you think?" Benny asks.

"Hmm?" I tear my gaze away from Kate and try to recall the words he just spoke.

"You'll be honest if you hate it?"

"Yeah, yeah, sure."

"Full honesty, man. That's all I need." Benny pats me on the back and disappears into the row of coats.

Like a moth to a flame, my eyes trail back to Kate as the girls gather their things and head to the checkout counter. Kate glances back over her shoulder and freezes in her tracks. Turning to fully face me, she waves eagerly, and her smile broadens, like the time she watched the sun set over the Grand Canyon for the first time—an expression full of joy and wonder.

A flicker of something passes between us, and it's the tiniest bit of confirmation I need to move forward and get my girl.

Full honesty.

Chapter Thirty

Kate

"So, you're saying when we eat cheese"—Claire's face twists with disgust—"we're eating fungus?" The class cringes at her question.

"I'm saying," I start as I shut my textbook, officially giving up for the day, "that cheese is produced through fungal and bacterial activity."

"Bacteria?" Tess whines.

I rub my temples and reassure the class. "It's just how cheese is made, you guys."

"No wonder you're vegan," Claire remarks, shaking her shoulders as if the conversation has physically accosted her.

"What about meat, then?" Travis shoots his hand up. I guess we might as well stay on this topic. I check my watch, praying the universe speeds up time. "Does it have bacteria?"

"It could, but it shouldn't be eaten if it does."

"What if it was roasted on a spit?"

"Dude, let it go." Devon tosses a pen cap at Travis's head.

"I can't! I'll probably never get a chance again!" Travis groans, attempting to throw his pop quiz paper at Devon. It flutters slowly to the floor between them.

"What are you—"

"Travis is just pissy he didn't get to see a pig roast at camp," Ethan murmurs from the back.

"Oh, why?" The class ignores my question, making themselves busy with their pen and paper. Whenever any of them are in cahoots about something, they do a terrible job at hiding it. Last fall, they really thought their plans to crash the school board meeting for Ellie and Benny would go unnoticed. Secret meetings in the chemistry lab were my first sign that something was up—most of these kids never set foot in that area.

Silence fills the room, so I ask the looming question, "What happened to the pig roast?"

The bell rings, and a wave of relief washes over their faces as they gather their things.

"No homework this weekend, but please have your final presentation topics chosen by next week. We will work in groups." My words are directed at an empty class as the students rush out as fast as humanly possible.

Tidying up my desk, I check my phone and see a notification from Derek, my newest online buddy. It feels weird calling him that, but there's no other way to put it. This online dating situation has flooded my inbox with so many options I can't fully wrap my head around it. So, in an attempt to sidestep the gnawing feeling of desperation that likes to make itself known anytime I scope the selection pool, I have elected to call them online buddies—people I'm getting to know, feeling out, with very open-handed expectations. A kind of judgment-free zone I've created for myself. It's made it more enjoyable these last couple of weeks. The less pressure surrounding this venture, the better. I'm pretty sure I already have everyone and their dog judging me. I don't need to judge myself too.

> **DerekL123:** Hey! Are we still on for today?

A smile creeps across my face as I respond with an eager yes. Derek has been the best of the bunch lately, very much wedding-date material—which, I will admit, has become a driving force for speeding this process along. Up until recently, it had nothing to do with Ellie and Benny's upcoming nuptials, but when Ellie reminded me that we have six months until the altar, I started to panic. Swiping right on every option with a full set of teeth was step one. Now I have to establish a relationship with someone and get to a comfortable place where asking them to be my date to the wedding isn't alarming.

Derek is an electrician, currently in school to get his MBA, with hopes to own and operate his own business one day. He has zero pets, zero dolls, and, so far, zero red flags. A perfectly harmless option.

I make my way down the hall to drop off some forms Emma asked me to handle before prom, noting the slew of prom-esque decorations lining the halls. Students have taken it upon themselves to decorate their lockers with memorabilia dedicated to their favorite literary works. I doubted the hype Emma's prom theme idea would get, but I am pleasantly surprised at how wrong I was. A few lockers have dedications to Jane Austen and Julia Quinn, while others have bats and faeries covering every inch of their locker door. I'm not sure what those are referencing, but they're all very warm and cozy in their own right. The ceiling is covered in twinkly lights weaved around vine plants, with book pages hanging by thread like they're floating.

The twinkle lights aren't lit yet, but I can already tell it will look magical in here come Friday night.

"What do you mean you can't get it done in two days?" Emma's snappy words travel out of the break room and into the hall.

I approach slowly and quietly, taking in the scene. Emma paces back and forth on the phone while Ellie and Benny watch her from the table with *another* banner attempt underway. Emma has vetoed four of Ellie's banners already. I wish she would just let it go. Margaret sits in the recliner, knitting a rather large sweater? Or hat? Something with a collar and three legs. Malcolm leans against the refrigerator, sipping his coffee and gazing out the large window. I sidle up next to him, doing my due diligence to avoid eye contact with Emma in her current state.

"What's going on?" I whisper, drawing Malcolm's attention away from the window.

"Something about an ice sculpture," he says into his mug, taking another sip.

Of course it is. Leave it to Emma to come up with these ridiculous plans days before the event. Who in their right mind can get an ice sculpture ready and delivered in less than forty-eight hours?

"I recommended a giant teddy bear instead, but she didn't appreciate that." Malcolm smirks, his piercing blue eyes lingering on my face. I can feel his eyes, like a gentle caress down to my pulse point, and I can feel myself longing for it.

Another reason to sludge through the online dating pool.

I can't keep getting sucked into these moments, making them more than what they are. Malcolm is my friend, that's it. His concussion was a fluke, affecting my brain more than his, contorting our friendly interactions and making them into something they aren't meant to be. And he still has no idea that we *kissed*. That his lips collided into mine like that was what they were created to do. My knees buckle next to him at the memory, and I have to cling to his elbow for support, jostling his coffee cup—*my* coffee cup—Hilda's face getting splashed with the strong stuff.

"Whoa there." Malcolm grabs my wrist while simultaneously protecting his drink. "It's too early in the day to assault someone." Even in his joking, he helps me stand up straight, and his eyes move all over me, a concerned wariness to them.

He's always been that way with me. A silly word or retort, yes, but his eyes are always watchful and his hands hover, as though they're prepared to shield me. It's like he's...protective...of me. The realization sends a hot, melty sensation down my spine with a flurry of goosebumps trailing close behind.

"I'm good, I'm good," I say, quickly shaking off the sensation.

"Alright, then!" Clicking her phone off, Emma directs our attention to the bulletin board on the wall. "Here are your jobs for Friday night. I don't want to hear any complaining about what you're stuck doing. It's literally for four hours. You can do anything for four hours!" She pins her gaze on all of us.

"Um, actually, I can't stand for that long," Bill reminds her, pointing to his hip, which I'm pretty sure should be healed by now.

"Ugh, fine. Bill can be on punch duty. I'll tell Ross he has to man the bathrooms."

"We don't need two for bathroom duty," Malcolm pipes in.

"Right, Malcolm, you're actually going to be on the floor," Emma says over her shoulder, eyes focused on the bulletin board.

"What?" The snarl Malcolm gives comes from deep inside his chest. The image of him enduring the mosh pit of dancing teenagers delights me.

"We need you on the floor." Emma waves him off.

"So I can get gyrated all over? No thanks."

I snort. "You'll be with us," I say, waving toward Ellie, Benny, and then myself.

"Yeah, it'll be fun!" Ellie says with an innocent gleam in her eyes. This is her first prom to chaperone. Homegirl has no idea what she's up against.

"Our definitions of fun are quite different," Malcolm mumbles into his coffee mug, the hand that was holding my wrist now tucked under his elbow.

"It won't be that bad," I whisper to him.

"Easy for you to say. Loud music and crowds are the worst combination."

I give him a supportive elbow nudge and pull my phone out when another notification from Derek comes in. I could be imagining it, but I feel Malcolm's body move away from me when I unlock my phone. Glancing up at him, I see he's now laser-focused on the banner draped across the table. The message from Derek is disappointing: *Something came up.* For some reason, I feel irritated and refuse to respond immediately. He just confirmed an hour ago. Why all of a sudden is he canceling? I shove my phone back in my pocket and focus on Emma, not the small balloon of rejection slowly inflating itself in the back of my throat.

"Everything is lined up. Be here..." Emma's words fade as my thoughts start to rush through—every conversation I've had on this little dating app replaying in my head like a broken record. This whole being-openhanded-about-it idea isn't that easy when you're constantly let down.

Everyone just leaves you, Kate.

The small voice of my mother lingers in the back of my mind, threatening to zap through every neuron associated with feelings and emotions.

"What's up?" Malcolm towers over me, his eyes doing that protective searching thing again.

"N–nothing," I stutter, abruptly turning to the cabinets behind me to hide the tears trying to escape. What is with all this weepiness lately?

"Kate, do you know what you're wearing?" Ellie asks as she steps up next to me and drops her palm tree mug in the sink—Benny's mug, actually. The notion that they share mugs, all couple-like, is another one-two punch to the gut.

"No."

"Are you alright?" She catches on too quickly.

"Do I look alright?" I snip, aggressively scrubbing the coffee remains from her palm tree cup.

"Nope," Benny says behind me, and I whip around to glare at him. I glare long enough to watch his eyes widen before he goes back to vigorously coloring the block letters on the banner.

"Do you want to talk about it?" Ellie whispers.

I finish drying her mug and place it in the cabinet above my head, then I grip the sides of the counter, letting my head hang for a moment. My messy curls drape down over my face like a curtain, blocking Ellie and Malcolm from view. Do I want to talk about this? Any of this? I don't even know what I would say or what I would need in return. I just know that I am *sick* of this ever-present despondent feeling that is affecting every aspect of my life. Unwanted and unloved. That's all I feel, even when I clearly have people around me who care. It looms over me like a black cloud, and no matter how hard I try to run from it, it follows me.

"I'll be fine." I abandon the mug I grabbed for myself and hightail it out of the break room. I need to get out of here. I need some sense and wisdom, something to help me trust that everything I'm doing is right. The universe seems to be of no help lately, so I will go to the next best thing.

There is one person who can speak some sense to me in times like these, and she has no other choice but to listen to my issues because she's currently on house arrest until cleared by her physician. Her physical choices lately don't indicate lifelong wisdom, but her words have always been a comfort no one else can give me.

When I pull up to Lola's house, my stomach twists when I see a red Mercedes parked next to her Jeep.

What is she doing here?

"Knock, knock." I open the door and peer in to see my mother sitting on the couch next to Lola. "Mom, what are you doing here?" The question makes it obvious how unenthused I am to see her, but I plaster a grin on my face to soften the blow.

"I'm here to see you." Mom smiles nonchalantly, as if her eight-month absence hasn't been meticulously cataloged by every aunt and uncle in our message group. "And to check on Lola." She grabs Lola's hand and squeezes. It would seem tender and sweet if it was anyone but her. I cross my arms and watch her, willing my eyes to stay centered instead of getting lost in the back of my head like they want to. Ignoring the fact that her own mother had a literal heart attack, she always has a motive for coming by. It's never a simple "I missed you" visit. There are stipulations for her stay, and my entire body tenses up with anticipation, never loosening until I watch the red of her car fade down the road.

"Yes." Lola pats her hand back. "We were about to have some tea. Would you like some?" She attempts to stand from the couch, but Mom squeezes her hand and gestures for her to stay seated. Lola eyes her, contemplating how much she wants to rebel, but she concedes and watches Mom walk into the kitchen and start preparing their cups for tea. I guess she can be good for something.

"Has she asked for anything yet?" I whisper to Lola, sitting on the floor at her feet. I lift her aging feet and rest them in my lap, rubbing her thin ankles. There's a purple tint to her dark skin with lines twisting and curving up and down her feet, and her soft skin feels frail under my fingers. Aunt Edna came this morning and painted her toenails a hot-pink color with sparkles. A smile pulls at my lips as I assess them. My lola has always been younger at heart than she really is. The fitness classes, the vibrant wardrobe, hosting a romance book club...all little things she does to feel young and alive, she tells me. Things that bring her joy and make her forget the hard things in life, like losing Grandpa or watching *Dateline* alone—which no one should ever do, by the way.

"No. Now, be nice," she whispers back, tsking me with a flick on the shoulder. We watch Mom pour three cups of tea at the kitchen counter, mixing each differently: Lola's with two Sweet'N Lows, mine with honey, and hers with a splash of milk. She remembers the way we like it. The small hole left in my heart from her absence tries to close a tiny bit at that.

"Kate, could you help me with these?"

I join my mom in the kitchen, collecting the mugs and a bag of chips from the pantry. As I head back into the living room, she stops me. "Kate..." Her words linger in the air, the inevitable favor waiting to hit me in the face like a pendulum. "I have something to ask."

"What's that?" I ask breezily.

"I was wondering if I could have your grandpa's antique tool set. It would work perfectly for an upcoming exhibit I'm helping organize!" She's practically giddy at the request, completely oblivious to how inappropriate it is. It's not even mine. It's Benny's.

I gape at her, dumbfounded. My face probably looks like one of those frozen-in-time moments that is so unflattering you have to burn the evidence. I try to speak, but my annoyance blocks my vocal cords, which is probably a good thing seeing as all I want to do is grab the woman by the shoulders, give her a hard shake, and yell, "What is wrong with you?!"

"Anna, that's fine. We can sort it out later," Lola answers for me, breaking the tense silence that was starting to build.

"Ahh, thank you, Lola!" My mom reaches around Lola, hugging her tight. "Look, I have to run a few errands. How about I pick up dinner on the way back?" Without waiting for our answer, Mom is halfway out the door with her purse slung over her shoulder. "Kate, will you join us?"

"I, uh…can't. Sorry, I'm busy." I keep my eyes pinned on the wooden bird clock hanging next to Lola's front door as the screen door swings shut. I wait, listening to the sound of my mom's wedges on the gravel and the closing of her car door, before I turn to face Lola.

"What the heck?"

Shrugging, Lola relaxes back into the couch and sips on her tea. Wincing once at the heat, she smacks her lips and raises a brow at me—a look that says I precisely know *what the heck* and how dare I question her. The wrinkles surrounding her eyes and lips deepen for a moment before she lets out a breath. "Katherine, sit."

I reluctantly plop down onto the floor, crossing my legs like a child, and pout at her. She's about to make me sit through an enlightening moment, wisdom thrown at me like bullets, and I'm going to have to deal with it.

"Why do you let your mother upset you?" she asks, and all I can do is stare at her, bewildered that she would ask such an obvious question. "Seriously, why?" she asks again.

"Um, because she's never here? And when she is, all she does is ask for something?"

"And do you think that's enough to be upset about it?"

My bewilderment takes on physical form as my mouth hangs open. "Well, yeah!" I finally say. "Does it not upset you that your daughter never comes around? That she'd rather go on her little trips than be with her family for Christmas?" The answers are obvious, but I still go up an octave to hone in on my point.

"It does." She nods, setting her cup of tea down on the rickety side table. A small black-and-white photo of Grandpa sitting on the edge of a boat rests next to a tiny box of tissues. "But it also reminds me of who my daughter is." I blink away from the photo and back to Lola. She's gazing out the front door Mom just walked out of. Her face is solemn yet peaceful. Accepting. "I have known your mother for fifty-eight years. And the one thing I have learned about her is that she will always, *always,* be the same. For years, I prayed she would change her ways, be more about the family, live the way we wanted her to. It never changed. But something else did." She looks back to me, gray eyes soft and warm. "It was my acceptance of who she is."

I scoff at that.

I am far from accepting that this is who my mother truly is. What daughter wants to feel unwanted by their own mother? Who in their right mind wants to feel like second place in everything? It's one thing to feel unwanted by *men*, especially those online who aren't always who they say they are—I'm talking to you, Larry, who was supposed to have hair. But it's a different thing entirely to feel that way with your own flesh and blood. The person who made you. To feel abandoned by the one person who is supposed to love you more than anyone else. When she's actually around, it's like I'm invisible to her, barely acknowledged. So, who can blame me for feeling a tad moody at seeing her this afternoon for the first time in ages after being let down by a man, *again*.

"Well, I haven't accepted it. And I probably never will."

"That's your choice. But I hope you remember this...you can't change people. People are selfish and will continue to disappoint you. The only thing you can do is change how you let it affect you. You can't make someone choose you."

I glance up at Lola as the weight of her words hit me like a ton of bricks. The corner of her mouth turns downward as she registers the feelings all over my face.

"I know you want to feel wanted, Katherine. For someone to choose you. And I'm sure it would be even better if it was the one person you've wanted since you were a baby, but life just isn't that way sometimes." She speaks so matter-of-factly, like she hasn't just gutted me with the truth. "Your mom will always be your mom, and I think the best thing you can do for yourself is to accept that. And then focus on the people in your life that do want you."

I scoff again, because that's the mature response right now.

"I'm serious," she says. "You have so many people who see the real you, all your faults and quirks. Your bright shoes and crazy hair. We see all of it and still want you. You are cherished by more people than you realize, and if you get over this thing with your mom, you might be able to see that."

"Being wanted by my seventy-eight-year-old lola and my crazy aunts and uncles isn't much to write home about." I curl my knees into my chest and hug them tight.

"There's more than that, and you know it."

"Benny is old enough now, so he's grouped in with the uncles."

She rolls her eyes and waves me off. "I'm telling you, if you opened your eyes, you'd see who I'm talking about. And you wouldn't have to stress about these little boys on these apps either."

What does she mean by that?

Chapter Thirty-One
Malcolm

"How are you doing today?"

"Fine," I say, which is the truth. I'm fine. Aside from the fact that I spent multiple hours of my day yesterday looking at sparkles and lace, then I had to endure a tiny woman poking me with safety pins to get things *just right*, I am peachy. "Today is fine."

I sit across from Dr. Ford in this sterile room full of muted tones that are probably meant to be soothing for troubled minds like mine. But I just find it annoying. Get a plant or something, lady. I fidget with a loose thread on the chair, feeling a little on edge as the clock ticks by overhead.

Alright, maybe I'm not fine. If I'm being honest, I woke up distracted, grappling with emotions I can't quite pinpoint.

"Do you want to talk about it?" She doesn't look up from her notepad. She rarely ever does. Her demeanor is much harsher than Ellie's, which is probably why I get along with her so well. If I have even an inkling of self-pity, Dr. Ford sets me straight, reminding me that pity is usually self-induced and projected onto others. And the only person I have to blame for those feelings is myself.

Do I pity myself? Unfortunately, yes. I'm hung up on a woman who views me as a friend. I'm just as much an option to her as Bill is. And I keep thinking about the loss of Brennan. He's been gone for eight years, but the memories are fresh and raw. Most of my days I can get through without thinking about him. Most days, I feel at peace with the loss. But then, on the rare occasion, I'm triggered by a sound or a smell, and it feels like I can't escape it, like my brain truly is my own worst enemy, and I'm suffocated by the memory of my friend. His laughter echoes in the corners of my mind—a gutting reminder of his life cut too short.

You can fight in a million battles, coming out the other side, but there are still wounds from it. Some you can't see. And some never leave, surging forth with new intensity when you least expect it. I've grown to accept that the wound of losing Brennan might never fully leave me, and even after all these years, the memory of him will always be lingering in the back of my mind, waiting to be triggered and let loose. I'll probably be eighty years old, sitting in my recliner for my afternoon nap, and it'll hit me—tormenting me, clawing at me to be relived. That's just the way it is.

"Not really," I finally respond.

She eyes me, speculating, probably aware that I just had a mini therapy session in my head. That's usually how this goes. Prying me for information never goes well, hence I don't see Ellie for this sort of thing. I'm also pretty sure that's a conflict of interest, no matter how often she tells me she can be professional.

"Do you know what today is?"

I didn't expect to be quizzed on the date when I walked in here.

"It's Thursday," I grumble. She looks at me over her glasses, waiting. "Uh...the 18th?" Her eyes soften as she pulls her glasses off, letting it sink in. April 18th.

The anniversary of Brennan's death.

Eight years.

Dr. Ford's voice is a distant murmur as I drift further into the memory, watching the helicopter collide with the ground, engulfing itself and its one passenger in flames on impact. I can feel the heat burning my face and neck, the breath in my lungs constricting, my heart racing. Everything around me starts to spin. I can see Dr. Ford's mouth moving, her posture changing, but I can't make out what she's saying to me.

Slamming my eyes shut, I breathe in for three and out for three, just as instructed in the past. It does nothing, and now my head is pounding. I feel my chest heaving as Brennan's face flashes in my mind, his dorky smile and kid-like stature. The image is haunting and suffocating. I try to breathe again, a little longer this time.

I hear Dr. Ford's voice become clearer, her words ringing in my ear. "Focus on something else, something peaceful." She lists off the typical peace-inducing scenes—a waterfall, a river, meditating in the green grass. In theory, they would work, but my mind focuses on something else.

Kate's face flashes into focus like a beacon, dissipating the darkness swirling around me. Her dark-brown eyes flicker at me, pools of warmth and understanding, anchoring themselves to me and holding me stable. Her gentle hands hold me as I tremble, confidently and without fear, like seeing me this way doesn't scare her. *"You can get through this,"* she whispers to me. Looking into her eyes, I know I'm not alone. Everything that haunts me fades. The ghosts of my past lose their power when she's near.

I realize, with sudden clarity, that she is the reason I've made it this far. Not the only reason, but one of the biggest reasons I've found any sort of healing at all. Dr. Ford is great and all, but Kate has been a lifeline in a sea of thundering emotions—a glimmer of hope, as cheesy as that sounds.

My breathing stabilizes, and my heart slows. "Kate," I whisper, almost to myself. "That's my peace. She is my peace."

Dr. Ford sets down her notepad, a different look on her face than I've seen before. She waits again, assuming I will expand. I rub my knuckles against my chest and sit up a little straighter, grappling with the truth I haven't let anyone hear yet.

"For the longest time, I thought she was a distraction. Annoying as hell sometimes. A little too quirky all the time. But it was enough." I shrug, and Dr. Ford keeps waiting. Damn this woman, wanting me to expand on my feelings. "It wasn't at first. I actually didn't see it coming."

"Didn't see what coming?" Dr. Ford asks, setting her pen down.

"This fireball of a woman wedging herself in. I thought she would drive me nuts."

Dr. Ford laughs. "But she does, yes? Drive you nuts?"

"The woman is maddening."

"And how is that helpful for you?" She clicks her pen, preparing to write down my answer.

I let out a huff and hesitate with a response. "I don't know. It just is." I don't have as many nightmares with her around, I don't think about Brennan as much, and the fear that I might never get through my grief has dwindled a tiny bit. I exhale and finally say, "Things just started to change the more she was around, so I forced myself to hang out with her more—a kind of distraction from the things I didn't want to deal with. She's a gorgeous woman, so it wasn't like it was miserable or anything. But over time, I realized she's not a distraction."

"I see, and what is she, then?"

"She's a safe place."

When these haunting thoughts have nagged at me, she's pulled me out of it. She hasn't erased the memories—I don't think anything ever will—but she's made them bearable. The truth settles the roaring anxiety inside me, calming it like a damn hurricane. In this silent war against myself, I've had an ally, anchoring me in ways I didn't realize I needed. "I obviously haven't fully healed, or I wouldn't be here, Doc. But Kate gives me the strength I can't summon on my own..." I pause, wanting to punch myself in the throat as realization washes over me. "And she doesn't even know it!"

Frustration swells inside me as my thoughts come flooding in—what Kate is to me, what she's done for me. I know I've loved her for a long time. Even when she accosted me about a chicken five years ago, I knew I would love her. But the depth of that love was never this weighty. It was never so intricately woven within me that it would be impossible to extract it. My love for Kate isn't something I can move on from. I can't sit here and watch her ride off into the sunset with someone she met on some app. My chest squeezes at the thought—the thought of doing any part of my life without her.

I close my eyes and settle into the quiet of Dr. Ford's office. Sometimes therapy is just this, me listening to the clock tick by until I talk. I'm grateful. Not that I can't elaborate my feelings, I just don't think they're important all the time. Words carry too much weight, and if I don't think through them clearly, they might not have a point, and I could end up drudging down a dead-end road.

My lips tingle as I inhale slowly, the taste of toothpaste and smell of lavender seeping their way into my brain for some reason. *Where is that coming from?* My head spins at a memory trying to break through, but it's still too unclear to focus on. I hate when that happens. Instead of dwelling on what I can't remember, I take another slow breath and focus on the things I can.

I am madly in love with Kate.

I miss Brennan.

These two things are weaved together in my brain. I don't know why. Probably never will. But I do know that any sort of healing can be a long process, and I just need to accept that. But I don't have to do it alone anymore. I can do it with Kate. I can share these things with her, and she can share her things with me.

"So, Kate is a safe haven for you?" Dr. Ford reiterates.

"Not just that."

"Then tell me, Malcolm, what is she to you?"

"She's everything."

Chapter Thirty-Two

Kate

"Can I get you anything else?" Sam, the owner of Wafflin's, voice cuts through the chatter of the diner as he sets down our orders—three towering stacks of waffles and one sad little pancake.

"No thanks," Ellie answers without looking at him. Her eyes are glued to the waffle tower. I wish someone looked at me the way she is looking at the melted butter dripping into the squares of that Belgium waffle. Pure, unadulterated breakfast romance.

"Should we wa—" I cut my own words off at the sight of Ellie shoving a forkful of waffle into her mouth like it's the source of all power. Clearly, asking if we should wait for her fiancé to start eating is a lost cause. If I were to ask Ellie to choose between Benny and these waffles, I would get a live reenactment of *Sophie's Choice* right here in the middle of Wafflin'.

"So," Ellie manages between mouthfuls, "do we have everything ready for tonight?" Her words are a bit muffled by the food being shoveled in like a conveyor belt, making her breathless and drooly.

"I, uh...I think so." My eyes dip from her mouth to her almost empty plate then back up again. I'm torn between watching her obliterate the waffle or focusing on the conversation. It's a struggle. "Have you checked with Emma?"

"Are you kidding me?" Another bite. "I haven't spoken to her since yesterday morning—as *instructed*." She points her fork at me, syrup dripping onto the table.

"Instructed?"

"Yes," Benny says, sliding into the seat next to Ellie and planting a kiss on her forehead. "Emma kindly informed her sweet sister and her *boss* that if we didn't have anything to contribute, then we should *stay out of her way*." Benny chuckles, grabbing one of the untouched plates from the center of the table. "Apparently, our banner attempts got us banished from the decorating committee."

Ellie scoffs at Benny's remark, as if it's a shock at how horrid her banner-making skills are. Surely she has some clue...surely.

"So, we're just chaperoning now." Benny shrugs, turning his attention to his food.

Ellie bristles at the notion, rolling her eyes and trying to stab at the pancake on the fourth plate. I swat her hand away, which earns me a pout. Benny, ever the gentleman, cuts his waffle in half and offers it to her. His eyes are soft and wistful as he gazes at her like there is no one else in this diner but her. It's heartwarming and nauseating at the same time. The sight tugs my heart in two different directions: happiness and envy.

I want what they have so badly it's starting to feel pathetic.

But I also wish they'd get a room.

Benny wraps his arm around her and toys with the engagement ring on her finger. Ellie reciprocates with a kiss on his temple, her unabashed smile growing as she looks at him. They're in their own little love bubble, and I'm just here—a third wheel in my own life.

I poke at my waffle, trying to drown out the laughter and shared affection from across the table. Beyond Benny and Ellie, I scan the diner. It's three in the afternoon, which is prime time for the early bird special. Other couples fill the space, lost in conversation and breakfast food bliss. One couple, the oldest of them all, sits on the same side of the booth, sharing a plate of waffles, and doing sudoku together. Even in the midst of company, the overwhelming weight of isolation crawls up my neck like a shiver. I try to physically shake it off.

Then, my mind goes back to seeing Mom yesterday, and it makes all of this feel a thousand times worse.

The absence of my mom's presence is usually bearable. Aside from the lack of birthday calls, I have grown accustomed to not thinking about her. Essentially, living life without her has become my new norm. And being on my own the last few years had also. I was so content, I thought.

Until these two googly eyed buffoons across from me started flaunting what they have right in front of my face.

I don't blame them, though. I would too. The empty space in my bed, the lack of shared moments with someone, being truly understood and loved by someone...these were things I didn't realize I was missing. But now I can't seem to shake away the weight it has on me. The longing for it. And seeing my mom yesterday was just a reminder that I'm nowhere close to getting past these feelings.

My phone dings with a notification, another *score* from Playing the Field, another pitiful chance for a happily ever after awaiting at my fingertips.

I greeted one of them *"howdy doody"* the other day.

Not my proudest moment.

My attempts are starting to feel desperate, but the ache to fill the void is shoving me deeper and deeper into the palms of other men—metaphorically, of course.

I'm aware that finding *"the one"* isn't black and white. I know that love isn't as easy as a swipe on a screen. Putting yourself out there and falling in love takes effort. And patience. And sometimes a lot of time. But these are things that don't come to me naturally. Patience? I scald my tongue on hot French fries almost daily. Patience is not a Stanley trait.

My thumb lingers with hesitation above the notification from *Hunter007* when another notification pops up, tingling my cheeks.

> **Malcolm:** Will Emma fire me if I refuse to wear a tie?

A small laugh bubbles out of me at the image of Emma yelling at Malcolm over a tie. The tingling sensation moves across my body in an instant. Another *episode.* This time, it's just at the thought of Malcolm. He's nowhere in sight, and I feel his closeness as if he's right next to me in this booth. I'd be lying if I said I didn't feel his presence around me all the time. He's always there, and when he's not, my mind seems to always drift to him, like a security blanket.

"Aye, did you not save us some?" my Uncle Jerry's voice booms across the diner as he storms over to our table with Lola on his heels.

"What are you doing?" I scold Lola. She dismisses me with a wave and takes the seat next to me without hesitation.

Uncle Jerry waves Sam over to order and pulls up a chair. "I had to get her out of the house. She was driving me crazy with the reely things." He groans.

"It's reels," Benny corrects with a chuckle.

"I'm on house arrest. What else am I to do?" Lola snips.

"Stay. At. Home. That is the sole definition of house arrest," I retort.

She shoots a glare at me, but I refuse to let her know how intimidating the look truly is and focus on the soggy pancake in the center of the table before responding to Malcolm.

> She might try, but I think you can outrun her.
>
> I ordered you a pancake btw!
>
> **Malcolm:** No time, gotta finish this banner. See you tonight
>
> Aw ok! See you later!

I cut a piece of pancake and smother it in syrup, watching as it drips slowly off the edge of my fork. The slow drag of maple is about the same speed that I analyze and contemplate my feelings as I watch my family around the table, exchanging loving glances and laughs. My mind drifts to picturing Malcolm here with us. My best friend, exchanging the same looks, fitting into the mix of it all like he always has. Like the Florida sun baking my face on that beach, Malcolm is a warm and steady feeling, clinging to me like rays of sunshine.

Have I lost that warm, steady feeling?

"What's troubling you?" Lola whispers to me, munching on her tuna melt. She refuses waffles every time—another form of rebellion on her list of many.

"It's nothing." I turn my phone face down and force a smile.

Lola eyes me, my smile faltering under *that* look.

"We're going to go get ready. We'll see you in a bit," Benny says, placing cash on the table for the way too many waffles his fiancée just inhaled. As they leave, Uncle Jerry finds himself interested in the group of elderly ladies playing cards in the back corner.

Lola shakes her head. "Aye, those poor women." We both laugh at his failed flirting attempts from afar before he quickly diverts to sit at the bar and harass Sam. "Poor Sam." Lola chuckles. She turns back to me and eyes me *again*. It gets exhausting how often she gives me that look. It's even more exhausting that it's had the same effect on me for thirty years.

"What?" I groan.

"How are your internet boyfriends?" she asks, pulling a mug of coffee up to her lips. Her smile lines deepen as she rolls her lips to fight the laugh trying to burst through.

"Aye, Lola," I grumble, stretching her name out.

She shrugs innocently and sips on her decaf coffee. "Is Malcolm taking you tonight?"

"No." I set my fork down and settle in for a long conversation. Anytime Lola talks to me about Malcolm, it's never quick. She tends to linger on how amazing he is, yada, yada. "We're chaperoning. It's not like we're actually going to prom."

"But you're dressing up?"

"Not really. Just dressy-*er* than our normal." The orange number I have set out would beg to differ. I still can't believe I let Ellie convince me to wear something other than black this year. For the last four years, I've worn the same dress pants and blazer with my sequin high-tops as the statement piece—a classy yet very practical choice.

"I bet Malcolm will enjoy it." She gives me a wink. I throw my head back and groan, turning every head in the diner in our direction. Lola shrugs again, unfazed by my reaction. "I'm just saying, he will."

"Will you let it go? It's never going to happen." *Right?*

The words left my mouth quicker than my brain could compute them. I white-knuckle the sides of my mug and gnaw on my lip. A million questions race through my head as my cheeks and neck flush with heat. There's no hiding the redness that is now plastered to me. Lola continues to stare at me. *Stare* at me, like I'm a lunatic.

Questions and assumptions pang around in my head like a pinball machine.

Is something with Malcolm possible?

Does he even want that?

Why is it so hot in here?

Has this table always been this wobbly?

I let out a gush of air, which makes me feel lightheaded and sends stars swirling around my vision. Putting my head in my hands, I focus on the crumbs of the pancake and the blob of butter that has now melted into a puddle. Lola's soft, fragile hands encircle her mug, now empty, with a small pink lip stain on the rim.

"Katherine," she whispers, releasing the mug and reaching for my hand. "What are you so scared of?"

"What? No, I'm not scared of anything. It's just annoying how much everyone *loooooves* Malcolm." I wave a big circle in the air to emphasize that it is literally everyone.

Lola's hand trembles weakly as she squeezes mine, showing her delicate age in a small motion.

On a quick breath, I say, "Just the thought of Malcolm, as more than my friend...it's just, just...I don't know. It's crazy!"

"Why?" I look up to see Lola cross her arms, eyeing me defiantly. A duel in her mind—one she intends to win based on the purse of her lips and the tapping of her fingers against her arm. "Tell me why it's crazy, Katherine. Why is it so crazy to be with a man who treats you the way you deserve to be treated? A man who is tall and handsome and fixes your elderly grandma's squeaky floors? What is—"

"Wait, what?" I hold up a hand to pause her rant. "Malcolm has been fixing your house? Malcolm? He's your secret handyman boyfriend?" The shock in my voice carries, drawing Uncle Jerry's attention from the reels he's showing Sam.

"Of course!" Lola says, as if this shouldn't be a surprise.

"Wha— Why? How? Why would he do that for you?"

It's a stupid question.

I know why. Because Malcolm is wonderful and would do anything for anyone, no matter how much they drive him crazy. Aunt Edna has a new shed for her romance-novel writing in her backyard because of Malcolm. I guess a small part of me assumed it could have been Malcolm who painted the door and fixed the sink, but another part of me didn't want to believe that he was that good. Part of me didn't want to admit that a man like Malcolm could give so much of himself to me and my crazy family. That he could love them so well.

Even when he wants to convince everybody he's a loner who only worries about himself, I know the truth. He's the good—the good feelings, the good parts of the day, the good you want to see in the world. He's the brightness that creeps in through the curtains in the morning. He's the sweetness in my nightly ice cream. He's the fresh air that fills my lungs on the track. And he's the one person that makes me feel seen, and wanted, and—

My thoughts screech to a halt. The realization feels like a nudge in the arm.

Whenever Malcolm is around, I don't feel alone. Being with him fills the emptiness in ways I didn't expect. Like a grizzly bear shimmying his way into a cold, dark cave for hibernation, Malcolm has made himself comfortable in the back of my mind.

The thought warms me from the inside out, chasing away that lingering chill of loneliness and filling me with something I'm unfamiliar with, something I don't think I've ever felt.

"Why is it so crazy to think that you could be with your best friend for the rest of your life, Katherine?" Lola draws my attention back to her. "You deserve that. You deserve a life with someone who shows you a consistent type of love. Stable. Uncomplicated. Someone who is sure of you. Someone who shows up. Someone who fills that little hole inside you that you've wanted filled since you were a child." She jabs her finger at me, swirling it around in the direction of my heart. As if her hand is pulling at a string attached to the beating organ, it flutters and pounds against my sternum. "How can you give your heart to some stranger on the internet when there is already a man out there waiting? A man who has shown you they're worthy of a heart like yours?"

My throat feels thick with emotion. The loneliness I've felt, the loneliness I've been so fixated on, the hole she's talking about...it's felt so suffocating that I've overlooked what's right in front of me.

Hell, it had to be thrown at me in a concussed-wrapped bow for me to see what I've been missing: a future where Malcolm is more than just a friend.

Is it possible that, for all this time, I really haven't been that lonely? That maybe the constant tugging in my heart and longing for shared glances, and inside jokes, and lingering touches, could have been within reach this entire time?

Is this feeling love?

Do I love Malcolm?

Does he even love me?

More panging inside my head and chest. I have to physically shake it off and focus. I have to look at the facts. I'm basing my information on a seventy-five-year-old with a TikTok obsession. Now, yes, history has shown she's never been wrong about this sort of thing. She knew the moment she met Ellie that she would end up with Benny.

"*Love is easy,*" she'd always tell us. And maybe she's right.

But she could be wrong. As much as she denies it, Lola doesn't know everything. It might not be as easy as she claims. Love hasn't been easy for me—ever. Loving Eric wasn't easy. Loving my mom sure as heck isn't. How can I know loving Malcolm will be any different?

As we leave, Lola's probing questions linger, and I start to wonder if she's onto something. Maybe it's time to stop searching for love and embrace the possibility that it's been right in front of me all along.

Maybe.

But how am I supposed to tell Malcolm that?

Chapter Thirty-Three

Kate

"Can you chill out? You're going to ruin your manicure," Ellie snips at me, swatting my hands away from my face.

"I'm sorry. I'm freaking out!" What an understatement. I've used an entire box of tissues to wipe under my arms and the back of my neck since walking into this gym. "Why is it so hot in here?" I groan and flail my arms about as I pace in front of the ticket table.

We finished setting up for prom with ample time to spare. Music and lights are waiting to be turned on moments before the doors open, because it will add to the *excitement of it all,* according to Emma. The place looks amazing. String lights cover every inch of the gymnasium ceiling and wrap around the banisters on the second level. Vintage books Emma found at Goodwill are used as centerpieces and accents in different areas. The wooden sign Malcolm made has been set up by the door for entrance photos.

My stomach feels like it's full of acid as I pace back and forth as nauseating nerves boil up inside of me. About thirty minutes ago, I decided I'm going to talk to Malcolm.

I have no earthly idea what I'm going to say. I just know I need to talk to him. I need to tell him what's going on inside my head.

Do I know what's going on inside my head? Even if I don't, I need to talk to him, right? Gosh, quit talking to yourself, Kate.

"Seriously, you're making me dizzy," Ellie presses her fingers into her temples as her eyes follow my pacing feet.

"Where is he?" It's 6:48. Malcolm was supposed to be here twenty minutes ago.

"Maybe he's finishing up the long list of crafts Emma had him do." Ellie mimics a hair flip, her tone shrill and sarcastic. She doesn't handle jealousy well, poor thing.

"And here is where we have the sign-in table." Benny gestures to our table from the opposite end of the gymnasium, leading our newest hire around on their first official tour of the school.

"Hey, Stanley!" Coach Daniels beams at me, wrapping me in a hug. It startles me at first, the affection, but I realize he's just *that* friendly. I guess helping carry a concussed Malcolm across the field really brings people together.

"Daniels, hi!" Returning the hug then stepping back, I assess his getup. "You look great!" I say, gesturing to his blue suit with a green Kirby t-shirt underneath. I evaluate it a second longer, pondering how he's able to pull off something so odd. But it suits him.

"Wanted to make a good first impression." He delights, his smile beaming bright under the string lights.

"Daniels, you'll be on bathroom duty with Bill. Figured it would be a good baby step." Benny directs him toward the door that leads to the hallway.

"Well, I'll catch you guys later!" Daniels jogs off with a literal pep in his step and disappears down the hall.

"Sure is nice to have some fresh blood around here," Ellie says.

"Just so you don't have to be the new girl anymore?" I ask, giving her a sly wink. I take a seat next to her, preparing myself for the craziness about to burst through the doors.

"Alright, ladies, pick one," Benny instructs as he approaches the table with both of his hands pulled tightly behind his back.

"Um, left." Ellie points, a giddy smile whipping across her face.

He pulls two corsages from behind his back, handing Ellie the left one and me the right. Both of them are white roses, one with a silver bow and the other with a green bow. I open my box and pull out the wristlet, admiring the intricate green bow tied on one end. We each look at our choices, then to the other, and quickly swap—the green for Ellie, and the silver for me. Benny lets out a singular laugh, and we shrug. Ellie helps place mine on my wrist, and Benny places Ellie's on hers. The moment is tender and almost sweet enough to distract me from the goal of the night.

Talking to Malcolm. Who *still* isn't here.

Emma barrels through the front door, a line of students forming behind her. She slams the door in their faces, yelling, "Not yet!" Grunting and groaning, she hurries to the table and drops off two buckets: one for prom king and the other for prom queen. "No funny business this time." She points at Benny and Ellie accusingly. "Only students can win!"

"That wasn't our—"

"Oh please." Emma waves off Ellie's attempt at defense. Benny and Ellie, two faculty members, were awarded homecoming king and queen last fall. It was hilarious to watch them be crowned, but Emma is still not convinced it was all the football team's doing. "Now, we open in three minutes, everyone!" she yells over us to the other teachers scattered around the gym. They mosey off to their assigned stations, which seem to have changed since our last faculty meeting: Ross on punch, Margaret and the assistant librarian on the back exit, and Bill heads to the bathrooms. The rest of the faculty line the walls for dancefloor duty. Looks of dread spread across each of their faces, knowing what's to come. Having to be the one to break up the bumping and grinding is never fun.

I thank the universe for ticket duty.

"Now, does this mean I have two prom dates?" Benny winks at us.

"Ew, gross." I wince.

Benny leans over the table to plant one on Ellie, big and passionate, before the students come in. Ellie's eyes flutter when he moves away, like she's lost in the moment. "I think Kate has someone else in mind for her date." She shoots me a wink and a shoulder shimmy, causing Benny's eyes to dart to me, widening ever so slightly.

"No. No. I don't have a date."

"Then what did I get all dressed up for?"

I whip around in my chair to the soothing deep voice behind me and see Malcolm standing in the center of the gymnasium. String lights sparkle above him like stars. He's dressed in a sleek, black suit with no tie. Something about that little detail sends a tickle all the way down to my toes. It's insanely attractive—and a tad rebellious. The suit fits him like a glove, accentuating the broadness in his shoulders and strength in his legs. I feel my breath catch when my gaze trips over his clean-shaven face, his strong jawline and tiny chin dimple on display. I let out an audible gulp that feels like sandpaper in my throat and realize my mouth has been hanging open.

Ellie kicks my ankle and shoves my chair, encouraging me in the most painful of ways to go talk to him.

I stand on wobbly knees. I guess that's what Malcolm in a suit does to my limbs. Inhaling slowly, I make my way across the gym. It's only thirty feet, but it feels like the length of the football field. Malcolm, dressed up, underneath the stars and floating books, is now an image burned into my brain forever. Something I will picture anytime I'm sad or lonely or when I need to picture the love interest in my next read.

"Hi," I breathe.

"You look..." He trails off, eyeing me up and down. The silvery blue of his eyes dances all over me, and I feel a spark of energy when they finally settle on my neck. One look, *that* look, fills me with the confidence to tell him everything I'm thinking. Right here, right now. He clears his throat twice and rubs his jaw, like he's trying to summon the strength to finish his statement. "Kate, you look—"

"It's time, people!" Emma bellows from the front doors. As she opens them, a crowd of students pile in, overtaking the ticket table. The music switches on, playing some K-Pop band, and the disco lights flicker on. In an instant, Malcolm's words are drowned out as kids start flooding the dance floor.

"Crap, I have to..." I glance at the table then back to him. Desperation is an understatement for how I feel. I need to talk to him. "Can I come find you later?" I tug at the hem of his suit jacket, the velvety fabric smooth against my skin.

"Please do." He tugs lightly at a piece of my hair, trailing his thumb across my collarbone and down my arm. "I really need to talk to you."

The crowd starts to close in on us, and he pulls his hand away. I see his shoulders dip forward as if his entire body deflated, probably internally sulking about the gyrating slowly starting to suffocate him. He gives me a salute then disappears into the sea of dancing teenagers.

The first hour of the prom is a chaotic whirlwind.

Ellie and I man the ticket table, Benny assists with the photo booth, and Emma barks out orders like it's the apocalypse. When the line to enter dies down, we finally sit down and take a breather. Music and dancing happen behind us in a blur. I glance around, looking for Malcolm, but he's a ghost, nowhere to be found.

"I'm going to get some punch!" I yell over the music to Ellie who has taken to playing Wordle on her phone.

Weaving my way through the bodies, I find the drink table and Ross on high alert. He really is the perfect person for the job. Volunteering for the police department ignited this spark inside of him. Protecting and serving—even at the high school prom—is what he lives for now.

"Hi, Ross!" The music booms around us, muffling my voice. He nods in greeting as I fill up my cup. "Have you seen Malcolm?" I yell in his direction, eyeing the mess that has overtaken the table. Ross shakes his head as he watches the table suspiciously, as if I, a teacher, will spike the punch while straightening the cups and napkins. Dusting the cookie crumbs off my hands, I collect my punch and turn toward the dance floor. There are no openings—a barrier of bodies swaying and jumping blocks my path across the gym. Sidling up next to Ross, I sip on my punch. Making conversation is useless with the noise, so we watch the madness around us.

"Hey, Ms. Stanley!" Garrett, dressed in a hot-pink suit with a black bowtie, pushes through the crowd. Ross steps closer to the table, glowering at Garrett as he pours himself some punch. "Are you going to get out there?" He smiles at me, chugging his punch like it's a shot.

I mouth, *"No,"* and he pouts. "Teachers don't need to be out there!" I wave my hand dismissively as Garrett points over the crowd at a short woman bouncing and sliding side to side in the midst of the teenagers. Margaret. A song even I don't know blares through the speakers, and Margaret is shaking everything she's got—off beat.

One arm goes up, the other goes forward. A slide to the left, and a slide back. It's a poor attempt, but she is fearless. My cheeks pinch at the sight—the sheer joy she has out there. And then, in one swift motion, Bill is on the dance floor, sidling up next to her, matching her energy like it's his own. My heart swells at the sight of two people so in sync and unbothered by everything around them.

"Whew, they're getting it!" Travis Van gives a single clap as he breaks through the barrier. I have to stand on my toes to keep watching Margaret and Bill as the crowd circles around them. *Did Bill leave Daniels alone on bathroom duty?*

Sarah and Ethan find their way to the table as well, holding hands and looking adorable. I refuse to let the sweetness of young love cloud my judgment of her date choice. *I'm watching you,* my eyes say as he fills two cups with water.

"Where's Geer?" Ethan asks the group. They each stand on their toes, scouring the crowd with no luck. They all linger around the table, Devon and Charlie abandoning their dates on the floor to join them.

For some odd reason, I feel the need to use this opportunity for intel. "Hey," I yell. Their faces are beet red from the dancing as they face me. Travis throws his hands up and steps away from the table as if I'm accusing him of something. "What happened at the restaurant?" They all look at me, confused, so I clarify, "Why did you guys crash my date?"

A wave of fixed expressions marks their faces—straight, taut lines, fighting any emotion or giveaway. Setting my hands on my hips, I wait. A few of them attempt to back away, probably hoping the crowd will swallow them. I jab my finger in the air at them, halting them in their tracks. "Spill it."

Devon sighs, stepping closer so I can hear him. "You really don't know?"

I shrug, unsure how to answer. I have a hunch, but I need confirmation. I need reassurance that my feelings aren't the only ones going wild right now. "We did it for Geer. He was freaking out about your date, worried about you. At first, we did it because none of us liked

Sanders and wanted to ruin it. But a day or so later, we figured it out." Devon shrugs, like that answers my question.

"Figured out what?" I ask.

"Coach, have you ever considered that maybe Coach Geer views you as more than a friend?" Garrett asks. "All the things he does for you and no one else? And that thing with the pig—I mean, come on."

"Wait, what thing with the pig?" Confusion mars my face.

"We were at a luau," Travis whines, "and we didn't even get to see the roasted pig. Coach had the kitchen staff move it to the other side of the party so we wouldn't see it—so *you* wouldn't have to watch them roast it. We had front-row seats and everything." He wails despondently, like this situation ruined his entire week at camp.

"Wh—why would he do that? I could have easily stepped away," I defend.

"We know." Garrett nods in agreement. "But Geer was determined. He even helped them move the thing. It was disgusting."

That was why Malcolm was late.

I stand there, unsure what to say or ask now. So, Malcolm ruined a luau *for me*. He crashed my date. These could all just be kind gestures you do for a friend. Maybe he'd do something like this for Benny.

Ethan and Sarah are the first to head back out to the dance floor, Travis and Charlie following suit shortly after. Devon waits, watching the crowd blur in front of us.

"Look"—Devon tugs at my elbow—"a monkey could tell how he feels about you. And you're out there trying to meet random guys on the internet." He waves a hand at the crowd, as if it's a clear representation of the number of online date-ees I've encountered. I glower at him, pursing my lips. "I'm just saying, the guy is so crazy about you. You'd be insane to not know!"

"You don't know that!" I defend again.

"Kate, ask anyone. You won't find a single person here who thinks otherwise."

Well, I clearly won't be doing that. I don't need to ask everyone. I just need to ask Malcolm.

An opening in the blockade appears, and I abandon Devon at the table and make my way through. Arms, hands, and even legs are obstacles as I break through the other side. Ellie and Benny are cozied up near the booth, swaying to a slow song that now plays overhead.

"Hey!" I snap them out of their trance, anxiety heating my back and neck like a furnace. "Is Malcolm in love with me?" My question is shocking and more aggressive than I intended.

"Um..." Benny hesitates. "Why do you ask?"

That is a good question. Why am I asking? Do I want to know the answer when I'm not even sure how I feel about him? I run my hands through my hair, curls breaking apart and falling over my face at the motion.

Ellie breaks away from Benny's arms, linking her arm with mine. "What's going on?"

"I just need to know!" I demand, my voice booming over the steady beat of the song. The lights flash around me, pulsing along with the pressure now building in my head. "I just... Ugh. It seems like everyone else knows how he feels, but me!" I pinch my eyes shut and practically yell, "I need to know if Malcolm is in love with me or not!"

"Why don't you ask me yourself, then?"

Chapter Thirty-Four
Malcolmm

Kate goes rigid. Her shoulders are basically touching her ears, and her fists are balled so tight I can see the muscles straining in her arms.

"Yeah." Benny's eyes are saucers, darting back and forth between us. "Ask him yourself, Kate." He reaches for Ellie and pulls her to the dance floor.

I step closer to Kate, who refuses to face me. Stubborn. The lights and music are suffocating, but being near her, I can breathe. I fight the temptation to drag my eyes down the edges of her burnt-orange dress and say, "Go ahead. Ask me."

Her dark curls hit me across the cheek as she whips around to face me. Her face is set in stone, one eyebrow raised and her lip tucked between her teeth. I follow my impulses and pry her lip free with my thumb, which makes her suck in a breath. Her eyes are filled with a thousand questions as she stares at me, unblinking.

"Where have you been?" She crosses her arms over her chest defensively.

"Is that really what you wanted to ask me?"

"Well, you are supposed to be manning the floor, so yeah!"

I'm confused at her tone, but I'll roll with it. "I switched with Bill. You know I hate crowds." I rub the back of my neck, observing her. "Is that alright with you, your majesty?" I eye her, unsure what's going on in that beautiful head of hers, but I also can't resist giving her hell when I see the anger twitch in her eyes. She doesn't say anything, and the auburn tint of her eyes flickers restlessly as they dart all around the gym. Frustration starts to simmer inside me with the silence. *Talk to me!* I grab her wrist, tracing my thumb across the small divot in the center. Her pulse pounds rapidly. "What is going on with you?"

"Are you in love with me?" Her words are like a strike to my windpipe. I knew what was coming. I should've been prepared. But hearing it come from her lips still startles all the air out of my lungs.

"I, um...what?" I release her wrist and feel my anxiety spike. This conversation needs to happen, but my heart might actually stop beating altogether if it happens in the middle of this sweaty sparkle prison.

"Malcolm..." Her voice is soft and tender. "Are you?"

The pounding of the music reverberates in my ears, adding to the headache threatening to break through at the next bass drop. I can't do this here. Grabbing Kate's hand, I lead her out of the gym.

"Where are we—"

"Shh, just come on." I pull her behind me, down the hall and out into the cool summer air. Our shoes pad across the paved parking lot, all the way to steps leading down to the football field. The stadium lights are on, and the smell of fresh-cut grass swirls around us as we land on the fifty-yard line.

"Malcolm"—Kate squeezes my hand—"please answer me."

I release her and try to take a breath. My nerves move down into my throat and choke me. I have to clear it three times before I can even look at her. She tries to whisper my name, but I hold a hand up. *Please wait.* I settle myself and take her all in. Her olive skin has a deep richness to it against the orange silk of her dress. Loose, dark curls graze the top of her collarbone. Just one swift motion of my hand and I'd see the beautiful curve of her shoulder perfectly. Those damn curly strands are just a tease. I clench my fists and fight every fiber within me telling me to reach for her.

She crosses her arms, growing more impatient by the second. I don't blame her. I'm kind of freaking out right now.

"Alright," I finally say with a long breath. I rub the back of my neck and decide to just lay it all out there. I can't cling to the hopeful idea of us anymore. She has to know how I truly feel, and I have to know if she feels the same.

"I like your hair." *You're an idiot.* She sighs, raising an eyebrow at the world's lamest lead in to someone professing their love. "I like your hair, Kate. I like your sparkly shoes. I like your vegan coffee creamer. Things I wouldn't usually focus on, I do, because they're a part of you." I let out a shaky breath and look at the turf, forcing myself to press on. *Use your words, Malcolm.* "I like watching you coach and support the kids. I like the way you bite your lip when you write on your chalkboard and how fiercely you love your wild family. I like how passionate you are about so many things. I like everything about you, even your obsession with the Jonas Brothers." She laughs, and I clear my throat. "But somewhere along the way, years ago...years ago, that *like* became something deeper. Something I can't shake." I pause and take a deep breath, feeling my heartbeat thrum erratically in my chest.

She doesn't move or speak. She just stares at me, hugging herself.

I rub my knuckles across my chest, attempting to ease the ache settling there. "Kate— I, ugh...God, yes. I am in love with you. I have been for a while now."

The confession feels heavy and thick on my shoulders. I thought I'd feel better by putting it all out there, but Kate's silence is fizzling that hope like a poorly tended campfire.

"How do you know?" she asks, keeping her eyes pinned on my chest.

"What? How do I—"

"How do you know you're in love with me, Malcolm? How can you be so sure?" She moves her eyes up to mine, still hugging herself. Her strong posture falters in the silence that follows.

"Well..." I pause. "Clearly, I prefer being by myself." I gesture to the empty field around us. Kate lets out a small laugh that mixes with the wind whistling around us. "I can think better and work through my issues better when I'm alone. It's peaceful. And other things aren't. I just, ugh...I get tired of everything, ya know?"

"I know you do." Kate suppresses a smile as she bites her lip.

"But I never get tired of you," I confess.

Kate's breath hitches, and her arms fall to her sides.

"I never get tired of you, Kate. I'd rather be with you every moment, of every day, all the time, than have a moment alone to myself. That's how I know I'm in love with you."

She's silent again.

At this point, I could really use a lightning strike to the head to get me out of this. Why isn't she saying anything? Maybe I can just leave, walk right back up those steps and back inside. The blaring noise and perspiring adolescents might actually be more fun than this.

"Look, I—"

"How— Ugh," she cuts me off, pinching the bridge of her nose and taking a deep breath. "How do you not remember our kiss?"

"Kiss?" Vague memories of kissing Kate have been piecing themselves together in my brain, but I wasn't sure if it was real or a dream. I've had too many dreams like that to know what's real and what isn't anymore. "We kissed?"

"Yes!" she yells so loudly it echoes across the field. "At camp!"

The feel of her curls tangled around my fingers and her lips pressing into mine rush through me. The memories are broken and scattered in my head, blending with different moments. I was concussed—of course I don't remember kissing her. I don't remember calling Steven *sweetie pie* either, but apparently, I did.

"Kate, I had a concussion." I press a palm into my forehead, rubbing the ache growing there. She lets out a trembling sigh and runs her hands through her hair. "Look, I don't know if me telling you all of this is freaking you out, but I had to, okay?"

"I don't know, Malcolm..." Her words linger in a whisper so quiet it's almost swallowed by the wind rustling past her.

"What don't you know?" I grip the back of my neck and exhale. *She does know.* She feels the same way, but she's scared as hell to follow through. I get it. I don't want to lose her either. Kate would rather risk a little with some stranger on an app than risk everything with me. Our lives are so intertwined. Extracting her from mine would cause me physical pain. And I have a feeling losing me from hers might be worse for her.

"Kate, what scares you?" I break the silence, asking her the same question she asked me at camp.

"I don't know," she snips, offense plastering red on her cheeks. "I just want to understand."

"What else is there to understand?"

"How this can be happening!" She yells it like a statement to her universe, voice cracking slightly. "How someone like you"—she waves a hand in my direction—"can love someone like me!" Pressing her hands to her chest, she looks up at the sky, and I can see the edge of her jaw tremble. When she finally looks back at me, tears are streaming down her face.

"Hey..." I take a step closer as she turns her face away and wipes at her tears. It kills me to see her like this—not believing the good things about herself or that she's worth loving. The tears slow, and she takes a slow breath, still not looking at me. "Kate, look at me."

"Why?" her voice cracks as she slowly turns to face me.

"May I?" I hold out my hand, and she takes it. I squeeze, and her shoulders relax, like the small touch relieves the tension that was there. I tug her close to me and wipe her wet cheek with my thumb. "Kate, I'm sorry."

"For loving me?" A weak laugh flows out of her, and I tug her closer, a reassurance that that is far from what I'm saying.

"Never for that." I cup her face in my hands and level my gaze with hers. "I'm sorry that people in your life have made you believe you're hard to love. I really am." She sniffles but doesn't look away. "But you have to know...you are not. You, Katherine Stanley, might be the weirdest and most outspoken person in the world, but you are *not* hard to love."

"Are you—"

"Ask if I'm sure, I dare you. I have never been so sure of anything in my life."

"Your whole life?" she asks in disbelief. Gosh, this woman can really get under my skin. "There's nothing else you've been more sure of? Not even the time you took the wrong exit to El Reno, and you were *positive* you'd find a new way there?" A mischievous glint flashes in her eyes, both irritating and irresistible as she looks at me, challenging me.

Her breath tickles my neck as I close the distance between us completely. "You drive me crazy, Stanley."

I grip the sides of her face, feeling her cheeks twitch with a smile against my palms. Her body stiffens for a moment when I press up against her. Then, as if a dam of restraint is broken between us, we're kissing. My hands tangle in her hair, and she grips my suit jacket, both tugging each other closer than humanly possible, like it's not enough.

Being this close to her, with her lips on mine, isn't enough.

Everything around me goes still. Quiet. As if the Earth itself is slowing down so I can soak up every part of this. The glide of her strawberry lips against mine, the smoothness of her cheeks against my rough hands, the fit of her delicate body against mine. All of it burns into my brain, wiping out every other pipe dream I've had about this moment. They don't compare.

The muscles in my body practically turn to Jell-O as she wraps herself around me. Something inside both of us releases under the relief of it all, like we've been starving in the desert for years and finally found water. I have been starving for her, but something about the wait makes this feel that much more satisfying.

Delayed gratification in a sense. And damn was she worth the wait.

Just when the taste of her is starting to consume me, something cold and wet trickles down my face. Slow at first, then it hits me like a rocket—repeatedly blasting me from every side. I blink at Kate, who is also getting hit. I turn around to see what is happening, getting drenched in the process.

The sprinklers.

Chapter Thirty-Five

Kate

"*I am in love with you.*"

Malcolm's words ring in my ears like the bridge at a concert, being chanted by thousands of people. I feel them rumble all the way down to my toes. But like being at the concert, I still can't believe I'm here, experiencing it. I can't believe this man standing in front of me feels the way he does...about me.

I pester him—I mean, how can I not? But I need to know for sure. Malcolm isn't a liar. I'm just not a believer. Not fully, anyway. I need proof.

A sign.

Something from the universe telling me that all of this is real, and I'm not dreaming.

Like *Joe Jonas barging into my high school and offering me VIP tickets to his concert in Europe* kind of dream.

And then, his lips are on mine.

Now, let it be said, the concussion kiss was every bit as spectacular as one might think. It was uncontrolled and passionate. But this kiss... This one is different.

It's all Malcolm. It's every bit of him that I didn't know I needed.

A rugged intensity at first, then a slow tenderness. The moment he's been truly waiting for is here. I can feel his body snap into the moment, like chains being broken and he can run free. But instead of becoming a wild man on the loose, he takes his time, soaking in each moment like it could be his last. I think about someone seeing a sunset for the first time, the colors blending together in a hypnotizing fashion. You can't look away. You're itching to run to it, reach up and touch it, but you also know it could be gone in an instant, so you slow down to soak it all in—the universe orchestrating something so breathtaking right before your eyes. A symphony of light and color that can be so fleeting you want to savor every second of it. You commit your first sunset to memory. Isn't that what you want to do with all your firsts?

That is how Malcolm is kissing me. Right here in the middle of our football field, he savors every second of this first.

I melt into him too, realizing that every part of me wants him just as badly. His breath trembles as his hands move into my hair. I used to think his joking obsession with my hair was just that, a joke. But based on the continuous gliding and stroking of his fingers through my wild curls, I realize it's not. He truly loves them, and something about it makes me ache.

Him loving something about me that I don't. Something that took me so long to accept, even if it is something as small as the texture of my hair.

Is this really happening?

Kissing him and questioning actually kissing him is enough to rip me in two, but I can't seem to stop my lips from moving with his. As he pulls me closer into his chest, I almost snap like a rubber band. The agony of wanting this but also not really knowing what I wanted releases inside me. Just as I'm about to accept that this really is happening, and I have no reason to question something that feels so right...my face is blasted with water.

Then my legs.

Then my back.

Before I know it, I am soaked from head to toe, curls falling flat against my cheeks. Malcolm turns around, attempting to block me from the field sprinklers, but it's too late. We're surrounded.

I press my head against his back and want to cry. "This can't be happening," I whine to the cosmos.

Malcolm laughs, pulling me to the sidelines. "It's just a little water."

"It's not!" I stomp my foot and yell at the sky. "It's a sign from the universe!"

He lets out a deep sigh and runs his hands through his wet hair. "I don't think—"

"It is!" I snap, pointing a finger at him. "The universe is stopping us before we go too far, before we get mixed up in all of this and ruin everything."

"Kate..." his voice is a defeated whisper, like my words are breaking his heart one by one. "Please don't do this."

"I'm not doing anything!" I lie because I know exactly what I'm doing. I'm sabotaging the moment. The possibility of something with Malcolm is too precious and wonderful, and my brain thinks the best way to react is to torture any chance it has at happiness. "I'm just stating facts. Of course we would get blasted with ice-cold water in the middle of everything. The universe is clearly sending us a sign," my voice wavers as I try to sound convincing—for his sake or my own, I'm not sure.

"Do you really think the universe is worried about us kissing?" he muses.

"I *think* the universe has a way of directing everything, and I *think* if this was meant to work out, it wouldn't be so difficult." Water droplets drip down my face as I glance at him. His face is blank as he watches me. "I just mean...ugh. Loving someone shouldn't be so difficult, right? Can't we just kiss and have a happily ever after without getting hypothermia?" I shiver. The cool air and the cold water aren't a good mix.

"You're right," he says as he takes off his suit jacket and wraps me in it. "Loving someone should be easy. But what about after that?"

"What do you mean?" I nuzzle deep into his jacket, inhaling the smell of his oaky cologne and fresh body wash that comes with it.

"What about life after you start loving someone? Falling in love might be easy at first, but staying in love is totally different. Life isn't easy, Kate, and no amount of talking with the universe can make it that way." He sighs and clenches his jaw as the shimmering blue of his eyes focuses on me. I feel vulnerable and safe all at the same time. "Falling for you was the easiest thing I've done... But hell, Kate, staying in love with you hasn't been."

I scoff at him, slightly offended, but I get it. I'm a lot for some people.

"But I have. I've loved you, regardless of the circumstances. And it's not because the universe or some higher power has made it so. It's because I *choose* to. Your family loves you because you're family." *Ouch,* I think. "Your future children will love you because you're their mom. But me? I don't have to love you. Some days, I think I'm crazy because of how much I love you, but I do. And I choose to keep loving you every day because you are everything to me, and that will never change."

He pauses for a moment, and I try to speak, but he keeps going. "Yeah, loving is easy at first, but as we grow old, life changes, and my love will change too. But I'm not going to doubt it. I'm never going to doubt how amazing you are. Or how damn lucky I am. I'm just going to keep loving you until you tell me to stop."

"Malcolm, I..." My lips quiver as tears fill my eyes. I swallow hard, the overwhelming emotions threatening to spill over if I speak any more.

"Look..." He rubs his jaw and shifts his weight from one leg to the other. "We can—"

"Hey!"

We're interrupted by Charlie as he barrels down the steps, flailing his arms at us like he's running from a bear. "Coach! Coach!"

Malcolm heaves a deep sigh and rakes his hands through his wet hair. "Henders, what seems to be the problem?"

"It's Bill!" Freaking Bill. "They think he broke his hip again!" Charlie pants. "We told him not to do it, Coach, but he didn't listen. He just did them."

"What did he do?" I ask, disgruntled and a tad snappy as I wipe under my eyes.

"The splits." Charlie winces.

Malcolm whips his gaze to me, and his eyes are a mix of irritation and obligation, morals and desire battling it out right there in his retinas.

"Go." I nod toward the school. Of course, there are a plethora of people in there that can handle the situation, but anytime someone gets injured, Malcolm seems to be the one they run to. I guess I can't let our little field excursion get in the way of our responsibilities, no matter how much I want it to. *We should've gone under the bleachers.*

"I'll be right there," Malcolm sighs, and Charlie speeds off back toward the gym. Turning back to me, he pulls me into a hug and kisses the top of my head. He lingers against me for a moment, resting his chin atop my head and holding me against him like we were made to fit together. "This will work if you give us a chance," he whispers.

Without missing a beat, he kisses me again, quickly this time, and races up the steps. I feel physical pain as he disappears into the gym. Loneliness tries to settle all around me again, like the black cloud it is. I replay every second of what just happened. The memory of his lips on mine tingles my mouth like it's a new sense. The desire to hone in on that sense and feel it over and over is strong. But something even stronger whispers to me in the back of my mind.

You can't lose him, Kate.

It's been a solid eight hours since I've seen Malcolm. He rushed Bill to the hospital and stayed with him until early this morning when Margaret recuperated enough to get there. Apparently, jostling her aching joints all over the dance floor wasn't the best idea for someone with rheumatoid arthritis. By the time Malcolm got home, it was 3 a.m. and I was passed out.

Probably for the best anyway.

Because I am freaking out.

It's now 8 a.m., and instead of rushing over to discuss last night's field trip, I am headed over to Lola's to check in on her first. I just about lose the smoothie I had for breakfast when I see her climbing into her Jeep and starting the vehicle.

"What are you doing?" I screech to a halt at the end of her driveway and race to her driver's side window. "The doctor said no driving! It will stress out your heart!" I yell at her through her closed window.

She narrows her eyes at me and rolls her window down an inch. "I don't need a babysitter to go to the store, Katherine."

"Yes, you do." I attempt to open the car door at the same time she locks it. Glaring at her, I cross in front of the vehicle, keeping my hands firmly planted on the hood. For some reason, I think this is the only way to prevent her from backing away. It works, and I reach the passenger side, jimmying the handle for her to unlock it and let me in. "I'm going with you."

She unlocks the door reluctantly. "I don't need your help getting potatoes."

"Deal with it." I buckle up, and she peels out of the driveway aggressively.

We drive in silence, and she huffs dramatically in my direction a few times. "Don't you have other people you can harass?" she asks.

I scoff. "I didn't think caring about your well-being was considered harassment."

She rolls her eyes and continues driving. Barely a moment passes before she bombards me with questions. "So, what is wrong with you? Did you hit your head? Did I not give you enough water as a child?" Her accent is thick as she ponders over the thought of neglect.

"Lola," I sigh and put a death grip on the door handle as she changes lanes without a blinker. "What are you talking about?"

"Well, something must be wrong with you for you to be acting crazy." She waves me off, changing lanes *again*. It will be a miracle if we make it to the store.

"Crazy?"

"Yes, crazy. You kissed Malcolm, yet you're here harassing me."

"I'm not hara—wait. How did you know?" I glance at her and back at the road. She rolls her eyes at me as if what happened last night is common knowledge across all of society.

"I have eyes everywhere." She changes lanes again, and I really start to feel that smoothie move up into my esophagus. "And those eyes think you're crazy. You have a wonderful man waiting on bended knee for you, and you're leaving him high and dry like last week's pancit."

"Bended knee is a tad dramatic, Lola. And I'm not leaving him *high and dry*," I emphasize with air quotes. "He had a long night, and I was going to go see him later."

"Ah..." She waves me off again and misses our exit to the store entirely. Instead, she races ahead, cutting a highlighter-yellow Corvette off in the process. "You're being stupid."

"Ouch." I swat at her arm. "And you missed the exit."

She ignores my directions and continues driving. "You're stalling." She lets out a breath, looking every bit as tired as she's saying, the deep lines around her mouth turning downward.

"I am not," I lie. I'm definitely stalling. "I can't lose him, Lola," I whisper. The thought of losing him clings to the back of my throat and squeezes.

"And who says you're going to?" She raises a brow at me. "He's not your mom, Katherine. He's not that one guy. Malcolm isn't going to leave you for some work retreat on the beach or some job across the country."

"Can we not talk about this?" I whisper, looking out the window at the passing cars. *Where is she going?*

"Fine." It's as if the word is an NOS button, because she speeds up and whips across four lanes of highway road like it's a video game. My stomach plummets into the seat as I brace for impact from every direction. Then she takes a familiar exit.

"Lola, why are—"

"If you aren't going to talk to me about this," she says, silencing me, "then you will talk to him."

I grumble at her as she pulls down a gravel driveway and parks in front of the small brick house I know all too well.

Malcolm is outside...chopping wood.

"Lola, I cannot talk to him like this." I wave in his general direction at the same time he notices our car. With the ax overhead, he chops another log and tosses it to the side before propping himself against the ax to watch the crazy women thirty feet from him. "There's no way!" I note the glistening sweat pouring off him and gulp dryly at the sight. Yeah, no. I can't have a levelheaded conversation with him looking like a sexy lumberjack.

"Go talk to him, or I will give myself another heart attack."

"That's not how it works."

"Try me." She glowers at me, and for a moment I think it might actually be possible for someone to trigger a heart attack. If anyone could do it, it would be her.

I grumble again, loudly and dramatically, as I slide out of the Jeep. Gravel crunches under my feet as I land with a thud. Ungraceful, that's my style. I don't know how to walk forward, so I just stand there, blocking the sun with my hand. Malcolm's silhouette comes into focus, muscles at peak performance after the ax wielding.

I can't do this.

I reach for the door handle to the Jeep, but Lola has already locked the doors. She smiles innocently at me and then proceeds to back out of the driveway. The woman is leaving me here.

"You gonna chase after her?" Malcolm calls to me as I stay firmly planted in place.

Chasing after her might be an option.

Alright, don't be ridiculous. Just go talk to him, the voice from last night echoes in my head. I replay the sound again, noting a familiar depth and drawl to it.

My grandpa's voice. It comes from deep in the back of my mind, nudging my feet forward.

"Gosh, where did you come from?" I quietly ask the voice, which is technically asking myself, since it's my brain talking to me.

Malcolm watches me warily, looking from my face down to my slow, shuffling feet. *Let him love you,* Grandpa whispers to me.

"You good?" Malcolm asks. He glistens in the afternoon sun as beads of sweat cling to his forehead and neck.

"I, uh...don't know."

He raises an eyebrow at me. "You look like you've seen a ghost."

"Feels like it," I joke half-heartedly. I can't really tell him my grandpa has decided to start talking to me from the great beyond...and that's the only advice I've truly needed this entire time. That's not crazy at all.

"Well, then..." He pauses, dropping the ax to the ground and grabbing the hand towel tucked in his pocket. Please don't dab yourself right now. "How are you?" he asks with a dab to his chest, then neck, and then a wipe to his face.

"Well, other than being forced here against my will, I'm fine." My mouth feels dry, as if him wiping himself has the ability to strip my tongue of any and all moisture.

"I see..." He pauses. "Well, if you don't want to talk..." His voice is thick and hesitant as he saunters off to grab a feed bucket and heads toward the back of his house.

"Ugh, I do! I just don't know what to say." I follow him as he heads toward his chicken coop that is now overflowing with almost fifty chickens. "Whoa. Where did these guys come from?" Last I checked, he only had thirty or so. I lean over the edge of the gate surrounding the coop and start counting. Malcolm hands me the bucket, and out of habit, I toss feed in for the little chicklets.

"Nugget!" Malcolm whistles, and our pride and joy rounds the corner of the coop. The oldest and most senile chicken of the group. The chicken he denies trying to kidnap from me five years ago. I swear I see the other chickens part like the Red Sea to let her through. Malcolm gives her a piece of melon and scratches the top of her head.

"Spoiled," I giggle, rolling my eyes and emptying the bucket for the others.

A beat of silence passes, and I realize Malcolm isn't going to force this conversation. I have to take the leap, or we will be on this carousel of silent feelings for the rest of our lives.

"So..." I drag out the word, "how's it going?" I lean against the gate as gracefully as I can, but it's flimsy, so I lose my balance and almost fall into the coop.

Malcolm grabs me by the elbow to steady me. "Careful there, Stanley."

His hand lingers on my elbow, soft and gentle. I glance down and see his thumb twitch against my skin before moving down my arm and resting at my wrist. A shiver moves up my arm and across my sternum in response.

I suck in a breath. "I don't want to lose you."

Encircling his hand around my wrist, he doesn't look at me. Eyes pinned on our hands, he lets out a shaky sigh. "Me either."

The truth sizzles inside me, waiting to be unleashed, but I feel distracted. I squeeze my eyes shut and block everything out—the feel of his fingers grazing my palm right now, the taste of his lips as they pressed into mine, the sound of his rumbly morning voice—all of it, I block.

"Are you processing?" Malcolm asks, because clearly he can read my mind and probably knows everything I was just thinking.

"Yes," I mumble. "I just...ugh, I just can't lose you, Malcolm. I physically can't." My words are weak and vulnerable, and I hate it. The goal of being a strong, independent woman deciding her own future feels so far away. I didn't want to be that person who clings to another person so much. All that's ever done is get me heartbroken.

"You won't." Malcolm's hands are on my shoulders now, gripping me as he rubs his thumbs back and forth.

"How can you—"

"Kate," he stops me. His face is serious, and his eyes are focused, and every single doubt lingering inside of my heart fades away. I know this man. I know who he is right to his very core. The man who was so afraid to make new friends or have a relationship because he was afraid of losing them like he did Brennan. The man who has never once gone back on a favor or a promise. The man who, no matter how miserable it makes him, will go prom dress shopping because it matters to someone else.

Why am I doubting his love for me when he's never given me a reason to?

"The only way you are going to lose me is if I get lost in the wilderness or when I die at ninety-six."

"That's specific." I smile.

"Hush." He smiles back. "I have been here, and I will always be here. And I will show you every day that I mean it." He brings my hands up to his mouth, kissing each one tenderly. "And I know you will do the same."

"It's not going to be easy, loving me forever."

"So? Easy is boring." He smirks, pulling my hands behind his head and resting them around his neck. A beat of silence passes, and he says, "Please don't make me beg."

"Well, now that you mention it..." I muse, giving him a wink.

He pinches my side before sliding his hands around my waist and pulling me against him. "Please, Kate. Let me love you the way you want—the way you deserve." It's not begging, but the pleading in his eyes grips every piece of my heart that's left. The pieces I gave up on. The pieces left by others. The pieces longing to be put back together.

"Okay," I whisper, "only if I can do the same for you."

Dazzling blue and silver beam at me as his eyes dilate slightly. "Is that a yes?" The smile on his face grows into a wide, childlike grin as I nod.

"That's a yes."

He kisses me without hesitation. Without fear. And without any sign of ever wanting to stop. I feel his smile as his lips are on mine, grinning wide and bright against my own. Between kisses, he says, "I will love you forever."

And for the first time in a long time...I believe it.

Malcolm

Eight Months Later

"Don't look at me like that." I direct my scowl at Nugget, who is perched atop my bed, as I retie my tie for the fifth time. "I'm nervous, alright?"

She chirps at me, then proceeds to peck at the loose thread on the corner of my comforter. Elvis Presley singing "Blue Christmas" drifts through the door from down the hall, accompanied by multiple voices singing along. It's almost distracting enough to suffocate the nerves building in my chest.

I reach for my tie again, shaking off the tremors settling into my fingers, and pull the knot loose. Half way through another tying attempt, I forget everything and pull the Santa covered silk off entirely.

Of course, today I would be freaking out.

The most important day of my life.

A knock on the door jolts my attention, and Nugget's.

"Babe, can I come in?" Kate whispers on the other side, sending the nerves up into my throat.

She opens the door, wearing a bright red turtleneck with reindeer antlers nestled in her dark curls. Blinking ornament earrings dangle next to her pink cheeks. Stepping into the room, she shuts the door quietly behind her, muffling the chatter and music from the living room.

"Are you alright?"

"Yes." I crack my knuckles. "No. I can't…" I gesture to the balled up tie thrown on the bed.

In one quick motion, Kate grabs the tie and whips it around my neck, mastering the Windsor without hesitation. "There." Her brown eyes glisten as she smooths out the silky knot then gazes up at me.

An unsteady breath trembles out of me. "Thank you." I take her face in my hands and stroke her cheeks, feeling them swell under my thumbs.

"It's going to be great." She kisses me. A soft and quick peck, like she's done everyday for the past eight months. It's second nature to her to be so openly affectionate with me, and my stomach still dips every time.

Another knock at the door and Kate answers it.

"She's here." Ellie, donning a giant snowman sweater and ribbon-tied pigtails, beams at us.

"We'll be right there!" Kate bounces on the balls of her feet before turning toward me and giving my arm a tight squeeze. Her excitement for the night is palpable, and almost contagious. *Almost.*

But the nerves in my throat seem to have tripled in size, constricting my airway and making it near impossible to feel anything but terrified.

I shove the feeling as far back as I can and head towards the front door, with Kate at my side. Kate's grip around my arm loosens as she rushes to greet our last guest of the evening.

"We're so happy you could make it!" She hugs her tight before pulling her toward me.

"Mackenzie, hi. Thank you for coming." I hug her and guide her into the living room.

"I wouldn't miss it," she says, smiling.

"Let me introduce you to everyone."

I direct her attention to the living room, introducing Benny and Ellie, Emma, Bill and Margaret, Gary, and even Daniels who goes a little greenish-pink with the introduction.

"This is everyone," I wave to the group again, "everyone, this is Mackenzie."

Confusion seems to work its way across the room at whoever this person is. I gulp, dislodging the nerves and clear my throat.

"My sister."

A collective *oh's* and *ah's* spread across the room as they swarm my tiny, innocent sister with questions. Mackenzie takes it in stride, partaking in the overly personal questions from Margaret, and even the philosophical questions from Gary, without hesitation. She's always been good at that, being friendly. Growing up she could talk to anyone, and she talked to me most. As a teenager, I hated it, but after we lost Brennan, I've looked forward to those conversations like when we were kids. It took me eight years to man up and get back to the way things were with my sister. Just hearing her voice, grieving the loss of her husband and my best friend, broke something inside of me bit by bit. I didn't ever consider that she might actually be alright one day.

I can be ignorant.

Or as Dr. Ford would say, *"lacking in knowledge."*

Basically, I'm the worst, and I assume if I'm struggling with something, then other people surely are too because there's no way someone else can cope with the loss of someone better than me. Especially my baby sister.

But last month, I found out she was doing well. Surprisingly well. I can't imagine being a twenty-eight-year-old widow, but somehow she has overcome it. And knowing that helped my own healing in its own way.

I watch Mackenzie take the invasive questioning in stride, feeling a sense of pride swell at how far each of us have come.

"Can you help me in the kitchen?" Kate's arms wrap around my waist as she tugs me away from the crowd. "She'll be fine," she assures me as we disappear around the corner.

Not missing a beat, Kate stirs the Crockpot, pulls a pan out of the oven, and pours me a glass of brandy. "You can relax now."

Relax. She has no idea what's coming in just a few hours. I won't be relaxing for a while. It's honestly a miracle I haven't collapsed from the insane amount of adrenaline coursing through my veins.

She strokes my cheek once, then drags her hand down my neck, chest, and arm, before interlacing her fingers with mine.

"I'll try." I say, feeling the tingle of her touch down the path she just made. Like an electrical shock that just blasted through a powerline, it sizzles deep into my skin.

I tug Kate closer, feeling her flush against me, and push a curl out of her face. Her eyes flutter closed as I rest my hand at the nape of her neck. On the other side of the kitchen wall, we can hear music, laughter, and clinking of glasses—noises that would usually be overstimulating and suffocating—but being wrapped up in Kate right here in the middle of our kitchen, they're not nearly as overwhelming. She squeezes my waist tighter and rests her chin against my chest.

My heart stutters, and she fights a smile. I know she can feel it practically skip a beat anytime she touches me.

A timer dings, and I look around for what else could possibly need attending to in this small space. Every inch of the counter is covered in holiday dishes and spreads, with garland, tinsel, and Christmas lights intertwined throughout. My well-used cast iron and stained coffee pot stick out like a sore thumb mixed in with the vibrancy of Kate's dishes—pinks, yellows, and greens cover each piece, along with small birds and flowers scattered across some of them. A stark contrast, her and I. Opposites. But it works. A warm sizzle moves down my throat and across my chest at the picture of seeing these little things everyday for the rest of my life.

"You've outdone yourself," I whisper.

"It's our first holiday party as a couple," she shrugs, "I had to."

I bite my lip as sheer joy threatens to break me in two. "I don't deserve you."

Brushing her cheeks, I pull her face to mine and kiss her. The sensation of her soft lips sends a zing deep into my belly and settles there as she kisses me back, bringing her arms up around my neck. With one hand sliding around her waist and the other tangling in her hair, I pull her against me as close as humanly possible, feeling every curve of her body with my own.

The goal of the night still lingers in the back of my mind.

I would usually get lost in a moment like this, forgetting anything and everything I had on the docket.

But tonight is too important.

Kate's body trembles under mine and it jolts my insides with a sense of feral want that shouldn't happen when we have guests. A small chuckle in the doorway snaps us back into our wits, and we reluctantly break our lips away from one another.

"Oh no, please don't stop on my account," Mackenzie rolls her eyes and smirks at us.

Kate clears her throat. "So sorry. I was just, uh, bringing out more punch!" She scurries across the kitchen to the punch bowl and pours a few glasses, spilling a few drops in the process. Giving an awkward, singular laugh, she rushes past Mackenzie and into the living room.

"I really like her," Mackenzie says, helping herself to the punch.

"I do, too."

"I'm very aware," she chuckles, wiping up the punch droplets off the counter.

I let out a shaky breath, still reeling from kissing Kate, and grip the edge of the counter. "Did you bring it?" I whisper.

Mackenzie downs the punch like a shot and gives me a reassuring nod. "I did."

My heart threatens to burst out of my chest as she pulls her giant purse onto the counter and begins to dig through it. For a few seconds, we both alternate between looking at the purse and over our shoulder, ensuring no one is coming, until finally Mackenzie says, "aha," and pulls out a tiny green velvet box. It's covered in lint, and has a rip on one corner, but it's still perfect.

"Here you go," Mackenzie hands me the box, and I see her eyes getting misty as she watches me for a moment, before turning to look out the kitchen window.

"Are you sure—"

"Yes, I'm positive. I clearly don't need it, and no offense, it's taken you way too long to find someone to give it to, so now is your chance." She gives me a playful punch in the arm. "Plus, it's just been sitting with my stuff for years…it's time."

"Alright," I nod.

I pause, noting the acceptance in my sister's eyes before I open the tiny box. Inside it sits a gold-banded, vintage wedding ring that belonged to my great-grandmother.

The last six years of my life flash before my eyes in the reflection of the small pear shaped diamond—pink high-tops, chickens, curly hair, and dark-olive skin—every moment that has made me feel whole again plays like it's a highlight reel. Everything that has brought me to this day swells inside me like a balloon, making me feel lighter.

"I don't know," I hear Kate say in the other room, "Ross just said it was urgent."

Her footsteps, skittery and unmistakable, get closer to the kitchen and I snap the ring box closed and shove it into my pocket. Mackenzie's eyes go wide as she watches me, then whips around as Kate barrels into the kitchen.

"Ross called, said there was an issue at the football field," she pants, rushing around the kitchen and covering the dishes. "We should hurry."

"Of course," I clear my throat and glance at Mackenzie, whose all-knowing smirk is borderline obvious as she backs out of the kitchen.

A few clanging of lids and readjusting of dishes happen before Kate grabs her purse by the door. All of her fluid movements happen like they're in that damned slow motion movie again, graceful and beautiful and distracting in every possible way. She stops short of the front door and looks at me, confusion moving across her face as I watch her.

This happens way too often. These moments where I find myself watching her every move, as if I haven't seen her do the exact thing she's doing a million times before, as if it's all new to me.

"You ready?" she asks, pulling the front door open.

"So ready," I say as I follow her.

"What do you think happened? On the field?" Kate asks as she climbs into the cab of my truck.

"Who knows," I lie, "maybe someone was playing on it."

The worst response you could come up with, Geer.

A chortle bellows out of her. "Remember that dating app I tried?"

"I tried blocking that out," I wink at her.

"It really was a terrible idea." She laughs, her eyes filling with memories as she gazes out the window.

"I wouldn't say that," I reassure her. "You had to get out there and make some plays to score." As cheesy as I sound, I know it's true. I hated it at the time, yes, but the reality is Kate had to put herself out there and see the possibilities to figure out what she wanted. And I had to get out there and make all the right plays.

"Well," she rests her head against the seat and closes her eyes, "I scored big time, then."

"Me too," I reach in my pocket and grip the tiny velvet box then whisper, "the biggest score of my life."

Acknowledgements

First to thank is YOU. Yes, you, the one reading this right now. It's because of you I have had the opportunity to write not one, but now TWO novels. What even is this life?! I am eternally grateful for anyone taking the time to read my lighthearted stories, and even more so for the ones who truly connected with the story. I hope you loved your time with the Glendale crew and plan to come back NEXT TERM!

My beta and ARC readers — thank you so much for taking the time to read, critique, and provide feedback. Your input was priceless and helped shape this story in a way I would never have been able to do on my own. Seriously, I should have paid some of you for the work you did (cough cough MJ and Jessee)

Cindy — your cover art is perfect per usual. Thank you for putting up with my constant changes and bringing Kate and Malcolm to life the way you did!

My friends —the people who I dedicated this book to — Kenzie, Shelby, Sarah, Steph, Ash, Ronnie, Chad, Dalt, and so many others — I am beyond blessed to just be in your presence, but to be your friend is something I will never take for granted. You fill my life with such joy and also give me so much content to write about, hehe!

My writing group — Stefanie, Cindy, India, and Michelle — you all are a gem of a find and I am deeply indebted to each of you for your constant support, advice, and sanity saving.

Mom — I hope you know how much I love you, even when don't talk as much as we should.

My babies – life with you is wild and sweet and absolutely perfect. I wouldn't be the woman I am today without you and I hope, if you ever read something written by your mom, it makes you proud.

David – there are not enough words to sum up my gratitude for you. Writing about love is easy when you're loved so well. Thank you for this sweet life you have provided for us and making a way for me to raise our babies and write some books. You are one in a million and I love you most.

My Lord and Savior – because of you I have new life and I am endlessly grateful.

Hugs,

Grayson

About The Author

Grayson Long currently resides in her home state of Oklahoma. The love she has for her family runs deep, and the love she has for Nutella might be just as strong. Her childhood dreams of writing were thwarted by a fear of failure. But turning the ripe age of thirty, she realized no better time to try than now. Grayson wrote her first novel in three months, writing in the late hours of the night, or during her daughter's naps. When she's not spending time with her family or finding time to write, Grayson can be found working as a Registered Nurse. When you read a story written by Grayson, her hope is that you smile, laugh, kick your feet, or a combination of three. But more than that, she hopes you leave the story feeling lighter and happier than when you started. Because that's one of the great things about reading—to escape to a brighter place for a bit.

Made in the USA
Columbia, SC
18 June 2024